ewa anderson

Sābanto

The Crimson River

Edited by: Maylon Gardner www.rightyourwriting.com

Cover Design by: Ana Chabrand Design House www.anachabrand.com

Publisher: Catalie Press www.cataliepress.com

Ebook ISBN: 978-1-7780186-0-2

Paperback ISBN: 978-1-7780186-1-9

Hard Cover ISBN: 978-1-7780186-2-6

The world is glowing
There's beauty in fire my love
Creator of ash

PROLOGUE

"W_{E HAVE FAILED}," _{THE} man said, propping himself against the head of a long table as he stood in front of a seated audience. He paused lengthily, waiting for his words to sink into the minds of the listeners. "Countries failed to maintain order. Politicians failed to maintain peace."

The lights in the room were dimmed except for the faintly glowing strips illuminating the floor for the safety of the occupants. It was hard to see the speaker's face, but all present knew who he was.

"Many years back, natural disasters crumbled and devastated our cities. Multitudes died or were displaced. It created global unrest which led to an increased conflict of interest between the most powerful countries—who wanted, at all costs, to expand their worldwide influence. That's how the fifty-year war started." He let that sink in before continuing, "Now, two years after we signed the peace treaty, the world is still in ruins."

The man took a slow stroll to the side of the room, making some people swivel in their chairs or turn their bodies around so that they could keep him in sight. He appeared to be weighing and reflecting on his words, and he expected the others to do the same.

"We fought for our freedom, poured our hard-earned money into weapons and ammunition. We sent our best to the front to die as heroes, but we failed to save what we had at home. Local governments and structures fell. Social order was destroyed. Gangs and mafias took over our streets. Neighbor turned on neighbor. Families turned against each other."

The man looked at the people in the room. They were listening, but the information wasn't new to them. The presentation was just a formality; a way to remind them of what they already knew and expected.

Each person in the room was dressed for the occasion in high-end tailored suits and pencil dresses. Their well-pressed attire was a statement on the importance of the moment, and on them as individuals. A symbol of status they showed with pride.

"Fifty years of war brought destruction, death, and famine to every corner of the world. Poor living conditions, malnutrition, and non-existent health care continue to bring illness and death to many. Our land is bare and no longer fruitful. Prosperous cities have turned into slums where only the fittest and most quick-witted can survive. Pain and suffering is all around us. But!" The speaker lowered his voice and said, with conviction, "We will rebuild."

The room was silent, except for the faint hum of the ventilation system pumping cool air into the room. They were contemplating the words just spoken, and some lowered their heads as they felt the pain and suffering in their own lives.

The speaker lowered his head as well, looking down at the table in front of him. Then he said, his voice growing louder with each word, "It's an opportunity. An opportunity to start anew. Like a phoenix from the ashes, we will rise!"

He circled the table and stopped at a chair where an attractive woman sat. Her amber hair fell on her shoulders in perfect curls, styled that morning by an attentive servant or personal stylist. He looked her in the eye. They were green, and she looked embarrassed, nervously toying with her diamond necklace. It wasn't clear if she was just shy or if it was the speaker who made her uncomfortable by fixing his eyes on her.

"We," he said, "we will be better than our ancestors." He broke eye contact with the woman and strolled back to the head of the table, stopping by an empty chair without sitting down.

"We have knowledge and tools that we didn't have before. We will use them, and we will use them well."

The listeners nodded and looked at each other in agreement.

"Think of your kids." The man looked at everyone in the room as he continued, "Think of the generations ahead." He adjusted his white shirt cuffs decorated with gold cufflinks.

"Do you really want them to face this again? Do you want to go through all this again? Is that what you want?" he shouted. The echo of his words lingered for a moment.

"I can see it on your faces. Each one of you wants what's best. You're eager to make a change. To make a difference. To stand up for what's right!" His voice was strong and passionate; his words heartfelt.

"Now, and for all. Together," the man said, leaning forward on the table, "we can end this. Together, we can ensure no homelessness. A world with no hunger, no crime. A life without fear."

The men and women in the room listened, anticipating what would come next. The speaker looked at everyone and punctuated each sentence by tapping the table with his index finger as he continued.

"We owe it to our people. We owe it to our children. We can—and we will—rebuild the world. We will unite for what's right. We will stand together! That's why I gathered you here today. To bring the means to make a difference. To bring you . . . " he straightened and said, "Sābanto."

1

S TEVEN WHITE GOT UP early in the morning, when the horizon to the east was still just a shade of dark red. The house was quiet, so he tried not to make much noise as he got dressed. He didn't bother to alert the staff—it would only cause unnecessary hustle, and he wanted some time alone.

He looked at his reflection in the mirror, at his short salt-and-pepper hair and long face. He was already in his late fifties, but he didn't feel his age. He was still fit and full of energy. He picked a nice, dark suit from a hanger and paired it with a blue shirt and a set of cufflinks he'd bought a long time ago. The design of them pleased him. He liked the way the gold shone, and they'd only cost him a thousand tickets.

War caused hyperinflation. Governments, already with one foot out the door, continued to spend more and more, fueling the conflict, trying to hold on to the influence they still had. Prices started to rise at an astronomical speed. When people were no longer able to afford food, a decision was made to start selling meal tickets to feed the hungry. He was just a child when people had stormed the banks, trampling each other to get rid of their worthless money in exchange for a few days of lousy meals. Now, decades later, tickets were their own currency.

He walked up to the window and looked through the glass at the dawn breaking. He could make out the rooftops of the town in the distance. "My Covedale," he murmured to himself and smiled. The city was his life, the purpose of his existence, his pride and joy. He'd spent the last thirty years protecting it, building it, and making it better. "What would you do without me?"

One day there would be lights shining at night. Electric lights. The power plant was his longtime dream. What a luxury it would be for everyone if he rebuilt the power lines that had been downed during the war. Bringing light to the townsfolk could be his life accomplishment, something that people would forever remember him for. His legacy. A legend of Covedale. He smiled.

He walked away from the window and through the door to the dark corridor. He passed his daughter's chambers and stopped for a moment. She was still sleeping, he was sure of that, and he didn't want to disturb her. It didn't seem like that long ago he'd held her in his arms at night, singing her lullabies, or carried her on his shoulders through the woods that were part of his vast property. Her childish giggles still rang in his ears. How he'd love to have those moments back. She'd been so small back then, doing her homework or practicing her ballet poses under the eye of her governess.

His daughter was a woman now, however. He, a man of status and power, felt weak for a moment as he thought that soon enough his daughter would meet someone, fall in love, get married, and move out. She'd leave him here, alone, in this big house. He looked around the dark hallway. He'd tried to delay this as much as he could to have more time with her, but Covedale needed a male heir. It was time for him to help her choose a husband wisely. A beautiful woman like her could attract a man that could destroy what he'd worked so hard for. He couldn't allow that. An arranged marriage would be best for her. It wouldn't hurt if he took a look around for a potential candidate on his next business trip.

He walked again towards the curved, marble stairs. There was more light shining now through the floor-to-ceiling windows and he didn't light the big crystal chandelier hanging in the middle of the staircase.

He slowly descended. The kitchen staff were preparing breakfast already and the smell of freshly baked buns was coming up from the basement. His stomach rumbled, but he'd wait for the servants to bring his food when it was ready.

He turned right when he got to the main floor. He paused by the fountain covering the height of one wall. The water fell down the stone surface, quietly humming as it made the journey. The liquid was so clear that only the bending light gave it away. His daughter wasn't yet a teen when she'd noticed this art piece in a gallery. How could he have refused her? These sculptures had to be eighty or a hundred years old. After all industry switched to support war, nothing with the sole purpose of pleasing the eyes was made. The fountain hadn't been that expensive, which had surprised him. Less than five thousand, and it continuously brought his daughter joy to look at it.

He passed the dining room where an immense table stood that could sit at least twenty. He never had that many guests seated at once for dinner, but the size and style fit the room perfectly. He admired the carved table legs and the backs of the chairs—Neo-Renaissance, he was told—and he showed it off proudly to everyone who visited.

As he was walking past the servant's staircase towards the door to his study, a young girl emerged, hurrying up from the basement. She almost collided with him, barely managing not to drop the silver tray she was carrying.

"Watch where you're going!" his voice thundered, echoing in the spotless hallway.

He didn't care to remember the servants' names. There were so many girls working in his house, wearing the same white apron and bonnet, that it was impossible to remember them all.

"I'm sorry, sir." She curtsied in front of him, lowering her eyes.

"Coffee in the study," he ordered, opening the door in front of him.

"Right away, sir." The girl curtsied again and hurried away. Whatever she had on the tray made a clinking noise as she walked.

The room on the other side of the door was still dark, except for the glow from the low fire in the fireplace. He walked up to the window and pulled the heavy curtains aside. Faint silver sun rays were already illuminating the ocean in the distance, promising a lovely day. He opened the sliding door a notch to let the fresh, cool March air in. With the morning air came the sound of the power generators.

Turning, he walked to the large desk to sit in his leather chair. He turned on the lamp and the faint light reflected from the top of the table illuminated the bookshelves encircling the room, reflecting off the spines of the books.

He couldn't imagine life without electricity. The diesel required cost him twenty tickets a day, but it was a small sacrifice for his daughter's well-being. He never dimmed the lights, even if it might save energy. He could afford the fuel, and he wouldn't have anyone coming to this house thinking less of him.

He picked up a paper that was on his desk and read it silently. It was a ledger showing the last month's income and expenditure for the city.

Fees from docks: 200,000 tickets.

That wasn't bad for a month's worth. He brought his head up from the document and looked ahead for a moment, thinking how these numbers could improve. He then lowered his head to read the next line.

"How many tons?" he asked out loud, frowning. "Fifteen *thousand* tons of food to be shipped to Riverlea?" He paused for a moment. "Okay," he calmed down and his face relaxed again as he read further, "So we only sent ten, and we're still to deliver five." Weren't there crates of onions that had been stuck at the docks for the last couple of weeks? The carrier still hadn't paid the dues. He grabbed a pen that was lying on the desk. *Send them onions,* he wrote on the side of the ledger and smiled to himself. He'd turn these notes into an order later. Let them complain about how he ran the business, he dared them. He put the pen down.

His father had taken over Covedale when the government structures fell at the beginning of the war. He had been the only one who could pull it off. He'd moved his associates from Riverlea, the downtown district already trained and equipped with guns to protect Covedale on the mainland, in the old city suburbs.

Stock markets were over; the world was in a deep recession, and people had less and less to spend. He'd moved quickly to occupy the portion of the river where the banks were low and accessible, which promised some trade with cities upriver. When the bridges between Covedale and Riverlea went down during an air raid—some claimed that his father had helped make that happen—there was no longer easy access to the downtown core, which had trapped people on the island that was Riverlea. All food and medicine had to pass through Covedale to be loaded on boats and shipped to Riverlea. It had been convenient and profitable for him to instate a heavy toll on these goods. It still was.

A knock on the door made him look up before reaching the end of the document.

"Come!" he exclaimed.

A servant girl walked in. She brought in the coffee, and quickly, but carefully set it on the desk beside him. She then curtsied, turned around and left, closing the door behind her.

He picked up the porcelain coffee cup and took a sip of the bitter liquid, continuing to read the document in his other hand.

Only four locked up? That should increase. Having empty cages would just make the town think of him as weak. Leo would have to do a better job of this. He was the security officer and should know better than to leave the jail empty.

He put down the coffee; the cup clinked against the saucer. He picked up the pen again. A farmer on the outskirts of the town that refused to pay for his protection. *Let him go free*, he wrote. He had a good heart after all. He then added, *Have thugs steal his harvest*. If White didn't find a buyer, he could distribute the crops in town as a last resort. Townsfolk loved gifts, and it always increased their respect for him.

He moved to the next item on the list. *Any trespassers in Covedale are to be executed,* he wrote on the side. The tree by the river needed some fresh meat hanging off it. It had been a few days since the last execution, and whatever was still hanging would have been picked over by vultures.

There was something missing from the report. He stared at it for a moment, trying to recall what it was he was thinking about. "Right," he said. *Do something with Tom*, he wrote on the bottom before putting the pen down. Tom was his nephew, and he was sick of hearing of his debts to others. He didn't need that kind of trouble in his family or his city. There had to be a way to stop Tom from doing any more harm. Fixing his deals was probably no longer possible, but writing his name down would help him remember to give it more thought.

He finished reading the report and turned on the radio sitting on the desk. It was time for his morning routine of listening to the latest news. The radio was the best medium these days for information from afar. The only printed words were in books and magazines, but those had stopped production with the start of the war. Newspapers were a thing of the past, long gone even before then.

"People are out on the street everywhere," the anchor said cheerfully, live from a Chicago broadcast. "Some are planning to celebrate the end of the war for the entire week." The sounds of celebration could be heard in the background.

The phone on his desk rang. With towers down, only a few could afford the satellite phones for communication. This room held the only such device in the whole of Covedale. He picked it up without hesitation.

"Yes?" He knew who was calling.

"People are laughing and dancing all around me—" the anchor continued. White turned the radio down a bit.

"Yes, I just went through the ledger," he replied to the person on the other side of the phone. "What do you mean you need more tickets?" He began to frown as he listened. "I can't pay much more than that." He was annoyed. His superiors always got most of the money from the docks, and the only other major source of income for Covedale was trade with the neighboring Riverlea. He couldn't agree to pay more. Running the city was expensive.

In the background, the radio continued faintly. "We've been waiting for this moment for fifty years!"

"Sure, I can do you a favor," he said calmly and sat up in his chair. He had little choice. Either he paid the extra fee or did what he was told. These were the usual terms, so he wasn't surprised.

He listened for a moment as the person on the other side explained, giving him directions. "Who is he?" he asked, then listened intently. "With all due respect, sir," he cut in, "I think it *is* my concern."

He felt his anger rising. He knew that there was no point in arguing with the man he was talking to, but he at least wanted to make a show of resistance. He didn't want it to seem like he would always just agree to everything.

"Yes," he finally said with disappointment in his voice. He hung up but kept looking at the phone.

The noise of a street party could be heard on the radio as the anchor continued, raising a toast. "A local syndicate has donated ale for everyone. To the new world!"

White felt defeated and his morning's energy had suddenly evaporated. Welcoming a stranger into Covedale was the last thing he needed right now.

He sighed and sat back in his chair to listen to the radio.

"Our ports have welcomed yet another ship coming from Europe. The veterans of war are coming back, and there are still many more waiting to make the trip. With the war over, families can finally be reunited!"

"Home!"

Oliver shook Eric who was lying on one of the bunk beds in a huge cabin that had been housing tens of men for the past week they'd been sailing from Europe. They were getting closer to the small port in Rockland. They were supposed to go to New York or Boston, but the ship had been diverted. They said it was because of poor weather.

Eric didn't move. His face was turned towards the wall, and Oliver knew it was pointless to press him. The man was constantly on edge, avoiding his presence at all costs since they'd boarded the ocean liner. At night, Eric tossed and turned, having nightmares, and often woke everyone up with his screams. During the day, they'd find him sitting on the open deck alone and shivering from the cold, staring at the empty sea.

Oliver looked around the large room full of tall bunk beds and at the men sitting or lying on them. Most on this ship had been broken by the war and by what they'd seen. All hoped the return home would heal them. Death, torture, and mutilation were common at the front and the experience crushed many souls.

When he'd met Eric, they were still young, not knowing what the future would bring. They'd been on their way to the front, riding in the same truck, when they'd spoken for the first time. They'd shared a slug, a hand-rolled tobacco cigarette. Eric had been a fragile kid without adequate training who hadn't enlisted for war, Oliver recalled. He hadn't wanted to go, but he'd been drafted.

They'd stuck together through the twelve years they'd been away from home. They'd shared many experiences of the front and the POW camp. The worst they'd endured, however, was after they'd escaped from enemy hands. While they were trying to cut through the front lines to return to their fellow soldiers, they had been captured somewhere in the Ural Mountains by what looked like local militia and put to back-breaking work manufacturing ammunition. The ten years spent there as slaves had taken a toll on both of them, but they'd always helped each other when they could. The hardship of that place, however, had been too much for Eric. It made Oliver sorry that they were parting in such sad circumstances, but he didn't hold it against Eric that he couldn't deal with a goodbye. He hoped that Eric would make good use of the little token of appreciation Oliver had given him.

Oliver turned around and got his backpack from the locker beside the bed. It contained nothing of value: An old shaving kit, a piece of soap and a change of underwear. The only set of clothes he owned he was already wearing.

This was his chance to separate himself from the past and the years he'd spent at war. He loved the idea of starting his life anew. He smiled to himself at the thought. Finally he was free. Once off this ship, he'd be able to do whatever he pleased. No one was there to control him and tell him what to do.

He felt the need for some fresh air again. The emptiness of the open ocean was calling him and he needed to see it one more time. Oliver grabbed his belongings, not intending to return to the cabin ever again, and exited through the metal door. They were deep in the belly of the giant machine. The rumble of the diesel engines was loud and sent vibrations through the walls that cracked and moaned metallically from the strain. He turned right and passed a few other cabin doors until he reached the steep stairs.

It took a while, but he got to the main deck and opened the heavy storm door to the outside. A cold March breeze blew across his face, but he walked to the railing and faced the wind, looking towards the land. The seagulls were already circling, hoping to find food in the currents made by the hull of the ship. He stared at the shore for a moment, then turned his back to the wind, took out a slug from his pocket, and lit it. Almost there. He puffed smoke.

It took the crew most of the day to finally get the ship doors open and start allowing people to disembark. Oliver was one of the first people to get off. The men working for the port directed him to the port registry office as soon as he stepped onto solid ground.

The room was a concrete box with no windows and peeling paint on the walls. There were two scratched up chairs and a desk made from a piece of wood set on a pair of sawhorses. A small radio was faintly recounting the recent news about the end of the war.

"Name?" barked the surly man behind the desk. He was wearing a military-style uniform with 'Port Authority' written on his breast tag. He had a piece of paper in front of him that he was filling out.

"Oliver Conway." He spelled out his last name. He wished he could use a different name, but when he'd gotten on the ship the officials required his soldier ID number, and he didn't want to risk being held back in Europe.

"Who are you traveling with?"

"No one," he replied. There was no reason to tell him about Eric. It was time they went their own ways.

"Destination?"

Oliver wasn't prepared for this question. Going back to his parents' house was an option, but that would mean returning to a life he'd hated so much that he'd enlisted for war. Maybe having them think he died was better.

There wasn't really any other place he really knew of, except maybe . . . "Riverlea," he replied. Karl—the man he and Eric had worked under—had told him to visit Mark Rodden, an accountant friend of his in Riverlea, once he was back in North America.

"Where is that?" The man threw a map onto the table for Oliver to look at.

He didn't know. He stared at the map for a long time, looking for the town by chasing the rivers with his index finger. Oliver knew it had to be there somewhere; he imagined a small town by the river with a meadow surrounding it. He started with the east coast, but the man behind the desk grew impatient.

"I can't find it," Oliver replied, annoyed. He was also getting frustrated not knowing where Riverlea was. He hadn't had the opportunity to ask Karl about it when they'd last seen each other.

"What was the name?" The man was watching the digital clock on the wall. He probably didn't want to wait the whole night for Oliver to find the place.

"Riverlea." He spelled it out.

The man walked up to the ancient-looking computer in the corner of the room and typed the name into his system. He looked at the display for a moment.

The quiet sound of a radio broadcast was audible in the room. "Limited available housing and food forces the government to implement a new strategy. Any fresh settlers will require special permits in the most populated areas."

The man got up and looked at the map. It didn't take him long to find it.

"Here it is." The man pointed at a location on the opposite side of the continent from where Oliver had been looking. "But I can't put you there. It's not in the list of authorized destinations. The best I can do is this adjacent city." The man pointed at the map. "Covedale."

"Covedale it is, then," Oliver replied. That town was farther than he thought he'd need to travel. It was at least a week away, even if he was able to catch an unlikely car ride. He hoped he wouldn't have to walk the whole way.

"You have no permit to settle here in Rockland," the man added. "We require you to leave the city within twenty-four hours." He took out a bundle of money and counted out one hundred tickets in blue bills of ten. "That's the payment for your military service." The man passed over the money and a copy of the completed arrival document. "You're free to go."

Oliver left the small office and stepped outside. He was finally free. He smiled to himself as he looked around. Behind him stood the rusting ocean liner, towering over ten stories above sea level. The other people still on the ship were lined up, leaning over the railings, ready to disembark. Oliver smiled and blew them a goodbye kiss as he turned around and started walking towards downtown. It was March and the ground was still partially covered in snow, which crunched beneath his shoes.

The money they'd given him would last him for two, maybe three months. It wasn't much. His thoughts went to Riverlea, as his life depended on it. He hoped that he'd find what Karl had promised him.

He crossed the port gate into the town. There was no one waiting for the war veterans. The town was quiet. It felt deserted. The fear of newcomers kept people away.

He set off towards the red of the setting sun. He was a lone man walking down the street, holding on to his only coat, which barely kept him warm enough. He felt free.

Eric turned in bed and looked around the room. The ship bounced as it docked. There weren't too many people left inside as most were already up and ready to get out of this rusty metal contraption that had kept them jailed for about a week. All of them were tired of the war and the trip, ready to finally put their feet on solid ground.

He sat up in his bed for a better view. He looked at the lockers and noticed that Oliver's bag was missing. He sighed with relief. He'd anticipated Oliver would be one of the first to disembark, and Eric didn't mind being the last. He wanted to keep as much distance between himself and Oliver as he could.

He jumped off the bunk bed onto the metal floor of the room. He walked up to the lockers and grabbed his bag. He turned around and noticed one of his fellow travelers still packing his belongings. He gave him a firm handshake and a wide hug as a goodbye before leaving himself.

Once he reached the main deck, he looked out at the dark, frozen town of Rockland below. The sun was already setting, tracing the contours of the roofs of the buildings with its red rays. He looked down onto the shore and noticed Oliver crossing the port gates and sending a kiss back to him. There was no way he could've seen him from so far away and picked him from the crowd, but Eric thought the kiss was for him and his eyes became moist, but not because he was sad. They were tears of happiness.

2

TWO MONTHS HAD PASSED since Oliver disembarked the ship, and the spring sun rays were strong enough to heat the concrete buildings and pavement. He had his usual smile on his face as he walked down the streets of Riverlea on what had once been a sidewalk. His posture was straight and self-assured, his long strides rhythmic, as though he belonged there on that street and had no worries on his mind. He wore a torn black t-shirt and old jeans that were stretched and hung on him like a sack, with unevenly-worn sneakers. An unflattering look for a man in his thirties.

When he'd arrived in Covedale and looked at the other side of the river—at the ruins in the distance—his heart had sunk. He'd traveled across the continent to be there, catching the occasional wagon ride or hopping onto empty cargo trains, only to see what little remained of the city. The tall skyscrapers were mostly gone, but still remnants stuck out like giant thorns rising from the ground that a strong wind could have toppled down.

What struck him as odd, however, had been the ferry that took people and goods across the river once a day. He'd wanted to go to Riverlea and see what was on the other side for himself, so he'd paid the fare of one ticket. He'd figured he had nothing to lose taking the trip, and still wanted to believe that Karl had been telling the truth about his connection there. When he'd arrived—about two months ago—he'd found that the city was alive and a home for thousands of people. Finding the accountant he'd been referred to, though, turned out to be harder than he'd thought, but he hoped to finally meet him today.

He passed building ruins and paused for a moment by a destroyed store-front to see his reflection in a piece of remaining glass. He ran his fingers through his dark hair to ensure all was in place and winked at himself. "You got this," he said out loud. Nature had been kind to him by giving him charm, confidence, and wisdom. The last piece of what he thought he needed—the money—was within his reach, closer than ever before.

He continued his walk, passing the city slums set up in what looked like a former park. The poorest of the poor he'd ever seen occupied Riverlea. People looked like they had lost everything and ended up in this shack city. He greeted an old woman sitting on the sidewalk as he passed by. Her face was wrinkled like the old paint still stuck to the ruins nearby. She returned the smile; a kind, genuine smile.

The dirty kids that ran past him barefoot, or the ones playing in sewers, would never have a normal life. Some were already addicted to drugs and alcohol by the age of ten. The local gang would absorb others and put them to long hours of work for little money scavenging the ruins for raw materials or making garments in the local textile factory. Mothers cooking the only meal of the day on the firepit in the middle of the makeshift city or hanging the washed rags to dry in the sun were selling themselves during the night to feed hungry mouths.

The entire city was a place of misery and unattainable dreams, but against all odds, people still laughed and smiled—either because the war was over, or because their situations were so helpless they no longer cared.

He walked about a block further to a few narrow houses in the middle of the wasteland of the city. He stopped in front of a storefront with boarded windows covered in old graffiti and burn marks. It looked abandoned, but with the housing shortage in Riverlea, nothing still standing remained empty. He knew this was the place he'd been referred to. He tried the door and found it unlocked.

As soon as he stepped in, he heard the hum of a charged gun behind him in an otherwise quiet room. It was dark, with no windows to let the light in, and his eyes hadn't yet adjusted to the change. The air was hot and heavy, with no breeze, and the sour smell of sweat was overwhelming.

"I come in peace." He brought his hands up before he was asked to do so. There was no worry in his voice. He knew any reputable operation would be wary and untrusting of a stranger.

"Whatcha want?" the male voice behind him asked.

"Let me introduce myself," Oliver began. Still holding up his hands, he turned around and boldly faced the charged gun. "Oliver Conway." He smiled. Normally he would've offered a handshake and asked how the day was going, but he knew it wasn't wise to make such moves at this time. His actions, however, were smooth and confident, which took his aggressor by surprise, and Oliver had the moment he needed for his vision to adjust.

The man in front of Oliver was average in appearance. He was gripping his gun a little too tightly, like it was the first time a stranger had just stepped in unannounced.

"I'm looking for an accountant," Oliver said calmly. He thought it was obvious why he'd entered the building.

"An' who the fuck are ya?" The man gestured towards the front door with his head suggesting that Oliver should leave.

"That's not very nice of you to just kick me out like that," Oliver said, still smiling, but with a bit of annoyance in his voice. "I believe this is the establishment of Mr. Mark Rodden, and I believe he'll be happy to speak to me—"

"Why would I?" asked another voice to Oliver's right. He hadn't been aware of the third person in the room.

"A friend of ours says that I can help you," Oliver said, turning his body towards the unknown voice standing in the shadows, still holding his hands up as the lethal weapon remained pointed at him.

Rodden walked to the center of the room. He was a short and slim person with some gray in his hair. He started to pat Oliver down and found a gun. Oliver didn't flinch; he was expecting this and didn't feel threatened. Rodden put the gun on the table before continuing, revealing two other items.

"This is a family heirloom I got from my father," Oliver said, as Rodden removed a small black satin bag from his person and placed it beside the gun. "Sentimental value."

The final object Rodden found on him was a small metal box called a jammer. There was nothing written on the device and it featured only a single button.

Rodden looked at it and kept it. He then turned to Oliver. "This way." He pointed at the closed door and gave the man who was still pointing a gun at Oliver a sign to stand down.

They entered a small office where the air felt fresher but much drier. There were many surfaces in the room covered with stacks of papers that hadn't been touched in many years, now thickly coated with dust. It was clear that this room wasn't used often. Even the desk in the middle was very messy, topped with paper and garbage and an ashtray that looked like it hadn't been emptied in months. Mark must have had another place where he conducted his usual business, because the room they were in didn't feature any of the necessary equipment. Oliver suspected that it was Rodden himself who had led him here. This room was clearly where Mark met with unwanted visitors.

Rodden signaled Oliver to sit down in one of the two chairs in the room and shoved papers off to the side of the desk to make space for the jammer. He then opened the desk drawer and took out his own identical device and put it on the desk on the opposite side of him. "I don't trust you," Rodden said.

"Of course not. And thank you for allowing me to speak with you."

They both turned on their jammers and leaned in. They knew the devices would only protect them if they sat close to them and whispered. As long as they were careful, no one would hear their conversation or be able to record it.

"That thing costs a fortune," Rodden said, pointing at the device. "Who sent you?" Having two of these on a single desk was very unusual.

The device had cost him nothing. He'd been fortunate enough to steal it from one of his fellow travelers while the man was sleeping on the crossing to the continent. Those who had enemies—and almost everyone did—wished to have such a jammer in their possession. "I need to take care of some business and our mutual friend Karl pointed me to you." Oliver leaned back in his chair.

"I'm in no mood to do business with you," Rodden said. "We're done."

Mark reached for the device to turn it off, but Oliver was quicker and, to the surprise and displeasure of the accountant, caught his hand.

"Why don't you hear me out?" Oliver asked and released Rodden's hand. "I'm not looking to do business with you. I'm looking for you to take care of my business." He paused for a moment and then added with a smile, "For a profit, of course."

"What do you want from me?"

"We both need money and I know where to find it."

"The world is drained of wealth," Mark said. "Nothing is worth the trouble for a few greasy tickets—"

"Now I feel a bit insulted that you think I came all the way here to discuss any small amount," Oliver said and shook his head in disapproval. He sat back in the chair and took out a slug.

Rodden leaned forward to the jammers and signaled Oliver to do the same. He complied.

"What business did you want me to do for you?"

"I know where the money is. I just need a little help to get it." Oliver smiled widely. He wanted to encourage him to consider his request.

"How much?"

"Well, I haven't seen the books in a while, but it'd be something around . . . a billion tickets," Oliver said with a wink and a smile.

Rodden froze for a moment. "No one has that much money except those who meddled in the war." He looked at Oliver suspiciously.

"What would be the benefit of lying to you to make you help me out? I'm not a war criminal." Oliver said, his smile turning into an annoyed grimace. "Then again, who came out without some kind of scar? I could incriminate you and prove that you're a bad guy just by looking through that," he bluffed, pointing at the stack of dusty papers sitting on the chair. "No one comes out of this war and goes to fucking heaven, Mark. The war is over and it's the choices we make now that will shape our future. You can turn all humble, move to one of the stinking slums—like the one I passed on the way—and await your death," he said, then paused. "Or you can let me help you be a better man. Whatever money you get from this partnership is yours to spend, and you can redeem yourself by helping others if you wish."

Rodden was lost in thought for a moment, but finally replied, "Where could this money possibly be hiding if you can't get it yourself?"

"Russian Central Bank—"

"What the fuck!" Rodden shouted, but quickly went back to a whisper and added, "Damn, I almost fell for it." He laughed.

"Mark, I'm telling the truth," Oliver continued. "I know the money is there because I put it there. All I need is some help to get the money from there to here." Oliver smashed his finished slug into the overfilled ashtray.

"Okay, let's say the money is yours, which I doubt. Russian Central Bank? That's fucking impossible," Rodden said dismissively.

"C'mon, you won't even try?" Oliver goaded.

"How on earth could a freaking billion be transferred?" Despite his tone, Mark looked like he was already trying to process a plan.

"Just to make it easier," Oliver said, "I don't need all the money at once. I'm fine with installments."

"Even if I could bring the money in in batches, it'd have to be laundered. Now that the war is over, they're planning to rebuild the cities and restore order. There'll be more people snooping around and looking at finances and transactions," Rodden said with some worry in his voice. "That amount of money won't go unnoticed . . ."

"That's why we need to act now, when there's less oversight. All I need from you is to get the money here and I'll deal with the rest."

Mark got up from his seat and walked to one of the boarded-up windows and stared at it, lost in thought. Oliver sat back in his chair and took out another slug and lit it. He waited patiently in silence for the decision. Oliver was right-handed, but he always held his nicotine fix in his left hand—a habit to keep his right hand, the steadier one, free at all times.

After an awkwardly long time, Mark sat back down and leaned forward. Oliver leaned in as well to continue the whispered conversation.

"How much do I get?"

"I was wondering the same. How much is your fee?" Oliver knew Mark's mind was set; they just had to work out the details.

"After deducting costs, I want ten percent."

"Well, well," Oliver said, and grinned. "Do we have a deal then?"

"I can look into it, but I'm uncertain I can do it."

"I believe in you," Oliver said as he wrote something on a piece of paper and slid it across the desk. If Karl believed in Mark, Oliver felt he could believe in him too.

Rodden grabbed the paper and glanced at it. It contained the account number of the Central Bank, as expected, together with security details.

Oliver had memorized the two account numbers Karl had given him. He recited them in his mind each time he went to sleep and each time he woke up. He knew Karl might take control of both deposits, but there was a chance he'd do what he promised.

After a moment Mark nodded. "Where are you staying?" he asked.

"Bayside Inn," Oliver said. It was a rundown hotel on one of the major streets that was mostly used as a brothel and often billed rooms by the hour, but a daily rate was also available.

Mark nodded. "Stay low," he said, knowing the building Oliver was staying in. "I need a few weeks to review our options and see what I can do. I'll call for you when I have news."

Oliver got up from the seat and extended his hand. Mark took it after a moment of hesitation. The deal was sealed and Oliver smiled. He collected his jammer off the table, along with the other items that had been confiscated from him in the main room, and walked out of the darkness into the daylight.

The sun was slowly setting. It was often dangerous to be in the streets of an unknown city after dusk, and he didn't want to risk it. He started to walk towards the Bayside Inn. Many people were sitting or sleeping on the sidewalks of what had once been the financial district of Riverlea, the coastal city's former downtown. These people could not afford their own shacks. The ill, the crippled, and the addicted had nowhere to go. Sleeping under the stars was the only option they had. Oliver felt some of their eyes following him and could hear the clinking of knives.

A big neon sign read 'Bayside Inn.' It wasn't lit and had probably broken decades ago, but it was still a landmark in the middle of the concrete-and-iron rubble that surrounded it. The inside was gloomy. Electricity was a luxury and generating your own power was extremely expensive. Those who needed it for their businesses conserved it any way they could.

The reception room was quite small and the lingering fog of cigarette smoke made it feel claustrophobic. Oliver noticed a half-dead plant in the corner and an old, dusty framed picture on the wall hanging askew. It was a yellowed print showing a field of golden wheat. A failed attempt to make the place welcoming.

"Another night?" the man behind the desk asked. "One for the room for the night; two if you wanna girl too," he recited. He was old and thin, his face weathered and dusty gray like the walls. His right hand was missing three fingers.

Oliver reached into the back pocket of his jeans and took out one of the blue ten-ticket bills he'd gotten at the port. He casually placed it on the worn-out desk. "That should be good for ten more days."

"Good," said the man behind the desk. He turned around, found the key to Oliver's room and threw it on the desk.

Oliver put the key in his pocket and entered the bar by the door on his left. He only had forty tickets and some change left of the money he'd gotten in Rockland. It wasn't much if he was to stay in the hotel. When he was traveling, he tried to save as much as he could by stealing the food he needed rather than buying it, but in Riverlea it was impossible to steal. There was no one to steal from. He hoped Mark would be quick with the transfer, otherwise he'd be forced to live on the street.

After a meal of overpriced watery stew and a few drinks that cost him half a ticket, Oliver went up to his room and sat on the bed. The room didn't smell pleasant. The tiny window in the corner hadn't opened for years so no fresh air ever made it in. Large yellow stains on the ceiling and peeling floor showed where the water pooled during the rain. No one that stayed in that room would ever be forgotten as the bed sheets, wallpaper, and even the floorboards permanently absorbed the sweat and smoke of the guests.

He reached into his pocket and took out the satin bag. He opened it carefully to reveal a shiny gold signet engraved with a dragon making a fiery attack.

He's eight and in someone's house. It's a small, dark room. Only a few rays of sun come through the slats of the yellow blinds in the dirty windows, illuminating the contours of the many objects in this messy house. Whoever lives here has accumulated a lot of junk that was strewn around in disarray.

"Be a man, kid," his father says. He never calls him by his first name. "You're a Conway and ya should act like one."

There are only three of them in the room. Oliver, his father, and a man sitting on the floor.

"I got ya the money!" says the man, crying and pleading.

"That's what ya tol' me two days ago," says his father, who turns to Oliver. "C'mon, kid, ya can do it. Remember the ring that I gave ya?" Oliver nods. "Be like that dragon."

Oliver stands there paralyzed with the gun in his hand pointed at the man on the floor. The gun is charged and unlocked—all he needs to do is pull the trigger, but he can't.

It isn't the first time he's been with his father on a mission to collect overdue money, but they usually finish with some beating and a promise that the money will come. This is different.

Oliver holds the gun tightly in his small hands.

"I don't have all day. Do it!" his father commands.

Oliver looks at the man, then closes his eyes and pulls the trigger. He hears the gun buzz for a brief moment then recharge again, but nothing else. There's no screaming, no begging. Just silence and the smell of something burning.

"Good job," his father says with a smile on his face. "Aiming for the chest, got him right in the head."

Oliver stands in place, eyes wide.

"Let's not speak about this to anyone," his father adds. "Not even friends."

Oliver looks at his father, then at the man on the floor. He nods. It's their secret. He then smiles, proud of himself, happy to please his father.

Violet moved the cloth that served as the door to the shack and peeked outside. There was a group of kids that lived in the alley who were amusing themselves with a knucklebones game made using rocks they had found. She noticed the neighbor opposite was sitting on a concrete block in front of her shack, chewing something that might have been tobacco. She glanced over at Violet and smiled warmly.

It was getting dark and her brother Mike wasn't home yet. He'd promised that he'd be back before daylight was gone, but he was nowhere to be seen. A few more minutes and it might be too late for her to go anywhere. The dark streets were not safe for a lone woman to walk.

Unable to see Mike anywhere in the alley, she retreated back inside and fed the tin can fire in the middle of their single-room place with a wood chip. She'd found a few of them in the ruins—tiny pieces of broken furniture— and brought them home for some warmth. The May night was cold again. Their shack walls, made from steel and tarp they'd found, were no longer than four meters each. The place contained what few belongings they had and was filled with smoke that stung her eyes.

Violet could hear the neighbors fighting again through the thin walls. The man was a drunk and violent when intoxicated. He beat his wife often, and sometimes the kids were not spared either. Nothing anyone could do about it.

Violet sat down on her rag-covered bedding that was placed directly on the packed-dirt floor. She covered her knees and bare feet with the robe she was wearing. There was nothing else to do but to wait. She suspected Mike was doing this on purpose—being late just to find a reason to keep her in and argue again.

She was able to hug herself for a couple of minutes, but jumped up when the cloth in the doorway moved and Mike stepped in.

"Leaving again?" her brother asked as soon as he was inside. His voice sounded more annoyed than angry. His gray eyes, just like hers, had a shine to them in the dark room as he looked at her.

She felt troubled by how much he cared she was going out. Just two years younger, at sixteen, her brother Mike was a tall, strong man. He was roaming the streets of Riverlea and she never asked if he was selling drugs or robbing people. He knew she was planning to be away for the night, so his question was to cause another fight. She didn't think it was any sign of him actually being concerned about what she was doing.

"Ya think he cares about ya?" he asked when she said nothing and moved to leave.

She was certain he did. "He buys me food," she replied, but it wasn't about the food. They spent a lot of time talking. It wasn't until a couple of weeks ago that he had kissed her. Last night his passionate lips had felt so good on her body. She was certain she was special to him.

He seemed to know a lot more things than she or Mike did. He was more experienced in life. His stories were so interesting, mesmerizing. She wanted to hear more of those, rather than listen to her brother complaining about how she should live her life.

"Right, that makes me the only one that brings in fucking money." Mike looked up and shook his head. "The roof is caving in, and the tarp has holes. Ya full stomach won't fucking fix those."

"Whatcha want?" she asked. She was impatient to get out.

"Ya to earn money and contribute," Mike replied, sitting down on his own mattress.

Before she could move the cloth aside and leave, he called, "Don't go by the river."

She stopped in her tracks and turned around out of curiosity. "Eh?"

"Covedale hung another guy," he replied.

She shrugged. She wasn't planning to go anywhere close to the river, but it wouldn't be the first dead person she'd seen. Another hanged man, that wasn't news.

Violet stepped out into the darkness. Shapes of the buildings were barely visible. She needed to be quick if she was to make it safely to the inn. It wasn't that far, but she needed to hurry.

She looked left and right down the deserted alley. Both kids and adults were already hiding in their shacks. She turned left and started to run.

Besides a single whistle she heard as she ran, no one bothered her. She stopped to catch her breath at the front of the inn.

"Fuck Mike," she mumbled to herself. "Earn money. Contribute." She crinkled her nose and tilted her head. "Be real. I won't find work." When they were traveling through the countryside, they'd found work on farms. They'd worked hard learning how to plant crops and harvest. Here in Riverlea, there wasn't even a single blade of grass anywhere. The entire city was comprised of piles of concrete and metal, remnants of tall buildings, and makeshift structures where people lived.

She looked around. The front of the Bayside Inn was busy. It was May, but a few women were standing around a metal barrel with a low fire burning inside it to keep the chill of the night away. Once in a while men approached them to talk, but she couldn't hear their conversations.

She didn't want to be outside for long so she walked into the inn and ascended the steps to the second floor. She knocked on the third door on the left.

An eye appeared in the peep hole and the door opened shortly after.

"Come in, my darling." Oliver invited her in with a slight courtesy bow and a smile, and locked the door behind her. He looked to be in good spirits and she smiled seeing him.

"I didn't expect you so late. Were you running?" He asked pulling her closer and giving her a brief kiss. She realized that she was still flushed from the run. "Did you eat already?" he asked.

"Yeah, I had some," she replied and moved away from him. She sat down on the only chair in the room as he remained standing. "Ya seem happy," she added.

She looked around the room and noticed a gun on the table with some money beside it. She didn't know how much it was, but she was sure she hadn't seen that much before.

"Remember that man I was looking for?" Oliver started as he circled the small room.

She nodded absently. "Ya found him?"

"I did, and I made a good deal." He stopped and leaned on the wall. There was a wide grin on his face.

"Well, that's good."

He noticed her lack of interest. "What's bothering you?"

"Ma brother was late again. That's all." She shrugged. It wasn't important to tell Oliver that Mike was doing this on purpose or that Covedale had caught another escapee from Riverlea. She'd probably learn who it was in the morning.

"Were you fighting?" He came over and slid between her and the chair. His arms embraced her waist.

They had met more than a month ago. She'd been sitting on the pavement by one of the ruined concrete building walls when he'd come by. He'd stopped right beside her, looking somewhere into the distance as though searching for something on the horizon. He didn't notice her until she gently pulled on his pant leg. She just wanted his attention as she extended his hand towards him.

She remembered his startled deep blue eyes as he looked at her, realizing her presence. He then smiled at her so she smiled back and stood up, keeping her hand extended, palm up. She didn't say a word to him, but he had to know she was asking. It was hard not to notice her sunken cheeks and bony arms. She hadn't eaten for two days. Normally people of Riverlea gave nothing to those who were begging. No one had any money or food to spare, but she was hungry and there was something different about him—as though he did not belong.

That's when he'd asked her to come with him. She hadn't been sure what he wanted, but she'd followed him into the inn. She'd expected him to take her to his room that night, but he didn't. He'd sat her at the bar inside and fed her with a stew he purchased for her, watching tentatively as she ate quickly, devouring the food in front of her. When she was done, he'd let her go and asked her to come again the following day.

Since then, she went to see him often. At first it was all about the food he so freely got for her. Later, she started to come for his company, and to—at least for a time—escape the tension that was growing between her and her brother.

"We always argue," she replied, not wanting to go into detail.

"What was it this time?" He moved her blonde hair from her face. His voice was soft and calming.

"Ya know we always fight 'bout money." She wanted to contribute, but there was nothing she could do to bring in money besides sell herself, and she didn't want to do that.

"Maybe I should talk with him." He held her hand. "It might be time we met."

"Nah, I don't think so," she said dismissively.

"Are you sure?" Oliver continued. "I could come visit you. Talk to him—"

"Not a good idea," she protested. She didn't want Oliver to see how poorly they'd built their shack. The only one that was crooked, stuck between the sturdier houses of their neighbors. She also felt that the less Mike knew about Oliver, the better.

She looked at him and put her arms around his neck. "I don't want to talk about it today," she added. "Today we celebrate ya deal."

He smiled at her warmly. She felt his left hand on her cheek, gently stroking it, then his soft lips on hers.

3

OLIVER WOKE UP EARLY with Violet still sleeping with her head on his shoulder. He smiled to himself and stroked her hair gently so as not to wake her up. Oliver had spent the past few weeks with Violet while he waited for Mark's message. She often came to the inn to avoid her brother and fall into Oliver's embrace.

They'd spent many hours talking in the darkness of the room about anything and nothing, the past and the future. She, a poor orphan, was always curious about the big world. She listened attentively, wide-eyed, captivated by his voice, as Oliver answered her many questions and told her the stories he'd heard himself when he was a child. She didn't hesitate to quiz him, showing her curiosity, not feeling judged.

"They can walk on two legs like humans?" Violet looked at Oliver with her brows drawn together, not believing him about monkeys.

He smiled at her. "And their whole body is covered in hair."

"Humans can be very hairy too," she joked.

"Monkeys also have tails coming right from their bums."

Violet couldn't help but laugh.

"And they use them to swing from the trees," he continued. He noticed that the more he described the animal, the harder Violet laughed. He could see tears forming in the corners of her eyes as she struggled to contain her laughter. It amused him and he started to laugh with her.

"And they have such big ears." Oliver pulled his own ears out and forward to show how a monkey would look.

"Stop that! Ma stomach hurts!" Violet said through her tears when she regained her breath. "Stop lying to me!" she accused him playfully, hitting his arm with her fist.

"I'm serious." He got up to jump around and make monkey noises, sending Violet into another fit of laughter.

Only a small ray of gray light entered the quiet room from the outside. The rest of the hotel guests were still sleeping deeply, tired from the drugs, alcohol, and sex they'd had the previous night. Those who got a bit of money as a payout for having worked flocked to an inn like this one. They celebrated their small fortunes by spending them here, in a short time, living their best lives. When their money ran out, they were back to nothing, just exactly what they had before, until their luck returned.

Oliver looked around the room and noticed the contrast of a yellowish piece of paper on the dirty floor by the door. He slipped out of Violet's arms carefully so as not to wake her and picked the paper up.

The note had only two words: *See me.*

It could've come from only one person, Oliver thought, and started to dress. The room was chilly and damp inside, so he decided to put on his gray, worn-out coat to protect himself from the expected rain outside.

He was about to open the door when he saw Violet wake up.

"Good morning, darling," he said. He walked up to her and kissed her. "I'll be back soon." He smiled and left the room to see Mark.

He walked towards the accountant's office. Due to rain, there were fewer people in the open, but he still hurried. He turned right into a small alley that provided a shortcut to the next parallel street on which Mark operated.

When he was almost halfway through the gloomy passage, a big man crossed his path. He was taller and wider in the shoulders than Oliver. At the same time, he heard the hum of a charged gun behind him, and he felt the muzzle press into his back. *Fool,* he cursed himself. The visit with Mark had distracted him and he had allowed himself to get ambushed. He felt his gun being pulled from the small of his back.

"I don't want any trouble," Oliver said to the man in front of him, but whoever was behind him replied.

"Us either," the voice said.

He was disarmed and incapable of fighting two men, one of whom looked strong enough to crush his bones with a single blow. Oliver brought his hands up. They could have the two tickets he had left on him if they let him go.

They frisked him, but found no other weapon on him. A hood was placed over his head from behind, and they pushed him forward to walk. The men grabbed him by the arms and kept the gun still pressed against him. They led him for a few minutes through the streets. The steps on the wet pavement echoed from the nearby walls as they went through a different narrow alley. Another turn left and they were again on one of the busier streets. Oliver could hear people passing him, but no one reacted to his abduction. Whoever the men were, they weren't disturbed.

Suddenly they turned left, shoving him forward with enough force that he almost tripped. He couldn't see anything through the hood. The gun was withdrawn from his back and he heard the sound of a door closing behind him. His hands were not bound, so he immediately took the hood off.

He was in a small room with tiny slits by the ceiling from which faint rays of light were passing through. There were three men in the room and it was full of tobacco smoke. Two were standing with guns pointed at him, ready to fire. The third man leaning against the wall opposite Oliver was clearly in charge. He casually pointed at Oliver and showed him an empty chair by the table in the middle of the room as an invitation for him to sit down.

"Who are you?" Oliver asked without sitting. It was hard to see the man's face in the poorly lit room.

"Gutters," the man said and pointed at the chair again. "Sit down."

Oliver slowly sat down. He'd heard of the Gutters. They were an underground organization, the militia of Riverlea, who apparently controlled everything that was going on in the city. He had no business with them, so he stayed out of their way, hoping that they would likewise stay out of his. Apparently, that was too much to ask.

"Do you know how many fucking people live in Riverlea?" the man started.

"The city is none of my concern," Oliver replied. He was more committed to getting off this island now than ever before.

"It fucking should be," the man said. "Half a million." He puffed some smoke. "But nobody cares. We don't exist in their eyes, so they don't have to help us or provide subsidies. Out of sight, out of fucking mind."

Oliver was laughing under his breath. This was madness and he still didn't know what he had to do with any of that.

"But the people out there," he continued, pointing at the wall behind him, "They all want to fucking eat."

It was the Gutters controlling the distribution and prices of food. Why would they kidnap him to tell him that the people of Riverlea were starving? Hunger was everywhere in the city and everyone knew about the food shortage. The Gutters were to blame for the conditions. Was he apprehended because of the money? Who told them? Mark?

"It isn't easy to fucking feed them. We either need money or reliable shipments," the man said. "I was contemplating taking a share from these transfers that Mark is giving you."

So this meeting was about the money. He'd been a fool to assume no one would know about his dealings with Rodden, but the information lifted his mood. Mark must have completed the first transfer.

The man continued, "But I got a better fucking idea. See, we know who you are." He pointed his finger at Oliver.

Oliver's heart skipped a beat, but he concluded that the man must be bluffing, trying to intimidate him. It was impossible they knew who he was. "We won't interfere with your dealings with Mark. I can keep a secret." The man threw an envelope on the table. "In return, we'd like you to do something for us."

Oliver picked up the envelope and opened it. There was a small piece of paper inside with a few words written on it. He read the note, suppressing some surprise. He waited, rethinking his options.

It puzzled him how someone here in Riverlea, practically nowhere, would know anything about him. It had been twelve long years since he had enlisted to join the war at seventeen. He had hoped it was enough time to separate him from his past, but he was clearly mistaken.

"Seems like you're not giving me an alternative," Oliver finally replied after a long pause. He wasn't interested in doing anything for the Gutters, but they were still pointing their loaded guns at him. The soldiers were alert, anticipating any sudden moves.

"It's a good deal."

"I will need time," Oliver replied. "I need to orient myself."

The Gutter nodded. "How much time?"

Oliver took a quick glance at the soldiers in the room before he replied. "I don't know. Weeks, maybe months." He then directed his words at the man in front of him. "I don't do things hastily, without preparation."

"We'll be watching."

Oliver put the paper back into the envelope and put it inside his coat, agreeing to the terms. If the rumors about the Gutters were true, they wouldn't hesitate to send him to the other world right from this room he was sitting in. Taking the envelope meant he kept his life and his money and that appealed strongly to him at this particular moment. He had many questions and concerns, but he didn't want to stick around longer. If there was one thing that he was sure of, it was that he needed to get out of Riverlea today . . . right after he got his money.

When he arrived at Mark's office a while later, he wasn't greeted with a gun pointed at his head. The room was still as stuffy and gloomy as before, but Rodden's bodyguard nodded and looked at the door, indicating for Oliver to just walk in. Mark was expecting him.

Oliver put his jammer on the desk and turned it on. He wondered if he really needed it since Mark was just freely passing information to the Gutters. The accountant didn't take his own device out, which he also found suspicious.

"So I got the first transfer," Mark whispered, nodding to Oliver who was sitting silent. "Everything checked out, and the money you spoke of . . . the account has not been accessed in some time, so I had to be extra careful. Neither of us wants people sniffing things out."

Oliver nodded. Was Mark not aware that he had just met with the bad guys?

"It took longer than I thought, but here it is." Mark passed a piece of paper towards Oliver, who grabbed it and looked at it. The paper featured information on the transfer, as well as the remaining balance on the account.

Oliver stared at it for a moment. Despite his troubles earlier, he began to smile. He put the paper back on the desk and Mark grabbed it, lit it on fire, and placed it onto the top of the pile of fossilized remnants of tobacco slugs. The paper slowly burned as Mark continued.

"I didn't see a tail, but I'd suggest you be careful." Oliver wanted to laugh, but then Mark placed six rolls of money in front of him. "Cash was the safest to get once I made a deal with the cartel," Mark said.

That's why the Gutters knew about the money. That made more sense now, but it was a risky move for a man like Mark. He should've known better than to involve the cartel.

Oliver looked at the money in front of him, within his reach. He'd never seen so much in his life. All he needed to do was to grab it and leave.

"Why did you go to the Gutters?" Oliver asked after a moment. He didn't think he could trust Mark. He needed answers.

Mark looked at him and must have noticed the judging look on his face. He sat back in the chair with a sigh. "I had to use their assets to ensure the money was safe," he said. He appeared equally unhappy with how things had turned out. "I know what I set up for them in the banks is reliable."

"Instead of setting up new money transfer routes, you used theirs?" Oliver couldn't believe how foolish Mark was. "Karl said you were the best and I think he was mistaken."

"I can't make that claim and I don't know who Karl is. I don't know anyone with that name," Mark replied angrily. "A new setup would take months and it looked like your matter was urgent."

Oliver was surprised. Hadn't Karl said that he and Mark were friends? The whole situation angered Oliver, but Mark was right. He needed the money fast. He couldn't wait months for the first transfer. He recalled the two tickets he still had in his pocket that weren't taken from him during his kidnapping. His gun, however, was gone. It might cost him a hundred tickets to replace it.

"I guess it shouldn't be surprising that you're fucking working for the Gutters. It's clear now why you live here rather than in Covedale," Oliver said and looked around the dusty room.

"I don't work for them, or for you," Mark said, annoyed. "What the Gutters want from you is none of my business. If you had a better plan for your money, why didn't you do it yourself, or go somewhere else?"

Oliver felt defeated. He had no clue how Mark was doing the transfers. He felt stupid for trusting Karl and coming here. The promise of that much money had blinded him. He could have at least made friends with the Gutters during his stay in Riverlea. It could've made things so much easier for him.

"No Gutters means no laundering of the money. The money I gave you is safe to spend but other transfers wouldn't be," Mark continued. "You'd need to invest it in something."

Oliver had no choice but to agree to the terms. He needed Mark, and the harm had already been done. The accountant knew where the money was. Canceling the agreement and going somewhere else might anger Mark, and it'd be just a formality for him to steal the money. All of it. He knew all the security details required to make the withdrawals. Losing the money wouldn't release him from the promise he'd just made to the Gutters, either. "I'll take care of the investing," Oliver said.

He picked up the rolls of money from the desk and put them into his coat, glad he'd worn bulkier clothes that morning. "I'll be leaving Riverlea for Covedale," he informed Mark.

Mark nodded. "I'll find you there." There was no worry in his voice, so he had to have connections.

As Oliver was walking back to the inn, he touched the outside of his pants pocket to feel the bundle of money. Mark had given him almost ninety thousand tickets, an amount some people would never earn in their lifetimes. Some who lived on less than one ticket a day would've had to save all their income for over two centuries to have that kind of fortune. He smiled to himself. Finally, after all these years of hiding and suffering, Oliver was no longer poor. He finally felt like someone.

While Oliver was out, Violet snoozed, using the entire width of the narrow bed all to herself, holding on to his warmth lingering in the sheets. It was still quite early, and she'd grown accustomed to staying up late in the night and getting up when the sun was already high above the horizon.

She dreamed. Her mind brought her back again to the time when she was just seven. She'd lived a good life in a one-room farmhouse. They'd kept a couple of goats, and it had been her morning routine to milk the animals before breakfast and release them to graze on the little grass shoots that came up in the early spring. The goats, Ella and Jade, and a few chickens had been enough to feed her and her family, so it was an honor for her to get up at the crack of dawn to help at the farm.

It had been one of those early mornings when Violet had been at the barn tending to the animals when she heard an argument outside. She'd watched, frozen and helpless, through a crack in the door as strange men beat her father. Quiet tears had fallen down her cheeks while she watched her dad suffer.

It had been her first close encounter with a group of the bad people who roamed around taking money and food from the farmers. Violet recalled her mom saying that if she saw anything suspicious, she should run far away from the house into the forest and not look back. So she had, once she regained control of her legs.

In her dream, she ran into the forest until she could no longer catch her breath. Her bare feet took her almost to the other edge of the woods despite the pain and injury they suffered tripping over sticks on the forest floor. She hid behind the trees until the next morning, quietly crying, too scared to sleep or make noises. She wasn't sure what frightened her more: the dark forest or the men that might've been looking for her.

When morning came, she quietly walked back. The men were gone, and so were the goats and chickens. They'd burned the little house she shared with her family down to the ground and slaughtered both her parents, who were lying out front in a pool of drying blood. Violet had no more tears left to cry over the death and destruction around her. She sat down on the ground, her mind an empty void. She'd lost all that she loved. She was alone, and she didn't understand why this had happened to her and her family. If she hadn't run, she'd have been with her family already, somewhere in heaven. She felt scared because she was truly alone.

She didn't know how long she'd been sitting like this when she felt a hand touch her. She jumped, startled, and was ready to run again, but as she turned around, she found her little brother looking at her. He was even more frightened than she was. Violet hugged him tightly, not wanting to release the boy from her arms for a long time. She'd been certain he'd been in the house when it had burned and perished in the flames, but he'd found refuge behind the firewood pile and survived. She was no longer alone and that meant there was still hope.

She took her brother's hand and they started walking just as they were, with no money or change of clothes. All they had was each other, and she promised to never let him go, but she felt him drifting away, his hand slipping from hers . . .

Violet woke from the nightmare with a gasp when Oliver opened the door. She wanted to run to him and find comfort in his warm arms, but he wasn't paying attention to her. Each time he'd gone out for a drink or a walk, he'd always made her the center of attention when he'd returned. He'd always been ready to kiss her and make her smile, but not this time. His attitude had changed, and he looked to be in a big hurry, packing his things in his bag.

She was shocked, because she knew he was leaving her. Another person in her life she'd become attached to was abandoning her. She felt her eyes welling with tears.

Oliver must have realized that she was looking at him for answers on why he was suddenly so cold, and stopped what he was doing for a moment. He sat on the bed beside her and took her hands in his. "I'm sorry, but I have to leave," he said. "It will be too dangerous for both of us if I stay."

He reached into his backpack before she could say anything and took out a few bills.

"This is for you, Violet." He pushed some money into her hand. "Use it wisely."

He held her chin and wiped the tears from her cheeks.

"You're a smart, beautiful girl. You don't belong here," he added.

He got up, picked the backpack from the floor and checked his pockets to make sure he had everything with him. He hastily turned to the door and touched the knob, but froze for a moment and lowered his head. He didn't look at Violet who was sitting motionless on the bed with the money he gave her.

"I'm sorry," he said as he opened the door and left.

Oliver left the inn and walked towards the river. His steps were light but hurried. He was done interacting with people in Riverlea.

The path to the river that ran beside empty lots piled with rubble and the ruins of old industrial buildings had been cleared. The locals must have used it often, but today it felt too quiet. The people of the streets were hiding from the rain, leaving the road unexpectedly empty. There was no other sound besides the slowly-falling rain and Oliver's shoes on the gravel. He looked behind him every so often, but there was no one following him.

He crossed the old, unused train tracks and found himself at the river. The open ferry from Covedale, the only one operating to Riverlea, was just docking to the bank when he arrived, so he was right on time to get on the next sail. But he wasn't the first. There were many people waiting at the shore for the ferry to arrive. More than the ferry could take.

Oliver's heart sank. When he'd arrived in Riverlea months ago, the area had been deserted. He hadn't expected so many people to be waiting in the rain to get on the ferry, and he didn't want to be in the crowd fighting for his spot or getting into arguments.

With the bridges down due to the war, there was no other way out of Riverlea but to take this vessel. Those who wanted to escape from the city needed to cross the river here because most of the other side of the riverbank had cliffs that were too tall to scale, and the waters around them were too treacherous to navigate.

He waited patiently with the rest of the travelers until the ferry arrived, curious what would happen.

The ferry stopped, and the crew started unloading large amounts of boxes. The crates probably contained food and alcohol that had to be imported to Riverlea. Only a couple of people on the ferry had arrived at their destination, and they were allowed to disembark. No one was moving to get on. People remained seated on the wet grass and rocks and were silent; only the waves made noise, swishing against the shore. People were waiting for a big, older man with a long beard falling to his chest to come up and speak to them. He was the ferry operator from Covedale and was accompanied by two men standing behind him with guns.

"Fifty," the bearded man said to the crowd.

A wave of hushed voices arose. Some were discussing the price with their travel partners or a group. Some simply shook their heads and left, possibly to be back the next day to see if the price was lower. Oliver remembered paying only one ticket for the trip to Riverlea that took at least thirty minutes on the wide river, fighting with the strong currents. The return fare, however, fluctuated between thirty and a hundred tickets per trip. Some people speculated that perhaps the fare depended on the diesel price of the day and its availability, or that maybe the Covedale mafia was dictating it, but Oliver didn't think they really knew for certain.

Most of the people here hoped that one day they would be lucky enough to get to the other side and escape the hell of Riverlea, but only a handful of people from the crowd got up and walked to the ferry. Oliver followed their steps and issued the requested payment that allowed him to step on board. The ferry's engines started shortly after, echoing loudly from the building ruins. Oliver felt movement underneath him as he took a tobacco slug out of his pocket to light it. He was on his way and finally felt at peace.

No one bothered him throughout the journey, and Oliver also kept to himself as he stood at the edge of the vessel, smoking and looking over the railing. The creaking metal boat made waves in the dirty brown water as it moved along, a gray foam of industrial pollution forming behind it.

The image of the slowly-burning paper in Mark's ashtray occupied Oliver's mind. A vision that was, in part, a memory of the event and a creation of his imagination.

He'd known it was a lot, but the information he'd gotten from Mark about the remaining balance surprised him. That amount of money could get him anything he'd ever wanted in life. There would not be any more worrying about where he'd sleep or what he'd eat. No more watered-down whiskey. He smiled to himself.

"Eric, you'll be safe here," Oliver says.

"Don't do it, it's not worth it," says Eric, pleading for Oliver to come to his senses. "It's suicide."

"I can't just fucking leave it," says Oliver, just as an explosion rattles the ground. "It's ready. I just need to press the button."

The factory is under heavy fire, but Oliver turns around and runs towards the building, against the river of people trying to escape it. He bumps into a few of them and almost falls to be trampled by the crowd, but regains his stride.

He runs up to the factory offices. He opens the console, a piece of equipment that used to be military-issued. He takes one last look around the room to make sure he's still alone and presses the button.

The transaction is quick, but every second is a matter of life-and-death and he keeps nervously looking around until it's completed. He closes the console and runs through the building again. There are no crowds anymore as most of the current shift is already outside. He just has to make it out himself . . .

A sudden jolt of the boat interrupted Oliver's daydreaming as it reached the Covedale side of the river. With one look, he realized how much he'd missed the green of trees, the tall grasses that grew at the shore, and the wild rose bushes that were blooming with their pale pink flowers. Covedale looked so different—fresh and inviting. It put a smile on his face.

While waiting for the ferry to moor, he took one last, good look at the city he had just come from. Riverlea had been at the height of its glory just a few decades ago, but now all you could see were ruins, darkened by the rain and covered in a thin blanket of fog. Between these piles of stone and metal lived people who had been lured there by the promise of a better life. They came from smaller cities and rural areas, hoping to stand a chance against the terrible hunger. Somewhere else was always better than wherever they were at the time. Once they had arrived and taken this ferry to the other side, they were trapped. There was no possibility of finding enough money for a trip back, something that no one had warned them about. Newcomers found no work, no prospects, and no hope of survival in the city. They were prisoners, locked there by the power of money they didn't possess.

4

BIG WILLOW TREES BENT over the Covedale side of the river, almost touching the slowly-moving water with their strands, giving about a dozen women much-needed shelter from the day's rain as they sat or squatted on the rocks. Each of them had a basin with a washing board and worked vigorously to get the soap working through the cloth fibers to release the dirt trapped in the fabric. The cold water and harsh soap made their hands red and every little joint in their fingers felt stiff, but they laughed and chatted enthusiastically despite the pain.

"Look who's coming," a woman with deep chicken pox scars on her face said, looking at the road behind them.

A middle-aged woman with her hair tucked under a brown scarf appeared, walking out from a narrow alley between the rows of buildings and carrying a wooden basin filled with dirty clothes.

She slowed down while crossing the sidewalk and nodded a greeting to the barber on her right who was standing in front of his shop waiting for his next customer to arrive. She then hurried to cross the road and join the other washers.

"A bit late now to come and wash when we're almost done," one said, concentrating on her work and not looking up.

"She comes when she wants," the first woman said and laughed, the rest joining her.

"If ma daughter gots married, I'd feel special too," added another washer.

"Not many good men is still around. We women needs to take care of ourselves."

"Who's still available?"

"Old Jay is still for grabs," one of them noted, and they all burst out laughing.

They worked quietly for a short time, until an older, bony woman said under her breath, "Ma Ivy won't find anyone." Ivy was the woman's second child, born twenty years after her brother. The washer considered the child a miracle, since she hadn't expected another pregnancy after the difficult labor of her son. She was constantly worried about her as a result.

The woman sitting beside her heard her well. "Nonsense. She find someone—"

"Nah if she working the whole day."

"Ivy's good, they won't let her go from the factory. Ya should be proud."

"I am, but what a life is it? Soon it'd be too late for her," said the older woman while she forcefully rubbed the clothes against the washing board.

"A woman like her is a gem these days," the other woman said. "She'll attract lots of boys. Nah need to worry."

"Twitchy Andy got attacked on the way to the market!" one of the washerwomen from the end of the line announced suddenly.

Everyone knew Twitchy Andy. When he'd come back from the front, he'd never been the same. Everyone laughed at him for how easily frightened he was by loud noises. He'd eventually chosen the solitude of a small piece of land outside of town. The kids still chased him and teased him whenever he showed up at the market, banging sticks on tins.

"He get a little battered, but he be fine," replied another. "His vegetables get stolen. Months of hard work—"

"He won't survive the winter."

The women present voiced their strong opinions, talking over each other.

"Where did it happen?"

"Oh, outside of the city—"

"It's the guys from Riverlea!" one of them shouted angrily.

"Time for Andy to move inside the city—"

"Soil here ain't good for growing—"

"There ain't a place for him here. What's he gonna do? Beg on the streets?" The woman shook her head.

"He can't 'cause the boys'll put him on the ferry—"

"Sure thing!"

"These disgraceful people belong to Riverlea, so why they coming this way?" a woman said angrily, pointing at the ferry that was docking on their side of the river. "We don't want them here!"

"All they wanna do is to rob us like they did Andy. All need to hang on the tree—"

"They're taking our jobs!"

"We don't go there and they shouldn't come here—"

"They can keep their drug addicts—"

"That one coming our way, look how happy he is!" one washer said, and the other women turned their heads towards the road above them.

"Disgrace!" said one of them in reply.

"We better stop these ferries."

A short woman stood up and took the basin under her arm.

"I complain to ma brother. He knows Mr. White. They need to do something about it," she said and walked up the steep bank onto the road. She paused right in front of the newcomer and stared bravely and with contempt into his eyes before spitting on the ground. She then turned and, with a sense of pride and accomplishment in her steps, continued walking across the street, her body bent on one side to balance the weight of the basin full of wet clothes to be hung to dry.

Oliver felt fresh energy inside of him. His encounter with the washwoman didn't take him aback. Distrust of strangers was expected, and he didn't let it affect him or his mood. Parents told their kids the same stories they'd heard in their youth, tales of the wandering witches turning kids into stones or of kidnappers who took people at night right from their homes, and these stories were passed on from generation to generation and were now imprinted in everyone's minds.

It was hard not to notice how different Covedale was from Riverlea, with clear sidewalks lined with trees and no one sleeping on the streets. He walked around with his head high and his usual smile, passing rows of short buildings and noting the storefronts of local businesses. He strolled by the market where the poorer people shopped and where the sellers were loudly pitching their crops and merchandise.

The town was buzzing with people. Servants looked at him as they passed, some taking rickshaws, hurrying with errands for their masters. Page boys were ringing their bicycle bells, not intending to slow down, forcing pedestrians to make way. Owning and maintaining a car was very expensive so it did not surprise Oliver that he saw none in town.

He noticed small, dirty kids staring open-mouthed at the display of sweet pastries in the bakery's window, but the store owner quickly shooed them away. Soon he'd be able to step into that store and get one of these buttery treats himself. His smile grew at the thought.

Closer to the bay he found an overpriced room in a hotel offering running water. It was a two-story structure that was quite old, but looked like it had a good caretaker and had been repaired as needed. Missing bricks had been patched with different-colored bricks or stones, and broken windows had been boarded up or repaired. The reception was quite dark, but there was a pleasant, fresh breeze of wet, rainy air passing through.

The rooms were definitely past their prime—the furniture was scratched up and the air was filled with the smell of tobacco smoke—but they were clean. The bedsheets were yellowing and overused, but smelled much better than they looked.

The water pipes in the building appeared to be original, but the water was coming from big containers on the top of the hotel roof. There were no water lines in the city. If there wasn't enough rainwater, they pumped the liquid straight from the bay using a diesel pump. The water had the faint yet distinctive smell of fish and algae, but Oliver was glad to wash off the dirt from the past few months.

He went out again feeling refreshed. A grumpy old man gave him a much-needed haircut and a shave. Oliver was certain that the man had charged him more than the locals for the service, which was mediocre at best. He was new, a stranger, and the barber didn't hide his displeasure in serving him.

He then visited the stands of the open market he'd passed earlier during the day. Farmers from outside of the city were flocking in every day for the opportunity to sell their produce, and the place attracted people from different areas. Many options for freshly charred meats and fish, ready-to-eat fruits, and freshly brewed beer were available, but the stall owners didn't welcome Oliver. The news of him, coming from the Riverlea side of the river, had traveled fast.

Eyes followed him during his visit to the market, but he smiled at them even when stall owners rudely shooed him away. He agreeably moved, not getting upset.

Some vendors took pity on him or were simply in need of money, and he was able to get some food. He also stopped at the only stall with household items and used-but-still-wearable clothing. Among the piles of useless garbage the stall owner referred to as antiques, he found and purchased a small navy velvet box that caught his eye.

After returning to his room, Oliver took a ring out of a satin bag and placed it in the box he had purchased earlier on impulse. It was a good fit.

Oliver sits at a kitchen table with an open book in front of him. His mother is sitting beside him, slightly bent over, looking at reading exercises with him. Oliver's father is also in the room, his back turned to them.

"The lion got up to lead them to the water," he slowly reads the sentence. His voice is unsure as he hesitates and stutters through some of the words and sounds.

See, it has the word 'to' in front of it. It means it's the infinitive form of a verb, so you say 'lead.' Lead is a mineral," says his mother, stressing the vowel sounds. He's making a lot of progress and she's proud of him.

"Can I go play, mom?" Oliver doesn't have his usual concentration for studying today.

"Okay, you can finish this later, but don't forget to do your math when you come back." Oliver is already heading out the door when she shouts after him, "And stay away from the ruins!"

On his way out, he pauses outside the kitchen door to listen to his parents. They don't know he's there.

"Ya spoiling him with this. Ya know he'll bring a book from the ruins. Can't he be like other kids?"

"Only a small portion of his generation will read. It will be to his advantage," she points out to his father.

"But he won't have life skills. He needs more time training. He has no muscles 'cause he stares at books. He needs to read people, not paper."

"Why can't you accept that maybe he needs both?"

"He's weak, just like ya father was."

"My father was a strong, intelligent man."

"Until the fool got himself killed!" he shouts at her.

"Don't talk about my father like that," she replies calmly.

"I'll call him what he was! He thought he could fix the world, and that got the bastard killed."

"The world needs heroes like him."

"I don't want the kid to be a hero. I want him alive!" says the father, pausing for a moment to think. "I take him on the streets tomorrow."

"He's not ready. He's only six!" she protests.

"Exactly! Time for him to see real life. He can't read that from ya books."

"I can't let you do that!" she says, this time with anger.

Oliver hears his mother gasp, and he's anticipating his father's heavy hand on her again, but he speaks instead, saying, "Stop me."

Oliver heard a knock on the door to his room. He wondered what the innkeeper wanted from him at such a late hour. He closed the box and put it back into his backpack before opening the door.

5

I T WAS LATE SATURDAY morning and Steven White was in his office at the side of his house attending to town matters, rather than in his study. His large two-story house had bay windows in front and a path at the end of the driveway which led through the neatly-cut lawn to this small office.

The room didn't have the splendor of the rest of the house. He saw it as a waste of money to decorate it. He only met here with town merchants and his immediate staff. The office featured a clean but worn-out wooden floor, plastered walls and a pair of old, scratched up sofas. There was a window to the side, but a large evergreen growing just outside obstructed the incoming light. Only a few sunbeams came in, and the lingering tobacco smoke additionally distorted them.

At the end of the room there was a large desk at which White sat, toying with a glass of amber liquid in front of him. There were currently three people in the room, besides him.

Leo Woodham was a man in his early thirties. His tall, slender body was topped with messy brown hair, long enough that it occasionally fell into his eyes. The man had been working for him for over fifteen years. He himself ensured that the town operated smoothly and Leo, as his officer, was responsible for protecting him and his interests from interior and exterior threats. It always made White smile when Leo stressed that he didn't work for White. When asked, Leo always said that he worked *with* White, even though it was White who paid Leo.

Another of his men—just a soldier—was pointing a gun at a man kneeling on the floor, his hands bound behind his back and his face bloodied and bruised. White was certain he was a stranger, even though it was hard to see his face under the crusted blood.

"He entered from Riverlea by ferry," Leo said, pointing at the man. "He crossed the river paying the regular fare. Checked in at the hotel by the

45

bay, the one opposite Jim's bar. That's where we found him. He wasn't even hiding."

"Name?" White asked.

"Oliver Conway."

"I've never heard that name before," White said after a moment of thinking. "So he had the money to come over here and rent a room, but he's not selling drugs, guns, or stealing anything? What is he, a spy?" He wasn't pleased with this development.

"Tree?" Leo asked, suggesting that the man be hanged.

The stranger could be the one he'd been waiting for, White thought. He'd have to risk assuming he was, rather than make a mistake that might cost him dearly. He feared even Covedale itself could be on the line. After a moment, White turned to Leo and said, "We can't be unkind to people we don't know and assume the worst of them."

Leo looked at him and scowled.

White knew it was out of character for him to make such an exception, but in this case he didn't think that Leo needed to know the details. Covedale wasn't an interesting place, and he hoped that the stranger would soon be on his way and no longer his problem. "We already gave him a nice welcome, but we're good people," he added. "We mean no harm to anyone who doesn't threaten us."

Once the soldier had pulled the man to his feet, untied his hands, and shoved him out the door, White turned on the radio. The voice of an anchor filled the air, providing the current news. White listened to it every morning.

"Due to large number of deaths and mass migrations, many people no longer know or understand their national identity. No more nations! Nationalism—never again!"

He looked at Leo, who walked up to the table on the side that had a carafe standing on it. He picked up the glass bottle and sniffed what was inside. Leo had to know it was rum, because that was what the servants always prepared for White.

"World United government agreed!" the speaker on the radio continued. "We'll continue the existing language of trade. The official world language is English. The whole world will adopt the metric system. There will be no more misunderstandings!"

Leo poured himself a tall drink. He then downed it in one long gulp, slumped himself onto the sofa and put his feet up onto the table as the radio continued.

"Our priorities: Organized crime has to go!"

Whoever is going to run the new government should learn from me, White thought proudly. There was no crime in Covedale.

"We condemn the fights that are still erupting in Africa! Time to unite the world under one government: the World United."

The broadcast finished with a short melody and the radio went silent. White stood up and turned the device off.

"We found the guy that attacked Andy," Leo said without getting up. His eyes were closed.

White didn't want Leo to question the decision he'd just made, letting this Oliver Conway go. He was glad his officer didn't bring it up.

"He had the loot, so there was no doubt it was him," Leo continued. "Once the boys are finished with this piece of shit, he'll hang on the tree by the river."

White saw Leo stirring and gave him a quick nod. His officer was making sure White wasn't planning to make another exception. He decided to ignore Leo's concerns as though nothing out of the ordinary had happened.

"Does that make me bad?" White wondered aloud as he sat down. Leo stirred. His eyes were closed again, but he was listening. "When the city council members got assassinated and the mayor left, someone had to fill the void. Someone had to protect the people living here. Could have it been someone else? Maybe. Would they be better than me?" White looked down at his shoes contemplating whether he should call one of his servants to have them polished. After a moment he added, "Just look at those boneheads on the other side of the river. They don't care about their people like we do in Covedale. They let people die on the streets, starving, take women to be their slaves and rape them like animals. There's no humanity in them. They're the bad people, not me."

White took a sip of his drink, then said, "I don't control people here. I encourage them to make a living on their own or join our troops and protect people. If a woman wants to make some money on the side by selling herself, who am I to forbid it?" Prostitution was profitable for Covedale. "All I want is to maintain peace and a sense of normality for us all. I have values and I stick to them. Those in Riverlea have none." He shook his head. "They come here any way they can. You'd think they would've run out of materials for their rafts by now," he digressed and smiled to himself. "The fools think the river is treacherous, but they don't know that the real danger is me." He pointed at his chest. "A limping dog won't make it across and enter Covedale without us knowing. We fish out those the river doesn't pull under. We capture them so they don't sell drugs to our kids. We can't sit and do nothing." He paused, but Leo kept quiet and allowed him to continue. "That's why the guy needs to hang, and he needs to hang right on that tree by the river—" White pointed his finger in the general direction of the tree he was referring to "—so that the other side can see that we're serious. That they shouldn't be messing with us and that we won't tolerate them here, trespassing and breaking our laws." White took another sip of the drink.

"What do you want to do with Tom?" Leo asked, taking advantage of a longer pause in White's speech.

White recalled putting Tom's name down on the list a couple of months prior. He still hadn't put too much thought into how to resolve that matter. "I haven't figured out what to do with that deadbeat." He shook his head and gestured dismissively for Leo to not worry. One of these days an idea would show itself. Maybe Natalie was the problem here. A good wife knew how to control her husband and keep him out of trouble.

6

OLIVER SPENT A COUPLE of weeks in his hotel room after the unexpected meeting with White and his associates. Once the bruises on his face healed up, he decided to venture out. He recalled seeing a small bar across the street from his hotel. It was close to the edge of a steep drop to the ocean shore below. He decided to check it out and grab a quick drink.

The place was quite busy. The interior looked pleasant, but the potent smell of burning candle wax and tobacco made Oliver consider staying outside. He sat down at the bar on the side that was open onto the street, but shielded from the cool breeze off the water.

"Whiskey—neat—if you have it," he asked the barman once they had made eye contact.

The barman nodded as he hid the money presented and poured Oliver a glass from a bottle that he fetched from underneath the counter.

Oliver took a sip of the drink and said, "That's better," out loud to himself, ignoring the curious heads that turned to look at him. He smiled and took another sip. He felt the strong liquid warming his throat and stomach.

"Any good? The whiskey?" a man sitting beside him said, pointing at Oliver's glass. An empty stool separated them.

The man himself had a clear-looking liquid in front of him that might've been gin or vodka. He looked to be in his forties, sitting tall in his stool. He didn't sound poor or uneducated, but his slightly-worn clothes made it clear he wasn't rich either.

"I've definitely had worse," Oliver said as he smiled at the stranger, raised a glass, and took another sip.

"I'm sure," the man said. "New in Covedale?" He didn't hide his surprise.

"I got here a couple weeks ago." He extended his hand. "Oliver."

"Tom." They exchanged a friendly handshake. "Where are you from, Oliver?"

49

"Nowhere, I guess," Oliver replied laughing. He took another sip of his amber drink before adding, "Just got back from the front."

"I was in the army for so many years myself, it no longer feels like I really belong anywhere," said Tom. "I'm lucky they shot me in the leg and I was sent home."

"Where were you deployed?" Oliver was skeptical about Tom's story. They only sent back the ones who could no longer hold a gun. Tom didn't have any visible wounds. Oliver didn't expect him to even have a limp, despite his supposed injury.

"I did my time here in America, Europe, and Asia."

Oliver's mind traveled briefly to the front and the vast wasteland with no trees or shrubs. There wasn't even grass, just bare land broken up by a maze of corridors. He'd slept on the ground of the trenches in the same clothes he fought in. There were no buildings in which to take shelter from the heat of the sun or onslaught of the rain.

Oliver shook his head and said, "Some parts of Asia saw the worst of it. I lost too many friends there." In the first two weeks, he'd lost five men and couldn't even bury them properly.

The enemy hit them regularly and they never knew what weapon would be used or when. They used gas dropped by drones, direct-energy weapons shooting microwaves, lasers that cut through flesh faster than a sword, and strikes from precision missiles. The shrieks from the strikes were mixed with the screams of people and military officers shouting commands. He was never sure if the blood on his uniform was his, or if it belonged to the soldier fighting beside him.

"So it was. You might come out of there alive, but never sane," said Tom, smiling nervously. "It fucks with your mind."

Oliver got a glimpse of the barman rolling his eyes. "I served east of the Caspian Sea. A place that I never want to see again," Oliver replied.

"I bet. I was at the north front, saw the flattened cities and crippled people," said Tom and ordered another round for both of them before finishing the drink still in front of him. Oliver jumped in to pay, putting a bill on the well-used bar top. Tom didn't protest.

Oliver didn't believe half of what Tom was saying and the man would probably stay and talk just to keep him paying, but the stranger at the bar was the first friendly person Oliver had spoken with since he'd arrived, so he was willing to keep the conversation going. He might still be able to get some useful information from the man. "What do you do now in the city?" he asked.

"Not much, mostly buying stuff and reselling it," Tom replied. "With the war over, there've been some products starting to show up that we haven't seen for a while, and they're slowly getting put back on the market. For example, proper cigarettes." Tom pointed at the slug Oliver had out and had been about to light.

"Here, try this." Tom handed Oliver a perfectly rolled cigarette and lit it for him.

Oliver inhaled deeply before saying, "Not bad."

The quality of the tobacco was much lower than what he had in his slug, but he admired the construction of the perfectly round cigarette he was now holding in hand with a smile. He couldn't recall if he'd seen something like this before.

"Not the best, but people are buying it," said Tom. "It makes them feel less common. People will pay a fortune for a chance to hold a bit of luxury from the past."

Oliver recalled the yellow, sometimes half-burned pages of books or magazines he was able to find in the ruins when he was still a kid. They showed neatly-dressed people with perfect haircuts and men with neatly-trimmed beards. Few were smoking in the images, but Oliver found the perfectly rolled cigarettes appealing. It felt right somehow to hold one of these.

Mark had told him to invest the money in something. It'd be best to get into something profitable. Cigarette production might've been interesting, but already seemed to be taken. He wondered what other luxury items from the old times would make good returns.

"I'm looking to invest, but I haven't found the right fit yet," Oliver replied after a moment. He noticed a spark in Tom's eyes and added, "Trying to learn about the city first. For example, who lives up there?" Oliver pointed at a faint light in the distance coming from the top of a short cliff. Not much was visible now in the dark, but he knew from painful experience that some Covedale big-wig lived in the guarded mansion overlooking the bay. He wondered if this Tom fellow knew anything more about the man.

Tom looked at where Oliver was pointing. Rotating his body back, he said with disinterest, "That's White's house." He then changed the topic, more interested in the previous conversation. "Trade or production?"

Oliver stared at the distant lights of the house for a moment. Tom wasn't interested in talking about White, so there was no point pressing him further. "Haven't decided yet," he said. He puffed some more of the cigarette, turning his attention back to Tom to add, "Hopefully something with quick returns."

"I know some folks. My wife Natalie invited some friends over tomorrow night." Tom wrote his address on a piece of paper. "See you there, I hope." Tom got up, finished the rest of his pale drink in one gulp, and walked away, swaying slightly. A woman crossed his path, and after a brief discussion she convinced him to change direction. He allowed her to lead him while resting his hand on her hip.

Tom was clearly interested in new investors. He might've been a grifter from what Oliver deducted, but if he were to stay in Covedale, he needed to make some connections. Building trust was always the hardest part of starting a new life.

Oliver sat at the bar for a bit longer to finish his drink and the cigarette. The bar started to quiet down, and the windup radio on one of the bar shelves sounded clearer. "Our new government is committed to the economy, but you, world citizens, are the frontline. We need you! No matter your age, there's work for you . . . " The signal trailed off, but Oliver wasn't paying much attention to the news.

The novelty of the rolled tobacco was interesting, but it was hard to get a good feel of the market. He hoped Tom was right about having connections in town. It might get him the necessary foot in the door.

He looked around and found people still sitting at the mostly-dark tables with burned-out candles. Oliver could hear some of them talking loudly and bursting into laughter from time to time. Those who passed out on their tables were quickly kicked out by the owner. When it got too chilly, Oliver got up and left. He noticed the guy from White's office, the one who'd given him such a warm welcome, slip away from one of the dark tables in the corner and follow him. It didn't surprise Oliver to have a tail following him around, he'd expected it, but he hadn't thought White's officer would do such surveillance himself. He made a mental note about it, but decided it was best to pretend that he had not seen him.

It was just a typical Saturday when Tom was in town, but Natalie always dreaded the evenings. Her husband never passed up the opportunity to invite someone over and tell tales of his journeys. Tom was often gone for weeks at a time chasing new merchandise and new contracts with neighboring cities. When he came back, it was time for celebration in their home with plenty of food and drink.

She enjoyed seeing their friends and gossiping with them about what was new around town, but Tom would get drunk and the gatherings rarely finished on the right note. Many times he made promises to others that he couldn't keep, made bets and lost the money he'd just brought in, or anger got into him and he kicked his guests out. There was no way to predict how the evening would end.

She and Tom were already sitting at the table and entertaining their guests, a couple they knew very well, when there was a knock on the door.

She excused herself from an ongoing conversation at the table and opened the door, which made a familiar squeak. She found a tall, handsome man standing on the other side who startled her.

"Good evening," the man said, smiling. She smiled back and froze for a moment. She was sure she hadn't seen his face before in Covedale; she would not have forgotten it if she had.

"Yes?" she asked shyly.

"Oliver Conway." He bowed a little as he replied.

Natalie felt his piercing eyes on her and quickly glanced down at what she'd chosen to wear this evening. She checked everything on her was tidy and in its place, feeling scrutinized by the man's deep blue eyes and subconsciously wanting to make sure his first impression of her was positive.

Oliver noticed her hesitation. "Tom asked me to stop by for a visit."

"That's my husband, please come in," she said. She smiled shyly and gestured for the man to enter the apartment. It wasn't the first time that Tom hadn't mentioned inviting someone over, and she didn't think twice about letting Oliver in. Tom spotted his guest from across the room as she was closing the door.

"Welcome, Oliver, I'm so glad you could make it! Let me introduce you to my good friends, John and Susan," Tom said. He sounded cheerful due to the alcohol he already had in his blood. "And you've met my wife, Natalie," he added when she entered the room behind Oliver.

"My pleasure," Oliver replied. With a smile on his face, he firmly shook hands with John and Susan, and took a seat beside Tom, who reached for the open bottle of vodka.

"I was at Jim's bar yesterday and I met Oliver there." Tom was recalling the events of the previous night. "He's new in town and he told me he's looking to invest in something, so I thought why not invite him tonight. Let's celebrate."

It was better to never let Tom know you had money. The entire town knew this. Oliver was clearly unaware, and it had been unwise of him to mention any plans of investment. Her husband was drawn to money like a moth to a flame, and she knew that befriending Oliver was his way of getting closer to his wealth.

Tom was ready to pour some of the alcohol into Oliver's glass, but Oliver stopped him.

"Can I join the ladies?" Oliver asked. He pointed at a bottle of wine at the table and smiled at Natalie and Susan, looking for their approval that they would share some with him.

"Of course," Natalie said, handing him the bottle. "It's just a fruit wine from the market—"

"No whiskey in this house," Tom said mockingly.

Oliver topped up the women's glasses, then poured some wine for himself and took a sip. "Let us have wine and women, mirth and laughter," he said quoting Lord Byron.

Natalie recognized the classic she had once read. He looked straight at her, making her uncomfortable, and she averted her eyes.

"You're an investor, you say," John commented. "You think going into wine is profitable?"

"It'll take time before the vines go back to producing the finest grapes," replied Oliver. "Definitely a good business to be in if you can wait for the grapes and for the clients to grow to appreciate them—"

"I gotta build the business now," John said, dismissing the idea. "Who knows if the war will start up again? Now's the time to make money. The tides might turn for the worse in a short time."

John and his wife were in their late fifties, with gray hair and weathered faces. John enjoyed spending time in Tom and Natalie's house with the flowing alcohol and carefree environment they were able to provide. After a few drinks, John's face turned red and he became very talkative. His wife Susan, however, was always quiet. She looked down more often than not, avoiding eye contact with anyone except Natalie.

"What do you do, John?" Oliver asked.

"I own the textile factory at the docks."

The docks were situated on the delta of the river on a man-made island, which was connected to Covedale by the only remaining bridge.

"Mr. Leggett, I presume?" Leggett's company in Covedale was well-known in Riverlea as well, being the only major industry in the area that was still operational. "I've heard good things about your factory."

"It used to run great during the war," John replied. "We had good money in contracts sewing military uniforms and coats, but that's dried up now since the war is over. Making textiles for the public isn't even close to the guaranteed income of the war. Readjusting the entire product line isn't easy. Production is expensive, and you need new buyers."

"War didn't touch us as much in Covedale, but it destroyed many families and businesses by confiscating the wealth to fund the conflict," Susan said, speaking for the first time since Oliver's arrival. "We're glad that Mr. White spared our factory and—"

"I put in a lot of work to keep it under our name," John interrupted, taking credit for the company's well-being. Susan lowered her eyes again.

Helen, their housekeeper, walked in and brought some simple appetizers and snacks to the table. She was short and thin, with white hair tied up in a bun. Her long skirt and blouse were very old and had been noticeably repaired in many places. She had a smile on her face as she walked in, but as soon she met Tom's stare, her smile vanished and she hurried to continue serving.

Natalie noticed that Oliver was the only other person in the room who saw the tension. The rest were used to it and dismissed it. "Helen has only been with us for a couple of months," Natalie said to Oliver as the housekeeper left the room and went back to the kitchen. "She's a wonderful cook—"

"They always want more," Tom barked. He was eyeing the food on the table, deciding what he wanted to eat. "They never appreciate what they have."

"Tom, it's probably not a good time," Natalie pleaded.

Tom was never satisfied with anyone doing their housework, though Natalie never had any complaints. When she'd once offered to cook and clean to save money, saying that it wasn't much work to take care of the two of them, he complained that he wasn't some screwup who couldn't afford servants. Natalie never brought it up again.

"See, my wife's too kind," Tom said, looking at Oliver. He took another shot of vodka and added, pointing at Natalie, "I think my wife would rather I talk behind someone's back than right in their presence—"

"Dear," Natalie cautioned, trying to stop him, but her husband ignored her. She decided not to press it anymore rather than risk him becoming angry with her.

"I want people to know the truth about what I think of them." Tom spoke clearly and loudly to make sure everyone could hear him, including Helen who was working in the kitchen.

Natalie frowned, unhappy that Tom insisted on discussing this in front of a stranger.

"What happened?" Oliver asked, his curiosity about the situation making her even more uncomfortable.

"She's useless," Tom continued. "Came for a few hours to help and then she had the guts to ask me for an advance. She should be glad she's not living on the street—"

"I'm sure she had a reason. She could repay it with work," Oliver broke in before drinking more of the tart liquid from his glass.

"People like us have to work hard and make a living, but their kind just stick out their hands and wait for something to fall into them."

"I agree," John said. "My workers don't appreciate what I'm giving them, either. They should be glad they have work at all. They only have to work twelve hours and I give them a day off every week, but they're sour about it, and never punctual."

"What's the daily pay now? One ticket?" Oliver asked, but he didn't get an answer.

"It's hard to cope in times like this," Susan said, but her husband gave her the stink-eye and she fell silent again.

"You should come over, Oliver, and see how we operate," John suggested, stuffing his mouth with a sausage.

Natalie wondered if John was also hoping Oliver would invest in his business, otherwise it made little sense to invite him to see the factory so freely. It would be fun to watch John and Tom wrestle over the money. The thought made her smile.

"I'd love to," Oliver said, nodding. He then turned towards Tom to ask, "What exactly do you trade, besides cigarettes?"

"Rare items. I often work on commission, but I take opportunities when they arise."

Anything that smells like money, Natalie thought to herself.

"You're doing well if you can afford a place of your own," Oliver said as he looked around their small but cozy apartment.

Natalie followed his eyes. She and Tom weren't rich, but they lived much better than most of the people in Covedale. They had a tiny apartment—one room, plus kitchen—on the upper floor of a squat old building close to the city square. The walls had large cracks and were long overdue for a fresh coat of paint, making the place look darker than it had been a couple of decades ago. The bed had been shoved into a corner to accommodate a table that could seat the current company. The large window was covered with heavy drapes separating them from the view of the street below and from fresh air, even though the window was open. The town was busy even this late in the day, with the sounds of rickshaws and conversations coming from below.

"What's the street tax?" Oliver asked.

"If you do it right, you pay none," Tom said. His voice was hushed, though Natalie wasn't sure why. It wasn't a secret that Tom wasn't paying street tax. Being White's nephew didn't give Tom the right to ignore the local laws though, and Natalie was certain there would be consequences. She just hoped that when the day came, she wouldn't be dragged into it.

"I guess one can easily be fooled," Oliver said, pausing for a moment. He clearly knew Tom was full of shit. "How does one get a property around here?" Oliver asked.

"You'd need to talk to White about that," Natalie replied without hesitation, then noticed Tom staring gravely at her. He clearly wasn't happy she'd said that. She bit her lip and looked down, away from his eyes.

"You might make a deal with him," Tom replied. Then added condescendingly, "He's sunk a lot of money into his pet power project and he's not even close to getting the power plant started up."

John nodded, "Nothing to show for what he's already spent and people still burning diesel to run generators."

"That's just it," Tom agreed.

"So, who would've thought we're in the new industrial revolution," John said. He knew very well that talking about White in Tom's house could quickly get out of control. Tom was constantly upset with his uncle because he never shared the wealth of Covedale with him.

"History is repeating itself," Natalie said while John and Tom each took a shot. Oliver declined.

John replied, "That's right. Until we get power back up, we again rely on human labor—"

"Is that why they did it?" Tom asked, interrupting.

Natalie welcomed the change of subject, but sighed quietly. She hated politics and talking about the past.

"Who did what?" Oliver asked with genuine interest.

"Started the war," Tom said, sharing another shot with John.

"Think about what happened fifty years ago," John continued. "Natural disasters, unrest, protest, crime—all led to war. In the beginning, the people with wealth and power attempted to contain the problem." John pointed towards the kitchen where Helen was still working. "But those people . . ."

"They didn't want any help," Tom said. "They wanted to ruin everything and everyone in the name of equality."

"People were going hungry and fighting for their basic needs to survive," Oliver said. "You can't blame them—"

"Fools! Look around and see where it got them," John said, leaning forward and laughing.

"All the governments needed to do was share the wealth and get people back on their feet," Oliver said, sipping his wine. "Why didn't they?"

"I have to agree with Oliver," Natalie said, jumping into the conversation. "Maybe they took the wrong approach and the leaders shouldn't have distanced themselves from the issues of the world—"

"People were apparently fighting for the government to improve their lives, for drinking water, food, shelter, while they didn't even bother looking for work." John said, taking another sausage. "The rich walked away from the unrest because they were clearly not welcome. They were accused of being unjust—"

"They did what anyone would do," Tom said. "Retreated to their homes and kept themselves safe."

John nodded. "No one can blame them for having their pride and not wanting to be part of the poor's agenda." He paused before continuing, "If I had enough money to leave the rest of the pathetic world behind, I'd do it."

"The world's elites weren't welcome. What else could have they done, but watch from their yachts and drink?" Tom said, and poured more of the clear liquid into John's glass.

"World leaders were smiling back then," John continued, "Hugging and shaking hands. Just look at the old pictures. There was no hostility between the countries."

"It wasn't the governments that started the fucking war that ruined everyone," Tom agreed. "People blamed them for not doing enough to stop the bloodshed—"

"I hope World United fixes it," John declared, way too loudly.

"I'm skeptical," Tom said, sneering. "Think about it. One government to oversee the entire world from some ivory tower . . . "

"The new world order," John said, "is trying to bring all the regions together as a sign of peace."

"The good and bad will sit together to decide our fate. What the fuck do they know?" Tom said.

John started to reply, "We gotta stick together, because the future is in our hands—"

"And where will the head office be located?" Tom scoffed. "Karben, of all places. Where the hell is that, anyway?"

On the other side of the world was what Natalie had heard on the radio. War reports used to be boring. They only talked about who had struck whom and how many casualties there were, but as soon as they'd reached peace, the broadcasts had changed. Those with windup radios were perpetually glued to them in anticipation of the new content. Everyone was interested in how the world would change. Much gossip and speculation circulated about the town.

"What's your plan?" Oliver asked.

"We need to get rid of all these stinky beggars on our streets," John replied, "and we shouldn't repeat what we did years ago because we'll turn around and have another war on our hands. It's their greed and demands that will get us into more conflict!" John's face was flushed from both anger and alcohol.

"Like dogs, they'll bite the hands that feed them!" Tom said.

Natalie looked at Oliver. She was certain he was knowingly adding fuel to the fire when he said, "I thought it was the greed of the rich—"

"Lies! That's what they want you to think, Oliver," Tom said. "All that nonsense about all the money being in the hands of the few was nothing but propaganda."

"We could argue one way or the other," Natalie said, trying to calm down the discussion, "but a new and better strategy is needed—"

"Exactly!" John shouted, pointing at Natalie in agreement. "If we choose the same path and give them a hand, they'll chew our entire arm off. The Russian revolution, started by the poor; the French revolution, started by the poor."

"The U.S. civil war, instigated by the poor," Tom added.

"Giving them what they want isn't an option! Not this time!" John pounded the table with his fist.

"Maybe not enough was done for them back then?" Oliver suggested.

"Not sure what world you live in, Oliver. Tell me, where do we stop?" John asked, leaning towards Oliver.

"There has to be a line, and they'll never agree to it!" Tom said.

"What if we don't draw a line, but instead we all work together? If there's no us and them, there won't be any conflict," Oliver said. "Maybe changing how people think is the way out."

"I think you're dreaming," John said to Oliver. "There'll always be us and them. We can't fix it. Socialism is not a solution!"

"One day you'll understand that you need to pick a side," Tom said

"Aren't you afraid that maybe one day you'll be them?" Oliver asked.

"Poor? That'll never happen!" John laughed and took another shot.

It was late when Oliver left Tom's place. The town was already dark as he navigated the streets to his hotel. He'd walked them before during the day and the buildings and occasional ruins and rubble were already feeling somewhat familiar. Oliver took out a slug and lit it as he walked. The air was still and quiet.

He's sitting secured to a chair in the ammunition factory. He can see a grim room through his swollen eyelids, and a man, Karl, sitting in front of him.

"So you disabled two of my men empty-handed," Karl says. "They're not good guys and they're sloppy in what they do. I don't like them either, but I can't say they aren't loyal." He pauses. "I wanted you to know that I'll send you some extra food and relieve you from work tomorrow," he continues, making hand motions. "I don't like what happened."

Breathing is painful. He has some broken ribs.

"I admire you," Karl says. "You're half their strength and you were able to take two of them. I was thinking about assigning them other duties," he says with a touch of sarcasm in his voice. "In order to do that, I need to replace them with someone . . . but who knows if they'll be any better?"

He heard something behind him, so he stopped and quietly stepped into the shadows, away from the path. The alley was dark, but there didn't appear to be any movement. He waited to see who was following him. No one appeared, and the street was still quiet. He waited for a bit longer just in case, but nothing happened, so he continued his walk.

He had taken no more than a few more steps when he distinctly heard light steps following him.

"Stop!" a voice behind Oliver said. It wasn't an adult's voice, but a child's. "Hands up!" the voice said, and Oliver heard a gun charging behind him. He grimaced, annoyed, but did as he was told. He couldn't see who it was, only the blue light of the gun about three feet away that blinded him in the darkness.

"What do you want, kid?" he asked calmly.

"Gimme ya money," squeaked the voice.

The heavy gun shook in the kid's hands. He clearly had no experience holding a gun properly. His arms were not accustomed to its weight and he couldn't keep it steady. Oliver left the slug hanging from his lips as he very slowly reached into his pants pocket to take out a bill. He extended it towards the attacker, saying, "Have it."

The bait worked. The kid lowered his gun to come closer, transfixed by the folded plastic bill, and reached for it. He gasped, caught by surprise, when Oliver grabbed the gun out of his hand, knocking him off his feet onto the dirt and pinning him down in one swift motion.

"What did you do that for?" Oliver asked.

"I got-got-gotta pay back the money." The kid's eyes were wide with fear.

"How much?" he asked, still holding the boy down.

"Two tickets, sir."

Oliver lifted the boy back onto his feet, but still held him tightly. "Don't run around with a gun again," he warned the kid as he pushed two tickets into the boy's hand. It was no longer a lot for him, but in the kid's life it might mean life or death.

As soon as Oliver let go of the boy's arm, the kid ran into the darkness, leaving his gun behind. He smiled to himself as he looked off in the direction the boy disappeared. The kid had no training and no discipline in him, and he'd probably be punished for losing the gun. There was, however, a chance he would grow up to be something else other than a killer. The world didn't need another shooter.

Oliver took a quick glance at the gun in his hand. It was an older model he was very familiar with. It was probably not worth more than thirty tickets with newer and better models available, but he felt a rush of confidence as he held it. He'd missed having a gun since the Gutters in Riverlea had taken his.

As he was putting the gun at the small of his back, he heard a noise in the distance. He looked in the direction of the commotion and saw an orange glow in the sky to the east. Fire. Oliver ran.

There were already many people at the scene. Small kids were rounded up together for safety, but anyone that could help was trying to contain the fire or save their precious belongings. It was a place of chaos and disarray. At least five shacks were already burning, but the fire was spreading quickly, even without the wind.

Oliver started to run towards the river to help fill the water buckets at the shore, one of the hardest jobs because it required plenty of upper-body strength. The fire was spreading quickly, and there were more than a hundred makeshift shacks standing side by side, all highly flammable. Without intervention, the whole place would be nothing but ashes in a few hours.

Oliver heard a woman screaming for help and he froze. He recalled the smoke in the ammunition factory and the shouts of people gasping for air, hoping someone would open the cages and let them out.

Screams echoed in his ears. Screams of people burning alive. There was no time to save them. There was no way. The guards with the keys had been the first to leave; the locks and bars had been too strong for any man to break. He'd have been killed if he'd tried.

A boy ran into Oliver by accident, bringing him back to the fire in Covedale. From where he was standing, he noticed a few men in charge of throwing water on the raging fire. They were moving as quickly as the full buckets were handed to them, but they were getting tired and would need to be replaced soon. Oliver saw this as an opportunity to make himself useful. The men welcomed the help, even from a stranger.

Oliver worked alongside the fire crew until dawn. Once the fire was under control, the men encouraged him to stick around and rest for a moment before leaving. Everyone around him was sleep-deprived and exhausted, but the adrenaline was still in their veins. People sat around on the grass in their dirty clothes, covered with soot and smelling of smoke, drinking a local brew being passed around. No one thought about leaving until all the stories had been told.

Oliver sat with the others and felt accepted as one of them. He no longer felt like a stranger and people recognized him for all the work he'd put in to save their houses. Only a quarter of the slum homes had been destroyed, and there were only two casualties, which he was told was a much lower toll than the last time a fire had erupted in town.

As he was sipping his ale, Oliver leaned towards a toothless old man who sat beside him. "What will happen to these people?" he asked and pointed to a group of fire survivors who were holding onto their rescued belongings.

"Mr. White will build them homes. He's a good man."

7

"**D**on't just stand there, Oliver." The short, middle-aged woman at one of the stalls at the Covedale market was fanning herself with what looked like a piece of cardboard. "Come sit with us."

She pulled a small wooden stool from underneath the stall. Oliver came over to the seller's side of the stand and carefully sat down, trying not to lose the juicy goat meat hanging from a stick that he'd just gotten himself for dinner. He went to the market every day now, indulging in foods he hadn't eaten for a long time. There were other places to get meals in town, but the market had lots of street vendors to choose from.

Since the fire, he was no longer a stranger. People smiled seeing him at the market, recognizing his face. They even liked his sense of humor.

"I swear you look younger every day, ma'am," Oliver said to the woman, smiling. "Your husband's a lucky man."

"Ya like to joke," the woman replied. She laughed loudly, showing the gaps in her teeth where some were missing.

"Just telling the truth," he teased, smiling and taking another bite of the meat.

"Have ya been to the public execution this morning?" the woman asked.

"No, I didn't go," Oliver replied. He wasn't interested in seeing the spectacle, seeming to have narrowly avoided that fate himself.

"Everyone in town shoulda been there," she replied. "It's a great lesson to see that stealing, even from Twitchy Andy, is punished. They lashed that thief bloody, then hung him."

An older, very thin woman from an adjacent stall bent over to join the conversation. "I hear from Mr. Paul," she began. Mr. Paul was the only one with a radio at the market. "World United is trying to reduce crime—"

"World United? Praise Mr. White for keeping the criminals of Riverlea away from us!" The woman working the stall Oliver was at interjected.

Oliver didn't take part in the conversation. He had his own opinion of Mr. White and he didn't think it would be well received. From what he'd heard so far, people liked the man and called him the protector of Covedale. Public executions weren't new and were effective in controlling people, especially when the public widely approved of them and deemed them necessary.

"Mr. White always give people a fair trial," the woman from the other stall said, nodding in agreement.

"We don't needa World United to tell us what to do with criminals."

The day was hot and there was barely any breeze passing through the market, but a straw canopy, which provided some shade, covered the stall. It was already July, and summers were usually very warm and dry in these parts of the continent.

"I couldn't sleep last night from this heat," the skinny woman from the other stall said, changing the topic. She then turned to Oliver. "How's the hotel?"

"It wasn't too bad, there was a cool breeze coming in from the bay."

"Living in the hotel gotta be lonely. Why don't ya move in with us?" the first woman suggested. "We make some space for ya."

"I'm actually looking for my own place," Oliver said.

"Build a shack, settle down. It be good for a young man like ya," the older woman said. "Betty looks at ya all the time. Ya go talk to her," she tried to cajole him.

"I might just do that," he said. Oliver smiled and got up. He had already finished his dinner, and was planning to stop by the clothing stall anyway—not to flirt with Betty, who was tending it; she wasn't his type—but to check if she had anything new.

"Here, take these," said a lady from the fruit stand, extending her hand towards him and giving him two beautifully ripe peaches. Her palms were dark and discolored by the soil pigments permanently filling the cracks in her skin. "No need to go to a girl empty-handed." She smiled widely.

Oliver grabbed the peaches, thanked the woman for her generosity, and gave one to Betty as he walked by. The young girl's stall had the same old rags hanging, which he had seen last time. They were of no interest to him, so he didn't linger. He walked to the other side of the market square to meet Mr. Paul, the man who had been kind enough to sell him the box he kept his ring in on his first day in Covedale.

The man waved him over as soon as he noticed Oliver. "I got a thing for ya. Found this yesterday."

It was an old magazine. Oliver opened up the yellowing pages and quickly scanned the images inside.

"I'll take it off you," he said, closing the magazine. He planned to study it later. His requested appointment with White was coming up. It was only a short walk from the hotel he was staying at, but he didn't want to be late.

Oliver wasn't sure if he wanted to stay in Covedale. Leo—the ladies at the market had told him the officer's name—was constantly following him, ready to step in if ever Oliver made a mistake or upset White. He needed, however, to be close to Mark and his money transfers. He couldn't go back to Riverlea and face the Gutters, and going to Clamerton which was two days' brisk walk away was not a good option either.

If White was controlling the transports to and from Riverlea, staying in Covedale could mean that he would be protected from the Gutters. They were afraid of White.

Oliver eventually decided that the Gutters were a bigger problem for him. White might have threatened him with the tree, but the militia from Riverlea actually put a loaded gun to his head. He decided to take his chances with White.

"I'm glad that you have given me the opportunity to meet you again," Oliver walked up to White's desk and extended his hand. White ignored it and coldly pointed at a chair, gesturing for Oliver to sit down.

"I didn't think you would dare come back here," White said. White had agreed to the meeting, but he clearly didn't intend to treat him with any respect. A lot depended on how this discussion with White would go, but there was no reason for Oliver not to act naturally. The more he was himself, and the more forward he could be with his plan, the more confident he felt that he'd achieve what he had come for.

Oliver sat down comfortably in the chair with his legs crossed, gently leaning back against the upholstery.

"What can I do for you?" White asked.

"I'd like to buy some property from you, sir," Oliver replied politely.

"And what makes you think I'll sell it?"

"I think the transaction would be beneficial for both of us."

White shrugged his shoulders dismissively, but encouraged Oliver to continue, gesturing with his hand as he spoke. "Go on."

"I heard that you're trying to start the power plant and you need money for that project. A little extra money for selling me a property would allow you to move forward."

White looked at Leo who was sitting on the sofa in the darkness of the room. The man didn't move, so White looked back at Oliver and replied, "I don't know what you're talking about. And what would the benefit for you be? First a property, then what?" White looked annoyed. "Why shouldn't I just have Leo here help you up a tree and be done with it?"

"I don't have any ill intentions towards you or Covedale, Mr. White. I have nothing to gain. You are the rightful leader of Covedale and I'll do nothing to disturb that."

"I govern the town to keep peace within the borders," White said. "And what I hear from you sounds like trouble. One day, sooner than later, someone else will show up in my town to settle some business with you. I can't allow that." He looked at Oliver without hiding his disgust and contempt. "How does scum like yourself even get a hold of enough money to seek a property?"

"I don't have enemies, and I didn't get the money by profiting off others—" Oliver tried to explain.

"Nonsense! Everyone has enemies. Dealing with Rodden is already an increased risk." White had good informers. "He's good at what he does, but if he makes a mistake, it could be catastrophic on both sides of the river. I don't know how much money you have, but your money smells like a problem, and too much money creates enemies. Friends can become enemies."

"I understand your concerns, Mr. White," he replied. "But how much money would it take for you to consider such a risk to be permissible? I'm planning to use White Covedale Bank services, and I can assure you it will be worth it. I'd be saddened if I needed to take my business somewhere else."

"Why does it have to be here?" White was annoyed.

"May I ask, why not here? Easy access to shipyards and docks. Lots of friendly people to do business with." Oliver paused and added, "I like it here."

"I'm certain everything you're saying is a lie," White said calmly after a minute. "But you've done nothing in the few days you've been here to upset me. You even helped with the fire and I appreciate that. I wouldn't mind some money coming into my pockets, but I'll be upfront with you." White sat up straight in his chair and leaned over the desk, looking directly at Oliver. "I'll be monitoring you closely, and I'll kick you out of my town as soon as I find something I don't like. You'll have Leo's soldiers," he said, pointing at the man sitting on the sofa, "keeping an eye on you at all times." He tapped his finger on the wooden desk. "We already have the best guys on the team. You won't be building an army of your own or snatching our people. You'll come to me to discuss in advance any business investments you're planning, in or outside of Covedale, and I reserve the right to veto. These terms are final. You can accept them, or go back to Riverlea, or . . . " White waved his hand as if shooing his guest towards the riverbank.

"Your terms are fair, Mr. White," Oliver responded. He was worried about having Leo's men around, but he would've done the same in White's position. For now, it wasn't a problem and it might even work to his advantage. "I accept them and look forward to working with you." He wanted to shake the man's hand as a sign of mutual agreement, but White continued to ignore his attempts.

"Tell me what you want to buy and I'll tell you the price," White waved his hand dismissively and busied himself with something on his desk.

It was quite late when Natalie knocked on Oliver's hotel room door. There was a pause, but she'd heard someone rustling inside before, so she knocked again. Her knock was light.

"Who is it?" Oliver's voice called from inside.

"It's me, Natalie," she said quietly.

Oliver opened the door, still buttoning his shirt. He let her in.

"I'll only take up a moment of your time," she said shyly as she walked into the room. She looked around the space, avoiding Oliver's gaze.

"How can I help?" he asked. He looked into her dark eyes when she turned to him. A shiver ran down her spine. She was afraid he'd see it, see her secret. See that she was a liar.

Tom was in dire need of money. A few weeks ago he'd come home beaten up, with blood on his face and a broken nose. He'd been shaken down for money that he needed to pay back quickly. Until Oliver had shown up, there had been no opportunity to get a large sum of money in a hurry. When a stranger, an investor, had willingly paid for his drinks at the bar, he knew he needed to get close to the man and seize the opportunity, so he'd invited Oliver over to their house to test the waters.

Tom had come up with the idea and said it was foolproof, but now Natalie doubted it. She knew Oliver wasn't the fool Tom thought he was. The stranger's piercing eyes fell on her and made her afraid that he could see right through her. She lowered her head to avoid his gaze.

"Actually, I've come to you with an offer." She shook off her thoughts and decided to stick to the plan.

"I'm all ears," he smiled at her.

She took a step back and slowly strolled through the room away from Oliver to gather her thoughts again.

"You said you were looking for a property in Covedale. You're new here, so we'd like to help. There are some properties that aren't worth investing in, and only a local would know." She paused for a moment before continuing, "There are also some people from Clamerton looking around who have similar ideas of investing here. Did you know that there are lots of people with money in Clamerton?" It was a neighboring major city, much larger than Covedale. It had been a popular spot for the wealthy. It wasn't a lie that some people in Clamerton could afford additional property, but talking about their interest in moving to Covedale was Tom's idea. "Covedale is a very nice town, not much destroyed by the war, so speed might be of the essence in order to get the best deal. Let us help you." She turned around and looked at Oliver with a smile she hoped looked genuine. "White is wary of strangers and he likes to execute trespassers. For a small share—ten percent, maybe—we can mediate with White on your behalf. He trusts us because Tom is his nephew. If you give me an advance now, we can arrange a meeting with White tomorrow."

Oliver sat down, lit a slug, and propped his elbows on his knees. He was deep in thought for a moment. She looked around the room while she waited, but she didn't rest her eyes on anything in particular. She mostly listened to her fast heart beat while she waited for Oliver to reply.

"It was his idea for quick money, wasn't it?" he finally said, looking at the floor in front of him. He waited for her to reply, but she had nothing to say, so he continued, "Here's where Tom got it wrong." Oliver looked at her and she knew he could see the fear and embarrassment in her eyes. She hoped he understood it wasn't her fault.

Oliver continued, "Given Mr. White's . . . enmity for strangers, Tom didn't anticipate that I'd have already met with Mr. White." He smoked his slug. "If Covedale was such a popular investment opportunity, White wouldn't be so desperate for money. I think the market is as cold as the river in winter. I'll take my chances without Tom's help."

He got up and walked towards Natalie and looked into her eyes. She stared at him, hoping that he'd take his words back, that he'd change his mind, but she knew it wouldn't happen.

"I can tell you now," Oliver continued, "eventually Tom's greed will ruin him. Why would a pretty girl like you want to go down with him?" He took her head into his hands. She didn't protest. She felt his warmth on her and she found it comforting. Why didn't Tom hold her gently like this anymore?

She knew his words were true, and they terrified her. He looked into her eyes. "If you ever need anything," Oliver said, "anything at all, please reach out to me." He paused, then added, "Take care of yourself."

She nodded slowly and left without looking back.

Leo sent Oliver a list of possible properties using a local pageboy. Oliver also took the officer up on his offer to show them to him. The man was clearly pretending to be nice and welcoming. Oliver didn't trust him, but sensed Leo would follow him around anyway, and Oliver wanted to keep an eye on him as well. Might as well make the best of it.

All the property locations were far from the busy center of Covedale, so they took a bicycle rickshaw. It wasn't comfortable transportation for two adults, but it was the only readily available way of moving around the expansive area of Covedale's city limits. The rickshaw had clearly seen better days, and one wheel squeaked as they rode.

As the day passed and they rode along the winding roads, Oliver grew more impatient. The sound of the rickshaw annoyed him, and he wasn't satisfied with the properties he'd seen so far. The houses were of adequate size and they appeared to be structurally fine, but none of them spoke to Oliver as places he could call home.

Finally, when it began to grow dark, the rickshaw driver stopped by the last place they were to see that day. It appeared down an old road, neglected and overgrown with bushes too thick for the rickshaw to ride through. The house was situated on top of an escarpment east of the Covedale city square.

"This one used to be the residence of a hotel owner," Leo commented. "The hotel in Riverlea burned down at the beginning of the war, and the man took his family and left Covedale. No one's heard from him or his family for decades."

It took a few minutes of struggling through the thick greenery for Oliver and Leo to walk about a hundred meters and arrive at the entrance to a building. The front wooden door had become partially unhinged and sat askew in the frame. The window beside the door had no glass, and it appeared to have been broken a long time ago.

The inside still had some of its original charm, with cathedral ceilings in the hallway, but the spiral staircase, a staple of the house, had missing steps. The tile floor was cracked in many places, and nature was taking over with weeds and saplings poking through from the ground underneath. It was late, and the house was dark, but Oliver walked further inside.

The next room had what had probably once been shiny wooden floors, but the boards were now bulging in many places, rotted by the rain water that had been entering through the glassless windows. The house was calm and unnervingly quiet. Even the pieces of torn cloth blowing slowly with the breeze from the windows made no sound at all. Oliver walked up to the fireplace mantel and admired the dusty wood carvings that were still visible. As he wiped them with his finger, he revealed the carved head of a dragon similar to the engraving on his ring. This place wasn't in any better shape than the others he'd seen, but it felt different—special, somehow.

Suddenly the red light of the setting sun shone into the room. He went out onto a large terrace, or what was left of one. The view from where he stood was breathtaking. There was a setting sun to his left and the remnants of the skyscrapers of Riverlea in the distance to his right, reflecting the sun's red rays. It looked like a fire descending from the sky onto a war-ravaged city. Oliver watched, transfixed by the beauty of the destruction before him, until the sun went down and a deep darkness set in.

8

WORD ABOUT OLIVER HIRING people to work on his house spread like wildfire through Covedale. He hadn't wanted to cause excitement in town and should've predicted that people would tell one another about the opportunity. The strict no-begging policy instated by White years ago had now also been mandated by World United. It was part of their promise to crack down on crime. Increasing lack of stable work in Covedale threatened people with hunger or deportation, maybe even to Riverlea.

He'd chosen a man who was experienced in security as his officer. They were all White's men, really, but he needed someone to be second-in-command. He'd test him and see if he was loyal, but it would take some time and effort. He could give him an assignment and see how he performed, but that would probably prove nothing. The best people showed loyalty only in real action. It wasn't a process he wanted to rush through only to be disappointed in the end, or even dead.

Oliver hired a foreman to oversee the renovations—an older man in his fifties. He himself had neither the skill nor the patience for such work. The ladies at the market had spoken highly of this man's attention to detail, and Oliver soon found out for himself that he was very capable. The work was progressing more quickly than expected.

Oliver gave the foreman free rein, trusting him to do the job well. "I want you to hire the best people," Oliver told him. "Use your judgment and give them as much as you think the work is worth. Don't stiff them. If they're committed and do the work well, don't hesitate to give them a bonus."

Just a couple of days after his purchase, Oliver had already moved into the only room in his house that was currently habitable. It was small, with a bed shoved into the corner to maximize the usable space. The wallpaper was peeling, exposing the rotten walls underneath. The workers had boarded one of the two windows up, darkening the room in some corners. It was a bit of a mess but it was home to Oliver.

He opened a drawer of the chest that had been prepared for him and a faint musty smell filled his nose. The furniture was clean, but old.

He took the small box with the ring out of his pocket and opened it. He'd left the ring behind in his parents' care when he'd enlisted because he hadn't wanted to take anything of value with him to the front. He had been reluctant to go back to retrieve it. It wasn't something he wanted to wear on his finger anymore. He wanted to be someone different. An opportunity to never become like his father.

He placed the box into the drawer.

He reached into his bag, took out a yellowing photo and looked at it.

Oliver walks towards his childhood house. He is curious how his father is doing after so many years without him. He is willing to forgive him for what he has done. The house, however, is no longer there. It has been reduced to rubble, and is overgrown with trees and weeds.

A neighbor tells him that, shortly after he enlisted, a missile hit the row of houses and killed his family. She holds for him, besides the ring, one more item recovered from the rubble: the yellowing photograph features the entire family smiling and having a good time. The last happy moments before it became a place he avoids. Before he finds it easier to sneak in and out of the house rather than have to deal with his mother's questioning eyes, wondering about the work he's doing and the girls he's sleeping with.

He propped the photo up beside the kerosene lamp on top of the chest against the wall, then paused and looked at the photograph more closely. Over the years, he'd learned that the dead needed to be erased quickly, forgotten, otherwise they might haunt you forever. He cared little about the people in the picture anymore—they were all strangers to him now—so he put it away beside the ring and closed the drawer.

Early in the morning, Ivy stepped through the broken door of a big house. It was her day off at the factory and she'd woken up at dawn, put on her best clothes, and climbed the escarpment to the east of the city where the ruins of the old hotelier's house stood. A friend had told her to come here about a job for a seamstress. She wore a knee-length gray dress she'd made from scraps and a braided rope belt around her waist, but her feet were bare and dirty from the dust on the road.

"Ivy?"

The man who greeted her knew her name. When she'd been younger, it had been hard to miss her playing with other kids in the neighborhood. She was recognizable by her fiery red hair, now tied in a braid, and her round, freckled face and narrow, wide-set eyes.

She nodded and said, "I'm here about a job."

"Wait here," the man said and left her alone, disappearing through the door.

Ivy looked around. She walked to the wall and touched the darkened pattern on the paper, admiring the texture and trying to imagine how it had looked when fresh and new.

From behind the closed doors, she heard the man talking.

"We should have the windows secured by the end of the day and the roof by the end of the week. We'll save what we can from the inside. Soon we'll start pulling out everything that can't be salvaged, ripping out the warped floors and moldy walls."

Ivy saw workers coming in and out through a large opening at the end of the hallway. She was curious about what they were doing, so she followed them into a large room with many windows, which the men were working on boarding up. She sat down on a piece of dusty wood and observed the workers with interest as they noisily set about with their tools. The room itself could have easily fit ten of the houses she'd lived in with her mother and her older brother's family of eight.

Living in Covedale felt monotonous for Ivy. Nothing much ever changed around town and she was constantly surrounded by the same boring people she knew too well. No one new visited Covedale . . . except maybe those who met with Mr. White, but she never saw them, just heard local rumors. Being in this house and seeing the workers showing their skills brought a rush of excitement. It made her forget she'd been told to wait by the front door.

Oliver was in the kitchen finishing his simple breakfast of scrambled eggs on dark bread with butter while his foreman gave the update for the day.

"Expenses are mostly labor. I spent thirty tickets yesterday, which leaves me with eighty-five. Should last me at least another two days. I might also need to add the seamstress to the daily payroll at one ticket a day. Her name is Ivy. If we want to keep her, we should probably tell Mr. Leggett."

Oliver had inquired about getting some help with his wardrobe. There were no clothes that interested him at the market. He was glad someone was willing to take the job. "I'll take care of Leggett," Oliver said, moving his hand dismissively then wiping his mouth with a napkin.

"The price of lumber is very high, and I hear on the radio that there's demand for it, which will drive the prices further," the foreman updated. "Some of the other materials are also proving more expensive than we budgeted for."

Oliver said nothing, contemplating this information for a moment. He recalled a pricey, but rather ordinary, set of brass plumbing fixtures Tom had found for them and he was even more certain that Tom was ripping him off. There were also rumors circulating about him having some disagreements with Leo.

"Do me a favor and find someone to replace Tom," he replied after a moment. "He can get stuff, but I'd rather not do business with him." He hoped to keep Tom as far as possible from him. He'd been useful for introducing him to other people in town, but that was no longer necessary.

"He's the only trader in town," the foreman replied.

Oliver shook his head. "I heard he just ripped Leo off," he said. Then added, "Some expensive shipment, I heard." If Tom was bold and foolish enough to risk Leo's retaliation, he'd probably overcharged Oliver for everything he'd gotten for him.

"Any suggestions?"

"If there's anyone that's willing to take his place, I'm willing to take the risk."

The man nodded and continued with the agenda. "Test the new girl. I heard she's good, but I couldn't tell ya. If she ain't good, we can send her back to Leggett."

"Let her in."

The foreman got up and left the room, leaving the door open behind him. The sounds of people working with saws and hammers became louder. Oliver heard the man hustling in the hallway and cursing under his breath.

After a moment he heard the foreman's irritated voice from somewhere deeper in the house. "Here you are! Mr. Conway is waiting for you!"

Shortly after, the man and the girl appeared in the kitchen. She stood still and quiet, looking around the room with interest, until Oliver invited her to sit down at the table.

"Coffee, dear?" The cook, a middle-aged woman, asked her while filling up the men's cups.

Ivy nodded with a full smile on her face.

"What do you do, Ivy?" Oliver asked.

"I work at Leggett, sir. I cut, mainly, but also sew while we wait for a new shipment of materials." The cook put a full cup of hot coffee on the table in front of her. Ivy immediately picked it up to smell the dark liquid with her eyes closed, cherishing the moment. It looked like she'd never had barley coffee before.

"What can you make?" Oliver asked, mesmerized by the girl's reverent enjoyment of the hot beverage.

"An'thing," she said and shrugged. She took a long sip from the cup, but suddenly realized Oliver was still silent, waiting for her to expand on her answer. She stared at the ceiling and nonchalantly listed off everything she could think of. "Sheets, shirts, pants, coats, skirts, dresses. Just tell me what ya need."

Ivy smiled widely, got up from her chair and spun around, showing off the dress she said that she had made. It wasn't anything fancy, but it was well-cut and fit the girl nicely.

"Give me a sample of something else you're good at," Oliver replied.

"Of course," she said, sitting down and continuing to drink her coffee. After a moment she added, "I seen materials at Leggett storage that we might be able to use."

"I was planning to visit Mr. Leggett anyway," said Oliver, smiling.

Leo looked around the single-room farmhouse. It smelled of rotten milk and animal shit. The shelf that stood by the wall was overturned. The clay pots that it had been holding lay on the floor, shattered. His men had torn the two straw mattresses in the corner to pieces, and the contents were all over the floor, trampled by their boots. The stone stove was now destroyed, but it still held a fire and a red-hot piece of metal. Leo left it there in case he needed to use it again, but he didn't think that would be necessary.

He was sitting in a chair by the table, leaning back and resting his feet after a long day. He was getting sick and tired of sitting here in this shack waiting for his men to finish their work outside. He took a slug out of his pocket and lit it. His movements were slow and relaxed. He had lots of time.

"You're thirty tickets behind," Leo said, and laughed at the naked man sitting in front of him.

The farmer was older, maybe in his fifties. His head hung low. Leo had bound him to the chair with a rope. His body was already covered in dark bruises and caked with his own blood.

The room was quiet. Only the muffled voices of people working outside were sporadically audible, but unintelligible.

"I pay. After the harvest," the man said faintly, gasping for air, making a lot of effort to speak. The last hit he'd received might've pushed his broken rib further into his lung.

The man was repeating the same words over and over again as though Leo hadn't heard him the first time hours ago. It angered him, but he refrained from hitting the man again. The man no longer had the strength to keep his head up. There was always a limit to how long people could scream. This man was already beginning to lose consciousness. Leo needed to ease up a bit to keep him alive for some time longer.

He remembered being in this house back in March when he'd thrown the man in jail. The farmer had failed to pay the monthly fee for protection. He'd begged to be let go and promised he'd pay later when he had the money, and White had released him. Someone had to plant and harvest the new crop. They watched the farmer closely, and once his wheat had been cut down, Leo moved in to collect the payment, just like White had ordered.

"Where is she?" Leo asked, but the man didn't reply. There were two beds, and he remembered seeing the man's daughter. Pretty thing. Eighteen, maybe twenty.

A dog barked outside.

No one disappears without a trace. He'd rather have the man talk—it was more satisfying—but there were other methods he could use to find her. The dog would know if she were somewhere here, hidden on the farm, or if she had run off into the woods.

Leo finished his slug, got up and pressed the remnants against the man's flesh to extinguish it. The farmer didn't flinch from the pain, but stirred when he heard the woman's shrieks outside and the dog growling and yapping.

"I guess they found her," Leo said, gagging the man before walking out of the house.

His men were standing in a circle, kicking and tearing at the clothes of someone on the ground. The dog was running around, trying to be part of the action and eager to be given the chance to bite the captive.

"What the fuck is the matter with you?" he shouted at his men and they stopped what they were doing. "Be gentle!"

"We found her under the house," one of his men replied, pointing at the spot: a piece of wood covering a hole under the stairs.

It couldn't have been more than a few inches high and right below the floor. Through the entire time he'd been working on her father, she hadn't even squeaked. He would've heard her. He liked the tough ones. They gave him more pleasure to break.

He came over and the other soldiers stepped away from the girl. One of them took ahold of the still-barking dog.

Leo bent over and looked at the girl's face. "Get up!" he ordered. She complied, holding what was left of her clothes in an attempt to cover herself.

"Get back to loading! I don't want to be here all night!" Leo barked at his men angrily, then took a step away from the girl and motioned her towards the house. She started to walk slowly. He shoved her forward so that she walked faster. He followed her into the dim room.

She immediately noticed her father sitting in the chair and tried to run to him, but Leo grabbed her arm and pulled her away. He looked at her. There was fear on her face. He looked her in her eyes, which were switching back and forth from him to her father. He traced her left jaw line with the back of his finger. Her face was as pretty as the last time he'd seen her. Even with the dirt on her cheeks and her dark hair in dis-array, she looked cute. He pulled her hand away from her chest, so that she could no longer hold her clothes. The men had torn her blouse and a small breast was peeking out. She shivered and held her breath as he touched it.

"Pretty daughter you have," Leo taunted. He grabbed her chin and directed her face to his so that she couldn't look at her father, who shook his head in resignation, unable to speak.

"Leave him be," the girl managed.

Leo laughed. "You're old enough to know there will always be punishment."

"If we had money, we'd pay," she replied. Her eyes were swollen with tears.

"But you don't and you didn't. All you needed to do was get a little creative and find the money."

"We pay ya, just let us go," she pleaded.

"Strip!" he ordered.

She shook her head and took a step back, away from him. Her eyes darted around quickly, like those of a cornered animal contemplating its choices. There was nowhere to run.

Leo took a short walk around the messy room. He stopped by her father and looked at him. "Let's make a deal," he said. "My men won't kill him."

He noticed how her neck moved slightly as she swallowed. She then took a quick look at her father's slumped body. He was shaking his head and moaning trying to tell her something, but no words were coming out of his gagged mouth.

Leo walked over to her and stroked her hair, then he pulled on it, watching her grimace in pain. She reluctantly brought her hands to what was left of her blouse and started to slowly unbutton it.

When Leo was done with her, he quickly pulled up his pants and watched with amusement as she slowly and awkwardly got up from her knees.

He walked over to the old man and bent over him, but the man didn't bring his head up to meet his eyes. He wondered what her father had felt, watching and listening as he'd humped his daughter right in front of him. *On all fours like a dog,* he thought, smiling. Shame the old man didn't care about her. Leo took out a gun and waited as it charged.

"If only you had come crawling to me," Leo said. He could've bought her and sold her for a good price as a mistress to someone, or to a brothel out of town. A young, tight ass like that might've gotten the old man the thirty tickets he needed.

Leo placed the gun on the man's temple and pulled the trigger. He'd kept his promise; he hadn't let his men kill the farmer. He preferred to do that himself.

The girl didn't realize what had happened right away, but shrieked in horror seeing her father's crooked head. She ran to the old man. *A loving hug,* Leo thought mockingly. He let her be with her father. He wasn't a monster. He sat down and watched her grieve, entertained by the performance.

One of his men, the second-in-command, came into the house a moment later. "All loaded!" he shouted.

Leo got up. Finally, he could leave. His job was done here.

He turned to the soldier as he exited the house. "Tell the boys they can have her," he said. Perfect way to boost morale.

9

T HE SUN WAS ALREADY high in the sky when Oliver took the trip to the docks. Once the men on guard confirmed that Mr. Leggett was expecting him, they allowed him onto the bridge. He was free to explore, so he took a quick stroll across the small island. It was his first time getting a look at the money-making operations of Covedale, with the big ship engines roaring and spitting clouds of black smoke as they came and left.

All the people who worked by the ships, and those who were resting before they had to turn on the engines again and continue their journeys, had to be fed and entertained right at the docks. No one wanted them roaming around the city and causing trouble. Watering holes, food vendors, and brothels were an integral part of this place, providing services around-the-clock for those with money to spend.

It was the perfect location for the Leggett building. Raw materials were delivered directly to the factory, and the final products didn't have to wait in storage too long. They could be sent out as soon as they were produced.

Oliver made his way towards the factory. He was surprised to see heavily-armed guards patrolling the grounds. Once he arrived at the factory entrance, John invited him inside for a tour.

Only dull rays of light came in through the closed, dirty windows into a huge hangar-like space. The inside was hot and stuffy, and smelled of sweat and urine coming from the hundreds of workers crammed together in the building. Women of different ages sat at their individual sewing machines. Some of these "women" were as young as twelve—if their legs were long enough to reach the sewing pedals and they were quick workers, they were employable.

It was only August, but production of wool garments looked to be in a full swing. John was filling up his storage for the winter market. The loud tick-tocks of foot-operated sewing machines filled every inch of the building.

Oliver felt sweat sliding down his back as he walked around the factory. There wasn't much to look at, but he politely smiled and nodded when John pointed at things and shouted explanations about the production over the noise.

"Don't the windows open?" Oliver asked as he was sitting down. He was glad the tour was over and that John had invited him into his office, which was much cooler and quieter.

"Maybe. I don't know," John said, shrugging. "As you can see, production is going well. The storage area will be full soon, so I just need some cool weather and *bam*—I'll sell it all."

John opened a cabinet, took out a bottle of whiskey and placed it on the desk. He poured the liquid into two glasses and raised one of them.

"I'm glad you could make the time to visit," he said, and they both took a sip of their drinks.

Oliver took the opportunity to light a slug to calm down and relax after the tour, which he'd found quite unpleasant.

"How's the market?" Oliver asked.

John put his glass down and wound up the radio on the desk. "Too early to tell. I'll sell some wool coats in the city, and then have some sent over to other places," John replied. "It's surprising how quickly the ships started leaving with goods. Trade with Europe and Asia is not out of the question."

"How much do you think the coats will go for?"

"I don't know. Maybe twenty or twenty-five. A modest price," John said.

The prices did not impress Oliver. Over ninety percent of the population in the city would need to save for months to afford one. For the rest, the product wasn't exclusive enough to be attractive. He wouldn't buy one himself.

"Plenty of sales opportunities," John added, in contradiction to what Oliver was thinking.

"Lots of sheep around these parts," Oliver noticed and laughed. John was clearly putting all the money into wool.

"I have a great contract with the shepherds on the islands," John said, smiling proudly. "For years, they've sold me their wool and lived like fucking kings."

"Are all the workers from Riverlea? I thought there was only the one ferry," Oliver asked, curious. "And the docks are closer to Covedale." The big ships passed the island on the other side of Riverlea and there was no bridge between the cities. The waters there were deeper and wider, but also more treacherous for cross-canal traffic.

"They're the cheapest labor here and they'll take any job. I built a private dock right on the factory grounds just for them and my boat gets the workers in and out twice a day," John said, but paused for a moment before continuing. "Accidents happen. We had one not too long ago. The boat sank, but I replaced it for a very small cost. People were already lining up to fill the open positions, so production didn't stop for long."

Oliver sat in silence, reflecting on what John had just told him, and took another breath full of smoke. The guards—no doubt placed there at White's insistence to keep the factory workers from getting ideas about escaping— seemed like an enormous expense.

Meanwhile, the anchor on the radio spoke: "Help your employer and he will help you. A free market means prosperity for everyone. There will be no losers!"

"What bothers me," John continued without paying attention to the radio, "is what will happen to the factory when I'm not here. You probably already heard that World United is forming a proper government. I got a message from them and they asked me to join the council, because I know what's what. They need an expert like me . . . But I can't just leave everything and go. I have no children to give the company to," he said, scratching his head.

"That's a great opportunity, John!" Oliver exclaimed. He smiled widely, then added, "I'm happy for you."

The men raised their glasses and drank to that.

"I know, but what will I do about all this?" John said, looking around the room. "This has always been my life. I can't just leave it."

"I think an opportunity like this might not come around again," Oliver said, looking into the whiskey in his raised glass as though he was drawing ideas from it. "You could find a partner, or just sell the factory?" he suggested.

"I'm uncertain if I want to sell. Susan will hate me forever if I do," John said, almost convincingly enough to give the impression that he genuinely cared about his wife's opinion. "I was thinking about a partner, but that's risky. If the partnership doesn't work, things could turn out badly."

"Why not partner with Tom?" Oliver asked.

"He's the last fucking person I'd do business with!" John responded angrily, which caught Oliver by surprise. He hadn't realized John had an issue with Tom. He could've fooled everyone with what close friends they seemed to be. "Better to burn the factory to the ground than give it that dumbass." John stopped for a moment then looked at Oliver and added, "Would you like to partner with me on this?"

"I'm not really partner material." Partnership with a man who ran a sweatshop was the last thing he wanted. He'd rather keep John at arm's length.

"I think you'd be a great partner, but I can't force you if you aren't interested," John said, sighing. "I might need to sell it then, but Susan . . . " he trailed off. Then said, "And finding someone to buy an entire factory would be impossible these days. I might as well decline the seat at the council."

"Declining would be foolish," Oliver said, looking around the old office. "What do you think this is worth?"

"I don't know. The walls cost little, but I have thousands invested in wool," John said.

"You could try and sell it. You never know."

John nervously picked up his glass and finished the drink, seeming to contemplate the idea.

"Large-scale production is our future," the radio said. "World United is planning incentives for businesses employing over a thousand workers."

John sighed deeply hearing the news, saying, "Nothing for me."

"Another reason for you to take the position and do something for the smaller businesses," Oliver said and finished his drink as well. It was time for him to thank John for the tour. He felt that he'd already overstayed, so he got up to leave.

"I have a request for you," Oliver said. "I heard you keep some unused material in storage. Can I buy it from you?"

"Whatever is in storage is no use to me anymore," John replied. "You can have it."

Oliver didn't want any debt that he'd need to repay in the future, so he passed a hundred tickets to John, whose eyes lit up. John took the money off the table and put it into his pocket.

Oliver closed his eyes, feeling the hot water envelop him as he took his morning bath. The radio was on in the background providing the latest updates.

"World United is still waiting for some prospective council members to accept positions," an anchorwoman said. The news was now being broadcast from Clamerton, the North American office of World United. Oliver remembered passing that town on the way to Covedale. It was just a two – or three-day walk away.

"The most recent addition is Mr. Benjamin Scholz, who has taken the position of Health Commissioner's office out of Karben, representing the European continent. He will work towards overcoming one of the biggest problems we're currently facing: the housing shortage. His office will also work on securing food sources and setting the first steps in a long path to rebuilding health care."

Oliver thought for a moment about the people of Riverlea and the conditions they lived in. Violet had never showed him how she and her brother lived, but he imagined the place was not much more than a crooked shack. One of the many inadequate living spaces in the overpopulated city. He wondered how Violet was doing now, but he quickly dismissed these thoughts. Going back to the island to get her was impossible. They had to go their separate ways. He couldn't risk running into the Gutters who might give him an *aggressive* reminder about his promise.

The anchor continued in the background "We're also waiting for a representative from the island of Japan to join World United."

"Ashita, Kazan wo kōgeki seyo," Oliver hears in a radio communication. He's back in the room at the ammunition factory in the valley of the Ural Mountains. He's chained to the chair again in Karl's office.

"I got rid of those two guards," Karl says. "I mean you no harm. I need strong people like you."

"That's Japanese," Oliver says. "They're attacking Kazan tomorrow. Aren't you running this for them?"

"Not at all," Karl replies. "They can go to hell."

"Then you're producing this for the enemies?"

"They can go to hell too," Karl adds, which confuses Oliver. "I hate this war just like everybody else."

"Then why?" Oliver asks.

"I'm just protecting my family," Karl says, then changes the topic. "Kazan's way south from us, so we don't have to worry."

The familiar chime indicating the end of the news broadcast brought him back. The water was getting cold, so Oliver grabbed a towel, got out of the bath, and turned off the radio. The barber was already waiting to give him a shave. The man was old, and Oliver didn't want to keep him waiting.

A couple of weeks had passed and World United was still looking for government positions to be filled, which reminded Oliver of John Leggett and his factory. Oliver had never been involved in production or been a businessman before. It was an idea, but he quickly dismissed it as foolish. He wouldn't even know what to produce.

He finished dressing and stepped out of his room right into the adjacent kitchen. He sat down in the chair the barber had pulled out from the table. The old man was ready to start his work. His tools were laid out nearby; the brush lathered, the razor sharpened. They'd been through this routine many times by now and the barber did his work in silence. The only audible sounds were the workers continuing the renovations and the scraping of the razor blade cutting hair.

When he was halfway through the shave, a pageboy entered the room. "Message from Mr. White!" he announced, his breathing quick and labored from scaling the hill on his bicycle.

Oliver raised his hand for the barber to stop shaving. The kid placed the note in his hand and Oliver read it quietly. It was an invitation to attend White's charity gala. The note stated that it was a gesture thanking him for his support and contribution to the efforts to start up the power plant in Covedale.

Oliver sat up straight in his chair. He couldn't afford not to go, and he was sure there would be others to introduce himself to . . . but he was distrustful of White.

Why now? A couple of months earlier, White hadn't even wanted to shake hands with him. Oliver had let it go then, and he'd kept his distance and the promise he'd made. Now White was extending his hand—an unusual move for someone in his position. White could have easily sent a thank-you note through a message boy for the money that Oliver had spent on the property. This money went towards the power project. A note would've been just fine, but an invitation worried Oliver.

He hoped his concerns were baseless, but everything seemed to be going too easily for him. Was it only his wealth that had prevented White from acting against him? After the welcome Oliver got on his first day in the city, White could have sent him up the tree, but he didn't. Oliver didn't think that White had had a sudden change of heart towards strangers. If it wasn't about the money, then what was it?

He sat patiently, allowing the shave to continue, hoping that the invitation was indeed a genuine sign of good intentions on White's part.

There was also still the matter of Tom. Oliver hadn't been able to find a new trader. Tom had to have some arrangement with White and others might have been too scared to interfere. Oliver decided to wait a bit longer, hoping for someone to take the job.

Meanwhile, Tom said he'd found a car for him that had been stowed away in one of the houses in Clamerton. Cars were rare and expensive to run. White was the only person in Covedale who had one. If there were others in town, their owners weren't using them. Having a car significantly reduced travel time. It would mean he'd be free to travel where he wanted. He could be in Clamerton in just a couple of hours.

Having a chop-jet might have also been nice. Oliver was sure White didn't have one of those. The vessel had a drone-like appearance and was technically called a vertical takeoff jet, but most just called it the chop-jet. Oliver had seen them before at the front. They were used for transporting food and ammunition, lifting off vertically to hover in place at low heights. Once in the air, jet engines can be engaged, giving the chop-jet the ability to move horizontally.

Maybe that's what White was worried about. Maybe he thought of Oliver as a threat to his status. White had the best house, the best men, the only phone in town, and the only car. Still, if he thought of Oliver as a threat, the invitation didn't make sense. It had to be something else.

When the shave was over, Oliver decided to leave right away to see about the vehicle. It was apparently an old car. There was no doubt Tom would rip him off, but he hoped it ran well and that the hover mechanism was smooth. With some of the roads destroyed, it'd be helpful to be able to take the car off-road without sacrificing the comfort of the ride. Oliver was also tired of the constant road dust that came with riding a rickshaw, and he looked forward to the change.

10

IT WAS SEPTEMBER AND the nights were getting chilly. Oliver was glad he'd worn a jacket. He took the long way to get to White's residence, enjoying the ride in his car through the town's wide, tree-lined main road, showing off his new purchase. The townsfolk were curious about the vehicle, and some leaned out of their windows or walked onto the street to see who was in it for themselves. Even the ladies at the market paused in taking down their stalls for the night to send him a smile and a wave.

He stopped the car and adjusted his suit before walking up to White's house. It was the first time he'd gotten to touch and wear something that he'd only seen in his youth. He wore a long-sleeved collared shirt, white and neatly-pressed, tucked into a pair of creased navy pants, alongside a matching jacket with skinny lapels and a breast pocket. Ivy had said that navy suited him better, and was more appropriate for the occasion than black.

Oliver had grown fond of Ivy. She'd proven to be a skilled seamstress. She was hard-working and produced results that pleased him. During the last week before the charity event, she'd insisted on sleeping on a straw mattress on the kitchen floor and working long hours, saving time on unnecessary commutes in order to meet the deadline. Oliver had been falling asleep to the tick-tock sound of the sewing machine and waking up to it each morning until she declared the project complete. Ivy was quick, resourceful, and full of ideas. He admired her ability to transform a magazine image into something real.

Oliver submitted himself to a search before walking into the well-lit hallway of White's house. At least a couple of large generators were being used to their fullest, because every light in the house appeared to be on. He adjusted his cuffs and proceeded into a much bigger and brighter main room. A few heads turned and looked at Oliver as he passed them, not hiding their curiosity about his presence in the house. He heard hushed voices coming from some ladies in the room, who didn't recognize him from any other events.

There were a couple dozen guests, and the large room was bright with chandeliers hanging from the ceiling above them. Two fireplaces on each end made the place look cozy and were keeping the ladies warm, some of whom were wearing clothes that showed more skin than they covered.

He noticed John and Susan Leggett standing at the side of the room, so he approached and greeted them.

"How's the World United?" Oliver asked, turning to John.

"I haven't heard much about it," John dismissed.

A server came up to them with a tray of tall glasses filled with some fizzy liquid, which they each accepted.

"I heard they're already holding meetings," Oliver continued. "Radio the other day said they're still looking for new councilors. Sounds like you should make your decision soon."

John sighed. Susan looked at her husband, puzzled, but said nothing. Clearly they weren't deciding together.

Oliver looked around the room in search of other faces he might recognize. He didn't care to spend the entire night talking with the Leggetts. He was more interested in the people he didn't know and the connections they might provide. The other guests were mostly older men accompanied by their wives or mistresses, some of whom were much younger.

He recognized some faces. There was the dock operator, whose name he didn't remember, and a man in his sixties holding a giggling teenage girl by her ass and constantly filling her glass with alcohol. There was the market owner, William Thompson, who made a living renting out small stall spaces on the market grounds for the modest price of ten tickets a day. He was accompanied by his plump wife, which made one wonder what happened to all the confiscated food when payment wasn't provided. And there was Miles Warren, a man in his thirties who profited from everyone's loss by overseeing all the gambling in the city, who'd come alone. He was standing by Mrs. Millner, whose husband ran a local brothel, and Mrs. Woodham, Leo's wife. Their husbands were not present.

The businessmen and local mafia were all in one room, but there was no one Oliver had had the pleasure of meeting before. He noticed that Tom and Natalie were absent; he guessed they hadn't been invited. There were too many rumors circulating around town that Tom owed Millner hundreds in unpaid time. It wouldn't be smart of White to invite someone like him.

At the snack table at the side of the room, Oliver noticed a young woman, probably in her late twenties, standing all by herself. Her knee-length turquoise dress fit her like a glove and contrasted pleasantly with the dark chestnut hair which fell over her shoulders. Oliver was intrigued by her presence and her beauty and he wanted to approach her, but just then a hush grew over the room. White walked up to the young woman, kissed her on her cheek, and then turned to the guests. It was common for a man of his status to marry a second time to a much younger girl or to have an official mistress, but Oliver felt angry seeing White's lips on such a pretty face.

"Thank you for coming," White started. "I'm glad that all of you share my passion for helping the community of Covedale. It's been my longtime dream to restart the power plant and bring light to our city." He paused for a moment. "We're now on the last stretch and we hope we'll bring electricity to some by December. This will make our streets safer. It will bring health and prosperity to the common people." He raised the drink in his hand. "And we wouldn't be here without you. Thank you!"

A round of applause erupted in the room and Oliver found himself clapping with the rest. He scanned the room, but he could no longer find the woman in the turquoise dress.

"Mr. Conway," he heard a voice behind him say.

He set his empty glass on the tray offered by a passing server, and turned around. White stood beside him, extending his hand.

"Last time we talked, we started off on the wrong foot and it was all my fault. I wanted to apologize. Steven White," he introduced himself.

Oliver already distrusted the man, and now he was also disgusted that a man like White was involved with such a pretty girl, but being in someone's house required manners, so he smiled back. "I'm glad to see you, Mr. White," Oliver replied as they shook hands. "Those were different circumstances."

"I was thinking about our last conversation, and I'd like to chat a bit more as friends," the man replied, extending his hand to show Oliver the direction they should walk.

They passed a couple of doors that separated them from the other guests and went into the study. Bookcases partially filled with books covered the walls, and the entire room had a faint smell of dust and leather.

Seeing Oliver's interest in the room, White commented, "I'm collecting books, but lots of them are now lost."

Oliver nodded and noticed Leo and another man already sitting comfortably in the room.

"Let me introduce you," White offered. The man allowed Oliver to come over to shake his hand, but he didn't get up. White introduced him as Peter Millner. Oliver finally was able to put a name to the face of the pimp of Covedale, who ran both of the local brothels—one in the city and one at the docks. He was a broad-shouldered, overweight man in his fifties. It looked as though the soft armchair was barely supporting his weight.

Neither of the men in the room were particularly interested in Oliver's presence and he didn't want to press it on them. He sat down in the empty seat closest to him, while White turned away from the group to pour some rum for himself and his new guest. Peter sipped on the drink he already had in front of him.

"I got a new girl for you, Leo, if you want to check her out," Peter said, looking at Leo sitting across from him. "Nice body. You'd like her, but come tonight or tomorrow because I won't keep her for long. She's there to work and not sit around and wait for you." Peter laughed, his belly shaking. The chair underneath him creaked under the strain.

Leo was wearing a thoughtful expression and casually arranging white powder on the table.

"I told you to quit that fucking shit," Peter burst out when Leo didn't reply to him immediately.

"Fuck off, Peter," Leo said, snorting one line into his nostril. He adjusted his back on the sofa and closed his eyes for a moment. Then with more enthusiasm he added. "Yeah, I'll come see your girl tomorrow—"

"You could've gone and fucked her today, but you'd rather get wasted," Peter said, sneering. "What's your fucking plan for tonight, anyway? To bang your wife?"

"Don't mind them," White said to Oliver, handing him a glass with some alcohol in it and sitting beside him. "They're never seriously mad at each other. I needed them to be in on this discussion. I prefer to keep them in the loop."

"Thank you for your contribution to the project," White continued. "I know I asked for a lot of money for the little bit of land you inquired about, but trust me, it went to the right cause. Since you were interested in the project last time we spoke, I was wondering if we could count on your help for the next phase we're entering."

Now it made sense to Oliver. This invitation and the meeting were all about the assets he had in White's bank. Mark had already deposited a significant amount.

"I'm glad you're finding new investment," Peter commented bitterly. "I'm already overworking my whores and I won't be able to contribute more than what I am already. Somebody needs to start buying the finished product."

White gave Peter a dirty look.

"Definitely put me down as one of your first electricity customers," Oliver said. "I don't see why not." He hoped they would speed up the construction. He needed a reliable power source for his house, and he didn't mind paying for it.

"We need infrastructure; we have no means to deliver the power yet," Peter said.

"My house is about ten kilometers from the power plant," Oliver said. They might as well build the infrastructure his way. "You can add connection points along the way in key areas. There are a few districts along the way, as well as the airport. Allow me to fund the ten kilometer stretch and connections to my house. I'll leave it up to you how you want to deal with the rest."

"How much do you think the stretch will cost to build?" White turned to Leo, who was already preparing a second dose of powder.

"It's hard to say, but it might be a few thousand," Leo replied.

"Why don't you just take it out of the account," Oliver said casually. "That amount of money is already available." He was fine to part with a few thousand. If that's what they needed to leave him be, he didn't mind.

They sat in silence for a moment. Leo turned back to his white powder and snorted the rest with his other nostril. Muffled sounds of the party down the corridor were reaching the study.

"I don't like this deal," Peter said. "It stinks. What do you want in return?"

"It's only ten kilometers," Oliver said and laughed dismissively. "Take it as gratitude for allowing me to stay in Covedale, plus I'll be one of the first with power."

The room was silent, so Oliver changed the subject. He turned to White. "There's one more thing, Mr. White. John Leggett is planning to sell the factory. I was thinking about buying it and I want to know what you think—"

"Your ideas stink like a fucking dirty whore!" Peter was unimpressed and angry.

"I know of Mr. Leggett's invitation to join the World United government," White replied calmly. "Since the factory's not ours, I don't think I have anything against this acquisition," White said, and the others didn't protest. "We'll, of course, have something for that transaction. Right, Mr. Conway?" He turned to Oliver who nodded in agreement. He expected that some of the money would need to go to White and he was prepared to pay this tax.

The door opened and the woman in the turquoise dress walked in.

"Father," she said, "your guests are asking for you."

"Yes, dear." White got up and turned to Leo. "Get me the cost of those ten kilometers." He motioned to Oliver as an invitation to leave the room with him. "Duty calls," he said, smiling as they walked out to talk and mingle with the other guests. Oliver looked around for White's daughter throughout the rest of the event, but he didn't see her lovely face among the others.

Oliver returned to a quiet house. The workers were long gone for the day, and he was also looking for some rest after a long evening.

He loosened his tie as soon as he stepped into the kitchen. He grabbed a glass and poured himself a couple fingers of whiskey. He smiled to himself, taking a sip and thinking about White's daughter. He recalled the gentle shape of her face and her sweet-sounding voice. He wished he'd learned her name. With time he would. There was no rush.

"Slug?" Oliver heard a male voice behind him and turned around on his heel as fast as he could.

A tall man stood in the door frame that led from the kitchen to his room. He had never seen him before. He could have been slim or muscular. It was hard to see his body frame as it was covered by an old coat. What was clearly visible, however, was the gun hanging at his side, which the man touched as a means of intimidation.

A neatly-rolled slug lay in the palm of his left hand, extended as an offering.

"Who are you?" Oliver asked, but he already knew the answer from how the man looked and carried himself. He had men monitoring the perimeter of the house at all hours. How had a Gutter gotten past them? "How did you get here?" The man in front of him was not small, but he had snuck in somehow. He would have to find out where the hole in house security was and make sure he wasn't bothered like this again.

The man pocketed the slug since Oliver didn't move to grab it.

"Fucking window was open," the man said, smirking and pointing his thumb behind him to Oliver's room without taking his eyes off him.

Oliver knew that the Gutter was mocking him and that he wouldn't reveal his path. "What do you want?" he asked.

"Being friends with White was na part of the fucking deal," Gutter replied. He suddenly got serious. His face muscles relaxed.

"I told you that I don't rush my work," Oliver replied calmly. He took another sip of his drink without a hint of nervousness, as though he had such conversations every day.

"Been fucking three months."

"I will take as much time as I need," Oliver said. He paused before adding, "Why do you need me, anyway? You could do it." He pointed at the man and gave him a quick look up and down, screening his ability and readiness for the job.

"Risky," Gutter replied. "They has fucking truth serum."

"You don't want to get caught?" He understood their hesitation to act. Once the Gutters were implicated, it would mean war and they might get smoked out of Riverlea island. They needed him, someone who was neutral in their pathetic conflict. He brought his head up and looked at the man in his kitchen. "Looks like we are both interested in anonymity," Oliver said. "I told your boss I needed to get close and test the waters. Don't rush me!" He said these last words in anger and pointed at the door for his guest to leave. The conversation was over. He wouldn't tolerate the Gutters coming into his house and disturbing him. The job would take as long as it needed to.

The man walked up closer to Oliver. "Boss said ya some kinda fucking big deal, but I not see it," he taunted, staring into Oliver's eyes and trying to intimidate him. "Ya has fucking tiny balls." He brought his hand up in front of Oliver's face, indicating their size between his index finger and his thumb.

Oliver said nothing, but he didn't flinch. He just wanted the man out of his kitchen. Responding would only prolong his visit.

"Make it fucking soon," the man said, then turned around and left through the front door.

11

Sunday dinners at White's house were a tradition that had been maintained even after the lady of the house had passed away. The cooks always prepared something nice to mark the day, and there was time for White to catch up with his daughter, whom he sometimes didn't see for days at a time. He hadn't remarried, not because there weren't any eligible women to wed, but because his work didn't leave him enough time to seek a new affair. He received women in his bed, but these were just flings that he didn't consider noteworthy. They were there to amuse him and be gone in the morning.

Some time ago he'd thought about adding a woman's touch to the house to help raise his little Sophia, but the longer he thought about it, the older he got, and the more independent his daughter became.

The servants brought a tureen of soup to the table and began serving it into the prepared dishes with a ladle.

It was usually just the two of them at dinner, but this time he'd asked Leo to join them as well. Leo got the first serving of food. He and his daughter's safety fell into Leo's jurisdiction. He knew Leo had handpicked the kitchen staff and servants and he treated them well, but White insisted that extra measures be implemented. There was no room for taking chances. Covedale had started to change after the war, and he didn't like the direction it was going. His head was on the line. Someone might try to poison him. He needed to be prepared.

Once Leo had a start on the soup, White picked up his spoon and signaled his daughter that she could have hers.

"Who was the man that was in your study, papa?" she asked, recalling the event they had held in their house the night before.

"No one of importance," White said dismissively, thinking she must be speaking of Oliver. She knew everyone else.

95

"I've never seen him before," she continued. Her spoon clinked lightly against the bowl as she filled it up with more soup.

"Just someone I'm doing business with. None of your concern, dear."

"You never invite your business partners into your study. Why him?"

White looked into his daughter's eyes. There was a spark of excitement in them he found concerning. His daughter's interest in Oliver was the last thing he wanted.

"Why are you suddenly prying into my business?" he asked, pursing his lips.

"I'm not, really. He just looked nice," she replied nonchalantly, bringing another spoonful of soup to her mouth.

"He's a dangerous man. Keep away from him and my business," he said, and they finished the soup in silence.

The plates were collected, and the servants brought in the second course. Roasted partridge in cranberry sauce with root vegetables. Again, Leo ate first. As they waited, the servants poured them some ale.

"There's a wedding in town next weekend and I'd like to go," Sophia said, changing the subject.

"I don't think you'll be going anywhere," White replied as he started on his meal after verifying Leo wasn't reacting to the food.

"You can't keep me in this house forever. I'm a grown woman!" Sophia said, toying with her potatoes rather than eating them.

"You'll do what I say!" White hit the table with his fist.

"It's not fair, papa," she replied calmly. "All I do is spend time with the old ladies—"

"There's nothing wrong with that. Also, there are no girls your age worth spending time with," White said dismissively. Her reputation would be at stake if she mingled with the wrong people. Prospective husbands might turn away from a girl who had no respect for herself. He took another sip of ale.

"Papa, I want to see life. I want to see cheerful people for a change—"

"You're being foolish!" he interrupted. Regaining his composure, he added, "Your mother would rise from her grave if anything were to happen to you." His wife, Claire, had died not too long after Sophia was born. She'd never recovered her full strength after the labor and had become weaker as the months went by. Sometimes she couldn't get out of bed even to nurse the baby girl. Their doctor said it was cancer and that it was terminal, but White hadn't believed him, and had done all he could to get the best doctors available to help his wife. When his contacts dried up, he went to people bigger than himself and fell into their debt, but even those doctors, top of their class, couldn't help her. Claire had died when their daughter was just two years old.

"Papa?" she pleaded with annoyance in her voice.

White turned to his daughter with anger. "No! I will not allow it!"

"I'm almost thirty!" Sophia got up angrily and left before the staff served dessert.

"You've been harsh on her, Steve," Leo said once she disappeared through the door. "You know she'll go to that wedding, regardless of what you say."

White didn't want to give up, but he knew Leo was right and that he'd lost control of his daughter a long time ago. Marriage, and soon, was the only solution, but he was still reviewing the candidates he'd learned about during his most recent visit to Clamerton. He should've done that ten years ago. He'd given Sophia extra years of youth by delaying her marriage and the inevitable shitty diapers, but she wasn't appreciative of any of that.

He got up and walked to the table with the radio. He turned it on, not with the intention of listening to it, but to kill the silence in the room and occupy his mind with something other than the state of his relationship with Sophia. The news was already in progress and the anchor was repeating some of the information he'd heard earlier in the morning. "We ask every citizen to do their share and pay taxes to the local authorities. We will distribute them back to everyone as much-needed services—"

"Speaking of taxes, I convinced a family to work the fields of that farm we expropriated last month," Leo said, taking White's mind away from his family matters.

"Peter thanked me for that girl," White replied with a nod of approval while returning to the table. "He said that after cleaning her up, he sold her off for a good price." White sat down and took a sip of his ale, then added after a moment, "That guy, Oliver. What do you think of him?"

"Why? Want me to get rid of him?"

"Eventually, but not yet," White replied. Leo had no sense of diplomacy. They needed to wait. "He's not giving us the whole story."

Leo looked at him with skepticism. "Maybe, but why did he have to put it all in your bank? He could've used banks in other cities. Can't you just fucking steal it?"

"I could, but I have a feeling that there's more money coming in and I'm waiting for the amount to grow a bit more." Leo could not know the truth about the promise he'd made. He'd ask too many uncomfortable questions White was not prepared to answer. "I might spook him too early and never get the rest," White added.

A servant girl interrupted by bringing in some golden apple cake for dessert, so they waited until she left.

"What about Leggett?" Leo asked.

"I'm not worried about him. The Leggett factory will still be in Covedale and paying our taxes, even if Oliver runs it. Meanwhile, John will have a chance to prove himself useful." Maybe Leggett would get some cushy position at World United, like a commissioner of trade. "He owes us a few favors."

The entire town was out in the streets for the wedding. It was already evening and the fire pits had been stoked for people to warm up by, but only a few stood beside them. The rest were warming up with the ale donated by White for the event, or by jumping and dancing to the beat coming from the lively band.

The bride's mother had invited Oliver in person. He didn't refuse her; he'd been preoccupied with the renovation work at home for too long and welcomed the distraction and change of scenery. The blue shirt and gray slacks he wore were adequate for the occasion. He didn't want to look too formal, but he still wanted to be noticed and treated with the respect he felt his new persona required. Oliver was no longer the same man who had stepped off the ferry just three months ago.

One side of the square rose above the other, and he sat down on the steps to one of the rare remaining stone houses, which gave him a splendid view of the party from above. He watched people laughing and singing, and listened to them as they gossiped loudly around him. He heard that the barber was having an affair with one of the market sellers, and that the Leggett factory was planning to lay off any remaining Covedale workers in favor of workers from Riverlea. With the new World United mandate to keep the water clean, they'd forbidden the washers to work at the riverbank, so they discussed how they would still use the river water for washing but dump the dirty water into the street in keeping with the new rules.

On the makeshift dance floor, people moved around to the music. There was an area to the side where the newlywed couple kissed every visitor that congratulated them. He had already done *that* ritual and given the girl a nice gift. Further, on the right, an enormous cauldron sat above a fire, gently bubbling with what looked like soup or a stew.

Oliver held a cigarette in his hand, which reminded him of Tom, who had apparently gone missing. Natalie was looking for him everywhere. Oliver was now working with a new trader who had gotten a hold of some silk and cotton. He'd been happy with his initial dealings with the man, and he anticipated that Ivy would also like the new fabrics when she saw them.

While he was enjoying watching people having a good time, he noticed a commotion in one corner of the square with kids gathering and taking special interest in something. He tried to figure out where the trouble was, but there appeared to be none. When he took a closer look, he noticed Miss White among the wedding guests. She was wearing the same turquoise dress he'd seen her in at her house. He got up and approached her to rescue her from the curious kids that surrounded her. She smiled at him when their eyes met.

"We didn't have the pleasure of meeting," Oliver said and introduced himself.

"Sophia," she answered with a shy smile showing a perfect row of white teeth.

He couldn't take his eyes off her. Her face was gently shaped in a way that reminded Oliver of statues carefully carved in stone. Her skin was pale and unblemished, undamaged by sun exposure, and rosy from the cool September air.

The band started playing a new, upbeat song and Oliver extended his hand to her. "Would you care to dance?" he asked her, and she smiled with her full, slightly pink lips. She took his hand, and he led her onto the dance floor which had been put together with wooden planks.

He knew the people's music and the style of dance it required. He'd danced this way before, so he led her through the steps and turns. She allowed him to lead her and kept up with his moves. She fell into the rhythm immediately. They danced in sync, as though they had rehearsed it many times before. He was glad she was laughing out loud; a laugh that was so contagious Oliver couldn't help but laugh as well.

Her presence hypnotized him. She was petite, jumping lightly on her feet, and holding on to him tightly when the moves were faster or more complicated. Her small hand was soft, unspoiled by hard work, and a little damp from the exercise. Whenever they faced each other while dancing, Oliver couldn't look at anything but her amber eyes.

The next tune would be slow. He knew not to let her go. He'd hold her close to catch the scent of her chestnut hair, and he'd have the opportunity to ask the million questions that were right now occupying his mind. But his daydreaming was interrupted by a bright flare high in the sky, followed by a clap of thunder and the screaming of startled people.

The music stopped abruptly. Oliver instinctively squatted down, close to the ground, taking Sophia with him and covering her with his body for protection. He wanted to make sure she didn't get injured. It might've been an unnecessary, paranoid reaction, but his mind took him to the front and the flare reminded him of one of the many air raids he'd lived through. Keeping Sophia's head down, he looked around, but there was no visible panic among the people and no further shots were heard. The screaming had stopped and people were loudly discussing what was happening. There didn't appear to be any imminent danger to him or Sophia.

"Are you hurt?" he asked calmly, releasing her slightly from his protection. She shook her head as a reply, but Oliver noticed her eyes were visibly frightened, either from the bang and the flare, or by his abrupt reaction.

"We should leave," he said, helping her back to her feet. He kept his arms around her protectively as they moved through the crowd. He felt responsible for her safety.

They overheard people passing information among each other.

"The exits are blocked by White's men."

"Someone snuck through the border."

12

NATALIE STEPPED INTO OLIVER'S kitchen with confidence. It was already October, and she'd been looking for Tom for a month now. She heard he'd crossed the border back into Covedale, but then had disappeared without a trace, never returning home.

After learning that he was missing, she'd walked to their empty apartment. She'd looked at the walls, the bed, the table in the middle. It was all too familiar, but felt cold and dead somehow. She was alone, directionless, lost in her own life. She'd thought before about leaving Tom, telling him that whatever they had together needed to end. He'd tell her to pack her things, and where would she go? Maybe a shack in the slums. How would she find money to live when she'd never worked a day in her life? Tom always said that she was meant for better things than hard work. Asking Millner for work was always an option—no experience necessary—and Tom would be happy to know she'd fallen so low. She couldn't allow him that satisfaction.

She recalled their first year together, when she and Tom had moved into this small apartment. How happy they'd been then. How he'd adored her and made her smile. Their love was unconstrained and passionate. Things changed when they tried for a baby and found she couldn't have one. Tom always wanted to have a family and it became a struggle for them to save their relationship. Was that why he had turned to other women? Maybe she should have fought harder to make things work.

For better or for worse, she'd made a vow. How could she break that promise? She couldn't tell herself that what they used to have had never happened. She searched harder for Tom, positive that she'd find him and help him to find a way out of whatever situation he'd gotten himself into.

First she talked to those who knew Tom well. She'd been friends with the girls he slept with—it was not their fault Tom had his flaws—but they swore he hadn't visited them. She then reached out to page boys who drove their bikes around town and offered them payment in exchange for information, but they didn't give her anything. Since she knew Tom had to be somewhere in Covedale, she risked scavenging ruins and old houses. She examined them for any clues. She didn't know what she would find—squatters, maybe people who were hostile or dangerous—but the buildings were empty. If Tom or anyone else were hiding, there'd be warm coals in a fireplace or food remnants, but she found nothing.

Later she talked with everyone of importance in Covedale. She even met with White to see if he had any information about Tom; he was his nephew after all. Leo was the only one who was able to give her a tip. All the soldiers reported to him, so he knew what was happening in the city. He confirmed that the rumors about Tom's whereabouts were true. She didn't think she had the skills to find him on her own, and if there was one person who could help her, it was Oliver. He had told her to come to him if she needed anything, and he was her last option.

"He's in Riverlea," Natalie said, her voice certain.

"How do you know?" Oliver asked. He was sitting at the kitchen table doing some paperwork. The workers upstairs seemed to be making a lot of noise.

"I talked with Leo and he told me so."

"And you believe his word?" Oliver lit a cigarette and puffed some of the smoke. He remained seated, but leaned into the back of the chair, giving her all his attention.

"Why would he lie to me?"

"Maybe because he's responsible for Tom's disappearance."

Natalie dismissed this and started to nervously pace around the room, saying, "That's nonsense."

"Is it?" Oliver asked. "Tom was lying to Leo about his smuggling business and cheated him on cocaine. That's evidence enough that Leo might've had his hands in it."

"I need to find him," she said, coming to stand beside Oliver and looking at him.

Her options for surviving on her own even in Covedale were limited. She was sure that she wouldn't be able to keep the apartment, regardless of what work she'd be able to find. It would cost more to remain there than what she would be able to make. If Tom were alive, the people he owed would look for him. Would she be accused of knowing where he was and asked to pay his debts? She didn't know how much he owed. It might be in the thousands. What if they took her as a slave to cover the debt? Millner occasionally sold his girls when he was pressed for money, and when he did, they were never heard from again.

She needed to find Tom and have him figure the best way out of whatever trouble he was in. He wasn't clever, but luck always seemed to be on his side. She hoped it still was.

"And how are you planning to find him?" he asked.

"I know you've been to Riverlea before. You must know some people," she argued, continuing to pace around the room. "You did some business there."

"That doesn't entitle me to ask anyone about Tom," Oliver replied angrily.

"If you can't help me, then I need to go to Riverlea myself," she rejoined. Natalie was sure of her decision. Oliver was trying to plant doubts in her mind, but he couldn't dissuade her from going.

"Are you out of your mind?" Oliver raised his voice. "That's madness!"

"I have no choice!" she yelled, exasperated, throwing her hands in the air.

"And what exactly are you planning to do there? Ask around where Tom is? Show people his picture?" Oliver crossed his arms.

"Whatever it takes."

"What if you don't find him?"

Natalie stopped for a moment and leaned heavily on the table with both hands. It creaked under her weight. "I'll search until I do."

"What if he's not there?"

"Then I'll come back," Natalie replied, taking another stroll around the kitchen.

"You know it won't be that easy." He took a breath of cigarette smoke.

"The ferry runs both ways, for fuck's sake!" Natalie's patience was running out, and she was getting upset with Oliver.

"Yes, you can get to Riverlea on one ticket, but the return trip is expensive. Did you know you might even need a hundred to get back?" Oliver said calmly. "You need two hundred tickets to make sure you get yourself and Tom back *if* you find him. You'll also need something to live on out there. It's already getting cold. Do you know how many people freeze to death every year?"

"I can take five hundred," Natalie said. She could take all the money she had for the trip. She was prepared to take all the savings she'd hid from Tom. That wasn't an issue for her.

Oliver rolled his eyes and took another breath full of smoke. "You don't get it."

Natalie stopped in front of him and looked at him with her dark eyes. "There's nothing to get, Oliver. You just don't want Tom to come back," she accused. Oliver's insistence upset Natalie. She knew he could help, but didn't want to. She knew Oliver didn't like Tom, otherwise why would he have hired a different trader?

"I wish him a happy return," he replied. "But if you start looking for him in Riverlea, in these ruins, we might not see each other again. That's what I'm afraid of." Oliver sighed, took another breath full of nicotine, then looked back at her. "Riverlea is its own world. You don't know the danger."

"I can hold my own." She walked away from him, feeling more confident in her decision. She was sick of people telling her what to do and pushing her around. The people of Riverlea lived there and survived. Why wouldn't she? She was not scared or helpless.

"I don't doubt that, but I can't help you find Tom and I won't be able to help you when you get into trouble."

"I'll be fine! You don't need to worry about me," she said. She walked towards the door without giving Oliver another look.

Before she crossed the threshold, she heard him say, "Remember that when the time comes and you really need me, I won't be there."

"Good morning, Mr. Leggett. Mark Rodden." The man extended his hand to John, who shook it.

John had heard of the man, but it was the first time he'd had the pleasure of meeting him. Genius with the money, he'd heard, but John felt some disappointment at how unassuming Mark looked. The man in front of him was shorter than himself and not that much younger. His clothes were clean, but looked old and worn. He heard White had used his services before, but he was skeptical upon seeing the famous Mr. Rodden in person.

"Thank you for agreeing to meet with me," Mark added.

John had no business in Riverlea, but he wanted to maintain good relations with the city because it was the home of the workers he employed. The

Gutters in Riverlea could, on a whim, forbid people to come to work, which would leave him and the company with no production until the matter was resolved. He didn't want to risk that, so he'd agreed to this meeting, rather than potentially angering the men from the other side of the river.

"Yes, please sit down, Mr. Rodden," John showed the man a seat at the worn-out desk in his office at the factory. "What can I do for you?"

"My client is interested in purchasing your factory, Mr. Leggett, and I was wondering if we could discuss this in more detail," Mark said. His voice was very authoritative and down-to-business.

"I haven't decided yet about selling," John replied, astonished. He'd never publicly spoken about it. Only a few of his friends knew he'd even been considering it. "Who sent you?"

"Sorry, sir, but my client would like to remain anonymous," Mark replied, which angered John.

"Then I don't want to do any fucking business with you or your client!" John shouted, getting up to escort his visitor out. This was an insult to him and his factory, and he didn't want to play games with Mr. Rodden.

Mark also got up, but clearly with no intention of leaving. He opened the old briefcase he'd brought with him, took out a piece of paper and placed it on the desk. John didn't want to look at the paper. He didn't want to sell, not now. He hadn't even had a chance to mention this possibility to Susan, who would certainly be upset, not that it mattered, but he felt on principle that he should at least let her know. He hadn't consulted with White on this topic yet, either. *Maybe in a few months,* he thought, but his curiosity won, and he picked up the paper from the desk.

The document was a sales agreement between himself and the buyer, but the buyer's name hadn't been filled in. John read the details and sat down in his chair to give his body the support it suddenly required. The number on the page made him sweat, and he took out a handkerchief to wipe his forehead.

"Is this a joke?" he asked after a pause, watching Mark sit back down on the other side of the desk.

"This is a legitimate offer, Mr. Leggett."

"I'll talk to my wife. We'll decide and let you know, Mr. Rodden," John replied. He suddenly felt much more inclined to sell than he had been a moment before, and this offer might even convince Susan as well. If his wife agreed, he could fuck off from Covedale. White was nobody outside of this town, and not a threat to him, he was sure of that.

"Mr. Leggett, if I walk out this door right now, this offer will no longer be valid," Mr. Rodden said calmly.

"Are you trying to intimidate me into selling?" John yelled. He was upset about being played like this. "What's this fucking game?!" His face turned red.

"My client is interested in buying, but I can't guarantee the amount on this document will remain the same if you don't take this offer now." Mark paused, then added, "I'm guessing it will be a lot less."

"I can't just decide now!" John replied angrily. He couldn't do this to Susan. It was really her factory, inherited from her parents, but it was his on paper and in name. The factory had always been a burden to him and he despised working with the suppliers, the dirty shepherds, and the sheep shit. During the war at least their finances had been in order, but right now the company wasn't doing well.

John picked up the paper from the desk to read it again. For this kind of money, he could buy something else if he wanted to. Start a more profitable business, maybe even in a different industry. Susan could have something in her own name while he went to World United and joined the council.

Mark took a pen out of his jacket and placed it on the desk. John watched him take a device out of his briefcase and open it on the desk while he reconsidered the offer. He didn't know what his actions should be, and his mind was empty, so he sat there motionless, letting the sound of the sewing machines echo in his mind.

After a moment Mark broke the long silence, saying, "I've set up the transfer, and if you sign the contract, you'll have the money right away."

John picked up the pen and looked at Mark, but saw no sign of emotion on his face.

"It could mean war with Riverlea if I sell," John pointed out. White would certainly retaliate if he sold the factory to someone who wasn't friendly with Covedale. If workers were laid off, the Gutters in Riverlea would be pissed.

"Since you're leaving, what do you care? Also, this matter has already been squared with White, if that's what you mean. No need to worry."

John sighed quietly, signed the paper, and shoved it a little too forcefully at Mark.

"You've made the right decision, Mr. Leggett," Mark said and pressed the button on the device. "I have transferred the money to your account." He packed his briefcase, got up, and shook John's hand. "Pleasure doing business with you."

After Mark left, John took out the bottle of whiskey he still had in his—not his office anymore. He poured some of it into a glass. It was still morning, but he didn't care. He had a drink and sat down to replay the events in his head. He frowned. The account number had been correct, but how had the bastard known it?

"Tell me how you do that," Oliver said. He'd been surprised to see Mark stepping onto his terrace through the window with a briefcase in his hand. He'd thought the man would be afraid to show his face in Covedale, but Mark looked confident. An accompanying bodyguard immediately began talking with the construction workers as though he knew them well.

"Do what?" his guest walked onto the broken tiles on the terrace, which made crunching sounds beneath his shoes. When he was halfway between the window and Oliver, he turned around and walked backwards for a moment. He looked at the back of the house and the moldy stucco on the walls.

"Play both sides," Oliver clarified.

Mark shrugged. "Fighting with me would ruin them all," he said. He turned around and looked away from the house. "Nice view," he said, looking at Riverlea in the distance. A large vulture was circling above the city, his wings open, the warm air keeping him afloat.

Oliver looked at Mark, not understanding him. "It looks like what they're doing to each other is ruining them already."

"See," Mark started to explain, leaning on the railing as he looked ahead admiring the view, "the Gutters need money, and White needs a scapegoat to keep the people of Covedale under control."

"That's it?" Oliver shook his head. He didn't believe the whole conflict between the two cities could be that simple.

Mark turned towards the house and took in the view. "Nice chop-jet," he commented noticing the vessel sitting on the grass not too far from the house.

Oliver smiled widely. "There was quite an uproar when I flew it here for the first time," he said. "I heard it was the first time people in town had seen one.

It's an older technology from the earlier days of the war, so it cost me only ten thousand tickets." It was a good deal he had made with the new trader. "It's not comfortable or fast, but did you know that the lower deck can hold a car?"

"I'm familiar with them," Mark said, but otherwise did not seem to share Oliver's enthusiasm about the purchase. "These are White's men around, aren't they?"

"White insisted."

Mark nodded. "White tolerates me because, without me, Riverlea would've been dead a long time ago. They both need me."

"Sweet spot to be in, but it's got to be hard to side with Riverlea with no consequences from White."

"That's why I don't," Mark replied dismissively. "I'm capable of doing business without getting involved in drama." He looked at Oliver before saying pointedly, "And that includes you."

"Explain this thing with Riverlea to me." Oliver was curious. He pointed at the city in the distance. The vulture was still making his rounds.

"That's not a secret," Mark started. "When the bridges came down, Max came over to me, asking me to fix the problem."

"Who's Max?" Oliver asked, frowning.

"You spoke with him while in Riverlea," Mark said. "He also wanted me to send you a reminder." Oliver opened his mouth to speak, but Mark dismissed him with a wave of his hand. "Don't tell me what it's about, I don't want to know."

Oliver nodded. "He never introduced himself," he said. He'd have to remember that name.

"The problem was that Riverlea was cut off from all funds," Mark said, continuing his story. "But White wants to collect his ferry fees. World United won't stop what White's doing. It recently gave free rein to all local authorities."

"So how does Riverlea even survive?" Oliver was confused.

"The Gutters came to me to try to find money somewhere," Mark continued. "I agreed, but I made sure that they would leave me alone in exchange. I didn't want to be the guardian of the city."

"You bring them money?"

"I find large quantities of money. A few million if it's a good month. Usually in abandoned accounts where people piled up their savings and then died without an heir, or accounts that became bank property. It's used to buy the food that's shipped there."

"And White?"

"White is always short on money, so he gets a payment for transporting any food that's shipped to the island. Hundreds of thousands in revenue for him."

"That's all?" Was that why the Gutters hated White so much?

"The arrangement has been working for years."

"What's there in it for you, then?"

"They leave me alone and I can do whatever I want. It works for me."

Oliver didn't know what Mark meant by that, but he concluded that as long he didn't get in the way of his business in Riverlea, Mark would leave him be. He decided he would honor that.

Oliver nodded, took out a cigarette pack from his pocket and offered it to Mark. Mark refused.

Mark was free to travel because White needed him. The most powerful man in Covedale couldn't act against him by hanging him from a tree for trespassing without losing valuable income for the city and Mark held a special status in White's eyes for the work that he was doing. He was allowed, unconstrained, to conduct any business he needed, and he was unafraid of coming to Covedale using his private boat.

Oliver piqued Mark's curiosity. There was something strange about this man having a similar untouchable status. It was out of character for White to allow a stranger to stay in Covedale. Selling a property to Oliver was very suspicious. Chop-jet? How did he manage that?

The Gutters had also confiscated no more money from Oliver than the usual cut Mark gave them for transfers like this one. Riverlea needed money, and it was an opportunity for the Gutters to grab a bigger share. They had the power to do that.

How had this man managed to make peace with both the Gutters and White? If Mark wanted, he could've done some digging on Oliver, but he concluded it would be best not to get involved. *Not your monkeys, Mark,* he told himself. A childhood friend had taught him that saying. Don't get yourself dragged into other people's problems.

"What brings you here all the way from Riverlea?" Oliver asked to break the silence.

"I was wondering what you were buying with all that money," he replied, putting his thoughts aside. "I wanted to see the house for myself. Maybe one day I'll move to this side of the river." Leaving Riverlea had crossed his mind many years ago, but he'd decided not to. The other side of the river was where his friends were. Riverlea was his home, not Covedale.

He was lost in thought for a moment, looking again at the state of Oliver's house. "You didn't get a good deal. It's all ruins," Mark bluntly concluded aloud. There was lots of land surrounding the house that had been part of the purchase, and the size of the property kept the place at a fair distance from any potential neighbors. The building, however, looked like it should've been demolished rather than renovated.

"White is a fucking skinflint," Oliver blurted out, taking another breath full of smoke.

A sudden reflection of light from the upstairs balcony caught Mark's attention as the window opened. He could not see who was there, but he caught a glimpse of copper-red hair in the sun before the person disappeared back inside the house. He turned his head to Oliver.

"I met with Leggett and I got the factory." Mark changed the subject. "We'll be laying off the workers tomorrow."

"That's a drastic move," Oliver said and stared at him, waiting for answers. It surprised Mark that he cared at all.

"The factory needs to lay empty for some time."

"We could produce something now rather than wait," Oliver suggested.

Mark shook his head. There was no rush to make money yet. "It needs to depreciate."

"I already paid for it, why would it matter?"

"What do you know about money laundering?" Mark asked, and when Oliver didn't jump to reply he answered his own question: "Nothing."

Oliver nodded, looking down.

Mark opened the briefcase he was holding and took out a piece of paper. He handed it to Oliver. "Here's your purchase agreement."

Oliver grabbed the document and carefully reviewed it. "December?" he said after a while, a little surprised.

"Right. Two months from now." Mark pointed at the spot on the contract. "Sign here and the factory is yours at the end of the year."

Oliver grabbed the pen from Mark, who had already taken it out of his pocket and was holding it out to Oliver. Oliver reviewed the piece of paper again, put it on top of the briefcase Mark was holding, and put his signature on it.

Mark took the document and put it away.

"What's next?" Oliver asked.

Mark shrugged. "Think about what you want to produce." He took another look at the view of Riverlea, then turned around and walked back into the house, almost colliding with a page boy who was hurrying towards Oliver with a note.

"Message from Mr. White," the boy called, still gasping for air after the ride up the hill.

13

For Oliver, it was just a short fifteen-minute car ride from his house to White's residence. He'd come using the direct route through the woods south of the town. The note had said the matter was urgent.

Mr. White greeted him warmly in the office at the side of the house with a glass of rum. Not Oliver's drink of choice, but he didn't refuse it. The room was dark and a fog of cigarette smoke lingered in the air.

Leo sat comfortably on the sofa at the side of the room. He was practically lying down on the soft upholstery, with his feet up on the table in front of him, crossed at the ankles. His head rested on the back of the couch so he could see the room without straining his neck. He was toying with something in his mouth, a piece of wood or a blade of grass, that stuck out of his grinning lips as he stared at Oliver. Oliver tried to ignore Leo's interest in him and wondered why White wanted to see him. What could be so urgent?

"We need to clear a few things up," White said, pointing at the armchair as an invitation for Oliver to sit down. "I'm not fond of your behavior. Friends don't do that."

Oliver sat comfortably in the chair. "I apologize for overstepping at the wedding. I shouldn't have danced with your daughter," he replied, assuming that's what White was talking about.

"Young blood is in her veins. She likes to party and she's been making poor decisions lately." White looked directly at Oliver before saying, "I've forbidden Sophia from spending time with you and I hope you'll respect that."

"I'll not be reaching out to her," Oliver replied calmly. Arguing with White on this matter would be foolish. White had the upper hand in Covedale and it was in Oliver's best interest to maintain good relations with the man, whose security services he depended on.

"There's another matter that I want to settle with you today," White said. "I need you to tell me the whole story about how you got the money."

"I don't think it's in either of our interests to talk about this," Oliver replied quickly. It was a Pandora's box he didn't want to open. From the corner of his eye, Oliver noticed Leo stirring in his seat.

"Yes," White agreed, toying with his glass. "You can try your luck, pretend to be the person you always wanted to be . . . but no matter how well you try to get rid of your past, it will always be there breathing down your neck. The more people who know your secret, the harder it is to keep it. If you share your secret with a big mouth, he'll spill the beans." He got up to take a small stroll around the room. "Once you're successful, people will start looking for you. They'll ask for favors and they'll ask for help. Some might even want to have you killed." He paused for a long time at the window, which had an uninteresting view of the evergreens outside, then sat down. It was clear that White wasn't finished. "All we needed to do was dig a bit. It wasn't hard for Leo to find out what military division Corporal Conway was in and who his friends were. From there, a quick search, a few people visited, some questions asked, and all the pieces began to fit together."

White puffed his cigarette while Oliver sat quietly, trying to understand what point White was trying to make. The man then pressed a button on his desk and a door at the side of the room opened.

Two soldiers entered the room, dragging a third person behind them.

"So we found the guy that breached our border," White said, staring at Oliver. "The one I had to break up the wedding over. It seems he came alone."

Oliver looked at the man held firmly by the soldiers. He recognized him, even though his face was swollen and bruised and dried blood covered his clothes. Oliver stretched his right arm, recalling the bruises Leo inflicted on him a few months back when he was in the same position. The man looked ages older than when he'd last seen him. He stared at Oliver with pleading eyes that were nearly swollen shut, but Oliver remained stone cold and disinterested.

"I don't know why you're showing me this man, Mr. White," Oliver replied after a moment and inhaled his cigarette. At least White hadn't broken up the wedding over him and Sophia.

"I was hoping you could tell me why this man came to Covedale asking for you," continued White. "I thought our agreement was that there'd be no trouble."

"That's still our agreement, sir. I haven't spoken with this man since my military service and I don't know why he'd be looking for me," Oliver replied calmly, not making the slightest twitch that might reveal the thoughts going through his mind. Leo was there to be a second set of eyes for White, but Oliver knew they wouldn't be getting the reaction they were hoping for. He wouldn't give them the satisfaction of reading him too easily.

Both of them could go to hell.

"We have our ways of getting information from people," White continued. "And I know he wasn't just your fellow soldier. It was quite a story he told us about Corporal Conway. It makes me wonder what exactly your involvement in this war was. I don't want World United to take a special interest in Covedale."

"I don't see him as a threat to either of us," Oliver said. "If you release him into my custody, I'll make sure he doesn't bother either of us again." Oliver was tempted to take a sip of his drink, but he didn't want White to interpret it as weakness or nervousness.

"He seems like a liability to you. I'm interested to see how you'll resolve this matter," White replied, then looked at his soldiers and motioned for them to release the man.

"Why are you doing this?" Oliver asked. "You could've ordered this man to be killed." Leo was trigger happy; he wouldn't have hesitated.

"If you're going to live in Covedale, you need to learn how to take care of your own business," White replied. "I won't order my men to do this for you. How you deal with this is your problem, not mine. Take Mr. Eric Finley here and do what you think is right." White waved Oliver away.

Oliver took Eric to his car and drove away from White's house and the town. He thought of what he'd just been told. *People will start looking for you. People will ask for favors.* He didn't want anyone looking for him. He was done doing favors. His dealings with the Gutters weren't finished yet, but after that he wanted to quit. One last favor and then he could live a quiet life.

He wanted to cut all ties with his former friends. White had a point. Money would put his name out there sooner or later, and there were people who knew who he really was. Someone would recognize him. His vision became blurry with rage and he failed to notice that he was driving dangerously fast on the empty road.

"Oliver!" It was the first time Eric had spoken.

"Keep quiet!" Oliver ordered harshly.

The car skidded to stop by a large grassland. He got out of the car and motioned for Eric to follow. They walked through the tall grass to a lonely tree in the middle of nowhere, and Oliver pointed for his companion to sit down on a large rock. The short walk had calmed Oliver, and he had regained his composure. There was a cool breeze coming from the water which combined with the already low temperature to make him shiver. It helped him cool his temper too.

"Are ya gonna kill me here?" Eric asked, distressed. "Just like ya killed the guards?"

Oliver got out a handkerchief from his suit and passed it over to Eric before he replied, "It's just a place where we can talk freely." He was calm, looking straight ahead at the gray of the ocean in the distance. "Why are you here?" he asked turning to Eric and watching him staining the cloth with the blood from his face.

"That's what I wanted to know. Why ya ask me to come?"

"I did no such thing." Oliver was annoyed, but spoke calmly. When he'd last seen Eric in Rockland, he didn't think he would ever see him again. "Tell me what happened," he demanded.

Eric recounted the story in more detail than Oliver cared for. Eric had been getting home from some work he'd been doing in Backthorns, a city up the river. He was hurrying to his wife, Ana, when a man stepped in front of him. The man asked him if he was Eric Finley. He'd told him Oliver had requested his presence in Covedale, but that Eric should use an old road to enter from the south, rather than the main road. He set out to take the trip a couple of days later, but there were already men waiting there for him. Eric was ambushed and taken prisoner. Leo beat him bloody, but Eric didn't know what he'd given up because they had used truth serum and the drug made everything hazy and out of focus.

"It was a setup," Oliver replied, stating the obvious. White didn't have to drag Eric all the way to Covedale to learn the truth. He and Leo had wanted to see Oliver's reaction, but why exactly?

"For the money."

"I can't tell you what to do with your share," Oliver said, still contemplating White's motive.

"I don't want the money," Eric insisted. "Ya shouldn'ta split with me—"

"Then what the fucking hell do you want from me?" Oliver tried to stay calm. "Just forget it ever existed."

"Knowing what we done haunts me—"

"What *we've* done? Or what I did?" Oliver pointed his finger at his own chest as he spoke. Eric had never risked his life to get the money, and he seemed to want to take credit for it.

"I can't sleep, Oliver."

"I stole a bit of fucking money from the criminals and agreed to share it with you. Looks like it was the biggest fucking mistake I've ever made," Oliver replied, clenching his teeth.

He was glad he didn't have his gun with him; after all, he'd kept Eric alive for so many years. He'd brought him extra bread when they were starving. He'd done all he could to make sure they'd both survived.

"I really didn't want no money," Eric said and shook his head.

"Why did you take it then?" He sat down on another stone and took out a cigarette. Nicotine always seemed to clear his mind. He offered it to Eric, but he refused.

"I'm not like ya," Eric continued, "I has a conscience. Every night I hear the screams of people tortured at the factory. Every night women cry for help while being raped. The hunger and hope for some sleep before the next shift starts. The smell of fear that someone gonna make a mistake and the whole place just go boom. That's this money. And look at ya. Fancy clothes, car. Ya not have any respect for those people?"

Sitting under the tree, the two of them looked like opposites. Eric was a short man who wore a faded old shirt and a pair of pants with torn pockets, while Oliver sat tall in his freshly-pressed suit, tailored for him by Ivy. Eric was younger than Oliver, but his body looked like it had been worn-out even before the beating that had left him black and blue. His face was wrinkled and unshaven.

"How do you think it would've helped them if I hadn't taken the money?" replied Oliver calmly. "Most of them perished anyway during the . . . liberation. Our allies didn't know they were mostly civilians making ammunition there, or that there were hundreds of people stuck in cages with no way to escape."

"Ya know nothing of life there, Oliver. Ya earn a cozy position. Ya attacked those guards, they took ya somewhere, and when ya come back, ya no slave like us. They flipped ya so fast." Eric paused for a moment. "Ya not the corporal I knew."

"That's true," Oliver agreed with Eric on this point. Karl had had plans for him so he wasn't forced back into his cell at the end of shift. Karl had trusted him, and he'd felt obligated to reciprocate that trust. It all started when he got moved to a lighter, more important job supervising shipping operation.

"Why did ya work with them? Blood is on ya hands too."

Oliver didn't reply right away. He sat there smoking quietly for a moment, contemplating the past and weighing his words carefully. "They wanted to find out how I was able to hurt the guards while I was in chains. They wanted to see if I was a suitable candidate to become one of them." He paused. "They thought that the promise of power and the drive for survival would be incentive enough to join them, but it wasn't. I didn't want any of that." He reflected on his own words. "I just got lucky when they intercepted a Japanese communication. I showed them I knew what the message said. I became an asset to them and I agreed to help them so I could find a way to infiltrate them. Maybe I could've found out what they were up to. Maybe even found a way out."

"All lies! Ya never knew Japanese." Eric frowned.

"I learned it in the POW camp before we escaped from there and were made slaves in that factory," Oliver said, surprised that Eric didn't remember. Maybe he'd blocked that time period from his memory. He recalled the lessons Aito, a fellow prisoner of war, had given him. He'd always been quick at absorbing information.

"Why we escape from the camp? It weren't that bad."

Oliver looked at Eric with wide eyes and replied angrily. "The fucking camp wasn't bad because I took care of us! If I'd known you wanted to stay there, I would've gladly left you!"

"Ya worked ten years, and ya never got us out?!" Eric replied in a similar tone.

"There was no escape. I tried," Oliver said calmly, inhaling some more of the smoke.

The factory had been at the end of a long valley, blocked on three sides with steep mountain slopes, riddled with landmines and a treacherous environment. There were some who'd tried to escape, but no one could outrun the guns and survive the mountains.

There was only one way in or out of the valley, and it was by using a road that followed a small creek. Attempting to leave that way was impossible, a desperate move. The entry to the valley was heavily guarded, and he'd seen an escapee shot and killed before even getting to the gates.

The trucks transporting people came in full every so often. Each time a new shipment of people arrived to be caged, put to work until their deaths, and then replaced. The transports always ran back empty.

The product, however, was transported out using a new technology. Men didn't operate the trucks and the vehicles didn't move from their bays. Instead, they simply disappeared for thirty minutes, reappearing on the same spot. Just enough time to load or unload it. Oliver wondered why no one was traveling with the load. One day he planted a rat in a cage during a transport, but the rat came back dead.

"Ya never wanted escape! Ya liked it there. Ya loved the power!" Eric shouted at him, still furious.

"If you think I'm so evil, why are you even here? Why would you come?" Oliver looked at Eric, waiting for him to calm down.

"Ya'd punish me anyway," Eric barked back.

"See, you're thinking about it all wrong. Leaving that money sitting there and doing nothing would've helped no one. It can't help the dead, but it can help so many other people," Oliver said, thinking for a moment about what he'd seen in Riverlea. "Have you thought about how much of a fucking difference you could make?"

Eric shouted. "Take ya money! Have it! S'all yours!" He got up.

Oliver escorted Eric to the border and wished him safe travels. Oliver didn't ask for his ruined handkerchief back, he left it in Eric hands as a gift. The last one he would ever receive.

Whatever friendship they'd once had was long gone. Oliver evil? That insinuation angered Oliver, but Eric wasn't in his right mind. His memories were flawed, and his hatred blinded him. The thing Oliver was certain of, however, was that Eric would no longer bother him. He wouldn't make this mistake again and seek contact.

1 4

WINTER HAD ALREADY SET in by December, and the late evening snow made the world look clean and fresh. The house was also quiet tonight with the workers having a day off.

Oliver stood at one of the large windows in his almost-finished bedroom, gazing at the dark ruins of the city in the distance, feeding his habits of nicotine and whiskey.

Leggett was now under his ownership, but it stood empty. Oliver still didn't know what he wanted to produce there. Making textiles sounded like the best option, but he had no experience in it, and John's wool coats were too risky to continue with. The Gutters agreed to wait a bit longer with collecting on his promise if the workers from Riverlea would be employed soon. At least some of them would have an income throughout winter.

Oliver turned around and looked at his room. It was the only decent room in the house; the rest were still being renovated. He was glad he'd been able to move out of the small chamber downstairs. This room was large and decorated in dark wood. The walls were covered top to bottom in walnut. The ceiling panels were the same wood and color and were set off with an elaborate chandelier that matched the look and feel of the room. It had been wise to get Ivy in on the project to design his chambers; she continued to amaze.

The room was well-lit. Electricity was finally here—the old, new luxury. Those who could afford it lit up their houses without the need for candles and the constant smell of burning wax. Oliver collected anything he could plug into the wall, from a radio to an electric shaver. He even got his hands on a video display panel, but Clamerton didn't yet have the capacity for an operational studio, so nothing was being broadcast. For now, the panel simply stood there and looked pretty, but Oliver hoped he'd find a use for it soon. The house had also become much quieter. He noticed the missing hum of the oversized generators.

He walked up to the wide bed standing in the middle of the room and touched the carved post, which featured the finest craftsmanship he could find. The light brown sheets with gold threads added some lighter accents and a feel of warmth to the room. Walking into this room when it was finished had made him aware of exactly how rich he'd become. The lifestyle he'd imagined was now a reality. He'd suffered a lot in his life, but he concluded now that it had all been worth it.

Oliver picked up a note from the night stand and put his cigarette out in an ashtray. The ladies' circle wanted him to join them for a casual evening to discuss their humanitarian efforts. Charities and helping the poor were the new popular pastime for the wealthy, but it consisted mostly of spending money on parties and dinners. None of the upper crust were very entertaining company, and these ladies would probably bore him to death, but he felt obligated to maintain the good relationship he had with them and their husbands. Burning bridges by ignoring the people in Covedale wouldn't be a wise move. He might need those connections later.

He walked to a door in the wall that had been disguised as a wall panel. The opening to the smaller chamber swung wide to reveal a windowless closet. Ivy had made him clothes for all occasions, in different colors and styles, and they were all neatly organized here, folded on the shelf or hanging. He grabbed a suit from a hanger that was good enough for the occasion— nothing from his best collection—and laid it on the bed. The evening with the ladies was scheduled to start in an hour.

The Millners lived on the southern end of town on acres of forest, about halfway between him and White. The lady of the house was a short and chubby woman in her fifties, just like her husband. Wisps of her long white hair escaped from a messy bun and framed her round face. Oliver greeted her with a small bow.

Contrary to the time listed on the invitation, the ladies had arrived much earlier to meet. They had already started on something stronger than an after dinner tea and were comfortably seated in the small guest room which had been well-illuminated, showing off the many paintings on the walls. Mrs. Millner was an art collector.

"I was just talking about my story from yesterday," Mrs. Woodham continued as Oliver sat down in a chair opposite. She was a thin woman, gesturing with her bony hands as she spoke. "I was working in the kitchen by the city square serving tins full of soup to the poor. I don't remember what soup it was this time, but it looked like some kind of squash and potato mix." She tried to remember the details. "Definitely nothing that I'd eat myself. All was fine until this man came in." She frowned when she said it. "He was so dirty and smelly, like he'd rolled in the sewers right before coming in. My head spun from the odor, and I thought I'd faint."

A young serving girl came in with a tray. She set a cup on the table in front of Oliver and poured some hot tea into it.

"That's unacceptable," Mrs. Millner burst out, troubled by the story.

"Then he came closer to me like he wanted something," Mrs. Woodham continued, fanning herself nervously with her hand. "I felt like I needed to protect myself, so I threw the full tin of soup I had in my hand at him and ran away."

"Was he ok?" Sophia asked, walking into the room behind Oliver unexpectedly and sounding concerned about the poor man. Oliver jumped to his feet to greet her. It was the first time he'd seen Sophia since the night of the wedding more than two months ago. She was the same beautiful, petite woman he'd danced with, but there was something different about her. She smiled at him as her amber eyes met his, but the girlish shyness Oliver had noticed before was gone. It was replaced with a certain confidence and elegance that Oliver hadn't expected from her, and he interpreted it to be cold and uninviting. He was now convinced that there had never been anything between them. That it had just been a figment of his imagination.

Sophia sat down in the chair across from Oliver as Mrs. Woodham continued, "I don't know. I went straight home. I was too afraid to go back today."

"Helping with food was getting boring already, anyway," Mrs. Millner said, waving her hand dismissively before turning to Oliver who was sitting back down. "That's why I decided to invite you to join us. You seem to have a way with the townspeople. I'm sure you can find something else we fragile old ladies can help with."

Sophia looked at Oliver and smiled, adding, "We know you're busy, so it wouldn't be nice of us to take up your time with something silly like this, but we would be very grateful."

"I don't mind at all," Oliver replied. He knew that anything they would be interested in and willing to do wouldn't serve anyone but themselves. "You ladies are a sample of what our world offers. You have the most charm and intelligence in our community." Mrs. Woodham appeared flattered by his empty words as he continued, "Trying to make a difference doesn't come easy, and I'd love to help . . . but if I may, I'd like to ask a favor as well." He picked up the cup full of tea from the table and tried to take a sip, but the liquid was still too hot.

"Anything, Mr. Conway," Mrs. Millner said.

"As you know, I'm the new owner of the Leggett factory," he began. He hadn't bothered to change the well-known name, but everyone seemed to already know it was his. There was no reason to hide it. "But men these days care little about their looks and how they dress. It's you ladies who are the customers, choosing between different sheets and colors of pillows, shirts and dresses, so I wanted to ask you: If you could have something special for yourself, something you've always wanted, what would that be?"

The ladies stirred on the sofa and looked at each other before replying.

"To tell you the truth, I have nothing," Mrs. Millner stated, shaking her head. "Everything I have is old and has been worn way too many times. I'd buy anything as long as it's something new."

"Imagine us walking into the hall in Clamerton," Mrs. Woodham said with a smile. "All wearing brand-new dresses, with all eyes on us. I'd pay anything for that."

"How about lingerie?" Mrs. Millner suggested, smiling to herself. "Something hot and sexy."

"I'm skeptical it'd make your husband stop banging that girl of yours," Mrs. Woodham mocked. Everybody knew Peter often selected the best girls from his brothel to sleep with, but recently he'd been choosing to spend nights with the house servant, who conveniently was also in the room and able to hear.

"I'll find a nice, young boy," Mrs. Millner replied, her voice dreamy.

"Not with that ass," Mrs. Woodham said, shaking her head, and Oliver caught a glimpse of the serving girl biting her lip to avoid laughing.

The ladies continued to amuse themselves with talk of how much their lives would be improved by being able to get themselves a change of wardrobe, and Oliver made mental notes. When they moved on to other topics, he excused himself to go out behind the house for a smoke.

The air was chilly. It was most likely below freezing and he'd forgotten to take his coat with him. He spent a brief moment finishing his cigarette and staring at the pond in the middle of the Millners' lawn. The thin ice that was covering it shone slightly in the lights coming from the house. Beyond the pond, he couldn't see anything but darkness.

When he was ready to head back inside, he noticed Sophia coming towards him. She was all bundled up in a fur coat.

"I'm sorry, I didn't know you'd be here," Oliver said. "I didn't mean to impose."

"I told Mrs. Millner to invite you," Sophia said. "They were looking for some new entertainment and I'm glad you delivered. Thinking about clothes will keep them occupied for weeks." She laughed. Her laughter was soft.

Oliver wasn't sure if it was appropriate for him to smile with her. She was sending what he felt were mixed signals, and he wanted to make sure they both had the same understanding of the situation. "Your father made me promise I wouldn't see you again."

"I know, but I needed to talk to you," she said, motioning for Oliver to walk with her.

They walked in silence along the wall of the house, away from the sitting room window and the prying eyes of the ladies. Sophia walked up to a dark sliding door. It looked like someone had left it slightly open on purpose, specifically for them to enter. Oliver followed her into the warmth of the house.

"My father sent me away shortly after that night," she began, looking at Mr. Millner's full cheeks in the portrait that hung on the wall as Oliver followed her with his eyes. The room was dark, but the moon's rays were highlighting parts of the walls and furniture. "He said he understood my need for some fresh air, to see other people and experience how they live. He sent me to Clamerton under the protection of John and Susan."

She walked along the wall of the room looking at the art collectibles the Millners had displayed on the large tables. "They've been doing well since they left Covedale. The Leggetts moved out right after they sold the factory. You know how Susan is. She doesn't tolerate change and inconvenience well, but she showed me around." She picked up a trinket from the table.

"We went out to parties, dinners, dances. I met many people when I was there. A lot of them were working at World United and living interesting lives. I admit, I enjoyed my time there, and in a way I forgot about Covedale." She put the item back on the table and continued. "One day, one of John's friends asked me to stop by his apartment to pick something up. It wasn't anything important," she added dismissively. "When I got there, he convinced me to stay longer to have some tea and cookies. He was nice, and my father's age, so I let my guard down. Then he touched me and I became paralyzed, unable to do or say anything, but when he tried to push himself on me and kiss me, I slapped him. My hand hurt so much after that." Her nervous laughter echoed in the room.

"I left for home the next day. I couldn't stand Clamerton anymore, but my father was angry with me." She had completed her circle and was back to where Oliver stood. "Not because I'd come back earlier than he wanted me to, or because I left John and Susan's place so abruptly. He was angry because I dishonored him. He said I gave the White family a bad name," she said with a hint of disgust. She looked at the painting above the fireplace. "He said he didn't blame me for rejecting that man, but he said I was too harsh. That I shouldn't have hit him or called him names. My own father told me I was too harsh in defending myself." She looked at Oliver, but he was unable to see the expression on her face. She was in the shadows, away from the moonlight coming through the window.

"I lay in my bed after that fight with my father. I felt lost and scared. I had always seen my father as someone who would protect me at all costs," she said. "But that man is gone."

She moved and he could see the moon reflected in her eyes. "It hurt me that he didn't take my side in this, but I remembered that brief moment when I'd been afraid and someone was there to protect me," she said, locking eyes with him. "Someone who shielded me with his body to make sure I wasn't hurt. I couldn't get your face out of my mind. I had to see you."

"I'd never let anything happen to you, Sophia," he said as he lowered his head to meet her lips. He confirmed, finally, that her hair smelled of almonds.

1 5

Mark, Ivy, and Oliver sat together and brainstormed ideas from the ladies' night, and soon came up with a plan.

The factory had a sizable amount of wool stored and there would be a constant supply of it if the contracts with the shepherds were to continue. It was Mark who had come up with the idea of making blankets to get the money laundered faster.

With production running around-the-clock, they came up with a figure of more than a thousand blankets a day, which they would sell for one ticket apiece in order to move the product as quickly as possible. It'd be the volume of sales that would bring in the profits. The blankets were not designed to be high quality. The fabric would tear with time and they would need to be replaced with new ones.

Oliver also insisted on paying the workers at the factory two tickets a day. He didn't see a reason to produce anything they couldn't afford to buy. This also pleased the Gutters, and he felt that it would keep them off his back for a while longer. He still didn't have a plan for how he would fulfill his promise.

In addition to this, Oliver used the society ladies' eagerness and vanity to help the cause and gave them an easy project so they could feel good about helping the poor. He asked them to do what they liked most: go out and attend parties, praise Covedale and the Leggett factory, and collect donations for the production of blankets that would then be distributed for free in Covedale and Riverlea. The ladies were skeptical about the charity at first because they expected people would be very reluctant to part with their money to help others, but Mark made sure the money flowed, channeling "donations" from Oliver's accounts through false identities and into the charitable cause.

They put Ivy in charge of Oliver's second idea of making customized designer clothes for the smaller wealthy population, but first she needed to find out what appealed to them. Oliver invited her to join the meetings with the ladies, and they loved him for it because Ivy had an endless collection of stories and ideas that kept the ladies occupied. This meant he could sneak off to another room to catch up with Sophia.

"I have a funny story," Oliver said to Sophia one night at the Millners' house when they'd managed to get some alone time together. They were in the same room where they'd kissed for the first time. The lights were on, and the Millners' collections were clearly visible. There were African masks on the walls between famous paintings by Monet, Picasso, and Rembrandt. On tables stood hand-painted porcelain tureens, colorful glass vases, and sculptures of various sizes.

The house felt quieter today. She sat on his lap with an arm around his neck, her touch slightly cool. One of his hands held her waist, but not too tightly—just enough to support her—while his other hand gently played with the fingers of her free hand. She watched him attentively, waiting for him to continue.

"We had a dog," he started. "A small one, a mutt. My sister found it some-where and brought it home—"

"You had a sister?" Sophia said with curiosity.

"Yes, an older one," he smiled. "Janet."

"I always wanted a sibling. It would've been great to have a sister. Where is she now?"

"She's gone," he paused. "Twelve years ago."

"I'm sorry," she gave him a long hug.

He waited patiently for her embrace to end before continuing. "So the mutt—Rex was his name—he was very energetic. He loved running around. Fetch was his favorite game, and he used to spring into the air to catch a ball or a stick. He was fast and jumped very high, his ears flapping as he flew through the air." Oliver moved the sides of his hair up to mimic the dog ears flying up and it made Sophia chuckle. "He was lots of fun," Oliver continued, "but we were kids—I was five or six—and soon the enthusiasm of having a pet passed, so we made him a door so he could go in and out of the house without waking us up early in the morning.

"Rex loved the freedom of being able to come and go as he pleased. Eventually he'd be gone for the entire day and just come back to sleep. He even brought fleas into the house once, and guess what, he decided to pack himself right into my bed," Oliver laughed.

"I've never had fleas." She grimaced.

"They're itchy." He smiled and ran his fingers across her back as though something were crawling on her.

"Stop that!" she laughed, getting up to get away from the imaginary fleas that were attacking her. She walked over to a shelf with statues on it.

"One day," Oliver got up and followed her, continuing his story. "It was late in the evening when the dog got back for the night." Oliver stopped beside her. "I was already sleeping," he continued, "but the screams from the other room woke me up. I opened the door. My eyes were still only half open, and as I tried to get them to focus, I saw my mom standing on the table."

"Was there a mouse?" she asked, picking up a glazed clay elephant from the shelf and inspecting it as she listened.

"No, she'd never scream at a mouse," he replied and smiled. "So she's standing on the table with a broom in her hand, pointing it at something in the corner by the ceiling." Oliver made a warrior-like stance as though holding the broom in his hands, making Sophia laugh at his performance. "My eyes weren't clear enough yet to see what it was. It just looked like a dark blob, maybe the size of a fist. Then it moved and flew right towards her, almost flying into her. She wasn't able to stop it with the broom. It landed on the other side of the kitchen, and she realized it was a bat." He flapped his hands, pretending to be a bat flying into Sophia and she laughed. "My sister came up trying to help catch the beast as well. It became a family effort. When my dad got in to end it, he couldn't get the damn thing out the window."

"Did you let it out?" she asked, expecting him to be the hero of the story.

Oliver smiled and shook his head. "I just fell on the floor, laughing until I got hiccups." He kissed her hair. "Rex had brought that bat in with him in his mouth."

Laughing, Sophia turned and tried to put the glazed elephant back onto the shelf a little bit too quickly. She gasped as she let go of the statue and it headed for the floor, slowly spinning as it fell. With quick reflexes, Oliver caught the clay statue before it hit the ground. He was fast, his hand gliding through the air like the bat he'd been describing.

"That could've been unfortunate," he said, smiling and holding the elephant in his hand for her to grab and put back on the shelf.

"We should get back," Sophia said. She was still in shock from almost destroying such a unique and fragile collectible. She put the elephant back in its place before hurrying out of the room.

White sat in the dark room waiting for his daughter to return home. It was no secret what she'd been up to since Mrs. Woodham had no filter for gossip. He'd been hearing for the past few weeks now that Sophia had been meeting Oliver and spending time alone with him under Mrs. Millner's roof until late hours.

"I know you're meeting with him behind my back. Are you sure that's what you want?" he asked when he heard her enter the house.

"Are you planning to give me some more fatherly advice?" Sophia replied mockingly while taking off her coat and laying it on a chair. The servants weren't around, but they would find her fur later and put it away.

"It wasn't fair of me to say those things to you. I want you to know that I'm sorry I acted the way I did."

Sophia walked into the room and sat down in a comfy chair beside him. "Do you really think I'll just get over it now that you've said that? Just forget it like that?" She snapped her fingers.

"No, but I want you to know that I still care about your well-being," White said with as much fatherly concern as he could muster. He sat motionless in the moonlight coming from the windows behind him. He'd feared this moment for a long time. For years Sophia had been drifting away from him, but now it felt like they were miles apart.

"It seems like you care more about your business than about me."

"I lost a big contract in Clamerton because of your actions. I was upset and said things I shouldn't have."

"Weeks have passed," she said with disappointment in her voice.

"That's my fault. I didn't know what to say."

"You could have at least apologized sooner."

"I still want you to know that I'm on your side." He knew he'd done wrong by blaming her for the lost business, but he still hoped she'd come around somehow and see the big picture.

"You're not very convincing." Sophia stirred as though she were getting up to leave.

"I told you, he's not who you think he is. Whatever he tells you isn't true."

"Your word against his! How can I not be torn, father?" She laughed derisively.

"You know nothing about him. What did he do before the war? Who are his friends, or enemies?"

"You have no proof, no basis for your claim that he's not a good man," she insisted and smiled gently as though she were thinking about something nice.

"I've always been true to you, except for that one burst of anger. Would you ignore the truth and disregard all the care I've given you over the years for that man's lies?" he said. His voice was calm.

"It will be difficult for you to regain my trust, even more difficult than it will be for him to lose it. You know that, right?"

White was painfully aware of what he'd done. "I know," he said, "but I care about you and I want you to promise me one small thing: That you'll ask him about his past one day, before it's too late. That's all."

Sophia got up and said nothing more as she left the room. She didn't want to listen to his lectures anymore.

16

IVY KNEW THAT IT was just a matter of time before Mark called her over to his office at the factory. Mr. Conway had made him a manager of the factory and he oversaw all operations.

Production was in full swing again and the hall was noisy with people working at their sewing machines. After the announcement of the re-opening and higher wages, many people showed up to work. Most of the floor was now dedicated to the blankets, and large quantities of them were already being produced. Over the past few weeks, she'd begun to see them everywhere. She heard some had even been spotted in faraway Clamerton.

Ivy had been given her own large room in the factory. She was glad Mr. Conway trusted her with the work. Her new role as head designer for the luxury clothing division sounded exciting, and she was eager to start on it. She decorated the room with wallpaper, drapes, and mirrors to brighten up the space and make it more inviting. She wanted to cater to the society ladies who wanted to wear things that were unique and fit their bodies and personalities. This was exactly what Ivy loved to do, and she became busy with projects very quickly as orders started to come in. She was also able to secure a large shipment of cotton fabrics to add to her growing collection of patterns and styles.

Mark was probably upset about her work, otherwise why would he have called for her? The only reason Mr. Leggett ever called anyone into his office was to yell at them. She must have made a mistake somewhere. The very thought terrified her.

"Please sit down," Mark said, pointing at the chair by his desk as she walked into his office. The noises from the production hall became muffled once the door closed. He was preoccupied, so Ivy looked around. She'd been in this office once before when Mr. Leggett had still owned the place. The room had been cleaned up since—the windows were no longer dirty and more light was shining through. The old desk was now filled with stacks of documents. "I wanted to ask you about this." Mark handed Ivy a piece of paper without looking at her. She recognized it as a purchase she'd made and the amount looked familiar, but didn't remember what it was for. "What does it say?" he asked.

Ivy's hands began to sweat, and she felt her heart beating faster. "Don't know," she replied after a pause. Mark stopped what he was doing and put down whatever he'd been holding in his hand. He looked at Ivy who immediately answered the question she was sure he was thinking, but hadn't yet asked, "I can't read." Ivy looked down.

"But I saw you count."

"I know numbers," she replied shyly. Her voice was quiet and Mark leaned closer to hear her. "I figure out what I need to measure and cut. I don't know letters."

"Does Mr. Conway know?" The chair squeaked as he leaned away from her.

"Don't know. Never come up," Ivy replied hesitantly.

"The position he gave you allows you to negotiate deals and contracts," Mark said calmly. "You have the power to make important business decisions and purchases. Do you know what kind of responsibility that is?" She expected him to be mad at her and raise his voice, but he didn't.

"I'm sorry," Ivy said, big tears beginning to roll down her cheeks. She was still looking down, afraid to meet Mark's eyes.

"I'm not mad at you," Mark replied calmly, bending closer to Ivy and propping his elbows on his knees. "It's not your fault, but we need to work this out. The purchase you made had an amendment you missed. You looked at the numbers and they looked right to you, but the fine print says that they might not deliver the materials if they don't have adequate supply. They got the money and we won't receive the product. It's not a lot of money, but we can't have it happen again."

"I promise. Never again." Ivy's voice was shaking even though she tried to control it. One hundred tickets was a lot of money to her. She felt ashamed of her carelessness.

"We'll work on this together. From now on, anything you do will require my approval," Mark said calmly.

"Thank you," Ivy uttered.

The alley was dark, even though the April sun was up. No rays reached this narrow passage with the ruins of two tall buildings on each side.

This wasn't the first such alley Natalie had explored in Riverlea during the past few months, following leads she got from the locals, trying to find Tom. The city was still new to her, and she remained cautious, scanning her surroundings for any dangers.

She thought she heard something and looked behind her, but saw no one. The lead she was following said that Tom had been seen working with a local drug dealer. She didn't think her husband had it in him—he only dealt with drugs when Leo asked him to. But he might've been pressed for money. She needed to find out for herself if the lead was right.

It had taken Natalie a few days to get to know Riverlea and how it worked. She'd felt scared seeing the raw and unwelcoming ruins up close. All her life, she'd only looked at the city from afar, from the other side of the river. Seeing the towering remains looming immediately above her was a brand-new experience. Buildings still occasionally fell down on people below, crushing or crippling them, but everyone saw this danger as just an inescapable part of their lives.

Hunger, cold, and desperation were visible in the eyes of the locals. Overcrowding had been a big issue in Riverlea over the winter, and spending time by the fire or getting something to eat required a fight. That seemed to have gotten a little better with winter's end.

She tried to spend as little of the money she'd brought as she could so she would have enough for Tom and herself to return to Covedale. She'd found a small hotel which had helped her survive the winter, but soon her body was covered in bites from bed bugs and fleas. She'd cut her long black locks with a knife to help control the infestation.

Something felt wrong about this alley and she looked around again. She was still alone.

Her search was slow. She was trying to make contacts without revealing how much money she'd brought with her. The people were not eager to share information—they distrusted strangers. She couldn't get any information on Tom; no one had seen or heard of him and she had moments of doubt where she wondered if he'd really come here at all.

A few days ago, she'd heard the name "Rodden" spoken in a hushed voice on the street. The man seemed important, from what she'd overheard. She figured maybe he'd know where Tom was, but was disappointed. Whenever she asked anyone, she was met with the same stare and the person would reply that they'd never heard that name before. She knew they were lying, so she became more persistent, and that's when she began to feel as if she were being watched.

She looked behind her and saw someone following her. She could see that it was a man from the way he walked. He was still a fair distance back, but she picked up her pace anyway. A few hundred meters and she'd be at the location her informant had mentioned.

There was always someone lurking in the shadows whenever she went out lately, but they'd never shown themselves so openly like that. Not until now. She looked back again and noticed the man was closer to her than he'd been before. She decided to run.

A few more meters and she turned the corner as fast as she could, but was forced to stop in her tracks. The rest of the alley was blocked by large pieces of rubble. There was no way past it.

Natalie turned around and saw the man standing at the corner looking at her. It was hard to see his face, but he was tall and thin. She looked at the rubble again in a panic, but she knew there was no way she'd be able to climb it.

"What do you want?" she asked the stranger, but he said nothing. He just came closer, put his hand over her mouth, and took out a knife.

Natalie shivered. Even if she screamed, there was no one out there to hear her. The alley was deep and narrow. No one would venture out to see what was happening. She'd heard screams in Riverlea at night, from men and women alike, and no one in earshot ever even seemed alarmed.

Ivy held onto Mark's hand. He could feel her pulse racing. She was clearly scared. It was evening, and she was looking at every shadow of the ruins of Riverlea. He'd asked her to stay after work to show her something and he was glad that she'd agreed. They took his motorboat from the docks and in a few minutes they were on the other side, walking down one of the large streets.

He'd had lots of experience with illiterate people. There were plenty of them; likely the majority of Riverlea couldn't read. Or count. This, however, was the first time he'd encountered someone who knew how to count, but not how to read. It amazed him that this had escaped his attention so easily when working with Ivy before.

She'd told him she'd never been to Riverlea, and that she'd heard terrifying stories about the place. From murders and kidnappings to people rising from their graves underneath fallen buildings at night. All were made-up stories designed to keep the kids afraid of Riverlea. He'd been sure that when he told her about going to the other side of the river that she'd refuse, but she hadn't. She trusted him. Mark smiled.

He walked down the street with confidence. He knew this place very well, and it knew him too. He'd lived and worked here since he was a teen. Being useful and doing occasional favors had helped him to live in peace with the Gutters all these years. Mark was quick, clever, and reliable, and he was an asset working directly with money. Illegal transactions, money laundering, untraceable transfers; these were his domain. Ivy didn't know that there were two heavily-armed men following them for additional protection.

They passed a large gate and turned into an alley beside it. They walked a few meters in and Mark knocked on a door on the right. A familiar face looked out and nodded. The door opened, and a man armed with a gun led them into a dark room, dimly lit by candlelight. Mark walked in confidently; he'd been here many times. He pulled Ivy in behind him, still holding her hand.

Mark greeted the dozen people who were already waiting for him inside. He pointed at a bench and asked Ivy to sit down. She was wearing a dress she'd recently designed under her light spring coat, and she looked a bit out of place sitting between strangers with unruly hair and old, dirty clothes. He found the contrast amusing, and he smiled at her.

She shyly smiled back at him and quietly sat down on the crooked bench Mark pointed her towards. She was still not sure what Mark wanted her to see. The room was silent as Mark took out a small box and put it in the middle of the table and turned it on. A blue hologram appeared showing the word "big" in capital letters and Mark said it a few times. People in the room repeated the word, looking at the image, trying to memorize the letters.

For the next hour, Mark introduced a few other words and short sentences that the students repeated. Ivy was shy at first, but repeated the words as well, happy to learn. She already liked Mark, and knowing what he did after work only increased the respect she had for him. The sound of his voice resonating in the small room drew her to him, and to his confident moves and gestures. When the class was over, she was surprised at how quickly the time had passed.

When most of the students had left, a blonde girl came up to Mark as he was packing to leave. She was very shy, and just a bit younger than Ivy.

"Mr. Rodden," she said awkwardly.

"Yes, dear," Mark replied while he continued to pack.

"Thank ya for helping us."

Mark stopped what he was doing for a moment, looked at her, and smiled. "You're most welcome. I enjoy working with you."

"Wanted to ask ya for favor," the girl said. Her face was red with embarrassment.

"What is it?" Mark sat down to listen to her.

"Sorry to ask—and if ya say no, that's okay." Mark patiently waited for her to continue. "Can ya tell me if there's work at Leggett? I know how to sew," she finally managed.

"I can't promise, but I can keep an eye out," Mark replied, nodding in agreement.

"Thank you, sir," the girl smiled and left the room.

Ivy looked at Mark once the girl had left and said, "We could find her something."

"We can't help them all, Ivy," he replied with no emotion on his face. He quickly added, "Let me take you back. I won't let you walk alone."

"Can I come again?" Ivy asked as they walked hand in hand to the boat, which was waiting at the river to take her back to Covedale.

"Of course. That's why I brought you out here today," Mark replied, smiling and squeezing Ivy's hand. "I've been running these small group classes for a few years now, and you can attend them if you like. I promised you we'd work on this together."

Ivy looked at him and smiled as well, feeling her cheeks grow warm. She wasn't sure if it was appropriate, but she took a risk and kissed him on the cheek.

When Violet left the reading class, she took a shortcut home through the ruins. It was dark and cold out there, but she knew every inch of this neighborhood because she'd explored it when she was younger. Even in the darkness she knew where there were sharp pieces of rusted metal sticking out that might injure her, and where the uneven stones would hurt her bare feet. Mr. Rodden's class had been good as always, and she was glad she'd joined it even though she had little time to study. There were new opportunities that might open up for her if she knew how to read, even if only poorly.

She'd been scared walking up to Mr. Rodden today to ask him for a job, but getting two tickets for a day's work would turn her world around. It would make it so much easier for her and her brother to survive in Riverlea, and she wouldn't have to rely on her brother so heavily anymore. Those who already worked there had nothing but praise about how the factory had changed under the new owner. The people in town said his name was, Mr. Conway, but she never heard that name before.

She jumped down onto the ground from one of the high stones that was always a pain to climb up onto when traveling in the other direction. Her shack was just down this alley and she wanted to hurry to keep warm, but in the darkness she tripped over something. She stepped back, bent down, and touched a leg. She retracted her hand quickly, but felt no movement. She touched the leg again. It was warm, and hadn't been laying there for long. She couldn't see anything in the pitch-black alley. She patted the body and found that it belonged to a woman. She located the woman's neck and found a weak pulse. She put a hand on her chest and felt faint movement. "Who done this to ya?" she whispered, but got no response.

She grabbed the woman's heavy body by the armpits and began dragging her closer to the street. She knew that if she left her where she was with temperatures dropping overnight, the woman would die.

17

DINNER WAS SET UP in Oliver's bedroom today rather than in its usual spot on the terrace. The night had turned chilly suddenly, and since the house was in a constant state of construction and disarray, it was the only room appropriate for a quiet evening with Sophia. The fireplace crackled quietly in the background. They hoped it was the last cold spell before the summer heat took over.

The table was filled lavishly, with more food than they could eat. Oysters caught that day and kept on ice. Lobster tails with garlic butter. Breaded shrimp. Lamb chops with rosemary sauce. Bacon-wrapped beef medallions. A feast prepared with great care, to celebrate an evening with his goddess.

Luxury food and spices were becoming cheaper and more accessible. World United had announced there would be no more taxes on goods shipped between continents in order to speed up the trade and globalization of the economy. Oliver immediately jumped at the opportunity, and he was glad to have something that others wished to have. A great way to impress his date.

"We're receiving a lot of donations towards our cause," Sophia said, very animated and excited. "I'm impressed." She took a shrimp and put it in her mouth, then looked at Oliver and nodded with approval in her eyes.

Oliver smiled at her. "You've all been putting out the good word," he said. His money was being channeled by Mark through the charitable organization and into his own pocket, so that he could safely spend tens or hundreds of tickets on lavish dinners such as this one. There was no need for Sophia to know about the details of his business.

"It was a great idea to do this. I've been seeing lots of the blankets on the streets," Sophia added.

"I don't think you've visited the factory to get something for yourself yet," Oliver said. He smiled softly, but he was annoyed. He'd hoped she'd share his enthusiasm for fashion and get something new for herself. He wanted her to look her best when they traveled to Clamerton in the summer.

"I just haven't had the time."

"We should go together then," Oliver suggested. "I wouldn't want you to feel left out of this whole fashion craze that Leggett has started."

Sophia nodded in agreement. She took a sip of her wine and grabbed a piece of charred chicken. Oliver put more food on his plate as well.

"I was wondering," she said after a long silence through which they ate their meal. "Oliver is not a common name. I feel like there must be a story behind it."

"It was my mother's idea. The olive branch is a symbol of peace and victory. I guess she thought I'd serve some higher purpose in life." Oliver laughed. "My father had little say." The truth was that his father hadn't cared.

"Sounds like she was a wise woman." Sophia smiled. "I think she was right; you've done more for these poor people than my father has in his whole lifetime. How long have you been in Covedale now, anyway?"

"Eleven months, I think." He recalled the day he'd showed up in Covedale with nothing but the roll of money he'd gotten from Mark.

"You created all this from nothing in a year. Your ideas and your determination are impressive. You've helped so many people in such a short time. I can't believe my father thinks you're an evil man."

Oliver didn't comment on Sophia's last sentence. He pretended not to hear it, but he wondered why White thought of him that way. What exactly had Eric told him? Everything Oliver had done so far in Covedale proved otherwise. Was it because he was new? Maybe it was because he was seeing Sophia. Technically he hadn't broken his promise. It was her who had reached out to him.

"Let's dance," he said in reply. He got up and turned on the radio after they were finished with dinner. Clamerton was now broadcasting all day with music and periodic news segments. The quiet hum of some old tune filled the room as he extended his hand towards Sophia.

Sophia took his hand. She recalled her talk with her father as she put her arms around his neck. They swayed to the music. Her father's request that she ask Oliver about his past seemed so simple, but there was never a good time. There was always something in the way, never an appropriate moment.

She worried it would spoil the mood. She smiled at him and said, "Covedale would not be the same without you."

Oliver gently kissed Sophia and held her closer to him. "Thank you for helping," he said, and went back to kissing her before she could say anything else.

He sat down on the edge of the bed and let her straddle him while they kissed. The bottom of her dress rode up as her knees rested on the sheets. She began to carefully unbutton his shirt. The fabric was crisp and smooth between her fingers, the small discs glided out one by one with ease. She put a hand on his torso. It was warm and firm, darker than her hand. She looked at him, feeling her heart beat faster.

He stroked her hair and tucked some behind her left ear, admiring her neck.

She felt his muscles flex under her hands as he laid her down slowly. She wasn't sure if these feelings she had for him were temporary, or if there was something more. It had been a few months since their first kiss at the Millners' and she always found herself waiting impatiently until the next time they met. Oliver clearly cared for her and she felt safe in his arms.

She was turning thirty this year, past her best young years, having been kept away from everything and everyone by her father. Cut off from the outside world, what options had she had in Covedale? Her father never would've approved of her seeing a boy below their class. She'd met wealthy men her age in Clamerton, but they were boring, full of themselves. Not worth her time. Oliver was different, and good-hearted. She found his stories intriguing; his life fascinating. She didn't understand why her father was against what they had. Why did he hate Oliver so much? He was exactly who she'd been looking for.

She sat up. The room was swaying a bit from the wine, but Oliver held her steady in his arms. She looked at him and put her palm to his cheek while he observed her, motionless. His face felt rough and weathered on her smooth hand. She traced his arm, lingering on his scars, but said nothing. He didn't move, just looked at her face; his eyes were lost in thought as she touched him gently.

It was now or never. She knew she should ask him, right at this moment, and honor her father's request, but she brushed it aside in her mind. The old man was paranoid and suspected everyone around him of being an enemy who would take Covedale from him.

She reached behind her for the zipper on the back of her dress, but it was hard to get a grip on it. He helped her, slowly and gently like he was untying the bow on a gift in anticipation of what was inside. The dress fell from her shoulders, exposing her bare pink skin as he planted small kisses on her shoulder. The room was warm, but she shivered. She could feel the blood pumping in her veins. She closed her eyes, her lips parted.

He kissed her again, gently at first, letting her have control, but this time there was more desire and passion from both of them. She lay down, pulling him on top of her, feeling his warm hands touching her firmly. The sound of the blood coursing through her veins was loud in her ears now, almost deafening, and it felt as though a warm gust of air was rushing over her body. She felt weightless. The feeling was powerful and intoxicating, and she welcomed it. She closed her eyes and enjoyed the sensation of falling.

For the next few days Sophia and Oliver were inseparable, spending every moment together, allowing their passion for each other to take over. They slept in, not feeling the need to rush to join the outside world and be forced away from each other.

Oliver lay propped on his elbow, admiring Sophia's delicate skin and breasts, tracing her body with his fingers as she watched him attentively. The radio was on in the background, but the music stopped in favor of the news. They listened in silence.

A loud female voice spoke. "World United will punish those who committed crimes against humanity during the war. Thousands perished while doing slave labor. Millions died from use of unauthorized, destructive weapons. Others had their villages cut off from their food sources and their drinking water was poisoned. We're creating a list of the war's biggest atrocities. Mr. Leggett, what's your opinion on this matter?"

"I believe we should bring war criminals to justice," he said pompously. Oliver froze for a moment. "There will be a death penalty for those found guilty, and the list of those who will stand trial is already growing. We should know whose names belong on that list soon."

Karl summons him again to his office and hands him a piece of paper with numbers and codes. Two sets of them. "Memorize it," he says.

Karl's plan is to destroy the factory to cover up any atrocities, and in the chaos of the next liberation attack, Oliver is to use the factory consoles to transfer the money to the account numbers that he's memorized. Karl promises he will leave one of these accounts for him.

"Is everything alright?" Sophia asked, sounding concerned. She had noticed his face change as he listened to Leggett speaking passionately from the radio.

"It was weird hearing John's voice on the radio," replied Oliver with a smile, his frown from moments ago suddenly disappearing. "How would you feel about visiting him?" He bent over her and kissed her again, taking their minds away from the news.

Later that day, while Sophia was out helping the other ladies with charity work, White came to visit Oliver. He was clearly trying to avoid running into his daughter. Oliver insisted he stay for a simple afternoon meal. There was no reason to do business on an empty stomach. The day was too beautiful to waste indoors, so they sat on the terrace listening to the birds singing in the nearby woods. The sun was high in the sky, showering everything with its warm spring rays, and the breeze was gentle and slightly refreshing.

White kept silent throughout the meal, and touched nothing on his plate. Once Oliver finished eating, he dismissed the staff so that they could speak freely. White still hadn't revealed the purpose of his visit, but he looked on edge. Oliver got up and poured some whiskey for them both. White looked like he needed to calm his nerves. When White offered him a cigarette, Oliver refused. He was trying to cut down. He'd promised Sophia he would.

"You're not a man of honor," White started, clumsily putting the rest of the cigarettes away. "You say one thing and do another. I told you to keep away from my daughter, and you promised to, but then you broke that promise. That's not what noble men do, but whatever's happened can't be undone." He paused for a moment, then continued with disappointment in his voice as he looked at the view of Riverlea in front of him. "I worked my ass off to line up great young men for her to choose from, but she decided to suck the dick of the first man she saw." Oliver frowned at the way White spoke of his own daughter. "She disregarded her father's wishes, something a dutiful daughter would never do," he said, shaking his head. His whole body was shaking with fear, not anger, Oliver was certain, because he'd learn to recognize the signs of fear. Oliver decided not to interrupt his guest. "If that's what she wants, she can officially move in with you." White paused again, feeling Oliver's piercing eyes on him. He turned to face him, "Marry her. I won't stand in your way, but don't think I'll leave Covedale in her hands for you to bring to ruin."

White puffed the cigarette, giving Oliver a chance to talk. When he remained silent, White continued, "She and I have our differences, and we've said things to each other that can't be taken back. But I have a hard decision to make. Should I let you live or not?" He paused again for a smoke, his hand shaking a bit. "If I let you live, you will eventually stab me in the back, ridicule me in front of everyone, and take over my Covedale. So maybe I should kill you . . . but then what will I do with Sophia?" He tilted his head as though rethinking his options. "You might have already knocked her up for all I know. She'd never forgive me if she found out I had anything to do with your death. So I waited. And guess what? Good things come to those who wait. I didn't like your friend Mr. Finley or the way you dealt with him, so I gave him a tail. A few months pass and, bingo, there's someone else watching him.

"Why do I see this as an opportunity, you may ask?" White paused again, and Oliver frowned, he was getting impatient for the old man to get to the point. "Whoever's looking for you won't give you any warning, like I'm doing now. They'll just find you and slit your throat. If they get past the soldiers and get to your bedroom, they'll kill you in your sleep. Convenient." He raised his brows. "Blood off my hands—but they won't leave witnesses behind, and there goes my Sophia, sleeping in your bed. So the choice is yours, not mine. You can do nothing, and both of you will die, or you can fix it."

There was a long awkward pause before Oliver finally replied, "Who are you so afraid of?" White didn't answer, so he continued, his voice calm, unmoved. "You have been contradicting yourself since the day I stepped into Covedale. I can't imagine what you'll come up with next. One day you're trying to get rid of me, the next you're fine with me staying. You're protecting little Sophia and sending her away, then a few months later you're giving us your blessing to marry. What's wrong?" There was no response from White again, so Oliver continued. "I see fear in your eyes, but I'm confused where that's coming from. I don't think you see me as your worst enemy. Who is it?"

"I fear nothing," White replied, but Oliver could clearly see it was a lie.

"Everyone fears something," Oliver said, looking White directly in the eye. "You have a secret. You're hiding something."

"So are you!" With that, White got up and left, his drink still on the table, untouched.

Oliver had nothing to say to this. He just nodded his head in agreement as White walked away.

Something was wrong with White and he was certain he'd figure it out soon. The message he'd given Oliver was weirdly delivered, but true. If his old friends were trying to find him, it'd cause a lot of trouble and ruin the life he'd set up here in Covedale. He needed to take care of it, otherwise it would always be there in the back of his mind, nagging at him.

"I heard my father was here for a visit," Sophia said after they'd had their dinner and were finishing the wine they opened earlier. She had overheard the servants whispering about her father being in the house while she was away. "What did he want?" she asked Oliver. She wasn't surprised her father hadn't wanted to meet with her, but she found it interesting that he wanted to talk with the man he claimed to hate so much.

"We just talked about the factory," Oliver said dismissively.

"What about it?" She wondered why her father had decided to come here in person, rather than sending a page boy. He rarely did anything like that.

Oliver opened his mouth to recount their conversation to her, but he was interrupted by a loud noise and the whole house suddenly shaking. Sophia had lived through many earthquakes, but this didn't feel like one.

"Wait here," Oliver ordered instead of answering her question. There was a shadow of worry on his face. His brows were drawn together. He threw the napkin he had on his lap onto the table and quickly left.

As Oliver was leaving the room, a servant girl ran in. There were urgent conversations coming from the hallway as the staff ran around. Everyone seemed distressed.

"What's happening?" she asked the girl, noticing fear and confusion in her eyes.

"Bomb in the car, ma'am" the servant replied, collecting empty plates from the table in a hurry and quickly leaving the room.

A shiver went through Sophia. She'd been in Oliver's car just that morning, visiting the other ladies about the charity work. The driver had parked the car in front of the house as he always did. The bedroom windows overlooked the terrace in the back of the house, so there was no point in trying to see what was happening. She decided to wait until further notice. Maybe the girl had been mistaken. Covedale was a safe place to live and she'd never heard of any bombs exploding here.

A moment later Oliver returned. There was an acrid smell of burning plastic and rubber that followed him into the room. He was no longer in a hurry, but he still looked concerned. He sat back down at the table to finish his wine. He tipped the glass and drank what was left in a single gulp as though it were juice.

"The car?" she asked after a moment. She looked right into his eyes. He was not volunteering any information and she had to know what had caused the fire. Had it really been a bomb? Had she been in danger earlier?

"There was a leak of coolant into the main energy chamber of the hover mechanism." Sophia had no idea what he was talking about. Learning how machines worked had not been part of her curriculum when she was growing up. Girls weren't taught these things.

"Car was old. I was planning to get a newer model anyway," Oliver added.

"What if it had leaked this morning?" she asked, concerned. Sophia was glad it was not a bomb and cursed the servant for talking nonsense. She wanted Oliver to reassure her that they were safe.

He leaned over and gave her a long kiss. "I should have replaced the car weeks ago," he said, and smiled at her.

She liked how warm his eyes were, and how they wrinkled at the corners when he smiled. She smiled back. She suddenly longed for his arms around her and that feeling of safety.

1 8

MARK ALWAYS SMELLED NICE. His shirts were clean and pressed, like they were supposed to be. Ivy knew he lived alone—he'd told her—so she wondered if he had a servant or if he was doing all the work on the clothes himself.

They were in his office at the factory, looking at a contract they were to sign. He bent over her, standing behind her while she sat, almost embracing her with his arms. He was trying to explain a table to her, but she was having trouble paying attention. She could touch him right now, but she didn't dare. She was paralyzed. Later at night, she'd hold his hand, walking with him through Riverlea, but not now, she kept telling herself. Not in the office, not where someone else could see them. Not that she cared about the other workers or their opinions, but maybe he did. He was her boss, after all. She contemplated this as her heart raced. She closed her eyes for a second, trying to suppress her thoughts, but she couldn't. The feelings she had and her awareness of the tension only became stronger.

They were running the company, the two of them. Mr. Conway rarely showed up, and when he did, his visits were brief. It was her and Mark, the two factory bosses working together, talking strictly about business. He was smart, not like the Covedale boys she knew. She'd been observing him for a while, his habits and gestures. He was always calm talking to her, never raising his voice. The more she discovered about him, the more she liked.

He stepped back. Maybe he was shying away from her; maybe he'd read her mind. Or maybe he'd simply finished explaining the contract in front of them. She didn't turn around to look at him, not right away. She didn't want him to see how flushed her face was.

Ivy always had work at the factory these days. The ladies from Clamerton and even Backthorn were streaming to Covedale in droves to have things designed for them, and Ivy's responsibilities were increasing. She'd had to skip some of Mark's classes recently because she'd needed to stay longer at the factory, but today she promised herself she'd go. She needed to study and couldn't keep away from Mark. She longed to see him, knowing that, at least for a moment, they'd be alone walking through the ruins. She wasn't afraid as long as she was with him. Maybe she'd steal another kiss, she thought, smiling to herself. On his cheek, like before. She wouldn't dare try anything more.

Their evening walk through the ruins was quick. They'd left the factory late, and had to make up the time. They had little time to talk, so Ivy held on to the questions she had for him that day. She'd ask him on the way back.

When in class, Ivy noticed the blonde girl was there again, the one that asked about the job a few weeks ago. "Come to Leggett, ask for Ivy," she whispered to the girl after class.

She felt Mark's piercing eyes on her, but she ignored them. He tried to explain to her later that there were too many people looking for work at Leggett—probably all of Riverlea was—and he didn't want it known that he could do favors, but it was too late.

The girl's eyes brightened when Ivy invited her, and she thanked her for her kindness. But just then, thunder rumbled outside and the girl rushed out, probably to get to her shelter before the rain started. Mark took a few more minutes to get ready to leave, and they opened the door to a wall of rain.

"It's a long walk to the river," Mark said, looking at the streets flooding with water. "Why don't you spend the night at my place?"

Ivy nodded. She wasn't keen about taking the long trip back to Covedale, either. They ran, but got soaking wet anyway. They were breathless and laughing by the time they reached Mark's apartment, though it was only a couple of streets away. They scaled a flight of narrow stairs to a small, windowless room. It held only the bare necessities: a small stove, a basin for washing, and a bed. The room was old and hadn't been spared by time, but the inside smelled nice. It was warm and, most importantly, it was dry.

"I'll take the floor," Mark said, noticing that she was surveying the place. They were both wet and cold, so Mark opened the closet door. "Let me find something dry for you," he said as he took off his wet shirt.

Ivy suddenly felt hot. Her heartbeat quickened and she felt the blood in her veins circulating faster, warming her inside and out. While Mark was occupied, she unzipped her dress in one quick move and let it fall to the floor. The soaked fabric that had been cooling her down was now gone, and the fire burning within her became even stronger.

She surprised herself when he turned around by pressing her naked body against his. She was no longer content with only kissing. She put her mouth on his and started to kiss him. Her hands reached down and began to unbutton his pants.

Mark hesitated at first, as though he wasn't sure what she was doing, but he didn't push her away. Ivy knew he'd made up his mind when he kissed her back, more passionately. He was hungry for her just as she was for him. He even helped her with his pants and pushed her against the wall. Her breasts pressed against his chest and his hands moved up and down her body, firmly gripping her hips and thighs.

They could hear the rain outside falling harder; big drops banged on the roof above them as they moved to the bed, still kissing madly. Ivy didn't dare interrupt the excitement, fearing that the momentum would be lost.

She felt her back falling heavily onto the old mattress and Mark's body pinning her down, making her a little breathless. Her thighs hugged his hips, squeezing them. Her heart raced as he slid into her easily, in one long move. Their bodies were meant for each other.

As he slowly moved in and out of her, jolts of pleasure passed between them and Ivy buried her hands in his hair. The bed swayed and creaked a little, but neither of them noticed as they moved faster with each rough stroke. The bed rattled its springs rhythmically with their movements. The rest of the world didn't exist. Ivy didn't care about anyone eaves-dropping; the neighbors were forgotten. It was just the two of them trying to last a little longer, desperately clinging to the moment for as long as they could.

Mark watched her gasp for air; unable to make a sound. Her eyes were wide open, her nails digging into his back, her muscles tightening inside and out. She arched her back and cried out.

He pulled out and came immediately with a groan, making her belly warm and sticky. Her whole body was still shaking. She watched him, admiring the way his skin shone from sweat. He bent down over her and stroked the wet hair off her face. "Thank you," he said, and kissed her, slow and gentle this time.

They lay beside each other on the narrow bed. He held her close. Their bodies were pressed together, sharing each other's warmth as they fell asleep.

Ivy woke up in the middle of the night. She smiled when she remembered she was at Mark's. Keeping her eyes closed, she examined the bed with her hand and found that he wasn't there.

She opened her eyes just a bit to see for herself if her hands were right, but the lack of windows made the room pitch black, except for a faint blue light shining from under the wall. She thought that was weird, so she got up to go to the wall and touch it.

The partition, floor-to-ceiling doors, moved so unexpectedly that Ivy jumped and gasped. They revealed a dazzling room that blinded her. Her eyes hadn't yet adjusted to the brightness and she covered them for a moment until she could make out some shapes.

The light was coming from a multitude of consoles and panels arranged in a room similar in size to the other half of the apartment. Ivy stood there for a moment, not knowing what exactly she was looking at. The monitors displayed colorful graphs and maps, but it meant nothing to her.

She noticed Mark sitting in the chair and motioning for her to come over. She smiled nervously and hesitantly walked towards him. The doors closed behind her. He sat her on his lap, hugged her, and placed his head above her bare breast as she put her arms around his neck. "I come here when I can't sleep," Mark said.

She looked around confused. "What's that?" she pointed at a display.

"That's just monitoring around the house."

Ivy nodded, recognizing the shapes of the buildings on the street. "And this?"

"Satellite camera stream of Covedale and Riverlea," he said, but she didn't know what that meant.

"Why do ya have all this?"

"I'm looking for my son." Mark took Ivy's hand in his and played with her fingers for moment, lost in thought. "I've been married before," he continued, talking slowly. "She's dead now. Riverlea was still a good place to live back then. Trees grew everywhere. Flowers." Mark looked at Ivy. "A stray bullet found her." His voice shook a bit, but he composed himself. "Three years ago, my son enlisted himself in the war. He was fourteen, so that would make him seventeen now. He hasn't come home yet and I'm still searching for him."

"Ya think he's alive?"

Mark stroked her hair and smiled. "'You,' Ivy," he corrected her.

"You think he's alive?" Ivy repeated, paying more attention to her words. She felt embarrassed knowing she sounded uncultured.

"There's no military record of his death. He's not presumed missing, either. The rest of his regiment is all accounted for, but not him. I'm monitoring news and communications. So far nothing, but I have faith," Mark replied.

"What's his name?"

"Daniel."

"Nice name." She hugged him, pulling him closer, and they sat in silence for a moment.

"We should go back to bed. You're cold." Mark opened the wall with the push of a button and carried Ivy back to bed.

"Why not move to Covedale?" she asked.

"Riverlea's where we raised him. He'll come back here looking for me," Mark replied. "I can't leave."

"He'll be back." Ivy tried to comfort Mark, but the odds seemed low.

Before they closed their eyes Mark turned to Ivy and stroked her hair, trying to read her thoughts from the way she was looking at him.

"You're still young and I'm an old man with baggage," he told her. "We can't be together—"

"Nonsense." She curled up beside him without letting him reply. She embraced him with her arm, pressing her forehead against his chest.

Mark put his hand gently against her waist. She felt comfort in his arms.

1 9

OLIVER SAT ON A shipping crate on Backthorn's river docks, looking at the water. It moved slowly, peacefully flowing towards the ocean. It was the same river that divided Covedale and Riverlea at the delta, but much narrower. The night was calm, and there was barely any wind, but the river didn't stop. It kept moving, swollen by the evening rain.

He'd brought five men with him. They'd taken the chop-jet. He wanted a quick turnaround, a couple of hours at most, so that Sophia wouldn't suspect he'd gone far when he excused himself in order to run some business errands.

The new car fit nicely in the lower compartment of the chop-jet. He'd purchased the vehicle recently to replace the one that the fucking impatient Gutters had blown to pieces. He'd taken the hint; they could have done it while Sophia was in it and had chosen not to. It was a warning. His time was running low and he had no clue how much longer he could hold them off.

He didn't want to be seen by anyone in town, so they landed on the outskirts. These docks weren't in a pleasant part of town, and no boats stuck around after dark. The area was deserted and eerily quiet. Only the crickets chirped in the grass.

He let two of his men go ahead while the other three surveyed the area and stood on guard to ensure the conversation he was about to have would be private. In half an hour, the two returned with another man, his head covered by a hood. They helped him out of the car and sat him beside Oliver before untying his hands, as they'd been instructed.

"Are ya out of ya mind?" Eric shouted, furious when he took off the hood and found Oliver sitting beside him with a cigarette in his hand.

"Sorry about that, I couldn't risk just visiting you." He offered the pack of cigarettes to Eric, who took one with a shaking hand. "I have no intention of harming you," Oliver said in an attempt to calm him down, but he spoke without smiling and his expression wasn't comforting.

"What do ya want from me?"

"I need to know who else knows about the money."

"I didn't even want it. Now look what it's going to cost me." He'd known sooner or later this day would come and that he would have to face Oliver once again.

Oliver laughed and said, "It was you who insisted we split it fifty-fifty." His tone hardened. "Who knows?"

Eric felt shivers going down his spine. "That man in Covedale—he's the only one I told, but that wasn't ma fault," he said.

"This goes beyond Covedale. Who else?"

Oliver was calm, too calm for Eric's liking. At least the other day he'd been angry with him. He knew this tone of voice; he'd seen Oliver like this back at the factory. It was the sound he made when he was displeased. Whenever he'd addressed people this way back then, they'd been escorted out by guards and disappeared, never to be heard from again. "No one! I swear!" Eric replied. He could almost feel the hair on his head turning grayer than it had been a second before.

"How much does your wife know?" Oliver asked.

Eric's jaw moved nervously. His hands were sweaty. "Keep her out of this. She's innocent." He tried to bring the cigarette up to his mouth, but his hands were shaking too much so he put his hand back down.

"How much does she know?"

"I had to decide. I only tell her I could get a hold of big money, but it's red. She tell me to bring none of it home," Eric said. "That's it."

Oliver thought for a moment, silent and motionless, then shook his head in disbelief. "You betrayed me, Eric."

"I swear she didn't tell anyone—"

"Maybe, but you have no proof, do you?"

Eric thought for a moment. He could've talked to Ana and made her swear that she'd said nothing about this to anyone. That would be enough proof for him, but it wouldn't be enough for this man.

Oliver took his gun out from the inside of his jacket and looked at it leisurely.

Eric looked at the gun as well. "Why not kill me there? No one gonna notice one more body in the rubble."

"For so many years, I thought that for some reason I had to protect you. That I had to bring you extra food when we were all starving, to keep the bullies in the camp away so that they were afraid to touch you. I didn't do it because I needed you. I would've been better off alone."

Eric had trouble paying attention to what Oliver was saying. The sight of a gun in the man's hand and the thought of what would happen next distracted him.

"Then, when we parted, I thought you'd be grateful for everything I did for you. The countless times I saved your life. I expected little in return, just that you'd keep your side of the bargain and keep your fucking mouth shut." Eric sat there without saying a word while Oliver charged the gun. It charged quickly. "Was that so hard?" he added.

Eric fell on his knees on the ground in front of Oliver, pleading, "Kill me, but promise ya spare my wife." He shook with fear and agony, his voice shaking uncontrollably.

Oliver looked straight into his eyes. There was no compassion and there would be no guilt, Eric knew. Oliver was cold and unflinching as he fired the gun right into Eric's head.

"You have always been a fucking coward, Eric," Oliver said, putting the gun away.

Oliver felt something he hadn't felt in a long time. A powerful thrill coursed through him, making his fingertips tingle. He knew it was a feeling most never experienced; it was special, reserved for a select few like him. The confidence and sense of power it gave him made him stand taller. He felt more in control of life than he'd felt a moment ago. He threw the rest of his cigarette onto the ground and went back to his men and the vehicle.

The gun was barely cool when Oliver arrived at a makeshift structure of wood and metal and knocked on the door. He heard rustling inside before a woman opened the door.

"Mrs. Finley?" Oliver asked. The woman nodded. "I'm a friend of your husband. We should talk."

She was a small, thin woman, older than Oliver. She had salt-and-pepper hair that was cut short. Her face was tanned and weathered with age. Oliver recalled Eric saying that her name was Ana.

The woman looked cautiously at Oliver, but opened the door wider to let him in.

It was a tiny one-room place, cramped with all their belongings, a basin with water, and a bed. Oliver sat down at the table and motioned for the woman to sit down as well.

"My name is—" Oliver started to say, but was interrupted.

"I know who ya are," Ana said.

It surprised Oliver to hear that, but he didn't show it. Eric might've told her more than he'd said he had. "I believe your husband is in danger," he said.

Ana didn't flinch. She sat up straight, looking at the intruder in front of her. She was clearly trying to act brave. "What do ya want?" she asked.

"I believe Eric told you about the money. Someone is very interested in knowing more about it. I need to find out who, before they get to Eric."

She nodded, unaware that Eric was already gone. "A man was asking. A year ago," she said. "Very interested in Eric's stories from the war. Asking too many questions. We told him nothing about the money."

"Did he tell him anything about me?"

"No." She shook her head.

Oliver nodded and sat back in the chair to think. It could have been anyone snooping around. It might've even been one of White's informants.

"Do ya think that man is after Eric?" Ana asked, breaking the silence.

"I know he is, and I don't know how to stop him, because he needs assurance that you'll keep your mouth shut. That makes you a target too."

There was fear in her eyes. She knew what her fate was even before he took out the gun, pointed at her and fired. Her body slid down from the chair and onto the ground with a small thud. He was using the latest model of charge gun. It fit better in his hand and didn't shatter its victims' brains and send pieces of them flying all over the room like the older models. It simply left a clean burn mark on their foreheads; no blood, no mess. He was glad he'd made the purchase.

The sun was high when Oliver led Sophia through the big glass doors of the Leggett factory. The waiting room was large and bright and Sophia praised Ivy's talent for decorating, amusing herself with the countless mirrors.

When Ivy greeted them, Oliver looked at Sophia, smiled, and kissed her. "I think Miss White needs something stunning to wear for an evening out."

"Please leave Miss White in ma hands—my hands, Mr. Conway," Ivy replied, cheerfully correcting herself. She immediately began to discuss ideas, fabrics, and colors with Sophia.

Oliver moved towards the entrance to the main hall. He had some business with Mark, and while Sophia was being pampered and measured, he wanted to use the time well. On his way to the hall, he noticed a small, thin, blonde girl working on something from the corner of his eye. Their eyes met, and they recognized each other.

It had been more than a year, but Oliver remembered Violet well. He could still feel her soft body in his hands, and hear her laughing about the monkeys.

He suppressed a smile.

Her pretty face looked different, more grown up and mature. He still felt something for her, and it frightened and angered him. What was she doing here, stepping into his life again to disturb what he'd worked for so hard? He was fed up with how things in his life were progressing lately, with threats that kept appearing out of nowhere.

The Gutters kept reminding him of the promise he'd made. First a brick hurled through one of the windows, then the bomb in the car putting Sophia at risk. They'd stopped his incoming money as well. He might not be able to push it aside for much longer, but he was trying to find a way to get out of the arrangement completely. It angered him that everything he'd worked on in the past twelve months was slowly falling apart, sending him down a path similar to the one he felt he'd already walked before, and rejected. He needed to regain control of his life. He'd promised Sophia he'd keep her safe and that he'd never hurt her. That was all that mattered to him right now.

Oliver turned around and asked Ivy for a word. "That girl that's working with you, the little blonde one, get rid of her," he said with urgency. "And make sure she doesn't get close to Miss Sophia." He left, not looking in Violet's direction.

A few minutes' walk from Oliver's house, there were woods that belonged to the large property, ending with a cliff drop to the West. Leo was not interested in the numerous lookout points along the bluff that provided a wide view of the river and city below, but in the large, open meadow in the middle, which was covered in tall grass.

He had heard from one of his soldiers that Oliver spent many afternoons in that spot. The man made no attempt to hide his visits, but he never took anyone with him. He was always there alone, away from everyone. Leo had sent some spies to learn that Oliver was doing target shooting. The report said that he was pretty good at it, and Leo couldn't rest until he saw the man in action for himself.

He stood behind the trees, hidden from view, surveying the area. He noticed Oliver bending over something in the middle of the clearing. It was a target launcher.

The pneumatic machine launched artificial targets into the air for a sharpshooter to take down. At one time they were made of clay, back when people used to shoot with shotguns and metal shells, but the technology had changed. The discs had been replaced with balls the size of his fist. They were made from a material that disintegrated when they were successfully hit by the beam of a modern gun. Whatever didn't get hit simply fell on the ground to be reused.

After Oliver loaded the launcher, he hurried away, putting distance between himself and the targets. The machine was set on a timer that gave the shooter enough notice to get ready, but Oliver was still walking away when the device began beeping.

A long beep sounded, and the machine shot the balls high in the air, one after another. There was a quick burst of about eight or ten of them. Leo didn't count as he watched every single target being destroyed in the air.

The loud sound of the balls exploding and the whooshing of the beam stopped. The forest was quiet. Even the birds had stopped their songs for the performance.

Leo clapped his hands loudly and slowly. He left his hiding spot and walked towards Oliver. "Excellent shots!"

Oliver noticed his presence and tossed a ball towards him as he got close. "Want to try it?"

Leo caught the small ball. He could handle a gun, but he'd never cared much for them; he enjoyed being close to people when he killed them. Shooting them from afar like a sniper made it less personal, less intimate. He looked at the ball he was holding. "Sure, why not," he replied and shrugged.

Oliver loaded the targets for him. "There's eight," he said.

He nodded and took out his gun. He readied himself to shoot.

After the three short beeps there was finally a long beep and the targets flew. Leo shot them all with ease.

"You're good!" Oliver commented.

"There's nothing to it," Leo said and shrugged.

"What do you think about a match?"

"First one to miss a shot is a fucking loser forever," Leo laughed. He was certain it wouldn't be him with that title, but Oliver's marksmanship was excellent. Most of the shooters working for Leo couldn't have hit all the targets as they were still flying upwards.

There was something suspicious about Oliver and Leo was determined to get to the bottom of it. He already knew that the man liked guns. He never parted with his and always kept it charged. Maybe he was concerned about the men Leo had planted in his house, or maybe he was afraid of White. But he never seemed scared. On the contrary, he seemed *too* confident.

Oliver bent over the machine and loaded it. The targets flew up shortly after and Oliver hit them all again.

Leo recalled Oliver showing up boldly at White's office asking to buy property. He never blinked. His posture was erect, his look serious, intimidating. It was almost as if Oliver had hypnotized White into allowing him to stay.

Now Oliver was trying to do the same to him, Leo thought. Making him look smaller and less important in order to manipulate him; make him lower his guard. White said he wanted to keep Oliver alive because of the money he brought to Covedale, but Leo didn't believe that was the true reason. What if White was keeping Oliver around because he feared him? Oliver must then be the enemy. But White would've had any threat to Covedale removed. His explicit instructions had been to leave Oliver alone.

"Ready?" Oliver called. The machine was loaded and waiting.

Leo nodded. As ready as he'd ever be.

When the targets flew, he hit all but one of them. He gave Oliver a moment of short-lived victory, then sniped the last target right before it hit the ground.

Oliver laughed. "Looks like we need to increase our distance."

The next one to shoot was Oliver and his score was perfect again.

"Who are you?" Leo asked in reply.

Oliver stopped in his tracks and looked at Leo. "What do you mean?" he said, and smiled. There was a confident smirk on his face that Leo immediately hated.

"My men told me about last night," Leo replied. They'd reported that they'd seen something change in Oliver after he'd shot that friend of his. Whatever they saw seemed to have spooked them.

"What did they say?" Oliver took a few steps back as Leo started loading targets for him.

"They were surprised at how clean it was." Whenever Leo killed, there was always a mess. He enjoyed seeing blood flow and hearing people scream. He took his time pulling souls out of them. The longer it took, the better it felt.

"The new guns are pretty good that way," Oliver replied.

They ran a few more rounds, increasing their distance from the machine each time, but both of them were shooting the targets perfectly. They were close to the limit of the range of the guns and still neither of them was missing.

"Killed many before?" Leo asked.

"The front was brutal."

Leo shrugged and clarified, "I mean in cold blood."

Oliver didn't reply as he walked towards Leo. They changed places and Leo walked over to the machine, loaded it up, and turned it on. The targets flew shortly after and Leo looked with satisfaction when one of them fell into the grass in the middle of the meadow.

"Where did you learn how to shoot like that, anyway?" Leo asked when Oliver was close, walking towards the machine with irritation written on his face.

"Why do you care?" Oliver finally replied.

Leo was convinced that his suspicion of Oliver was right. He was a great shooter who was trained with a purpose to kill. "Is that what White needs you for? Is that why he brought you here?"

Oliver stood in front of Leo now. His eyes were piercing as he stared at him. "What are you talking about?" he asked.

Was White not happy with how he killed people? Too brutal, maybe? He'd never complained before, so why now? Why wouldn't White just tell him he wasn't pleased? There was no reason to involve anyone else.

"White knows who you are, doesn't he? He knows someone is looking for you." How had White put it? *Someone will look for you, someone will ask for favors.* He couldn't recall the exact words.

Oliver squinted and smirked. "Who do you think I am?" he asked, laughing out loud like he'd heard a joke. He turned around to put more targets into the machine, readying them for the next flight.

Leo walked up behind Oliver and pointed his gun at him. "There can only be one killer in Covedale."

Oliver laughed loudly. "Is that what you think I am?" He turned around and faced the charged gun in Leo's hand.

"You don't deny it," Leo said. Oliver didn't even blink at the accusation. "No one fucks with me!" he added.

A beep sounded suddenly. *Why had he turned on the target device?* Leo wondered for a moment, not letting Oliver out of his sight. The match was over. He'd won.

"I promised to let you and White be. I agreed to all your terms. What else do you want from me?" Oliver was calm, but there was a hint of annoyance in his voice.

Beep.

"If you don't leave Covedale on your own, I'll fuckin' force you to," Leo threatened.

Beep.

"How do you plan to do that?"

A long beep sounded, and the targets flew upwards one after the other. They were loud, cutting through the air at high velocity. Leo took his eyes off Oliver for a split second, distracted, and suddenly felt something warm on the side of his face. He brought his hand up to his right ear.

He stepped back, touching his ear again. A piece of it was missing. What remained was still warm from being hit by the gun. Oliver now stood in front of him with a gun in his hand. *The bastard just shot me!* How did he get his gun out so quickly?

"You could've killed me!" Leo shouted.

Oliver just smiled.

Leo still stood paralyzed by what was happening while Oliver came closer to him and firmly grasped his arm.

"Nobody points a gun at me," Oliver said, and with that he left the clearing, disappearing between the trees before Leo could recover from his shock. He watched the targets stop at the height of their flight and then fall onto the ground.

2 0

JOHN LEGGETT ARRIVED AT the airport to pick up Sophia and Oliver and he looked surprised to see at least five bodyguards with them. Oliver, however, couldn't take chances. After Leo pointed the gun at him and lost an ear for his trouble, he expected that there would be consequences. Leo was plotting something.

White didn't seem to know where Leo was, which was surprising. Maybe White was pretending so Oliver would let his guard down? He couldn't believe that the officer would disappear without a trace. Oliver was sure the man would resurface unexpectedly and he needed to be ready.

"Welcome!" John greeted them when they got into his car. He then commented on the armed men, "There's no need for arms in Clamerton."

The car lifted off the ground slightly and started moving. There was no engine sound, and the movement of the car was smooth. The bodyguards followed them in another car they had unloaded from the chop-jet.

"Have you been to Clamerton before, Oliver?" John asked. Oliver shook his head no. "Let's do a quick tour, then," John suggested. "We have lots of time."

"I fell in love with this city when we arrived," Susan started. "I don't know why I never explored it before. It was always right there, so close, just a brief trip on a plane. I thought I'd never want to live anywhere besides Covedale, but Clamerton is very charming." She leaned slightly towards the guests from the front seat beside John. "Sophia had a great time with us when she stayed over," she added.

Sophia nodded and smiled nervously.

"Probably the least-destroyed city on this continent," John continued. "You can still see deterioration and neglect like everywhere else, but the original charm is still there."

The remaining intact old buildings were mixed in with recent developments, and the city had cleared the streets of any rubble. In a few areas, they'd even planted flowers by the side of the road to make the place more pleasing to the eyes.

"Here's the old city hall," Susan said, pointing it out on their right.

It was a brick building whose facade was being renovated. Scaffolding surrounded it. It featured a billboard, the first one Oliver had seen with his own eyes since World United had announced paying for them. They were planning to install them in many places to increase awareness of the newest government initiatives. The display was scrolling through a variety of information. One captured his eye as they passed: *World United listens! Air travel improvements are our top priority.*

"It's a beautiful city," Sophia told Susan.

They passed market stalls full of people and vendors selling fresh food. The city was alive, but the homelessness problem was also visible. There were people sleeping on the streets or in makeshift shacks in the city squares.

"I can see why they decided to have the affiliate of the World United here," Oliver said after absorbing the new views. The city was in better shape than Covedale and growing faster. White was less innovative in how he ran a city, Oliver noticed.

"Speaking of which. If it's alright with you, we've invited someone else to our dinner tonight. Ben is the Health Commissioner for World United, and he's here all the way from Karben in Europe on business," John said.

"I'm sure it will be a great evening. I'm looking forward to meeting him," Oliver replied and turned to look at the view. He wasn't happy with this development. He didn't want to upset Sophia and he'd agreed to go on this trip that they'd been planning for weeks, but he wasn't in a mood to entertain strangers.

"We still have some time. Don't know if you heard, but we bought a new company with the money I got from selling Leggett," John said. "I put it in Susan's name, Quinton."

"Thank you for taking over the factory," Susan joined in. "I was glad it ended up in good hands. You brought it back to its full potential."

"I agree. Selling it was a mistake and I should've known better," John replied, "but seeing it doing so well makes up for it."

"The factory is very profitable, even after giving everyone a raise," Sophia said. She put her hand in Oliver's and rested it on his lap.

"I was skeptical of the move at first, but it seems to work," John said. "Let's see my new purchase," he added.

The vehicle moved a little faster, and in a few minutes they reached the outskirts of Clamerton. The modern building had power and many bright lights illuminated the space. Electricity meant easier access to running water, so the place was cleaned regularly, unlike their old company. The dry smell of dust and lint that lingered in the air wasn't unpleasant.

"We're still working on getting electricity in the old factory, and we're not too far off," Oliver said.

"Believe me, electricity is a game changer," John said. "Here we have the traditional sewing method using electric sewing machines. As you can hear, the sewing is much faster, which means that we can produce more in the same time frame."

"It's also much quieter here," Oliver noticed.

"That's right. The only downside is that it's a bit more expensive, but with the increased production it evens out," John added. They followed John towards another portion of the factory. "And here's the future," John pointed as they walked through the door.

It was an open space, about a quarter the size of the production hall. There were only a few people walking around a couple of large machines. On one end, a giant roll of cotton fabric was being fed into the machine. On the other, a final product was returned. The perfectly stitched shirts and pants were then neatly folded, stacked, and packed into boxes. Robotic arms did all the work in between. They moved quickly and didn't make much noise.

"World United provides lots of incentives for investments in automation and robotics," John explained. "I needed to take advantage of them."

"Is that fully automated?" Oliver asked with genuine interest.

John nodded. "It takes a long time to set them up, but once they're running, they produce a consistently high-quality product, equal to at least forty people doing the same work manually," John replied.

"You must save a lot on labor," Oliver noted.

"Yes, it's a much better way to produce." John looked at his watch and motioned for them all to leave the factory. "Time to return to the city for dinner."

After a quick stop at the Leggetts' house to refresh and change, they arrived at the restaurant. Attendants opened the door for them and helped them out of the vehicle. Sophia wore the new dress that Ivy had made for her, and Oliver couldn't believe how stunning she looked in it.

The dress was designed to draw attention to the perfection of her body. The open back exposed her unblemished skin all the way down to below her waist. The green fabric hugged her curved hips tightly and moved with them as she walked. It was floor-length, with a small train at the back that lightly grazed the floor. Her look was accessorized with a gold coil around her arm, matching long earrings set with emeralds, and a gold clutch.

The staff greeted them nervously and led them to a private patio in the back prepared just for them so they wouldn't be disturbed throughout the evening. It had a round table set for six, surrounded by fragrant flowers and a small waterfall in the corner. Large sliding doors separated them from the other customers, making it a quiet and peaceful oasis.

Oliver later learned that the owner had objected to his bodyguards checking the restaurant before his arrival. The man insisted that there was no reason to do so as the place was safe, and his officer had been forced to have a frank conversation with the owner. This explained why the staff was so nervous.

Another couple was already seated at the table waiting for them. They got up to greet the rest of the party, their faces showing curiosity about him and Sophia.

"Mr. Ben Scholz and his wife Emma; Mr. Oliver Conway and Sophia White." John introduced.

"The love of my life," Oliver said. He smiled at Sophia and helped her sit down before taking a seat himself.

"Oliver is a distinguished member of our community in Covedale," John said, raising his freshly-filled wine glass.

"I've heard lots of good things about Covedale," Emma said. She was a pretty woman in her thirties. Her blonde hair cascaded onto the floral summer dress she'd worn for the evening. "What kind of business are you in, Mr. Conway, if you don't mind my asking?"

"Please, call me Oliver," he replied with a smile. "I own the old Leggett factory. The one John left behind to join the world of politics."

"Oliver made it better than it used to be," Susan added, proud that her family legacy was still doing well.

"How so?" Emma asked, looking at Oliver, but John cut in.

"I'm a volume person, so I always concentrate on making more and selling more. Oliver had a unique vision," John said.

Waiters interrupted them by bringing the first of many courses and explaining the dish that was being placed in front of them. Today's special was foie gras on a bed of paper-thin slices of celeriac.

"Most of the factory is still doing large-volume production," Oliver explained. "It's targeted towards improving the well-being of our community. The rest, which is more profitable, targets those who are looking for some additional luxuries in their lives."

"I've seen the Leggett blankets," commented Emma. "How do you afford to get them out to the poor?"

"We produce them on a budget and we receive generous donations to help the cause," Sophia replied enthusiastically.

Susan changed the subject, asking Ben and Emma about their eight-hour flight, and Sophia was curious about Europe and about Karben, the center of World United.

After the next course of seared tuna on a salad sprinkled with sesame seeds arrived, Ben returned to the previous topic of conversation. "How much did the blankets help the community? Do you know what the estimated death toll was last winter in Covedale?" Ben looked older than Emma, maybe in his early forties. His black hair and dark, neatly-trimmed beard showed patches of gray.

"It's hard to get the exact numbers, but we think it was about three percent," Sophia replied. She'd been watching the statistics with the other ladies at the charity.

"That's indeed below average. The world is trending at about five to ten percent dead by the end of winter," Ben said. "We don't get it back in birth rate. Infant life expectancy is very low."

"As I mentioned, Ben is a Health Commissioner for World United government," John said.

"The lower death toll is an outstanding achievement," Susan replied, and added proudly, "Oliver is such a mastermind."

"We're working on lowering the death rate worldwide and it's difficult. The winters are terrible in some parts of the world," Ben replied.

"I'm interested in helping," Oliver said. "We could use my factory for something. More blankets maybe, or something totally different. Also, the more people involved in this, the more ideas might come out of it."

They talked about John's work at the factory and the changes that World United represented as they enjoyed the following courses of duck, lamb, and braised meat. The recent worker riots and protests were a hot topic these days, and John wasn't shy with his opinions, condemning the protesters and calling them ungrateful.

A violin player came into their part of the restaurant in an attempt to entertain them. It annoyed Oliver that the man was allowed to disturb their dinner, but Sophia seemed fascinated by his performance. He didn't want to upset her, so he endured the music as the string instrument screeched some sad melody.

"I'm intrigued about the luxury items at the factory," Emma said when the player left and the elegantly decorated desserts arrived.

"We offer a unique take on clothing. You might even call it an experience," Oliver replied with a smile. "The goal is to bring style and sophistication to people's lives through bespoke clothes."

"How does it differ from a regular tailor?" Emma asked, confused.

"Regular tailors use templates," Oliver replied. "They produce known cuts and styles that don't draw attention when you walk into the room." He looked towards Sophia. "We can design a custom dress, one that looks so good that all the other ladies will immediately be jealous. And we haven't forgotten about her date, either. He needs to complete the look so well that separating the two of them would be a sin." Oliver raised Sophia's hand and kissed it without taking his eyes off her.

"I must admit, it's an effective sales pitch." Emma laughed, playing nervously with her hair.

"I should get some of these tailored clothes for myself," Susan said to her husband. "We should visit Covedale for a few weeks."

"I'm thinking about bringing our services here as well. I can see a potential market in Clamerton," Oliver replied, watching the ladies become excited about the idea.

After dinner, Oliver and Sophia excused themselves to go for a walk. As they were leaving the restaurant, a slightly drunk older man walked up to her. Oliver saw one of his men stir in anticipation, but the old man was clearly just drunk, so he signaled for the soldier to stand down.

"I want to apologize. My behavior was unacceptable," the man said. Sophia shivered and put on a fake, nervous smile, but didn't reply.

Oliver escorted Sophia away from the man. He sensed Sophia was a little shaken, but she relaxed as soon as they walked out of the restaurant and away from the stranger.

"Did you know that man?" Oliver asked her as they were leaving.

"Someone my father used to work with." She brushed it off as though it were unimportant and put on a fake smile again. It was enough for Oliver to deduce the man's identity.

The restaurant door exited directly into the city garden which was filled with flowers whose fragrances traveled through the warm evening air. Access to the fenced park was regulated, and the area provided a peaceful escape that made you forget about the outside world, about the poor begging and the homeless sleeping under the trees. They walked close together on the paved path, their hips swaying rhythmically. They passed a fountain, some art statues, and another couple sitting on the bench.

They stopped at a lookout point to watch the boats on the water. The sailors burned lanterns as they tied their boats at the riverbank. The water was calm, the evening breeze gentle.

He kissed her hair. "You look so lovely tonight," he said as she snuggled closer. He put his hand into his left pants pocket and took out a small velvet box. Sophia didn't see it; her back was turned to him. She continued to look at the lights from the garden reflecting in the water. He opened the box to make sure the contents were still in inside.

He'd had the engagement ring with him for some time now—he told the trader to find him an expensive one with a large diamond set in the middle—but he hadn't known how he wanted to ask her. He'd been thinking about having friends for a visit, hosting a grand event and declaring his love for Sophia in front of everyone. Seeing her today in the new dress, and how beautiful she was, made him reconsider. He needed to ask her, now, when they were alone and away from anyone's eyes. An intimate moment, the memory of which would be just for them.

Sophia turned to him when he dropped to one knee. He noticed tears welling in her eyes. She was anticipating the question that followed.

"Will you marry me?" he asked.

"Yes," she replied without hesitation.

She let Oliver put the ring on her finger, helped him up, and pulled him closer for a long and gentle kiss.

He was happy. Sophia was his treasure. He adored her and vowed that he would do anything for her. He would order his new officer to kill the man who had touched her last year. An apology couldn't make up for what he'd done.

It was already past midnight when the ladies finally retired to their bedrooms after a long day. Oliver was sitting with John in the man's study and working through a bottle of whiskey John had opened after hearing the news of his engagement.

"I heard you on the radio the other day," Oliver mentioned, sipping his drink. This was a great opportunity to learn more about John's job.

"There's lots of interest in war crimes, so they often ask me to comment on things. Additional responsibilities keep me busy," John replied without showing much interest in the subject.

"War crimes aren't easy to deal with, and you might never find out who was at the top of the chain."

"I was hoping to do something trade-related at World United," John replied wistfully, seemingly lost in reverie. "Something easy and comfortable. Trade in goods would've been nice, or even natural resources." John sipped his drink, then snapped out of his daydream, returning to the topic at hand. "They're still compiling the list of people and crimes they want to investigate. It'll take a long time to get through all the interrogations, maybe years." John looked at his drink with interest before taking another sip. He was lost in thought. "

"Any interesting names on the list so far?"

"There's a human trafficking case, there's use of chemicals and weapons that were forbidden by international treaty before the war, and there's an ammunition factory that burned down—"

"Did it blow up like fireworks? Sounds like there might be nothing left," Oliver interrupted, forcing a laugh.

"There were a lot of funds going in and out, apparently. My advisers say it won't be that hard to follow the money. They're already investigating some accounts in Asia."

"You'd need solid evidence," Oliver said, thinking about Mark and the transfers that he'd set up. He didn't want to be accused of war crimes because of that. He wasn't a criminal, but someone might see it differently.

"They estimate that the factory could make thousands of mines a day," John said "Can you believe that?"

Oliver nodded. That sounded about right.

Upon their return to Covedale, Sophia invited her father to join her and some of their friends to celebrate her engagement to Oliver. With renovations complete, they hosted the event in the house. Ivy had decorated the large room in calm cream and beige colors. Large curtains hung on the windows overlooking the redone terrace, which offered a view of Riverlea during the day. Above the restored fireplace with the original mantle featuring the dragon, which Sophia knew Oliver was very fond of, hung a painting by Pierre-Jacques Volaire. The painting was given to them by Mrs. Millner from her collection and it featured the eruption of Mt. Vesuvius.

They treated their guests with caviar and champagne for toasting because Oliver wanted to constantly entertain and amaze. Even though it was a small gathering, Ivy had presented Sophia with a red dress with carefully crafted slits, openings, and adornments that worked perfectly with the diamond jewelry she wore to accompany the ring.

Once the congratulations had ended, Sophia noticed Oliver disappearing into his study with a man she'd never seen in Covedale before. He was tall and wore a long coat. She thought she saw a gun on the stranger, but she was interrupted before she could investigate by Mrs. Woodham who wanted to hear the story of how Oliver had proposed.

"I thought you knew better than to set foot in my house again!" Oliver said angrily as soon as he closed the door to the study.

"So fucking emotional," the Gutter said, raising his hands in surrender. "Boss just wanted me to fucking congratulate ya."

"Get out of my house!" Oliver ordered, but the man sat on the leather sofa on the side of the room and put his feet up on the low table in front of him.

"What will ya do, Mr. Tiny Balls?" the Gutter taunted and laughed out loud. "Call ya guards and break ya party?"

Oliver didn't want to cause a scene. There was already the risk that White, being in his house right now, might have seen the Gutter. Calling the guards to take the Gutter out could clue White into the fact that he was up to something in Riverlea. He might even suspect it already. Confirming he was right would complicate things even further, and there was no need for that.

"Ya did good. More pay for workers, but it ain't the deal—"

"Trying to kill Sophia wasn't part of the deal, either."

"Leaving a fish head on your doorstep would've been a waste. Their heads are good in soup." The man smirked. He took a slug from his pants pocket. It might have even been the same one he'd put in there the previous year when Oliver had encountered the Gutter for the first time. He lit his match and looked at the flame. "We don't want to wait anymore," he added.

"I get it—"

"Do ya?" the man threw the burning match onto the carpet.

Oliver quickly ran up to it and stomped out the fire before it had a chance to ruin the carpet.

"Give me 'til the wedding," Oliver replied, looking at the Gutter sitting in front of him.

"Don't wanna lose ya little doll?" the man said and laughed loudly. "Ya know, we could tell her the truth. A note on her wedding dress. *Ya man has tiny balls—*"

"You wouldn't dare!" Oliver said with anger. Sophia could never know about his past.

The Gutter laughed out loud. "Boss is too kind." The man got up and pocketed the unlit slug he still held in his hand. "Put us on the guest list," he added before leisurely walking out of the room.

Oliver watched him until he disappeared in the corridor. He took out a cigarette and lit it. He looked under his shoe and found a mark on the carpet. Fucking Gutters. He hoped they'd burn in hell like the Riverlea rats they were.

Sophia had made her rounds, but Oliver hadn't returned yet from his meeting with the strange man. Her father was also missing and she decided to look for him. He was nowhere to be found among the guests, so she stepped out onto the balcony and saw him there, looking off into the darkness.

She went and stood beside him. "There isn't much to see at night," she said. "One day they'll rebuild Riverlea and we'll be able to see the lights in the distance." Her father didn't respond, so she continued. "We missed you inside. I know you don't approve of Oliver, but can you at least pretend to be happy for me?" Nothing.

"Are you still thinking about the money?" she asked. "The factory is doing well; he has a great mind for business. Can't you see the difference we're making for others, for Covedale?" Her father's silence upset her. "If we judged people based only on their pasts, what would that make you? You're a thief, a criminal, even a murderer. You yourself don't want to be reminded of it, so why are you so ruthless in judging others when you don't see yourself at all?"

She turned her back to the view and looked at her father. "All I want is for you to be happy for me," she said, and left to rejoin her fiancé inside. He was back now and talking with the guests.

White looked at his daughter as she walked away. The bottom of her beautiful dress was flowing to one side in the warm breeze. Her chestnut hair, just like her mother's, worn down and curled like springs, was accented with shiny hair pins. She was beautiful.

He recalled the death of his father. It had been a heart attack, they'd said, and he'd believed it back then, but later he had doubts. He, Steven White, was the only heir available to take over. The only son, too young to understand, too naïve not to be manipulated. His father had thought he'd have time to teach him the work—the politics involved in running an entire city single-handedly—but he'd underestimated his friends, who'd turned on him. An enemy, who had never identified themselves, had killed the old man. After taking his father's place, he'd seen plans to bring Covedale and Riverlea together. A peace treaty which never happened because *they* had stopped it.

White knew he'd made poor decisions, because of the terrible advice he'd been given. Unknowingly he'd sworn loyalty and silence to his father's killers. There had been no way out, not without knowing who surrounded him. He'd had no experience, no knowledge of how to find people he could trust, or how to unite them against the enemy. He was constantly being watched, directed, and scolded. Paddling against the river was pointless when the current was so strong. He'd ended up going with the flow, enjoying the luxury and peaceful life that came with it. He had done what they'd told him to.

His wife's sickness had added more nails to the coffin of his freedom. The golden handcuffs tightened even more around his wrists. Powerful ghosts, people without names or faces, were watching, day and night, and controlling every aspect of his life. Years passed, and he continued to be their puppet.

He needed his father's courage now, and his wisdom. The only thing he had left, his little Sophia, was now slipping away from him. He'd been instructed not to interfere with what Oliver was doing, but how could he do that to her? How could he just watch her throw her life away to be with a man she knew nothing about? A man who appeared to be no one, but who was of such interest to his superiors?

White had been on a tight leash, muzzled for decades, but they'd never directed his personal life until now. Who was the man Sophia was engaged to? What was the connection? What was the motive? All he knew was that she was in danger, making the same mistake he had made before—trusting the wrong people. He vowed to himself that he'd stop the wedding no matter the cost.

21

It was mid-July already, more than a year since the official announcement of the end of the war, and most of the cities were pulsing with new life once again. World United had offices all over the world, with the main center in Karben, in a brand-new building located in the middle of the European continent. The rumor was that numerous structurally stable houses had been demolished in order for it to fit into the downtown area of the city, leaving many people homeless. Oliver looked around before he entered, noticing lots of concrete and metal rubble still surrounding it.

The glass facade and curved walls gave the building a pleasantly modern look. The inside was spacious, too big for the few people Oliver saw walking around, and bright with the sun's rays glowing on the shiny floors.

Oliver stopped at the security desk and handed over his ID, announcing, "Oliver Conway. I'm here to see Mr. Ben Scholz." While he was here attending to other business, he thought it would be a good idea to stop in on his new connection in government.

"One moment please," the surly guard behind the large table said and turned his back to make a call.

As he waited, Oliver noticed an enormous billboard on the wall displaying the latest World United news. *Your tax dollars at work,* he read. *Instant teleportation: the travel of the future * New breakthrough in genetic research * Investing in large-scale enterprise to satisfy increasing demand.*

The guard turned back to Oliver, saying, "Mr. Scholz is expecting you, Mr. Conway. Second floor, unit 204 to your right."

Oliver nodded and went through the sniffer, a device that detected anything that might bring harm to people inside, including guns and explosives. He'd left his gun with his bodyguard, who was waiting for him in the car.

A short ride in the glass elevator and a stroll on the corridor to his right got him to Mr. Scholz's office. The secretary led him into a vast room with

171

floor-to-ceiling windows, but the shades were lowered to block the blinding sun. The office was fairly empty, decorated in light colors and featuring a large desk with chairs beside it. One corner was reserved for more comfortable, casual seating.

"Nice to see you again, Oliver. Please come in," Ben Scholz said. "What brings you here?" He motioned for Oliver to sit on the sofa and offered him a drink.

"I'm ready to expand my business. I worked with John and I got him involved in the blanket production and expanded the luxury clothing market into Clamerton. I'm a bit surprised, but the fashion business is really catching on. I'm hoping to bring some of that manufacturing here as well," Oliver replied.

"I'm glad to hear that," Ben said, putting one tumbler with whiskey in front of Oliver and another in front of himself before sitting down. "Making Leggett a worldwide company sounds like a good move. There's no place for small businesses these days with all the subsidies from World United. Gotta go big. And my wife would love you for bringing it here. She wouldn't need to travel such long distances to get herself new outfits."

"Indeed, ladies enjoy showing off their latest purchases," Oliver replied with a smile. "How have you been?"

"Been fine, I guess," Ben replied. "Never-ending work and deadlines. Can't resolve old issues, and new ones are piling up."

"How's that?" Oliver was interested. He sipped his drink.

"I remembered what you told me the other day at dinner. People donate money to manufacture blankets at Leggett, which are then distributed to the poor. This enabled you to lower the death rate significantly, but I'm having trouble expanding these types of ideas to other parts of the world. Few investors are interested."

"Maybe you need to look for other opportunities. What Leggett is doing might not be the right fit for other communities." There was a reason there appeared to be so many smart-minded people investing in his company. He didn't want Ben looking too closely into the blanket production at his factory.

"The problem is that fucking war left too many poor with nothing to live on," Ben said. He took a large swig of the drink before continuing. "Some cities are also dangerously overpopulated. The government spends a tremendous amount of money—millions of tickets—just to keep these people from starvation. With businesses and the market not recovering fast enough, the profits are pathetic. People don't want to pay huge taxes just to keep others alive." Oliver nodded as Ben continued. "When cold weather sets in, these expenditures increase further. While the idea of blankets is great and it helps Covedale, it's a temporary measure. What we need is a revolutionary idea that will permanently improve the situation. We can't afford quick-fix solutions."

"Is the main issue that the poor have no income?" Oliver asked.

Ben nodded and took another swig to finish his drink. "There aren't enough jobs for everyone and there's a portion of the population that won't be able to hold one. Companies are investing in automating their production because of the tax breaks they get—just like you and John do." Ben straightened himself in his seat and quickly added, "I don't blame you, but the simple jobs for the mostly illiterate population are diminishing."

"I currently employ close to a hundred people," Oliver said, "just to take care of me, my house, and the work at the factory. I pay them generously, two tickets per day, but I admit I don't care what they do with their money. I don't know what they eat and where they sleep. Maybe it should concern me . . . " Oliver contemplated. "Maybe the real revolution would be employing staff with a commitment to providing them meals, housing, and whatever they need to live on."

"That's an interesting idea," Ben replied, leaning forward. "Passing the responsibility from the state to an employer. But what about those who cannot be employed?"

"I'm sure we can figure out something."

"I'm being pressured by the government to lower taxes for people and businesses," Ben replied with disappointment and anger in his voice. "As of right now, I get only six tickets per person per year. If I lower it any further, I won't have enough budget to afford anything. What are we gonna feed them with? Fucking sand?!"

"With training programs in place, most of them might be employable, just like how it used to be. We just need to give it a chance," Oliver said.

Ben was unconvinced. "In the meantime, I can't have so many of them dying."

"What's the biggest expense right now?"

Ben walked to his desk and projected the balance sheet onto the wall for Oliver to see as well and sat back down. "Food."

"That would be lower if their employers start feeding them. Now they take their money for the work they do, and then collect food handouts. If employers provide for them, fewer people will need federal money."

"Good point," Ben replied. "The logistics of supplying the food are also a challenge. We could use those teleports, but there are too many locations for efficient distribution at low cost." Oliver nodded and Ben went to the next two items on the list. "The other issues are temporary housing during winter, and clothing."

"We could eliminate these with some initial investment—"

"I have nothing to invest. I can't pull miracles out of my fucking ass!" Ben said, distressed. He was angry, but his anger wasn't directed at Oliver.

"How many people do we estimate?"

"They say there are two billion left, worldwide. My department is responsible for them all, but only about a hundred million have the means to pay taxes and provide for the poor," Ben replied, calmly this time.

"How many people would be left after we employed the eligible?"

"Let's round it to one-and-a-half billion," Ben said. "Optimistic estimate."

Oliver did some calculations in his head based on what he saw on the budget sheet. "So they want to lower the spending from nine billion to, what? Six?"

"To fucking zero if they can get away with it," Ben said. "What they want me to do is impossible." Ben got up from the sofa and walked back to his desk. He took out a folder from the drawer and handed it to Oliver. "Here's what the council proposed I do. Does this smell like genocide to you?"

Oliver looked at the file and read it with interest. Meanwhile Ben nervously sipped his second drink. Oliver put the document down for a moment and lit a cigarette, staring off into the distance, lost in thought. He then picked up the paper and read it again, his jaw visibly clenching every so often. "Let me think about it," he told Ben. There had to be another way.

Violet had a few hours to herself and she spent it in their shack doing chores. It was rare for her to be alone these days and she didn't want to waste the time she had. She wanted to show Mike that she didn't sit around and do nothing the whole day, even though she was unemployed. She always found something to repair or clean.

She took the floor mat, made from woven rag strips, and carried it to the main street. She dusted it by beating it against one of the many inoperable light posts, putting a cloud of dirt in the air, and swept the floor with a small broom made from twigs she had found. The spring storms washed the wood onto the shore with other debris, and she scavenged the beach for them. She worked quickly, bent over low until she felt lightheaded. The heat of the day was making her dizzy. She sat down on the bedding—old rags placed on the dirt floor—to rest for a moment.

While seated, she looked around. The shack was small, with a low ceiling. It was a roof above their heads and she was glad they were so fortunate, but it always needed repairs. The metal sheets and plastic tarps used to cover the roof from rain were hard to find and they were very expensive to buy.

Violet had the money to help out, but she didn't know if she dared spend it. It scared her to think what Mike might do if he found out she had it. It had been more than a year since Oliver had pushed the money into her hand as she sat in his room at the Bayside Inn.

"I'm sorry, but I have to leave," he had said. "It would be too dangerous for both of us if I stay."

The night before they had laughed together, talking about something she couldn't recall now; they had talked about so many things. He had kissed her so gently on her body and went down on her, making sure she enjoyed it. His strong arms had supported her when they made love. Then he had held her, nice and tight, and the relaxing beating of his heart had lulled her to sleep right in his arms.

She had tried to remember his smell that morning—smoke from a tobacco slug, the sweat-soaked sheets on the bed—but scents were the hardest for her to recall. She had looked at the money in her hand. It looked like a lot, but she didn't know how much exactly. In her heart, she had wanted to cry from the pain of having a part of her world ripped away so suddenly, but she had also wanted to laugh. She'd looked again at the money she held, which was getting wet from the tears falling down her cheeks.

A lot has happened since that day, Violet thought. She noticed an ant crawling on the shack's floor. She wondered why this tiny creature had left the others behind, separated itself from the group. Aren't you lonely? She wanted to ask. Didn't it feel anything for the rest?

Violet recalled the pain of admitting to Mike that the man that she'd thought cared about her had left her. She'd had no choice but to ask her brother for forgiveness for not listening to him.

She had had to find work to keep peace with Mike and luckily Mr. Leggett had been hiring at the time. The whole city was buzzing about this, and Violet had gone with a couple of her close friends to check it out. She'd stood in a long line outside the factory, trying to get work. The chances that she'd be given the job were slim, but to her surprise, they had hired her. She'd learned how to sew pretty quickly, and thought she was pretty good at it.

One day, however, she missed work and lost her job. She'd woken up sick, nauseated, and couldn't make it. Once she realized she'd also missed her period, it became clear she was pregnant.

She had thought about going to the old woman who knew herbs and spells. Many women said that she had helped them get rid of their pregnancies, but Violet wasn't sure if she wanted to do it. Her brother no longer needed her affection. If the baby survived, she'd have someone who would return her love and who would never leave.

She had hidden her pregnancy from her brother because she knew he'd be upset. Many women in Riverlea had miscarriages because of poor conditions, and she wasn't sure if she'd be able to carry the baby to term anyway. No point getting him worked up.

In a couple of months, her belly had swelled and she could no longer hide it. Her brother had been furious and beaten her. He was very strong and his punches hurt. Mike had blamed her, accused her of losing work because she'd been sleeping around.

She wasn't mad at him for hitting her. He'd never done it before, and she felt he'd been right to call her a whore. He hadn't struck her on the belly and she didn't care about the rest of her body hurting for a few days. It would pass. Violet couldn't be upset at the hands that brought her food. She didn't dare to tell him the truth about the baby's father, or the secret money. She was glad that Oliver and Mike had never met.

Once the baby was ready, a midwife helped her, and after twelve hours of labor she gave birth to a healthy boy. She called him Seb, short for Sebastian, after the boy's late grandfather.

When she was able to look for work again, she'd found information about the classes Mr. Rodden was running and attended them while leaving Seb with a neighbor for a couple of hours. Then one night while on her way home from class, she'd found Natalie.

Violet had tended to the woman for a few days, changing the wet cloth on her face often, trying to control the fever. She recalled how terrified Natalie was when she finally woke up, not understanding what was happening to her. The woman kept talking about the money that was stolen from her, and Tom, the husband she was looking for.

Mike didn't like having Natalie around and he was constantly angry that she was living in their shack. He was right in a way, Violet thought, looking around the small space. There was not much room in here for three adults and a baby, but Violet enjoyed the bustling home. She missed the busy farm from her youth and she was glad that Seb would never fear being alone. Violet also didn't have the heart to ask Natalie to leave. The woman had nowhere to go. After Natalie fully recovered, she began to help Violet with some of the chores and take care of Seb. She had been helping out for three months now and Violet welcomed it.

When Violet had been working at the factory, she'd been making enough money to share some with Natalie, paying her to take care of the little boy. Shortly after seeing Oliver at Leggetts, Violet had been let go from her job. Mike once again became the only one who was bringing in money and feeding them.

"There's work," Mike said, coming unexpectedly into the shack. Violet snapped back to the present and jumped up from the bed. Mike had startled her and she didn't want him to think that she was slacking off. "A project outta the city. Gonna sign up," he said and started to pack his things.

"Ya leaving?" Violet asked, distressed. She nervously watched as Mike stuffed his clothes into a bag.

"Food and bed promised, and I ain't gotta see ya fucking dirty faces no more," he barked at her. Violet knew that he was upset about Natalie.

"What is this project?" she asked.

Mike shrugged. "I only know the name—Sābanto," he said and left with his belongings.

Violet looked at the dirty rag of a door hanging at the entrance, still swaying after he left. She sat down on the dirt floor and cried. She was suddenly terrified, wondering how she and Seb would survive with Mike no longer taking care of them.

22

ANOTHER TRIP, ANOTHER BUSINESS success waiting to happen. Oliver smiled as the chop-jet landed in Clamerton after a quick thirty-minute trip.

He had left Sophia in Covedale to continue the wedding preparations for the dresses, ribbons, and flowers. There was no reason to take her away from her planning. It was purely a business matter and he was expecting to be home later that same day.

White was quiet these days, avoiding him and any confrontation. He didn't interfere in Oliver and Sophia's relationship, for which Oliver was grateful. She was so happy about the upcoming special day that any action from her father would cause more friction in their relationship and spoil the mood. Oliver was happy that White wanted to keep a distance.

He still didn't know where Leo had gone after their confrontation in the woods. He was worried that White might blame him for the disappearance, but the man didn't even mention Leo of late. Oliver was initially cautious and aware of his surroundings, but Leo hadn't made any appearance and with all the wedding excitement Oliver was thinking less and less about White's officer.

Upon arrival in Clamerton, Oliver headed to the Quinton factory on the outskirts of town to see John Leggett.

"I knew working with you would work out well," John said when Oliver stepped into his factory office. It was a huge room with a desk and large sitting area. Not like the cramped office in the old Leggett factory. "I was skeptical about producing these blankets, but I see investors coming in," John added enthusiastically.

"I was in Karben a couple of weeks ago," Oliver said. "I'll be opening a new factory in Europe, too. I don't know the market, but every city seems to struggle with the same problem. We've proven that we can make a difference."

"Happy to see you grow," John replied. Oliver's own success ensured the prosperity of the Quinton company as well. Making the blankets was a great opportunity for John, and he abandoned the idea of making coats or winter jackets.

"Speaking of growing," Oliver digressed. "The Covedale factory is fully electrified now. I'm thinking about investing in these automatic machines and taking advantage of the incentives from World United."

"They do work well. Definitely a win," John said. "I could hook you up with the seller."

Oliver nodded in agreement, then changed the subject. "How is World United treating you? Still liking it?" he asked.

"I think the investigations are going well, but so much happened during those fifty years, it'll take another fifty to get it all accounted for." John laughed with disbelief. "As soon as we prioritize the list, we discover something new, an additional detail or evidence in the case." John sounded defeated. "I hate this job," he added.

"I still remember you telling me about that ammunition factory that blew up like fireworks," Oliver laughed, recalling their last conversation.

"Why are you so interested?" John looked at Oliver with suspicion, narrowing his eyes.

"I heard others talking about it. Getting those responsible punished is important to people and the World United," Oliver replied carefully. He was a fool for bringing unnecessary attention to himself. *I'll have to be subtler going forward*, he thought.

"Nothing really new on that one, but eventually something or someone will show up," John added.

They talked a bit more about production and the new Karben factory before Oliver left. He'd be back once John got him in touch with the sellers of the automated machines.

It was late, but the chop-jet wasn't ready to depart—some maintenance issue, he was told—so Oliver decided to stay at a hotel and head home in the morning. He didn't want to bother John and Susan with his presence at their house. The hotel wasn't bad; it had recently been renovated and equipped with bright lights. The rooms were expensive, but the staff changed the sheets daily so they smelled of fresh laundry. Rooms also featured a balcony with a view of the road and the small forest on the other side. The terrace was convenient for a quick smoke if Oliver needed to get his nicotine fix or get some fresh air.

After having a nice dinner in town, he called Sophia from his room so that she wouldn't wait up for him. He planned to spend the evening reviewing the plan for Scholz. If they played it right, they could find the savings that they needed.

After falling asleep on the hotel bed with his clothes on, staring at the numbers, Oliver woke up sitting in a chair with a colossal headache. He was no longer in his room. He was in a dark space with only a single light shining directly into his eyes. It felt as though it were burning his brain. Had he been kidnapped? He checked his hands and legs and found he could move them freely. The chair was soft and comfortable. He couldn't believe his men had betrayed him. He suspected White had something to do with this.

There was someone else in the room with him, so Oliver calmly asked, "Who are you?"

"A friend," the male voice replied. "Or, I should say a friend of your late father—and I'm sorry, but I needed to make sure you wouldn't know where you were in case our conversation doesn't go as well as I hoped."

Oliver looked up to where the voice was coming from, but he only saw the silhouette of a man. "What do you want from me?" His father had known many people, and anyone could claim to be his friend. He had had enemies too.

"The son of Conway is sitting right in front of me. I'm so pleased to see you. I forgot my manners. Call me Bob." He got up and offered Oliver a cigarette, but when he refused the man said, "Take one for later."

Oliver took the cigarette and put it in his breast pocket. He still couldn't see the man's face through the blinding light, but the headache was wearing off along with the drugs he figured he'd been injected with.

"Your father was great with a gun," the man said as he started walking behind Oliver. "When my friends had a job, he was the first to accept. It paid well, and he always did a good job. Clean. No hassle. He was the best." He smoked his cigarette. "When you enlisted, he got sloppy. Shortly after that, he got killed in his home by a fucking missile." Bob paused again before adding, "Unfortunate accident. We haven't found anyone like him since."

Oliver didn't respond and Bob continued, "I thought maybe he missed you when you left. Every time he took a job, he wanted you to be on it as well. You were, after all, a team. Inseparable." The man paused. "Then a few years later, I get a message from my dear friend Karl that he has a Conway in the factory."

Oliver took the borrowed cigarette out of his pocket. He noticed his hands were shaking. The man politely lit it for him as he continued.

"It's not an uncommon name, I guess, but what are the odds? The description fits." Bob walked to the front of the room and leaned on the desk.

Oliver tightened his fist for a moment. He clenched his teeth, but then relaxed and leisurely puffed the smoke out. He looked down at the only thing he could see well in the room, Bob's shoes. They were brown leather, neatly polished, and looked expensive. Size nine or ten, he guessed.

The man continued. "I told Karl, 'If he is who I think he is, don't you dare give him a gun,' but he didn't listen. He wanted to see your eyes as you killed those two guards. He praised your precision.

"After that, we put all our hope on you. We risked a lot, but it was all worth it in the end." Bob laughed. "As you can see, I'm a patient man. You made the transfers and then you met with Mark in Riverlea just like we wanted. You needed that money. I can't blame you. Your old man took everything you ever earned for himself. Just to be clear, Mark isn't in on this, so don't take it out on him. Our goal was to keep you in Covedale so that we could keep an eye on you."

Oliver's mind was reeling. He silently cursed Karl, Mark, and all of lice-ridden Riverlea. "Is White also working for you?" He needed to know who else to add to the list.

"He owes us some favors and we're slowly collecting on them. He was just told to allow you to stay in Covedale. It's a pleasant town. We kept it from being destroyed by the war. White doesn't know who you are, but he was so distrustful of you that he sent his daughter away—I have to say, she's a beautiful woman. Excellent choice," he said and nodded with approval.

"By the way," Bob continued. "I have to thank you for coming up with that idea to split the money with Eric. That made our work a great deal easier. Killing Mrs. Finley was all the proof that I needed. I knew it was never your father doing the terminations, it had always been you. A kid knocking on people's doors, pretending to sell cookies, then assassinating the entire family. Even the fucking dog!"

"The barking annoyed me," Oliver frowned, recalling the job and the stupid dog. He had been eleven at the time.

"I saw you later that evening. You never talked about what you did; you played and laughed like nothing had happened."

Oliver couldn't recall who he'd seen after that job. It was too long ago. "So after this many years, you decide to talk to me. What do you want?"

"You're not a businessman, Oliver, you never were. Friends needs you back on the job—"

"What if I say no?" Oliver asked, recognizing the name of the organization. He knew the answer, but needed confirmation.

"Then I'll have to ask for my advance back." Even if Oliver sold all he had, he'd still be in debt. He'd spent a lot of the money that was in the account in the Russian Central Bank that there was no way he'd be able to pay it off.

"I still don't get why me. You can ask any of your men to pull a trigger."

"I know what I invested in," the man replied. "And don't get me wrong, I won't need your services often. You can live your cozy life pretending to be a businessman, a respected citizen, but I'd like you to answer my calls. Friends needs to have assurance that no one steps out of line and that our interests are protected. Some jobs will be easy, some harder, others will need to be done yesterday. Once the job is done, leave it to us to clean up and make up a story that fits our narrative. That won't be your problem."

Oliver looked towards Bob, or where the sound of his voice was coming from. "I'll need men."

"The men you already have are at your disposal. They're loyal and know their duties."

His guards were in on this, then; the chop-jet trouble had been part of the setup. Everything suddenly made more sense to Oliver. White wasn't afraid of him or the Gutters in Riverlea; he was afraid of Friends, a group of the world's most powerful people whose true identities no one knew. It was his fear that continued to fuel the conflict between the cities, just as Friends wanted. White had never been his enemy, it had always been Friends. Friends, who were now telling him what to do and steering his life as it suited them. They were forcing him to be a killer again.

"Who?" Oliver asked, taking a breath full of smoke.

"John Leggett."

Oliver furrowed his brows. "Can't say I'm surprised." John's crime was being too eager to solve the war crime cases, but death was a pretty harsh punishment. Someone else, however, had already decided, and he was just a tool. The hit man. The death certificate was already prepared and laying on somebody's desk. It just needed a date stamp.

"One more thing," the man said. "I need to get rid of White."

"That's not impossible, but it will complicate my plans with Sophia," Oliver said calmly, but he was getting angry. Did Bob want him to kill all of Covedale? Why would they want to kill someone who was in their debt, and terrified of them?

"Poor choice of words," Bob apologized. "I want him to live a happy life as mayor. He might not need a lot of persuasion, but it's time he retires from playing mafia boss. We, the World United, don't want organized crime anymore. That's such a thing of the past. He'll be more useful to us in a new role."

Oliver nodded, finishing his cigarette. He knew that the Friends organization that ran the ammunition factory during the war had a long reach, but he'd underestimated them. They were dictating the lives and deaths of millions, and their powers weren't limited to the Ural Mountains or Riverlea. They now controlled the world.

He knew he needed to locate Karl and beat the shit out him, but taking care of John was a priority so he could get Friends off his back. His personal vendetta would have to wait.

"Until next time," Oliver heard Bob say somewhere behind him, then he felt the sting of the needle in his neck and everything went dark.

He woke up in his hotel room probably an hour later, again not knowing how he made the trip. His head was throbbing. He hated the drug they used, but it would wear off soon. He stepped into the bathroom and looked in the mirror with disappointment.

He'd enlisted because what he was doing wasn't working for him anymore; he'd done it as a way out of the never-ending cartel lifecycle. It was like being a passenger on a train that never stopped and was trapped on a circular track. The only way to leave was to throw yourself under it. That was what the military was supposed to be for him. He'd wanted to die on the front . . . but then why had he fought so hard to survive?

When he got back, he had been a fool to assume he wouldn't be going right back to where he started. *People will start looking for you. People will ask for favors.* The words were still ringing in his ears. He was mad at himself for getting played.

To fight against Friends, he'd need to make peace with the Gutters and honor the request they were still waiting on. The promise that he'd made and was delaying any way he could, but which he now doubted would make any difference for the Gutters or Riverlea. They wouldn't be able to defeat Friends.

He swept everything off the counter in anger. The complimentary hotel glasses fell on the tile floor and shattered.

There was no way out of this trap without a bloody mess if he acted now, irrationally, in anger. It would mean a war that he knew he'd lose. Revenge would be sweet, but he needed to prepare for it. It might take years to get to Friends, and for now he had no choice but to agree to accept the work. He knew how to do terminations cleanly and quickly. Sophia wouldn't even know. He could hide it all from her. He'd done it before, sneaking in and out of the house and acting sweet and happy at the family dinners. "She can't know," he said out loud.

He didn't go to sleep. He rounded up the men he had with him, three of them, and set the autopilot to take them to an open grassy field just outside of Clamerton. The men were confused when they arrived at the location, and Oliver wondered if they genuinely expected him to go straight home before settling this matter of his kidnapping.

When the chop-jet landed, Oliver took out a cigarette and lit it. He looked at the men in front of him. After a moment he motioned for one of them to take out a jammer dome from the overhead box. It was a device that, when turned on, provided interference to all listening and recording devices in a five-meter range from the center. Much bigger and better than the small jammers. There was no need to whisper with this one.

"Put down your weapons," he instructed calmly once the device was on, pointing at the table in front of him. He let them stand while he sat facing them.

The soldier on his left complied, taking his gun out and putting it down on the table. The other two hesitated. Hesitation here was wrong. It was just the four of them inside, and two of them were afraid to let go of their guns.

He stared at them unmoving until they complied. It was only fair that they would have their discussion with no weapons in hand.

"What happened?" Oliver asked. He sat comfortably and smoked his cigarette, genuinely interested in hearing their versions of events. He waited for an answer, but one wasn't forthcoming.

"How long have you been working for Friends?" Oliver asked. He saw confusion in the men's eyes. Was it real or feigned?

"Ya know we work for White," the man on the left said. The soldier was young, easily corrupted, probably ambitious, but not someone who would call the shots in staging a kidnapping.

"What about these two?" Oliver asked the man while pointing towards the others. "Can you vouch for them?"

"No sir!" The man straightened up.

Oliver noticed movement from the corner of his right eye while he was occupied with the soldier on the left. He grabbed a gun from a table and turned it on. He remembered it charged quickly, so he didn't wait before pointing it at the man who'd just drawn his backup weapon from a hidden holster. Oliver was quick. His speed and reflexes were faster than the time he'd caught that silly clay elephant for Sophia. It was only a split second before the man fell to the floor.

The soldier's mistake had been to wait for the charge to fully complete before shooting. The difference was between wounding or killing usually, but when one knew what to target, even a quarter charge was enough to be lethal. The secret was to be precise. Aiming at the eye, for example, created a direct passage to the brain.

"One down," Oliver said, standing up. "Don't fuck with me." The gun, already recharged, was still in his hand, in case either of the remaining two men were thinking about trying their luck. He looked at both of them, then walked to the other side of the table and leaned back on it. He was now standing between the men and their weapons. "An officer and a soldier left," he drawled, looking at them both carefully, trying to read them.

"Whose order?" He was calm, relaxed. He looked at his officer. "White is too stupid for this." He was just a pawn, but where was Leo? He hadn't seen that sleazy man since he'd taken off a piece of his ear.

The officer was in his forties, a strong, wide-shouldered man who had worked his way up the ranks under White. Oliver had considered him loyal, but the man served White and Friends. Oliver circled the two men. The officer stood boldly, unmoving, and the kid was sweating like crazy. Neither of them were talking.

"A soldier comes to my officer and says that god-knows-who needs to stage a kidnapping, and my officer says yes?" Oliver shot the officer in the calf, making sure not to hit the bone just in case he was wrong. Unlikely, but there was no need to cut off the man's leg for this. The man collapsed to his knees in agony, no longer able to hold his weight. "Who do you serve?" Oliver pulled the officer's hair back to see his face. There was no fear in the man's eyes, just contempt.

"Fuck you!" the officer replied, breaking a poison capsule in his tooth and starting to shake.

Oliver let go of him and looked at him with disgust. "At least you could've died from a gun with some fucking dignity." He shot him, just so he didn't have to see the body spasm anymore.

"What's your name?" Oliver asked the young man still standing in front of him, who was now clearly weak in the knees.

"Greyson, sir," the soldier replied, trying to stop his voice from shaking.

"Stand down and sit down," Oliver offered him a cigarette when he sat down by the desk. Greyson took it and lit it with his shaking hands. "You knew your officer had given the order, but you kept quiet even though it could mean harm for you." He walked to the bar, and poured two glasses of whiskey.

Oliver had become friends with death at a much younger age, but Greyson had potential. He could still be trained. There was also no one else, so he'd have to take this chance. As of now, he'd rather put work into a novice than trust another officer who would jump at the opportunity to betray him. They were all loyal to Friends, but the kid already feared him, and fear meant obedience.

Oliver put one glass in front of the soldier. "What's your allegiance, Greyson?" Oliver asked as he sat down, looking directly at the young man in front of him.

"Ya, sir," Greyson replied and looked up at Oliver.

Oliver nodded. "I'll be honest with you, Greyson," he said, sitting down opposite the soldier and taking a sip of the drink in front of him. "You'll get nothing for sticking with me. I can't make you rich or famous." He inhaled his cigarette, which was almost finished. "There's a war coming. A new one. A different one. The only thing I can promise you is death."

Greyson looked at Oliver, his eyes more mature than when he'd stepped onto the chop-jet earlier that night. "I'm a dead man no matter," he stated. It wasn't a question. He knew.

Oliver nodded. If Greyson wasn't with him, he couldn't keep him alive.

"What's this war?" The soldier asked.

"There are some powerful people who shouldn't be in charge."

"Friends?" Greyson asked, confused.

Oliver nodded. "They need to be stopped."

"Am I on the right side?"

"Why did you join White?" Oliver answered with a question.

"Covedale needs protection. I was to be a border man in a month." Greyson replied, looking confused about what Oliver was getting at.

"Then you're on the right side. We need to protect what we have."

"What ya gonna do?" the kid asked. Oliver wasn't sure if he understood or was just going along with what Oliver was saying.

Oliver replied with a smile, "Which of your fellow soldiers can you vouch for, Greyson?" He'd send everybody else back to White.

"I might know a couple," Greyson said quietly.

Oliver nodded, then got up and looked at the two bodies sprawled on the floor of the chop-jet, their eyes still open. "No one points a gun at me," he said under his breath, then turned to Greyson and said, "Let's clean this shit up."

23

OLIVER SAT IN WHITE'S dark bedroom, cigarette in hand, thinking about what he'd say to him when he woke up. He needed to test his abilities. Too much time had passed. He was no longer the small, skinny boy who could sneak through the shadows unnoticed, but he was pleased he still had some of that in him. There was no sound of alarm; no one was running around the house trying to find the trespasser. Oliver wanted to see White's face, his eyes wide open, when he discovered an intruder right in his bedroom, just like in the story he'd told him when he insisted he take care of Eric to protect Sophia. Oliver smiled to himself.

He'd been sitting here for a while, listening to the creaking of the old house, his own heart beat and the shallow breaths of the man sleeping in the room. His cigarette was more than halfway finished.

On the table beside him he found a wooden statue. It was hard to see it in the darkness, but it was about four inches tall. When he was ready, he tossed it towards the bed and it made a hollow thud when it hit the floor. It was effective.

The sudden noise woke White, and as soon as he stirred in his bed he heard a voice coming from within his still dark bedroom. "Don't turn on the lights." The voice was calm.

White recognized the voice. He had a gun in the nightstand, but he was too slow to reach for it. Now it was too late. He grabbed the sheets as though they would give him some protection.

"What do you want?" White asked as Oliver sat beside him on the edge of the bed. "How did you get in here?"

"I thought this fortress was impenetrable," Oliver looked around the room. "I met with Friends yesterday and they told me you're running for mayor—"

"The fuck I am!" White dismissed the idea bitterly. He wondered where the hell Leo was and why he wasn't protecting him. The man had missed their morning meetings for the past four weeks, with no word. That was odd. Where was that bastard? *Sleeping with the fishes, maybe*, White wondered, but brushed the thought away. If there was anyone who could take care of himself, it was Leo.

"I'm just a messenger," Oliver said. "It's your chance to keep Covedale. What you do with this information is of little concern to me." Oliver got up, straightening his suit. "Our agreement is over. I'll be sending your men back." He looked around the room again and added, "I'm not your enemy, Steven. Whatever you have against me is irrational. I'm willing to extend my hand. Next move is yours." Oliver opened the bedroom door and left the house through the main entrance. White was certain that wasn't the route he'd come in through.

In the morning they found two bodies on his lawn with a note that said, *Traitors*. White knew who'd left them there, and if that was Oliver's way of extending his hand, he wanted nothing to do with it.

It was the middle of the night and Mark couldn't sleep. Ivy was lying with her head on his chest, sleeping. Her breathing was slow and rhythmic. Mark gently freed himself from her embrace and got up, but paused when Ivy stirred. Fortunately she only mumbled something incoherent and went back to sleep.

Mark moved to the other room and sat down in front of the consoles. There was a woman who had been asking about him. Short, dark hair. He thought he'd seen her before somewhere. Anyone in Riverlea knew how to keep their mouth shut, so she hadn't been able to get a lead on where to find him. He'd captured her on the cameras outside his complex months ago and was looking over the images one more time.

He'd given her a tail back when he first saw her, but when he'd asked Ivy to come with him to the class the first time, he recalled the tail so that he could protect Ivy better in case something unforeseen happened. He'd lost track of the woman after that and she didn't seem to have resurfaced. Staring at the image wasn't helping him figure out who she was, so he closed the screen.

The display underneath showed a warning of some unusual activity. He hadn't looked at that panel for weeks and the warning was quite old. The activity was far away from here, half a thousand miles in an area that was not usually of much interest to him. He hadn't bothered setting up any audible notification that would've brought it to his attention sooner. He put it onto the big screen and looked at the satellite pictures it showed.

He stared at the large panel for a moment, not understanding exactly what he was looking at. "What the fuck is that?" he asked himself out loud. What he saw looked to be located south of Covedale. Probably a day's travel. When he zoomed in he noticed structures, partially built—clusters of white buildings or tents making up small compounds that were maybe five kilometers apart.

In the morning, Greyson rounded up other soldiers who were ready to pledge their loyalty. They were all kids with pimples on their faces. The oldest was only twenty-two. Expecting anyone older and experienced to show up was just a dream on Oliver's part.

The recruits stood at attention in a row. Oliver looked at them one by one, observing their movements and trying to read their thoughts. There were just six of them. Not enough, but it was a start. These kids were ambitious compared to the older men, but that would mean he'd need to get them in shape first and train them. He had already done one-on-one interviews with them all, which under other circumstances he might have left to Greyson, but the kid was clueless about what to look for. He wanted to make him an officer, but he needed to learn by example, and that was something Oliver would have to provide himself.

He stopped in front of one of the six and looked the boy straight in the eye. "What did Greyson tell you this work would be about?"

The recruit hesitated, but replied, "Protecting people and property."

Oliver looked at all of them. "If that's all you were looking for from this job, you can leave now and go back to White."

One kid stirred and Oliver noticed, so he walked up to him and said, "There's no punishment if you leave now. You can go."

The boy nodded, still a little unsure, but left the room.

The rest slouched rather than standing straight, but he ended up accepting them all once they pledged their allegiance. It reminded him of the day he himself had joined the gang, years back.

These kids, like everyone else, wanted to belong somewhere, to fit in. Youth had few opportunities besides following the criminal path in anticipation of power and money, but under White, they wouldn't get that. It'd be a painful journey for them for many years without seeing the fruits of their hard work, and Oliver knew these kids wouldn't have the patience to wait. He'd been there. Chances for them to get closer to the top of the chain were slim. They would quickly fall into bad habits and routines, and become apathetic towards the unjust system they were part of.

Oliver's agenda was personal—he needed to take Friends down to avenge the pain they had caused him—but he hoped to sow the need for justice in these young hearts. Friends' goal was to exploit people and make money from their suffering, just like they'd done at the ammunition factory in the mountains. Oliver hoped that, when the kids joined him in the fight, they would realize there was plenty worth fighting for. *How* to fight them was the important question that Oliver didn't have an answer for yet.

"I expect loyalty and silence," he told them. "In return, I will compensate you well. You and your families will be safe and well-off. If you betray me, you'll lose all that. I tell you now, it won't be worth it." They agreed by nodding their heads. "I won't tolerate drugs or rape from my people, so if you want to live in peace with me, agree to my terms."

They didn't object.

Once he'd dismissed them, he lit a cigarette. "Just five kids and Greyson," he said to himself. He wasn't sure what he'd do with them yet, but they had a long way to go before they were even close to being of help against Friends.

24

VIOLET WAS AWAY FROM the shack for a few hours and had left Seb in Natalie's care. It was her turn to shove her way through the sea of people to get the free food that was distributed daily at the square. She still had the money she'd hidden, and she trusted Natalie, but it'd be too easy to spend it all. When she really needed it, she'd have nothing left. She kept the money safe, and only took some when she was desperate.

"Look what I got," she said to Natalie with a smile on her face as she entered the shack, showing her the two sweet potatoes she'd acquired.

Natalie smiled back in appreciation of Violet's effort, but they both knew two potatoes for the whole day would leave them hungry again. Her smile wasn't a happy one. "I took Seb when you were gone and I talked with the scavengers," Natalie said. "They told me they only hire kids because they're small and they can get into small places. Ruins adults can fit into have already been looted. They wanted to recruit Seb in a few years, but have nothing for me."

"I asked the kitchen girls in the square. They shoved me away," Violet commiserated.

"Washers at the river were the same," said Natalie. "Most of the women here wash their own stuff, anyway."

Natalie grabbed the old aluminum pot, darkened and misshapen from years of use, and went outside. She came back a few minutes later, having filled it with milky water from the river. Violet was already waiting for her outside by the common area fire pit. They put the water there for boiling.

"Are the Gutters supplying the free food?" Natalie asked.

"Gotta be," Violet said, shrugging, then added, "Ya can't just apply to be one of them." The Gutters were part of the underground. Nobody else was allowed to go below to the old subway tunnels, even on the cold days in the winter. The Gutters were also living and keeping order in the parts of the city that had been assigned to them. Dave was the Gutter for their sector—his shack was much bigger and it exited to the common area they were now sitting at—but it was hard to tell how many others were actually living in this neighborhood. Thanks to the Gutters, however, Violet and Natalie didn't fear anyone would attack them in their alley and steal their precious food. Or worse.

The water boiled, and she threw the potatoes in.

"I can't live on these handouts," Natalie said with sadness in her voice. "We won't survive the winter."

"I can't work at Leggett, and ya don't know how to sew," Violet replied, recalling the fact that Oliver had recognized her and ordered her termination. "We can't sell drugs, we ain't scary enough," she laughed. The addicts would just steal the drugs and money from them.

"What about the girls in front of the inn?" Natalie asked. "How much do they get?"

"If ya got work every night, you can get three or four tickets a week." There was a girl a few alleys over she knew who worked there.

"I thought the guys had to pay a ticket for each night."

"They never pay for the whole night and the Gutters get half," Violet said, poking the potatoes with a stick. They were still hard. When she'd been visiting Oliver at the inn, she'd learned what the women who were standing in front of it were doing. She turned to Natalie and continued. "If ya want more, then ya screw many more guys for a quarter of a ticket or less, or steal when they ain't looking. Stealing gets ya a beating."

When her brother was still living with them, he had always brought some food home. They always had some potatoes, rice, or beans to eat. It wasn't much, but it was enough to feed the four of them. She didn't hold Natalie responsible for him leaving them. Mike was Mike, and their sibling relationship hadn't been good for quite some time. It was inevitable that her brother would leave her, and she was glad that she wasn't left all by herself. She had Natalie. Whatever happened, they would take care of each other and Seb.

Violet checked the potatoes again. They were ready, so she fished them out of the water. Once they cooled down, they fed Seb, then finished what remained, enjoying every piece, skin and flesh, of the only bland meal they had for the day.

Later that same night, Natalie went to the Bayside Inn and stood outside. It was the only option available besides starvation. The decision might have been too hasty, but she didn't have time to dwell on it. One of them had to bring some money from somewhere, and Natalie couldn't allow Violet to be the one taking her place outside of the inn. Natalie also needed funds to continue paying for clues and information in her search for Tom.

She looked at what she was wearing, a loose-fitting shirt and a piece of cloth wrapped around her waist to act as a knee-length skirt. It wasn't a very attractive look and it revealed none of her assets, such as they were now. Her curves were gone, and her bones showed through her skin in many places. Her cheeks were sunken, her skin pale. Even her shiny hair had become matted. Her breasts, once plump and well-rounded, now sagged.

There was an understandable lack of interest from the men who passed her. She barely looked like a prostitute. She lacked the confidence and attitude. Violet had helped her by tying her hair with a piece of rope, and had found a red dye to mark her lips. That was clearly not enough to get her noticed.

She was scared. Her mind raced through the possible scenarios of how this night might progress. Where would they go to do it? She didn't have the money for a room at the inn so that was out of the question. It had to be outside. In an alley maybe, but they were dark and smelly. What if she got beaten up again? Could she refuse a man if he came drunk or high? What if he was dirty or sick? What if Tom found her like this? She nervously looked around, but didn't see him.

Some men directly approached the girls who caught their eye, then disappeared with them inside the inn. They looked like they might've been regulars. Others looked each woman over first before deciding, like shoppers browsing merchandise. There were a few who wanted to pay with drugs or alcohol, but they were waved away by the girls.

It felt like just a moment ago that she'd had a home, a roof above her head. They hadn't been rich by any means, and Tom had his issues, but she would've been glad to return to that life, back to a time when she didn't worry about where her next meal was coming from.

Oliver was right, coming here had been a mistake. Riverlea was its own world where people were forced to behave as animals. Like coyotes scavenging the dump for food. Food. Food was what everyone in Riverlea was after. Food was like gold here. Food was on everyone's mind. She felt as though her stomach had caved in from the lack of it. She hadn't thought it was that bad here when she'd had money, but once it had been stolen from her, she had become a part of the misery that was all around her.

She felt ashamed at the possibility of Tom finding her here, judging her for what she was about to do. On the other hand she wished he were here to rescue her, to be her hero again like he used to be when they were younger and he'd still loved her. He had felt something for her at some point, hadn't he? She'd do anything to not be standing here all alone and so vulnerable, so scared.

"Ya scaring ma customers," a young girl who approached her said. She didn't look twenty yet. Everyone looked smaller here in Riverlea. Their bodies weren't growing at the proper rate because of malnutrition. The girl's shirt was unbuttoned, showing her small, braless breasts for anyone to see. She had also rolled up the front of her skirt, showing her underwear. She was so thin that her hip bones visibly poked outward. She inhaled the tobacco slug she was holding and blew the smoke into Natalie's face. "Get lost," she said angrily and walked away.

Natalie stood her ground. She refused to be intimidated by the girl. She looked around after the girl left and saw her talking with a short, wide-shouldered man. Glad she got a customer, she thought, but a moment later that same man stood in front of her. His face was serious, his eyes narrowed. Natalie realized he was a Gutter.

"Come," he ordered. When Natalie didn't move, the man grabbed her by the arm, digging his fingers in. "Deaf or stupid?"

"I'm not going anywhere," she said, but then another man suddenly appeared as though he'd risen from the ground. She had no choice but to allow them to lead her.

They turned down a dark alley and her heart skipped a beat. She recalled the night when she'd been attacked. She tried to get away from the man who was holding her, trying to pry his fingers off her arm, but he slapped her with his other hand. "Calm down, ya fucking bitch!" he shouted. He shook her violently and pushed her forward so that she continued to walk.

Her lip hurt and she tasted copper on her tongue. There was no chance she'd be able to get away from these men by herself, so she allowed them to lead her further.

They left the alley and turned into the open space of another major street. They followed it for some time, then turned towards stairs leading down into the darkness. Did the Gutters actually gut people? She shivered as she descended the steps. She didn't want them to think that she was scared, so she tried to pretend that it was the cold and dampness of the underground passage chilling her bones.

At the bottom, there was a rotting smell that filled the air. She couldn't see anything in front of her and she stumbled a few times on the uneven ground, slippery under her bare feet. Before her eyes could adjust, they stopped and put a blindfold on her, then continued to lead her deeper into the underground tunnels. There were turns, right and left, but she lost count of how many there were and how long she had walked. At least three times the men who were holding her changed. She could tell by the way they held her and how they walked.

The final door they went through led them to a place where the air felt fresher. The stench of death, sewers, and piss were gone, replaced by a mixture of old leather and tobacco. The man who was holding her let go of her arm, but then pressed down on her shoulder. "Kneel," he said, and she obeyed. The hard floor felt cold on her knees.

When the blindfold was lifted, she found herself in a spacious and well-lit room. It was decorated like an office, with old furniture that appeared to have been salvaged from skyscraper ruins. They had led her up and down multiple sets of stairs, but Natalie was sure she was still underground.

She was kneeling in front of a man in his early forties. He had dark hair that was cut short and a shadow of rough stubble on his face. He sat comfortably on the sofa with his legs crossed, staring at her. He wore fitted jeans and a clean, gray shirt.

"Ain't this the one?" the man who had dragged her inside asked.

The man nodded. He took out a bill from his pocket and extended his hand without making much effort to lean over. The soldier walked over and reached for the bill, but the man in front of Natalie didn't let go of it right away.

"Next time I ask for something, don't fucking break the merchandise," he said calmly and released the bill. Natalie knew he was commenting on her split lip, and she felt goose bumps on the back of her neck as she realized that the man had referred to her as though she were an object.

The Gutter nodded and left without another word. Natalie heard the door close behind him, leaving her alone with the man who was staring at her in silence. After a moment, he got up and slowly walked over to a side table. He returned with a glass of amber liquid in his hand and sat back down in his seat opposite her. He rested his elbows on his knees.

He looked at her with his narrow eyes, which were a very dark shade of brown. His stare wasn't threatening, but it was intimidating, and Natalie didn't want to look him in the eye. She chose to look at the plain, concrete floor she was kneeling on.

She felt his eyes on her and couldn't stand the silence. She didn't know if it was appropriate for her to speak, but she spoke up anyway. "Who are you?"

"They call me Max," he replied calmly, but that meant little to Natalie.

"What do you want with me?"

"Having a job is a privilege, Natalie," he said. His voice was matter-of-fact.

"How do you know my name?" she asked, shocked. She wanted to burst out in anger. It was her name and her right not to give it to strangers if she chose not to. She closed her eyes and tried to calm herself down.

She heard Max laugh as he leaned back on the sofa. "Because it's my fucking business to know what's happening in Riverlea."

"Who are you?" she asked again. *Tom,* she called in her mind, *if you're going to rescue me, now's the time.*

Max didn't reply to her question. He took a sip of his drink and crossed his legs.

"Why am I here?" Her knees were becoming sore on the hard floor.

"I was wondering the same. A Covedale bitch in Riverlea," he paused. "White doesn't have men to send around to spy anymore? And what made you think you could just decide one fucking day to be a whore?" Max replied in a much stronger, louder voice. "You thought no one would notice? That the whores wouldn't fucking complain about lost business?"

"What's it to you?"

Max laughed again. "Because the whores work for me."

She brought her head up and looked at him and the smirk on his face. "Being a pimp does suit you," she retorted, knowing it was risky. It didn't faze him.

"You know so fucking little." He laughed out loud. His voice resonated in the room.

A different Gutter came in suddenly and went to Max and said something, but she didn't hear it. Max nodded and took a ticket from his pocket, looked towards Natalie and gave the money to the soldier. He then got up from the couch and disappeared through a side door, ignoring her presence in the room.

The soldier told her to stand up and held out the ticket he'd received from Max for her to take. She looked at the bill with disgust, and she contemplated whether she should take it. Her knees were throbbing and her dignity was hurt, but it was still money. Money was food. She didn't feel she could show up empty-handed when she returned to the shack. She took the ticket, not for herself, but for Seb and Violet.

The man put a blindfold on her and they again took her down the smelly maze of the corridors and up to the outside. The August night air was much cooler now. She didn't know what time it was, but she knew it must be late. The Gutter took the blindfold off and pointed her towards the familiar alley she'd been living in with Violet.

"I pick ya up tomorrow night," he said, and went back down into the dark corridors.

What did he mean? Natalie was confused. Was she supposed to see that man, Max, again tomorrow? Why? Why did he want to see her? He hated her. She looked at the money in her hand and it terrified her. Was it an advance for something?

As soon as Oliver stepped off the ferry in Riverlea, he was stopped by two Gutters with guns. They searched him and found him unarmed. He wanted to show that he came in peace.

"I need to speak with Max," he told them. He remembered Mark telling him the name of their leader.

They nodded without talking to him and used their guns to direct him where to go. He didn't resist, and allowed them to lead him between the rubble of the buildings and into a small room with a peeling paint on the walls.

"What do ya want from him?" one of the Gutters spoke.

"I will only speak with Max," he said harshly and definitively.

The two men talked with each other quietly and one of them left the room in a hurry. Oliver probably could have overwhelmed the Gutter who was left, even with the gun pointed at him, but he had no intention of running away. He waited patiently for a long time, maybe even hours, before Max finally showed up with three more men. As Oliver expected, the Gutters were not pleased to see him.

"I don't like being fucking interrupted," Max said as a greeting when he stepped in. "Tell me what you want."

"We need to talk," Oliver said calmly.

"There is nothing to talk about. I'm ready to end this fucking farce right now. I have waited for too fucking long," Max said, gesturing for his men to shoot Oliver.

Oliver nodded. "I understand, but grant me a last wish," he looked at the men and guns pointed at him. "You know I wouldn't risk coming here without a good reason. Hear me out."

"Fine. Start talking, or they start shooting."

2 5

THE CLOSER OLIVER AND Sophia's wedding day grew, the more interested Oliver became in his factory. Ivy was assisting with the preparations, and he was happy to leave them to their planning. He empowered them to make wedding-related decisions without constantly asking for his opinion.

Blanket production was going well and more of them were being shipped out through the Covedale docks to Asia. Oliver started to think about expanding his company further. It felt like there was no limit to his business, which was nothing but successful.

Leo was still absent, and White never brought up the topic of his disappearance. *Convenient,* Oliver thought, but he didn't think the man had forgotten about his officer. He wondered if White didn't have any information on Leo or if he just didn't want to disclose it.

The latest message from Friends was to complete the task he'd been given before the wedding night. The work was urgent now, but the informers that Friends had provided him with still hadn't completed all of the surveillance he'd requested. He might need to risk it and complete the task before getting all the details.

"I'll be heading to Clamerton soon," Oliver said, stepping into Mark's office. "Do we need anything?"

"I don't think so. Most of the sewing machines have been replaced," Mark replied. "We're also changing to three shorter shifts, as you suggested. Light levels are no longer an issue with the new lighting."

"I was thinking about automation. I'm thinking about buying one of these big robots."

"We'd need to get the factory ready, but I don't see why not."

Oliver nodded. "I'll be back in a day or two. I'll see what I find."

Oliver got up to leave the room, but Mark stopped him, showing him a photograph. "Can you look at this?" he asked. "Isn't that the land you asked me to purchase?"

Mark had helped Oliver in securing a large, uncultivated swath of land in the south, but he hadn't told him what he was planning to use it for. Oliver looked at the picture pensively, then looked at Mark. When their eyes met, he nodded.

"I made a deal with the Gutters," Oliver replied. "Let's discuss this next week."

Mark nodded.

It would've been hard for Oliver to sneak in and out of Clamerton without being noticed, so he stopped at the Quinton company for a quick visit. If anyone saw him, he could say it was a business trip.

As always, John was happy to see Oliver when he stopped by. "Good move on trying automation. It never ceases to amaze me," John said. "Let me show you in detail."

Once at the machine in question, John explained each stage of the process. The machine pulled the fabric from a large roll, then stretched it to ensure it was smooth. Using sharp stencils, it cut out shapes that were ready to be assembled. The robotic arms quickly rearranged the pieces and stitched all the appropriate edges together. Once the fabric was turned around, the final product was neatly folded and packed into boxes by the dozen.

Only two people were needed to operate such a machine. One to ensure the fabric was fed into it properly and that the fabric rolls were stocked for the next batch of product; the second to ensure the dozen finished garments were correctly placed in the box and to stack the boxes to be moved to the warehouse.

The machines were making simple shirts, pants, and underwear. At the speed they were being produced, they could be put on the market at very affordable prices—less than a quarter of a ticket each.

"I'm still worried about the cost of purchasing such a robot," Oliver said as they got back to the office.

"You shouldn't. The machine is way more efficient than a human," John replied. "Check out Clamerton Dynamics. I've already talked with them on your behalf. They'll cut you a deal and even take care of all the benefits from World United for you."

Oliver spent the rest of the afternoon at Clamerton Dynamics company. It was an old military operation on the south side of the river that had previously specialized in war equipment. It had once produced exoskeletons, drones, and robots for the front, but had recently branched off into the civilian market. Oliver learned they produced a wide range of machines for different industries. There was a market for mining and manufacturing equipment, and the company had diversified as much as possible. His friendly hosts explained all the ways in which Clamerton Dynamics was making a difference, as well as the improvements they were working on in several key industries like food and medicine.

After ordering a couple of the machines, which he was warned could take months to arrive and then still needed to be assembled on site, Oliver stepped into his hotel room and had a quick takeout dinner with Greyson.

He double checked his gun to make sure it was charged—he didn't trust anyone with it, not even Greyson—and put it behind his back. The day was overcast, and it had been raining on and off. His coat would conceal the gun well.

After the meal, a quick shot of whiskey, and two cigarettes, Oliver was ready.

"Ya think Friends will fuck off?" Greyson asked.

"I need to keep them believing I'm on their side," Oliver replied, and his soldier nodded. He didn't think Greyson fully understood, but he went along with it. For now they just needed to stick to the plan. It was their first job together, and a loyalty test for Greyson. "If you do well today, I'll make you an officer," Oliver added.

They were in the same hotel that Friends had kidnapped Oliver from just a few weeks before, so he was familiar with the general floor plan and room layouts. He left through the balcony and climbed over the railing to the adjacent terrace to the room that John had reserved. He was glad he'd started exercising more to set an example for his new crew, but he still was far from his best strength. The workouts had also been great for losing the extra pounds he'd gained after all those lavish dinners, and Sophia seemed to approve of the results.

Greyson stood on guard monitoring the hallway. If something went wrong, he was to provide a distraction. Out on the balcony, Oliver was on his own.

It seemed like an easy assignment, but the preparations for it had taken weeks. Next time, when the time came—and he knew it would—he'd need to use his own people to investigate and oversee the work. Good intel always reduced collateral damage, and he was sorely lacking information. From what Bob's people had been able to find out, there was no good place to corner John. The intelligence collected by Friends mostly consisted of learning John's patterns, like when he was at home and how long he spent at the factory.

On weekends, John was a sitting duck at home, but if he were going somewhere, it was always with Susan at his side. Monday to Thursday, he usually left home at eleven and got to his office by noon. He spent four, maybe five hours there, had dinner with someone at one of the local restaurants with a river view, then stopped by the factory on the way home. Only on Fridays did he deviate from this routine. After work, he went to a restaurant for dinner with people from the office, like usual, but not to the factory or straight home. He spent a couple of hours in a hotel first. Each Friday he met with the same girl, fucking her always, conveniently, in room 216, which he booked ahead.

Greyson had rented the room beside it under a false name. Oliver and Greyson had broken into the John's hotel suite earlier and ensured the sliding doors to the balcony from the sitting room were unlocked.

John finished his dinner at the restaurant a little later than usual. He didn't want to break the heated conversation at the table. The local merchants and men working at Word United who joined him for the meal were discussing the government budget proposal and the planned reduction in taxes. They all complained that it was not enough of a change to make the businesses thrive, and John agreed with them, but kept mostly quiet, waiting for the right moment to excuse himself.

He had been invited to Oliver's wedding, which was taking place on the following day, but the night was still young. John knew he had enough time to get a good ride from the girl, go home, have a good night's sleep, and still be ready to leave for Covedale early in the morning. He hadn't changed his plans, and had reserved his favorite room as usual.

He rushed to get to the hotel as soon as he was free from his company, driving a little faster than usual. John didn't want his girl to be waiting. He parked the car by the front door of the hotel and took the stairs up to his room. He closed the door behind him and ripped off his tie in excitement.

The girl knelt in front of him, undid his belt, and unzipped his pants, which fell to his knees. She took him in her mouth; it wasn't the first time they'd done this together, in this room. She knew the drill. John's eyes rolled back while she pleased him, but he was ready and impatient to have the girl. He stopped her and pushed her onto the bed. He took off his shirt, laid on her, and pushed himself inside her. He wasn't a small man, but rather bulky with extra weight around his middle, and his body pinned the girl down so that she had trouble catching her breath in between his strokes.

As they were busy with each other, the overhead light went out, but John wasn't about to stop. Blackouts were common with the wires and transformers being old and poorly-maintained. In a moment the generators would surely kick in.

"Why do Friends want to kill you, John?" said a voice behind him. Someone else was in the room with them. A man.

John stopped what he was doing and pushed the girl away, who froze and remained seated on the bed.

"Who are you?" John said. The intruder turned on the gun in his hand, and a blue light illuminated his face.

The girl gasped.

"What are you doing here?" John asked, recognizing Oliver and covering his naked body with the sheets. Not because of modesty, but because the room felt chilly all of a sudden.

"I need to know what they told you," Oliver said.

"Who?" John was confused. His heart raced seeing the charged gun in Oliver's hand. What was he planning to do with it?

"Friends."

"I don't know who you're talking about or why you're even here." John was getting impatient. "Why are you in my room?" He needed answers; a reason for this intrusion into his private space. "What's with the gun?"

"Someone came to you and asked you to do something," Oliver replied calmly. "I need to know who it was."

"I saw no one. I got a written message. It said to remove an item from our list of war crimes."

"Which one?"

"The ammunition factory," John replied. "The one you were so interested in." *That was it, that damn factory,* John thought. *But what was Oliver's connection to it?*

Oliver nodded in reply but said nothing, so John continued. "You know who's behind it?" Oliver nodded again. "Help me!" he implored. Maybe if they worked together they could find a way out.

"I can't."

John went speechless for a moment. "Why not? You were always the good guy. You're always trying to help everyone, why not me?"

"If I don't kill you, they'll kill me and probably many others in your office at World United," Oliver replied. "That would also put Susan at risk."

"You can't be serious." John was sweating. He couldn't believe Oliver was capable. They were friends, business partners. The person dressed in black in front of him holding a lethal weapon that illuminated his face was unfamiliar, alien. A reaper. He trembled.

"I'm dead serious, John. I can't do anything for you now." Oliver brought the gun higher and put it up to the girl's head.

She began to cry. "Please, no!" Her voice was muffled by sobs, but Oliver remained unmoved. He pulled the trigger, and the girl fell to the bed right beside John.

He almost screamed, watching Oliver kill the poor girl. "What are you doing?!" he shouted. He thought about Susan finding his body in a hotel room. It would break her heart. She wouldn't be able to run Quinton without him.

Oliver fired the gun a second time, and John's crooked body came to rest on the headboard. It was a dead end. John had gotten a message. There was nothing that could be traced back to a person. Oliver was back to square one. Two bodies, zero leads. He left the same way he'd entered.

WHEN OLIVER GOT UP early the next morning, he turned on the radio. He listened to it while having his morning smoke, but there was nothing in the news about the previous night in Clamerton. The radio was reporting on a mob that had tried to enter an employer's mansion somewhere in Asia during a wage dispute riot. Five workers had been killed, and many were wounded. World United was promising solutions to end the unnecessary violence, but wage increases would not be mandated.

He needed little time to get ready for the wedding, so he took a long, hot shower. When he finished, he checked the radio again, but there was still nothing being reported about John's death. Ivy already had all his clothes prepared for him, so he quickly put them on. He was ready to leave at any time.

He opened a drawer and took out the picture. The distant, almost forgotten faces of his family looked back at him. His father smiled widely from the photograph. The older man's carefree face made him angry.

"Is this the life you wanted for me, father?" He said quietly to himself. "I don't know how much money they were paying you and what you did with it, but was it worth it?" He carefully tore the man out of the picture. "You set all of this in motion the first day you took me out into the streets. The first time you told me to kill, it was already too late." He lit the piece of the photograph with his father on it on fire. The flame quickly grew and turned the face brownish. The smile began to disappear. "Did you ever stop to think about what an eight-year-old wanted? Did you ask me? No. Otherwise you would've known that I just wanted to be loved. I killed for you. I killed for your attention." Oliver threw the remnants of the burning paper into the ashtray before the flame touched his fingers, allowing it to burn until nothing was left. "How painful was it for you to speak my name?"

He reached into his pocket and pulled out the envelope the Gutters had given him. He looked at the wrinkled paper. Oliver had been carrying it with him whenever he went, afraid of letting it out of his sight. Inside was proof that he had worked with the Gutters, which White could have easily used against him. He was glad it was no longer relevant. After some negotiations, Max had compromised and Oliver no longer needed to complete the favor they'd requested.

He lit the envelope on fire as well and put it on top of the ashes of the photograph. Its edges curled as the fire turned it to ash.

He then opened the small box with the ring. He'd almost forgotten it existed. There were lots of memories of his father imprinted on the ring, but suppressing them meant forgetting everything else. He didn't want to forget the wrongs of his father; he'd never forgive. It was a crime to teach a kid to hold a gun and kill in cold blood. He was a Conway, but he swore he'd never make his father's mistakes.

He looked at the familiar details of the engraving. A serpent-like creature with wide wings to soar the skies. Free to fly wherever it wanted. Claws strong and sharp to tear apart prey and enemies. Jaws open with fiery breath coming out like a tongue. Fire that doesn't spare anyone or anything when it rages, and leaves nothing behind. A dragon does not look back at what he's burned.

Oliver put the ring on. It fit him well; he had his father's hands. The weight of the ring on his finger was something he'd have to get used to, but it was there to remind him that there was only one way out. It meant a fight. It meant tearing Friends apart.

White had a plan. He was the father of the bride and would have an opportunity to come up to the podium and say a few words before the ceremony. It was his right to do so. Once there, he'd have everyone's attention, including people in high places—World United commissioners. He had proof that Oliver had killed his men and Eric Finley. Finally he'd expose the bastard for who he was.

He arrived at Oliver's house ahead of time, but the place was already swelling with guests. He saw Greyson, and they exchanged glances. Greyson, the traitor who had conspired with Oliver to kill two of White's men. The soldier who had been loyal to him was gone. White averted his eyes and went inside the house.

It had been two months and Leo was still missing. Leo's wife had begun to ask questions White didn't have answers for. If Leo didn't show up soon, he would have to promote someone to officer rank, at least temporarily. *Where was Leo?* he wondered. *Had Oliver killed him, too?* He shivered.

He grabbed some kind of alcohol at the bar—he didn't pay attention to which—and poured a tall glass. Probably a bit too much for an early afternoon, but he drank it in one gulp anyway. He then walked out onto the terrace and took a seat in the front row; a spot designated for family and close friends.

It was a nice day. Warm, but not hot. Sunny, but the clouds passing by provided lots of shade. Servants had decorated the place pleasantly, with bows and ribbons blowing gently in the light August breeze. The sweet fragrance of the flowers was mixing with the perfumes of the female guests.

White wiped his sweating forehead with a handkerchief. Now it was all about waiting for the right moment.

A tall man sat down beside him and crossed his legs. White didn't recognize him, so he assumed it was one of Oliver's friends and he shivered at the thought that there might be more of them in the crowd. He would not give up. He should've done something about this a long time ago, rather than waiting until the last minute.

The couple showed up together. Sophia looked so bright and beautiful. They walked hand in hand to the little platform that had been erected for the occasion. It was the moment White had been waiting for, and he wanted to stand up and let it all out, but he felt a heavy hand on his shoulder.

"I wouldn't do that," the man beside him said.

White's heart sank, and he suddenly felt ten years older. He didn't hear the vows or see the wedding ring being put on Sophia's hand. White closed his eyes and listened to his own heartbeat, feeling the sweat dripping down his back. He'd missed his chance.

When the applause erupted, he left.

His own house was quiet. The servants had been dismissed for the evening as he was supposed to be out, so there was no one waiting for him. He walked up to his room and relaxed his tie and unbuttoned his collar.

He poured himself a glass of rum and sat down on his bed. After a few sips of the alcohol, he put the glass down on the nightstand and took his gun out from the drawer. How do people do it? Do they put it against their temple or just point it inside their mouth? He tried holding it both ways and chose the one he found most comfortable.

He placed the muzzle between his lips. It was the first time he'd ever thought about taking his own life. He used to have everything: money, friends, and the respect of the people of Covedale. Over the past year and a half, he'd been downgraded to no one. They wanted him to leave his current life and become a mayor. And do what? Sit in a cozy office where his only job would be to sign whatever documents they presented him with? Not that he wasn't doing that already, but why change something that had worked well for so many years? He was no longer needed. They were phasing him out.

Sophia didn't need him anymore, either. She no longer belonged to him. There was nothing he could give her to make things right again. He wasn't a father, he was a failure, no longer trustworthy and reliable in her eyes. Thinking that she'd be back someday, running up to him with her arms open like she did when she was five, was unrealistic; a fantasy. Such thinking was selfish on his part. If Sophia ever came back to him, it would be when she was in pain from having her heart broken, and her eyes would be filled with tears. That would be the only circumstance in which she might want to see him again, and he didn't want to live to see such a moment.

He turned on the gun.

There was silence.

The familiar hum of a charged gun wasn't there. He took it out of his mouth and looked at it. The gun didn't have any power left. It had been in the drawer for months and he'd forgotten to check it. If he wasn't able to do something as minor as keeping his weapon loaded, was there anything he could do right in his life? He threw the gun into the corner of the room and it made a heavy sound as it hit the floor.

White got up and picked up the bottle of rum from the table and brought it to the nightstand. He sat down again and started to drink straight from the bottle in quick gulps, trying to drown any feelings he still had.

Oliver had been anticipating the news of John's death throughout the evening, but nothing disturbed the event besides Sophia wondering why John and Susan hadn't shown up. Her father's absence at the reception didn't bother her. She knew he was still mad and she'd given up fighting for his approval.

The news came the next morning, with an anchorwoman describing the graphic scene of two lovers brutally murdered that had been discovered in a Clamerton hotel. "The man's wife has identified him as War Crimes Commissioner John Leggett. There's no indication that the murder was political. The suspect, the woman's longtime boyfriend, is in custody and is being questioned as we speak."

THE GUTTER CAME BACK for Natalie the following day, as promised. He brought a stick man, which he'd probably made himself from wood and a couple of acorns he found somewhere. Natalie couldn't recall having seen any oak trees in Riverlea.

"Hey, Seb," he said. "I got ya something." He handed him his craft, and the boy smiled and happily picked up his new toy.

"I thought ya went to Sābanto." Violet kept an eye on Seb so that he didn't hurt himself with the sticks.

"Nah . . . I like it here," he said. "I got promoted, so I can't just leave."

"Ya always the smarter one," Violet said, laughing.

"You know each other?" Natalie asked.

"Riverlea is a small place," Violet said, then looked at the man. "She ain't in trouble, is she?"

"I don't know," the man replied, shrugging.

Natalie hadn't told Violet anything about what had happened to her the previous night. When she'd gotten back, she'd quietly laid down on her bed, unable to sleep. Her mind had raced through her conversation with the man, trying to recall every detail, every word. She'd tried to remember every fluctuation in his voice and laugh. When she finally drifted off as daylight peeked through the holes in the shack, she dreamed of being in the dark corridor. She was looking for Tom in the smelly tunnels. She heard footsteps behind her, so she ran straight in the opposite direction. She expected to reach the end, or an exit, but the corridor stretched endlessly. She continued to run, feeling scared, lost and disoriented.

When Violet had asked questions, Natalie had ignored them. They spent the money she'd gotten and ate a bigger meal that day, with eggs and rice. It was a good meal, but Natalie had had no appetite. She'd had trouble swallowing the rice Violet gave her. Seb had looked happy and innocent, and she'd convinced herself that what she'd experienced wasn't that bad and that it was worth it just to see him smile. She felt the need to protect the boy.

The Gutter looked at Natalie and she nodded that she was ready. She didn't want to go, but if Max had been telling the truth about knowing everything in Riverlea, she feared it might be her only chance to find Tom.

The soldier took Natalie down the same entrance she'd gone through the night before. At the bottom, he put a blindfold on her and led her through the tunnels.

"Why the blindfold?" she asked. "Isn't it dark enough here already?"

He laughed. "It makes ya confused."

"So that I can't find the place?"

"Or the exit."

Just like in the nightmare she'd had. She could run, but she'd never escape.

After the maze of right and left turns, ups and downs, he placed her in the same room as before and removed the blindfold.

An older woman in her sixties was there waiting for her. She gave Natalie a quick up and down, a judging glance, and asked her to follow. Natalie entered a bedroom with a large bed sitting just a foot off the concrete floor. It was made, and the room smelled of fresh linen. There was a small lamp on the floor in the corner, and a desk shoved against the wall. A rack full of clothes stood on one side, and she guessed they must be Max's. He'd clearly made the room look like home, but there was an unwelcoming roughness in the solid, gray walls.

She followed the woman to the next room, which was just as gray and cold as the other one. A claw-foot bathtub sat in the center, which was the only indication that it was a bathroom.

"Strip and get in," the woman said harshly. She wasn't skilled in pleasantries. The woman checked the water already in the bathtub and added a bucket of steaming-hot water to it. "It should be warm now." Natalie looked at the woman in confusion, so she added. "How many months has it been since you had a bath?" the woman asked. She didn't wait for an answer. "Don't think. Get in!"

Natalie stepped into the water.

The woman put soap on a rough brush and cleaned her with circular motions. She scrubbed Natalie's arms, back, neck, and belly until they were red. The woman even asked her to stand up so that she could clean her legs properly. She shampooed her hair, telling her to keep the foam off her face, because it was a lice treatment. The more she scrubbed Natalie, the darker the bathwater became.

"What does he want from me?" she asked, feeling her fingers wrinkling from the soap and water. She had an idea, but she hoped the woman would tell her something different.

The woman shrugged and said nothing.

Natalie felt lighter as she got out. She felt like pounds of dirt had been removed from her. When the woman left her alone, she dried herself with a towel and was reminded of home. She wondered for a moment how her apartment was, and if the people she'd left it with were watering the plants every week. Her little climbing plant—she could never remember its name— probably needed to be pruned. She would've done anything to be back there again. It felt so close but was so far away at the same time.

The woman interrupted her thoughts when she walked back in and brought her something fresh to wear. It was a short brown skirt and a blue blouse, neither of which fit her very well, but they were clean and smelled of soap.

She was then escorted to the big room, but this time she was allowed to sit in a chair. The woman left.

She had a moment to look around the room. The light gray leather sofa she was sitting on was old and scratched in many places. The metal table in front of her was empty with no dust on it, which indicated someone cleaned it regularly. A large desk made from dark wood stood at the other end of the room.

"I'm sorry I had to run off yesterday," Max said as he entered the room.

Natalie said nothing. There was a long silence as he grabbed himself a drink, then slowly walked over and sat opposite her in an armchair. He looked at her, his eyes piercing, judging again. She didn't want to meet his gaze.

"Aren't you going to say something?" she asked, breaking the uncomfortable silence. Her head was still hanging low, her eyes staring at the floor. Sitting in Max's presence wasn't any more comfortable than kneeling.

"I'm just fascinated," he replied, as though there were nothing wrong with his actions.

"Why?" she asked, but he was silent.

Max eventually got up and walked to the desk at the other end of the room. Natalie brought her head up and got a better look at him. His shoulders slumped a little when he walked, and his steps were heavy and his body swayed a bit. There was no grace in his posture. The way Max carried himself reminded her of Leo.

"What do you want from me?" Natalie asked as he walked away from her. He didn't reply, so she added quietly, "Just fuck me and let me go."

Max turned around and chuckled with amusement. "So eager . . ." he said, then his tone became angry, making Natalie jump in her seat. "You people from fucking Covedale think you can come here, spy! Steal the food handouts! Put people out of work!"

"My money got stolen," she said calmly, trying to explain her actions.

"I know," he said and leaned his back against the desk. "The guy spent it all and then fucking overdosed the next day."

"You can just send me back—"

"And fucking pay White's ridiculous ferry fee? Fucking Covedale! Tell me: What the fuck is there in it for me?" He paused for a moment, then continued his rant. "You want to go back? Sure. You can fucking swim!"

"I've done nothing to you," she said, for a moment trying to match his tone and anger, but she was certain he'd retaliate. It was a slippery slope from verbal to physical abuse; she'd learned that firsthand while living with Tom.

"Covedale! Covedale fucks with me every day! This Covedale bitch invites herself here, takes food away from the hungry. That's what you've done!"

"I never wanted to stay," she said. She felt scared, waiting for him to come over any moment and hit her. Her only crime was clearly just being from a different town, from the other side of the river.

"Did you know that the fucking sweet potato you ate, and the rice, are ten times more expensive than what they cost in Covedale?" he said, his voice calmer now. Max sounded like an instructor trying to convey a very important life lesson to a student.

"All I want is to find my husband," she replied. "Where is he?"

"How many times—how many fucking people—need to tell this Covedale bitch that he's not here, and he never was! Everyone was telling you politely to get the fuck out for fucking months!"

"That's not true. He is or was here—"

"Did you just call me a liar?" He walked up to her, bent over her, and looked straight into her eyes. "If a man matching his description had entered Riverlea, I would've known."

Max was inches away from her. She could feel his breath on her and she wanted to spit in his face, but she didn't. She was too paralyzed to move as she watched him straighten up and walk away from her. "Your word against Leo's," she said.

Max laughed out loud, almost hysterically, spitting his drink. "Fuck! I haven't heard that name in a long time." He composed himself. "How's that dick doing?" he asked. He sounded cheerful suddenly. "I thought he was already six feet under after all the snorting he was doing."

"He still does that," Natalie said. She wasn't sure why she volunteered that information, but everyone in Covedale knew about Leo's addiction. It wasn't a secret.

"He never learned that you don't use what you sell." Max shook his head in disbelief.

"He told me—"

"Whatever he told you was a fucking lie!"

"He told me that Tom went to Riverlea . . ." her voice trailed off.

"Do all Covedale bitches believe Leo?" Max asked in reply. There was a smirk on his face.

Before she could leave, he motioned for her to get up and lean on the table with her hands. He pulled her skirt up. She didn't have the luxury of saying no and she didn't protest. Used and humiliated, she earned herself another ticket.

There was a small funeral service for John, just close friends and family. Oliver and Sophia were present to pay their respects. They both comforted Susan and said kind words about the man who'd been cheating on his wife and been brutally murdered because of it.

Greyson was there too, acting as a bodyguard. He didn't want to be there, but Oliver had insisted, knowing that it would make him uncomfortable and be a good learning experience. This would be Greyson's first time pretending that nothing had happened after a major incident. Acting naturally to avoid drawing unnecessary attention was always hard, but the next would be a little easier now. As far as they knew, they were the only two at the service knew who the truth about John's death. Greyson was anxious the whole time and ended up throwing up under a tree at the cemetery in Clamerton, but he blamed it on food he'd had earlier.

"How do ya do that?" Greyson asked Oliver when they were alone. They were sitting on the steps leading from the terrace to the immaculate lawn at the side of the house. The gardener had already finished cutting the grass for the day.

"Do what?" Oliver replied, blowing some tobacco smoke into the air.

"So unmoved. Ya have any feelings about the man you killed? Any guilt?" The screech of cicadas filled the air.

"I do," Oliver replied. "John wasn't a great guy—he had his issues—but I don't think he deserved to die. Is that what you're asking?"

"Ya fooled me," Greyson said and leaned forward, putting his elbows on his knees.

"It was just a job. I've done it for almost ten years," Oliver explained, looking down. "It's all about how you deal with it in your mind. If you pull on that trigger thinking you will feel guilt, then don't pull the trigger. The feeling will eat you away from the inside. It will haunt you and destroy your life."

"How do ya suppress it?" he asked, curious. Greyson straightened himself and looked at Oliver.

"I usually forget it happened. When it's a stranger, I take one last look at the body, and when I turn around, the person is gone like they never existed." Oliver shook his head. "Don't be a monster like me." Being a killer was a curse. He never wanted to have to teach anyone how to avoid being haunted by the souls they'd taken.

Greyson nodded and looked directly into Oliver's eyes, asking, "Is that why ya don't talk about it?"

Oliver averted his eyes from the kid's gaze and looked ahead of him. "Keeping your two lives separate isn't easy. It's like having two wives— whatever you do, you don't want them to meet," Oliver replied, and took another breath full of smoke.

"How?" Greyson asked, trying to process the information he'd been given.

"Do you have a woman, a girlfriend, in your life?" Oliver asked after a moment, and Greyson shook his head. "So say you meet a nice girl, and on the first date, maybe the second, she asks you what you do. What would be your answer?"

"I am an officer under Mr. Conway," Greyson replied with pride in his voice, lifting his chin.

"So then she asks 'Is that a military? Do people report to ya? Why is Mr. Conway keeping an army,'" replied Oliver. "All awkward questions you don't want to answer."

"What do I say?"

"If you say that you're Mr. Conway's bodyguard, it suddenly makes all the difference. It explains why you hang out with me and why you carry a gun. You cease to be a guy running around shouting orders and having others do things for you. You become a person who can protect. Chicks like that." Oliver looked at Greyson who was nodding, then turned his head to look forward into the void as he added, "It's all about the white lies."

Max summoned Natalie almost every night. It was the same routine. First being led, blindfolded, through the corridors, then bathing to wash the dirt and stench of the slums from her body. She never saw the old woman again, but everything was ready for her each time she arrived. Sometimes, if he felt like it, Max would pour her a drink, then sit beside her on the sofa in the big room. He blamed her for everything that was wrong with Riverlea and called her his Covedale bitch.

Being in his presence scared her, but he never physically hurt her. He wasn't rough with her while taking her to his bed and using her body, but Max was as cold as the walls that surrounded him. It felt like he had no soul, as though his heart were just a block of ice. She recalled how cold Tom had been towards her, sleeping with other women just to show he didn't care. She'd hated him for that, but it didn't seem so bad anymore. She'd never complain again if Tom came back. Where was he?

Max rarely looked at her after sex. He usually just left the room, or turned his back to her, leaving her to change into the rags she'd come in with. He was done; she was dismissed. On rare nights he fell asleep, pinning her down with his arm so she couldn't move. These were the only times she stayed longer, until he moved in his sleep, but she never slept there herself. She used that time to try to figure out what it all meant and what she was doing there. What did she expect? A thank you? A goodbye? A 'Fuck you tomorrow, Covedale bitch?' She would've taken anything over the silent treatment. She was doing this for money. She knew she shouldn't expect much. It was just work, she told herself, a part-time job in a way; in and out. Wasn't that why she'd walked up to the Bayside Inn the first time? There was no passion required, and there would be no gratification other than seeing Violet and Seb fed.

When she lay on her straw bed in the shack—she didn't sleep well these days—her mind wandered. She longed for home, for Tom, for Covedale. Did they still remember her there, or had she been forgotten? The one thing she was sure of was that no one was coming to her rescue in Riverlea. If there was no Tom, if Max had killed him, there was no one who cared for her. She quietly cried herself to sleep.

When she had come here to Riverlea, she'd thought she could be a strong person, a warrior. A woman who wasn't afraid of any hardship. She'd been certain she had it in her, a willingness to fight for Tom and for herself no matter what, but Riverlea had snatched that feeling out of her. She was back to her old self; the version of Natalie who was content being submissive and cowardly. She still had dreams that Tom, her knight in shining armor, would save her . . . but now she was sure that he wasn't coming.

She'd reached financial rock bottom. She'd thought that there was nothing worse that could happen to her. She hadn't realized until now that there was another level below rock bottom, underneath the financial desert she was navigating. There was an underground of human existence. Each time she met with Max, she felt like she'd descended another step. She tried to act tough and thick-skinned around him, but the days left her feeling emotionally drained. She felt that one day soon she'd reach a deeper bottom and there would be nothing of her left, no tears to shed.

"T ELL ME WHAT'S WRONG," Violet said, worried. She'd noticed how absent Natalie had become, sleeping most of the day and sometimes refusing to eat.

Natalie shrugged in response. They were sitting under the tree watching Seb dig something in the beach sand. The tide was high, and the shore was just a narrow strip of land occupied by people trying to absorb the last rays of sun before the gloom of fall set in. Those around them were enjoying the day in groups or in solitude. Some lay on the sand trying to conserve energy before their next meal; others with no work and no prospects came here out of boredom. The salty waves moved loudly in and out of the land, leaving their wet touch behind on the sand and muffling the sounds of other people's conversations. Despite the hardships of Riverlea, there were random bursts of laughter.

It was late September, and the weather was cooling off, but they hoped to tire Seb out so he'd sleep better that night. A little cold sand wouldn't hurt him, they'd decided.

"Is he hurting ya?" Violet asked.

Natalie shook her head.

"Tell me. I'm worried about ya."

"I'm worth less than dust."

"I'm sorry," Violet said, giving Natalie a long hug. "Why don't ya just not go?"

Natalie shook her head again. "I can't," she said. "I can't eat for free. He'd know."

Violet nodded. It would be hard to hide anything from the Gutters. "If he cared, would that be easier?"

Natalie shrugged in reply.

Had Oliver cared? Violet thought he had, but she was no longer convinced. He hadn't taken her with him because he wanted to protect her; he'd said so himself when he'd given her the money. But then why had he been angry when he'd seen her at the factory? His eyes had burned with rage and his brows had drawn together in irritation. She'd never forget his face that day at the factory. She'd wanted to tell him about Seb—he was as much his as he was hers—but if he no longer cared about her, would he care about his son? What would she tell Seb when he got older? What was better, not knowing who your father was, or knowing that he didn't care?

They sat in silence for a moment.

"Anything ya can fix? What does he want from ya?" Violet asked, but then noticed that Seb had crawled too far out. She ran after him, grabbing him and bringing him back closer to where they were sitting.

"I just want to go home," Natalie said when Violet sat down again.

"Ya can't. Not with no money." Violet paused for a moment before continuing. "Left anyone back there in Covedale?"

Natalie shrugged.

"See the woman?" Violet pointed with her chin. "Got old and her son kicked her out from the farm. She came here. She wanted to go back, see her grandkids. Three years passed. No one is waiting for her. She knows. Now she watches people's kids for a potato or a turnip here and there. She's happy 'cause she can be useful. That man," she said, pointing at the man who had just walked by, "left his family. He got himself high. He couldn't quit and his family was starving, so he came here. He hopes his luck lasts, and he has his fix tomorrow. Here is his home."

Violet spotted her friend sitting under one of the trees in the distance. The girl lived just a few shacks over. They were peers and had grown up together here in Riverlea. A couple of days ago, her friend confessed how scared she was to go live with a man much older than her, but her parents had no choice but to agree to this marriage. They had no means to provide for her.

"A young girl's getting married tomorrow, she's born here." Violet continued watching her friend in the distance, but without pointing her out to Natalie. "This is her home, her world. There's nothing outside Riverlea. She dreamed—a child's dream—the pretty boy she knows rescues her from the marriage that her parents fixed for her. She's sitting at the riverbank, watching the waves. Husband will beat her, all of them do in Riverlea, but she's happy. He's a Gutter and she won't starve."

"Why are you telling me these stories?" Natalie asked, irritated. Her eyes narrowed.

"They changed, adapted with time. They're happy with what they have—"

"What do you want from me?" Natalie asked and pursed her lips, annoyed with Violet. "I have nothing."

"I watched my parents die," Violet said. "I grew up here, just me and my brother. We built the shack with our bare hands." Violet's eyes filled with tears as she spoke. "I only had my brother. I looked after him, and he grew up to be a man. When he was around, I knew I was okay 'cause he always protected me. But he's gone." She wiped her tears with the back of her hand. "I've got Seb. He's everything. I want to keep going and have the strength to protect him. I'm scared of what could happen to him." Big teardrops now fell down her cheeks, but she smiled and said, "I'm happy to see him grow. I want him to be a good man."

It was the first time Violet had opened up to Natalie. They'd grown close, but it was hard for Violet to open up and let go of all the things she carried in her heart. She tried to show that she enjoyed the life she had and always tried to look happy, but she held back tears every day. She did all this for Seb.

"Violet, I'm scared," Natalie admitted, her eyes also filling with tears. "I have nothing to live for anymore."

"We all scared," Violet replied. "Can't say what happens tomorrow, but see what life brings us, then we make the best of it. What's left for ya? Jumping off the building or into the river?"

"You think I should accept my fate?" Natalie asked, staring off in the distance at the open ocean.

"No," Violet said. "Make up your mind. What do ya want life to be? Wanna stand up to Max? Face it." If she had another chance, would she run out to Oliver and face him? She didn't think so, but it was the only advice she could offer Natalie.

As usual that evening, Natalie finished her bath and dressed up in the clothes provided. She reluctantly left the bathroom and walked into the bedroom. She knew how the evening would go, but she was never ready for it. As she hesitated to walk out into the main room, she heard a conversation through the open door. There was someone else there and he was speaking. She listened.

"There's still some money that I'm transferring, but it's drying up."

"So how much more will I get?" Max asked. His voice was calm.

"As we agreed, you'll get ninety percent of what I take, so I estimate it'd be nine thousand tickets," the guest said.

"I guess I have to ramp up my fungi production again and get new fucking buyers." Max sounded a bit annoyed, but not upset.

"There's another account Oliver has, but he doesn't want to touch it yet," the stranger said.

How many Olivers were there? She was hopeful. Maybe she could send a message to him somehow.

"He needs to get that money out for Sābanto sooner rather than later," the man continued. "He'll have no choice. The project will go over budget. That will be our chance."

"Do Friends know where we're getting the money from? If they do, it's a fucking risk."

"They know I get it, but they don't know I feed you with it. I'll keep it that way."

Natalie decided that she'd been standing there listening for too long and risked being accused of eavesdropping, so she walked into the room.

Max's face brightened when he saw her. "Have you met my ass?" he asked his guest, motioning for Natalie to come and sit on his lap. As she walked towards him, he added, "I found her in front of the fucking inn. A Covedale bitch. Can you believe it?"

"Mark," their guest introduced himself uneasily. He looked at her. "I think I've seen you somewhere before," he added.

She didn't think she'd met him before. "Natalie," she said as she sat down on Max's lap and let him put an arm around her waist. She looked at Mark. His eyes had a soft, mature look, so different from Max. He looked like the kind of person she might be willing to put her trust in.

"Let me know what he fucking decides. I need to plan accordingly," Max said.

Suddenly Natalie felt the floor underneath her move. It was only for a split second, but she got terrified knowing that she was somewhere underground, trapped in corridors with no exit during an earthquake. She stood up, but the tremor ended as quickly as it started.

"What the fuck was that?" Max looked at Mark. His eyes were open, his brows furrowed.

Mark immediately became preoccupied with some device he had with him. There was lots of commotion outside of the room and the Gutters suddenly began to come in and out. Both men started rapidly giving out orders. Natalie stayed out of the way. She leaned against the wall and watched what was happening.

"We got a building down, C12," she heard Mark say.

For the first time, Natalie noticed the display panels up on the wall. She was surprised this detail of the room had escaped her before, but they must have been turned off when she was there. She strained her eyes trying to make out the shadows and silhouettes that were now displayed on the panels. As the street barrels were lit, the view of the destruction became clearer.

"There," Max said, pointing at something on a display. Natalie could see that he was serious and concerned. He looked like he genuinely cared about what was happening in the city and to those people on the surface. Was he? Was there some humanity in the man after all?

"Damn, it fell on houses," Mark said, pointing at the display. "Redirect the Gutters from A2. I'll get my men to keep an eye on it."

Max nodded and barked an order to a soldier in the room.

When the dust settled, the surface was clearly visible on the display. The disaster had woken people. The stronger ones ran to the rubble, trying, with their bare hands, to free those who'd been trapped but who might still be alive. There was no sound coming from the displays, but it was clear that people were crying, trying frantically to find their loved ones, friends, and neighbors underneath the pile of steel and concrete. The Gutters were shouting orders, trying to control the chaos and organize the rescue efforts.

Some houses on one end were already engulfed in flames which were spreading quickly. All it took was a spark, and the wind created by the falling spire was sending hot embers from the common area pits onto flammable roofs. Women and kids tried to rescue their belongings from the shacks that were still whole before they lost all they had. Everything—rugs, blankets, pots—was crucial for the families to survive the winter. Nothing in Riverlea was replaceable.

"When was your last medical shipment?" Mark asked.

"Fucking next week," Max replied, sighing. "That motherfucker White is holding it. We'll have to make do with what we have."

After discussing some more logistics with Max, Mark turned to Natalie. She looked scared. "I'll take you home," he said. Max wouldn't have time for her until the rescue missions were over.

She nodded.

He escorted her outside and took off the blindfold, but before he could leave, Natalie grabbed his arm.

"Help me," she said and released her grip seeing his displeased stare.

"How can I help you?" Mark asked, mostly out of politeness. He remembered her from the surveillance videos around his house. She'd been looking for him months ago. He wondered what she wanted.

"I need to get out of here. I need to go to Covedale." She looked into his eyes desperately.

"I can't do that," he replied calmly.

"I came to Riverlea looking for my husband, Tom, and I have no money to leave."

"Tom, the trader from Covedale?"

Her eyes brimmed with hope.

"He's dead," Mark said bluntly.

"No. No, he can't be." Her heart sank. She felt sick. "Why would Max kill my husband?"

"Max didn't kill him."

"But he *is* a killer."

"Tom's body was found in the river last September," he said. "Why do I know Max had nothing to do with it? Max is many things, but he's not enough of a moron to throw a body into the river where Riverlea gets its water. Anyone who dies here is burned to control disease."

Her eyes widened. "What do you mean, they found him in September?" Natalie looked shocked by the news. "I got here in October!" she cried.

"Sounds like you missed him by a month."

"Please, get me out of here!" she begged.

"I can't." Mark shook his head in disbelief. He owed nothing to this woman. He didn't have to do anything for her.

"Why not?" Natalie asked, pleading.

"Everyone here wants to get out."

She tried to explain, "I'm at his mercy—"

"Aren't we all?" Mark was in a hurry to get back to his apartment. Ivy was spending the night with him and he'd left her by herself. She was safe there, but he was certain the shaking ground had scared her.

"I'm his sex slave," Natalie pleaded. Her eyes were begging, scared, scanning his eyes for some compassion.

"Didn't he say he picked you up off the street?" Mark asked, confused. Natalie hesitated to reply, so he continued, "His sex life is the least of my concerns."

"You have to help me!" She was getting angry, demanding.

He thought that she was going to grab his arm again and his bodyguard would have to intervene, but she didn't. "I live here," Mark replied in a slightly hushed voice. He wanted to calm her down. "I can't afford to have Max as my enemy, and I won't do anything behind his back. That's the end of this conversation." Mark walked away towards one of the dark alleys, but he turned around and found that Natalie was still standing in shock. He retraced his steps.

"Have you eaten today?" he asked. She shook her head.

Mark took bills from his pocket and pushed five tickets into her hand. "Don't try to find me," he said, shaking his head. He then turned around and left.

Natalie waited for a moment, watching Mark disappear into the darkness, then looked around. She realized that her last chance to get back to Covedale had just walked away. She'd been so distressed about Tom that she'd forgotten to ask Mark about Oliver. She blamed herself for it.

This was it. The end. There was nothing left to fight for anymore.

She should never have come here, she knew that now. Max had been telling the truth. Tom was never here. Leo. Leo had lied to her. *Why did he do it?* she wondered. Was he afraid that she'd learn the truth? She'd looked everywhere for Tom. She'd left no stone unturned in Covedale, hoping he was somewhere to be found. Was Leo afraid she'd find something that would point her to the real killer? The lost money, the lice, the hunger, the rape, it was all Leo. All this time, it was Leo.

What was this happiness Violet spoke of? Finding the good in the bad. Taking chances, facing things head-on. *Violet,* she silently called, *how does one find any happiness in these ruins, in this place where no one is truly alive? Wouldn't it have been better for us if you'd never rescued me?*

She turned around and slowly walked towards their shack, then paused and looked at the money. She put a ticket into her bra. *That's for Violet,* she decided. She knew she should've kept going straight, to the slum alley where they lived, but there was a voice inside of her that made her change her mind. She walked up to the Bayside Inn that was just a short walk away and stepped into the bar. It was deserted because it was late, and all the capable men were off helping with the disaster of the fallen building. Only a few drunk guests were still inside finishing their drinks. She sat at the worn-out bar.

When the barman came over, she threw him one of the remaining tickets she'd gotten from Mark. "Drink and smoke," she said, and the barman nodded. She didn't know how many shots the four tickets would get her, but she was determined to drink them all.

The usual watered-down whiskey arrived. She downed it quickly and asked for another. She lit the slug the barman gave her. She had only been a casual smoker before, so the first few breaths were harsh on her throat. She felt her eyes water, but the next drink helped numb the feeling.

A woman sat next to her and introduced herself. "Lita," she said. It was the young girl who had called her out on the street and reported her to the Gutter. She was also in a way the reason for Natalie's recent misfortune, but she didn't hate her. Lita was a victim of this town just like her, and like the rest of the people who lived here.

When Natalie said nothing, Lita added. "They watching ya."

Natalie looked around and met the eyes of a man in the inn. "Gutters?" she asked.

Lita nodded. "They kicked out one already." Natalie shrugged, but Lita continued. "Men say that they can fuck a wasted pussy for free."

"Watch me care," Natalie replied and sighed.

"He does," Lita said, smiling.

She hadn't said his name, but Natalie knew exactly who Lita was referring to. "He's controlling me. That's all." A third drink arrived, and Natalie downed it as well.

"Or maybe he gives a fuck."

"Stop shitting me," Natalie said and frowned.

Lita laughed. "Three girls I know have been fucked by him and score him high."

"Let me guess, they're all from Riverlea?"

Lita nodded.

"Then they weren't his 'Covedale bitch,'" Natalie said, ordering a fourth drink with her last free ticket.

"What do ya think men want?" Lita seemed to have some deep philosophical thoughts to express. "Money, power, and sex. Right?" She paused to see if Natalie was following her. "They want power to have sex or money to buy sex."

"Speaking from your own experience?"

"I been working at the inn for five years now," Lita said, and Natalie looked at her with disbelief. "Yeah, I know. I look younger, but I'm twenty-two." She smiled. "I fucked many guys, and they all cared 'bout one thing. Sex."

Natalie laughed. She'd come here to drown her sorrows, not to hear the memoirs of a hooker. When the bartender brought her last drink, she downed it almost immediately.

"Swear, all guys are same," Lita said. "Do ya know why the Gutter is eyeing ya?"

Natalie shook her head. She didn't really care.

"The real reason is that Max wants ya to himself."

"He's succeeding," Natalie replied and laughed bitterly.

"Not my point," Lita said and waved her hand in dismissal. "If he don't like ya, then why the trouble?"

"He's a control freak!" she barked in reply.

"He controls the whole city. Nothing wrong with that," Lita replied. "Ya struck gold. What more ya want?"

Natalie didn't reply. What kind of gold was this, she wondered. Abuse? Narcissism?

"Ma guy always comes around this time. If I'm busy, he goes away, but he'll be back. If he's broke, he hopes I suck him for free, but I'll say no. I have ma rules. When he got money, then I see him. He was a kid when concrete fell on him. Other girls didn't want to see him 'cause he drools and he talks funny, but when he came to me, I said why not. He is ma customer, and he never goes for anyone else."

"And your second name is Teresa?" Natalie mocked.

Lita laughed. "He's not scary. I fear the new guy. Ya don't know how rough he is. A hitter? A choker? Both? A girl got killed by one weeks ago. When Gutters moved in, she was already cold."

There was a moment of silence as Natalie averted her eyes from Lita. She recalled the night she'd been assaulted in the dark alley and how the man had held her. She was gasping for air, she recalled, thinking that she'd die that day. She almost did.

Lita noticed the change in Natalie and tilted her head closer to her. "Ya don't fit here at the inn," she said. "The devil ya don't know."

There was truth in what Lita said, Natalie thought. She couldn't do what these girls did every night.

Lita got up. "Ma date paid," she said to Natalie with a smile. The man who came in was broad-shouldered and looked strong enough to help with the rubble cleanup, but there was clearly something off about him. The drool coming from his mouth was visible, even from afar. Scars that looked like burns covered a large portion of his face. Lita motioned with her bony hand as an invitation for him to follow, and they both disappeared down the corridor that led to the rooms.

WHEN NATALIE WOKE UP, she didn't know what time it was. The underground room was dark and still, as it usually was. It could've been the middle of the night or the middle of the day, she couldn't tell. There was no clock she could see, or windows to guide her.

It had been three months since she'd started coming down here, and five weeks had passed since the collapse of the building and her talk with Mark. She believed what Mark had told her, and knowing that Max had nothing to do with Tom's death lifted some of the burden from her heart.

She turned in bed and found that Max wasn't with her. It wasn't unusual for him to get up and wander off. He seemed to sleep for only a few hours at a time, waking up shortly after the sheets got warm.

Acceptance of her new life in Riverlea was the only way to stay sane. Her fight to return to Covedale was over. There was no way out of here without having money, and there was no possibility of earning enough in Riverlea. She allowed herself to relax more in her new reality and tried to control as much as she could. The more she thought about her situation, the more she began to ask herself what was there for her. In just a few weeks, she'd gone from a helpless woman to a real Covedale bitch who knew what she wanted and wasn't afraid to take it. Max turned out not to be a terrible partner. She smiled to herself.

She sat up in bed and found the slug on the floor where she'd left it earlier and lit it. He'd told her not to smoke in bed, but he wasn't there to complain, so she ignored that. She was no longer scared.

Max had noticed the change in her and was smirking at her more often. He still called her names, and it seemed that his foul mouth was an integral part of him, inseparable, but his attitude seemed to have changed. She found he was somewhat nicer to her, accepting of her presence. She wondered if maybe he'd never been all that mean from the beginning and she was just now realizing it, or if she was simply lowering her standards.

She puffed the smoke in the air. If she stayed until morning, she might be given breakfast again. The thought made her smile. They said that the meat in Riverlea came from guinea pigs because it was easy to breed and feed them. Natalie used to be disgusted by the idea, but it didn't bother her anymore.

Max was insisting more often that she stay the night. The more time she spent with him, the clearer it became to Natalie that having her over was driven by his need for human contact. He told her he'd been here for over twenty years. Acting like a pretentious teenager stuck in an aging body. There was a price on his head so he hid here, in this coffin made of concrete, to stay alive. He left often, but only to roam the tunnels and corridors to attend to his business. He almost never went up to see the sun.

She puffed the smoke again and heard voices from the other room. Max had visitors at all hours. Sometimes heated conversations erupted, and she listened. She learned about the production shortage, of what Max called fungi, and about delays in food shipments that were once again stopped in Covedale. With the weather getting colder, there was a flu outbreak in B6, a riot at the food distribution center, and C2 had an increase in crime.

"Mark warned us that, before fucking Sābanto gets in, we need to get it out of here," she heard Max saying in the other room. "He says we have a few months, maybe a fucking year."

Their voices were muffled as they often were when Max and his guest talked quietly.

"Neither of us can take it out of here," the visitor said. "Not when they keep watching Riverlea." Natalie didn't remember hearing that raspy voice before. The man sounded much older.

Max replied, but Natalie couldn't hear him.

"Mark?" The old man said.

"That motherfucker is pissing me off. He already said he fucking doesn't want to have anything to do with this." There was a pause before Max added, "Sending a Gutter is a big risk. If any of them crosses on the fucking ferry, they'll hang on the tree in Covedale."

Natalie remembered the trees by the river where White hung trespassers from Riverlea.

There were some more hushed voices in the adjacent room, but Natalie couldn't make them out.

"I can't just fucking ask her to do that!" Max said.

"You've invested yourself too much in her," the man replied.

Natalie sensed they were talking about her. She got up and walked up to the door so she could hear better. She felt the cold of the room on her naked body as she inhaled the tobacco.

"Don't fucking tell me what to do!" Max said in anger. "You're not my father!"

The other man tried to say something, but Max interrupted him.

"You tried to be my fucking father for over twenty years, but all you did was to try to get rid of me!"

"You were seventeen when your parents were murdered. We didn't know how to help you—"

"All you did was fucking complain about me smoking and fucking!"

Natalie heard the familiar sound of the lighter flipping in Max's hand. He lit his slug just to spite the old man.

"I worked on this for thirty years. Now I'd need to destroy it." The other man's voice sounded defeated. "I made a promise to the old man—"

"I can never fucking agree to this!" Max replied, full of anger. There was a thud that followed, and Natalie thought he'd hit the desk with his fist.

"We could force her to take it," the man said. "If they give her truth serum, they'd know she was coerced. They might let her go."

"You fucking underestimate White!" Max was furious. "These assholes will fucking kill her just for knowing about this!"

"But, listen," the man was trying to make a point. "No one would suspect her. If she plays it right—"

"What if she fucking doesn't? What if that cokefiend Leo sees through her?"

"You said that she wants to go back to Covedale. We could persuade her, somehow. They think that you're keeping me captive here. I could act as a victim, ask her to do me a favor and send her back."

A pass to Covedale, Natalie thought. There was still a chance. She closed her eyes as if in prayer.

There were hushed words again that Natalie couldn't hear before the other man continued, "Why didn't you say that you killed her husband?"

"What good would fucking lying to her do?" Max paused, then added calmly, "She needs to know it was that shithead, Leo."

"Maybe she'd be more eager to leave?"

"And she'd take the fucking blueprints and go straight to fucking Leo to tell him about it." Max replied. "She needs to understand that Leo, that motherfucker, can't be trusted." There was a moment of silence before Max added, "I'll try to talk to her." He sounded defeated.

The topic changed, but Natalie could no longer hear the words. She went back to the bed which was still warm and put out the remnants of the slug. What was the valuable thing they wanted her to take across the river, she wondered. Blueprints of what? She closed her eyes thinking about the conversation and she drifted off to sleep.

Max woke her up later when he came into the room. He sat on the edge of the bed. There was a bottle in his hand from which he was talking large mouthfuls of liquor.

Natalie didn't know which part of the conversation had turned him to the bottle, but she noticed that he'd clearly had a few too many already. She knelt behind him and reached out for the bottle, which he agreeably handed to her. She took a gulp of the fiery liquid and continued to hold it in her hand rather than give it back.

"What's that thing you want me to carry?" she asked.

"How much did you fucking hear?" he asked calmly. He didn't seem too upset that she'd been eavesdropping.

"I know you want me to take something out of Riverlea and you don't want Leo to know about it."

Max nodded. "It's dangerous, and it might take fucking months before you're ready."

"What is it that it's so important?"

Max turned around to look at her and shook his head. "They won't stop looking for me or trying to find it," he said. It was clear that he didn't want to talk about any of the details at that moment.

In a few months, she'd be home in Covedale and sleeping in her own bed. Tom was dead and there was nothing she could do that would bring him back. She'd have to manage on her own, but this time she felt more confident that she would be fine. In a few months, she'd finally be free from Max and Riverlea. There was a light at the end of the tunnel. Finally, something to hold on to. She smiled to herself.

She didn't mind that there might not be anyone waiting for her on the other side of the river. She'd probably been forgotten, not expected to return. When she arrived, everyone would be surprised, their mouths agape. She would've survived Riverlea. Few came back to tell the tale. Any other hardships she might find in Covedale—lack of work, money or those that might still be looking for Tom to recover their money—felt like nothing compared with what she had already gone through.

"I'll fucking do it," Natalie decided, taking a large mouthful of the liquor.

Max looked at her for a moment, trying to spot any hesitation on her face, but he found none. He smiled and took the bottle out of her hand and placed it on the floor out of their reach. He then laid her down across the bed, pushed her thighs apart with his knees and placed his cool hands on her naked belly. He propped himself up on one hand and lowered his body on top of her to kiss her.

A few months, Natalie thought to herself as she closed her eyes. In a few months this Riverlea nightmare would be over. Until then she'd be able to make a few demands, she thought, smiling to herself. She was crucial to whatever it was they were doing. She felt new energy flowing through her veins. Her blood was burning, hot as the alcohol she'd just drank. It was her turn to be in control.

Through her closed eyes she imagined getting off the ferry in Covedale. What if Leo was waiting for her with a smirk on his face? How would he react if he found out that she knew who had killed Tom? Would he want her to pay Tom's debts? She shuddered.

Max stopped with his hand still on her inner thigh, surprised by her reaction.

She looked at him as though searching for answers, things that could be of use, in his dark eyes.

"Teach me how to use a gun."

30

A YEAR HAD PASSED since Oliver put the wedding ring on Sophia's finger, but since then he had only received two job calls from 'Bob' on the satellite phone that Friends had given him. One of them was for a minor paper pusher in Karben. She lived alone, so the job had been trivial. The other was a drug dealer in Lanton, a remote town up north. Neither of the hits appeared to be significant. They didn't even get mentioned in the news that was constantly reporting on World United's achievements and other propaganda. The victims also hadn't been able to provide any more information about Friends.

Besides that, he'd spent the year increasing the market for Leggett products, which now reached Asia, and working with Ben Scholz on his plans and concepts for helping the poor. Giving people housing and organizing the food logistics were their priorities. He expected that this project would take off soon. Everything was ready to go. They just needed the councilors to vote.

There was no reason to bore the ladies while Ben and Oliver discussed business and attended meetings in Karben, so they let them loose in the city for the afternoon. Emma was a great host, and she had planned out the whole day with Sophia. This day and the following one would seal the fate of the project that had been keeping their husbands so busy.

First there was a review in front of the council and a chance for discussion and questions. Then they were invited to a buffet dinner with all the councilors, accompanied by their significant others. A social evening before the vote the following day. They had already secured results, with most of the councilors agreeing with their ideas. The vote was just a formality.

"Thank you for presenting this today," Ben greeted Oliver as he arrived at the Karben office.

When Oliver had initially presented the plan to Ben, he'd been skeptical that it would work. It was risky and unpredictable. It would lower taxes and provide better security for the people, just as they'd wanted, but Ben hadn't been sure if the ends justified the means. Oliver's proposition, however, was still better than what the council had initially been suggesting, and if they got their way with tomorrow's vote, there would be hope.

Councilors were already gathering in front of the conference room for the meeting. The large billboard on the wall was providing information on World United's priorities: *Unions are hurting our economy. We mandate that labor organizations are now illegal.* Oliver looked around the room as the people gathered, but there were a few he didn't recognize.

"Which one of them is Councilor Johansen?" Oliver asked. They had appointed Lars Johansen to replace John Leggett to investigate war crimes, and Oliver was interested in making his acquaintance.

"The tall guy right there," Ben said, nodding towards Johansen as he happened to look right at him. The man was indeed tall, standing straight and confident. He looked to be in his sixties, his bald head shining under the lights.

"What a pleasant day," Ben said as the new councilor walked over to greet them. "I guess you haven't met my adviser yet, Mr. Oliver Conway."

"I don't believe we've met," Lars said, extending his hand to Oliver. The voice was familiar to Oliver, distinctive in tone. Lots of time had passed since he'd heard it. He was glad to finally put a face to it. Why he had taken the councilor position himself rather than steering a lower-ranking, expendable pawn, Oliver didn't know.

"I heard about the proposal and I'm intrigued," Lars said. "This will revolutionize how we look at the future." He was about to say more, but just then they were ushered into the room and asked to sit down at a large table. They'd reserved the head of the table for the speaker, and Ben gave it to Oliver while he himself took a different empty seat.

Once everyone was seated and the lights were dimmed, Oliver began his speech in a strong voice. "We have failed."

He touched on current challenges and how they could be overcome with Sābanto as the councilors listened intently. He tried to imprint the new vision of the world he and Ben were proposing in their minds, something that had never been achieved before.

"We owe it to our people," he said. "We owe it to our children. We can—and we will—rebuild the world. We will unite for what's right. We will stand together! That's why I gathered you here today. To bring you the means to make a difference. To bring you Sābanto."

It was no longer just an empty term; it was the revolution everyone was looking for.

"Sābanto is the way to make it happen." Oliver continued his speech. "It will ensure an adequate minimum standard of living for everyone, regardless of income. That there are enough homes. Enough food. As long as we all work together, Sābanto will ensure that no child sees poverty or violence on the street. Sābanto will serve our people!"

Oliver looked at the presentation that had been prepared and displayed behind him. It described in more detail, through words and diagrams, how the Sābanto project would proceed. He then took a few steps to the side to give the listeners a clear view and switched to the next slide.

"Stage one. We have already completed it," he said. His voice was strong and confident. "We have already provided housing and the means to live to millions of people. As long as a person has a job, they won't go hungry or cold. Sābanto has already succeeded there."

The councilors in the room looked at each other and nodded in agreement. They required every employer to provide these necessities and there had been no major pushback in implementing stage one from factory owners, businessmen, or farmers. They simply paid their workers less or nothing at all.

"Stage two will begin soon," Oliver pressed on with the presentation, "if we all agree that we want to proceed. Sābanto needs your vote tomorrow." Oliver said, pointing at a random person in the room. "We'll conduct a census of all who were not included in stage one. We need to know who can and cannot work. Those who can work will go through the work placement process. They'll be evaluated based on their skills and abilities and employed depending on the current demand." Oliver pointed to the stage one slide again to draw attention to it, demonstrating that those who were employable would be included in stage one results.

"The second group," Oliver continued, "will involve those who can't work because of age or disability. These are the people who are the most vulnerable and at the highest risk. These are the people who are malnourished and freezing to death on our streets. Sābanto will give them housing and allow them to live their lives with no fear of not making it another day."

Oliver took a sip of the water that had been prepared for him and continued. His voice was still strong, and resonated in the room. "Sābanto is the only way we'll fix the world and ensure lasting peace."

At the end of the presentation, both Oliver and Ben took questions and clarified the Sābanto processes. Only two of the twenty-one counselors weren't happy about the project, calling it exploitation of labor and the return of slavery, but the rest, who believed the money saved would be worth the method, overrode them.

The meeting finished and everyone left to freshen up and grab their significant others before the evening dinner. They all seemed more enthusiastic about the social part of the day than the formal one.

The dining room was on the top floor of the World United building in downtown Karben, and featured a green terrace with a view of the city below. Sophia was nothing less than stunning to Oliver, even though the dress she wore hid some of her curves, as well as her sixteen-week-pregnant belly. Sophia wanted to have fun at the party without discussing motherhood. She laughed that she'd still have lots of opportunities for that later.

The dinner featured a whole roasted pig, fruits de mer on ice, and a tower of cake that stood on display right beside an ice sculpture of a swan. After dinner, when everyone was mingling with cocktails in hand, Oliver left Sophia's side and walked out onto the terrace for a smoke. He looked down at the city. A bright billboard advertisement for a local plastic surgeon was visible amid the rubble, claiming he was capable of fixing anything and inviting the viewer to make an appointment for a consultation.

Oliver was soon joined on the terrace by Lars, who he had known before as Bob. "Living dangerously?" Oliver asked him, smiling coldly.

"This was the only way we could've united all Friends. After all, we want the same thing. For no one to dig, and if they do, it'll be six feet deep. Friends warned Leggett, but he ignored them, so they wanted someone who knew better. The death of another War Crimes Commissioner wouldn't go unnoticed, and this time around we might not have been able to find someone who would willingly admit to the slaughter. In case you were wondering, the murderer's family got a nice sum of money, and we made sure he didn't end up on death row for it. The girl's family was also taken care of."

Oliver nodded. "They didn't find the body until Sunday."

"I wanted to make sure you had a great wedding. You deserved it. White also wanted to have a moment of bravery, so we made sure we brought him back to his pitiful reality."

"The intel you gave me last year wasn't great. I need to do my own surveillance," Oliver said, and Lars nodded in agreement.

"You knew I'd be here today." He wondered why Lars had revealed his real name to him.

"Eventually you'd know my face—it was just a matter of time. Plus, now I know you'll take my calls so I'm not that worried. But I increased the number of my bodyguards," he said and laughed. He looked at the view of Karben from the terrace for a moment before adding, "I have a belated wedding gift for you." He put his hand into a pocket inside his suit jacket and took out a folded piece of paper. He handed it to Oliver who opened it. The note had an address here in Karben. No name and no instructions, but these usually weren't written down. "You won't be disappointed," Lars said as Oliver hid the note.

They stood there looking at the views and finishing their cigarettes until Oliver broke the silence. "What's up with Riverlea?" he asked. "I know you keep White on a short leash in Covedale, and you didn't want peace between the two parts of the city."

Lars thought for a moment, then replied. "Think of it as a sore or a wart stuck to a healthy society and no matter what you do, it will never heal. Sometimes you need to protect the rest of the body by excising it, even if it causes a lot of pain."

He threw his unfinished cigarette onto the pavement and walked away without giving Oliver another look.

Lars turned towards the entrance of the building. He was glad that Sābanto was to start in Riverlea. He'd wanted to deal with that place a long time ago, and now Oliver, unaware, was helping with the plan. He wished him luck with that little pet project of his, trying to evolve cockroaches into humans. Lars smiled to himself as he walked away. The underground in Riverlea had been a problem for Friends for decades, and finally there was someone who could smoke them out. Their investment in Oliver was already paying off, and the timing was perfect.

They'd set the vote for the afternoon, so Oliver went to check on the address in the morning. It was in a brand-new neighborhood of large houses with lots of land. Oliver and Greyson sat in the car for some time and waited, but no one came or went. There was no movement in the windows.

He didn't think Lars would send him into a trap after investing so much in him, but they were careful walking up to the door just the same. In his mind he explored all the possibilities of someone watching them, but saw no one. He rang the doorbell. Someone was there, he could hear them, but no one was opening the door, so he rang the bell again.

"Coming," the voice said, struggling to be loud. Whoever was there was taking their time opening the door, so Oliver rang again.

"Coming," the voice was closer and more annoyed now. The door opened. The man in the door was very thin with no hair on his head. An oxygen tank that he was pulling behind him hampered his ability to move around. Oliver recognized the man well, even with his dramatic change in appearance.

Without a word, the man walked back into the house. He left the door open for them to come in if they wished to.

Oliver took a quick look around the room when he entered, while Greyson swept the house. The place had none of the luxury of Oliver's house, but there was charm in its simplicity.

He walked into the living room and looked around for an ashtray to drop the ash that was hanging from his cigarette. He found one on the mantel that he used without asking.

"Have a drink," Karl said, pointing at the cupboard in the room's corner.

Oliver walked over to it and found a bottle of liquor and some glasses. He poured two, handed one to Karl, and sat down on the sofa.

"What the hell happened to you?" Oliver gestured at the man with a wry smile on his face. "You look like a ghost."

"To one spirit or another," Karl said, raising a toast.

"Really, what happened, Karl?"

"I've been sick for some time, it just caught up with me," Karl said as he tried to sit down. "Did Lars send you to kill me?"

"When he gave me the address, I assumed it was yours," Oliver replied, "but you look like my grandfather would if he were still alive."

"He blamed it on me, didn't he?"

"You say that as though you didn't have a hand in it," Oliver replied, annoyed. Shifting blame from one person to another was pointless. Someone had to pay for what had happened to him. Why would he put all the blame on Lars, when it was Karl who had made him sleep on a hard floor for all those years?

The old man nodded. "Didn't we all?" he said, but Oliver didn't reply. He continued, "I knew of your father, but I never met him. Hits were never my specialty." The room was filling up with tobacco smoke. Karl took a big, wheezing breath before continuing. "There's nothing I can say to you that would make things right."

"Why ten years?" Oliver asked. "You could've easily let me go and you didn't."

"Would you really have left Eric still trapped? You knew he wouldn't survive without you, and if I let both of you go, you'd have compromised the operation." Oliver frowned, but he didn't know what the answer was. Karl was probably right. "I always wondered why you left all those people to die," Karl continued.

"There wasn't time," Oliver said flatly. Karl said nothing. "If you'd told me about Friends, I could've helped you—"

"Could you?"

The question left Oliver speechless. What could he have done? How could he have helped himself or Karl out of that situation? He looked at the floor in front of him. The soft rug was dirty under his shoes. His mind raced. If Karl's family were in danger, what could they have done from thousands of miles away?

After a long moment, Oliver looked up at Karl and asked, "Did Lars tell you why he needed me?"

"Yes, he told me the story about you being the reputable killing machine."

Oliver grinned at the description. "Then I'm impressed by how calm you are."

"I have nothing to lose, do I? You frying my brain right now would be an act of mercy."

Oliver nodded. "I wanted to get out of this work, you know, but now you and Lars have made it impossible."

"As I said, nothing I can do to make things right."

"How about telling me who Friends are? Or should I say, World United?" Oliver was certain that Karl had to know something.

"I don't know. They're always sending you messages, calling you, but you never see them. There are never any meetings. Even the anonymous people you talk to are probably not them, just messengers."

"How much do they control?"

"I don't know, but I know what they don't control." Karl coughed again trying to catch his breath. Once his breathing was better, he continued. "They don't control Riverlea, but they would like to."

Oliver sat up. "Why not?"

"I heard the underground is too strong and too many people live there, but I don't know the details. I don't even know why Riverlea interests them. All I can say," Karl added, "is beware of their dirty tricks."

There was a moment of silence that Greyson broke. He seemed to be trying to understand the significance of Karl's words, so he spoke slowly, looking out the window and observing the road for any suspicious activity. "If there are too many people living in Riverlea, isn't Sābanto supposed to change that?" He looked at Oliver and was met with a grave stare. It was clear now. Coming to see Karl was a diversion from something else. Oliver downed the drink he had in his hand. They had to get back to World United.

31

THE ALARM WAS PIERCING. The noise coming from the system in the adjacent room woke Mark. He checked the time; it was close to two in the morning. He got out of bed, trying not to wake Ivy who was somehow still sleeping soundly through the alarm.

A year ago, he'd tried to resist her charms and keep away from her. It had been foolish of him to allow her into his life, he knew, but as time went by, he'd stopped resisting her. She'd wanted more from their relationship and eventually he gave in. How could he turn down her passionate kisses? He longed for the time they spent together and how she made him laugh. The more time passed, the stronger the feelings he'd developed for her became and the less he wanted to put a stop to things.

He opened the sliding door to the other room to check what the alarm was for. He looked through the images on the display with his eyes still half closed from sleep. What he saw on the satellite pictures coming from Covedale alarmed him.

As soon as the vote passed, hundreds of Sābanto men positioned themselves by the river. The road by the riverbank was full of them. There had been many people vying for those Sābanto jobs—it was their only chance to safely get out of Riverlea—but the sheer scale of the operation shocked Mark. It wasn't simply a police force to maintain law and order in the city; it was an army, and they were about to invade the island.

"Get up," he gently woke Ivy. "Get dressed," he added in case they needed to leave on short notice. There was an urgency to his voice. Mark knew Oliver had been planning to implement Sābanto in Riverlea. They'd agreed it would take months to sort out, so why would he order them to get Sābanto ready right after the vote? He looked for any transcripts from the summit but he couldn't find anything. Nothing had leaked yet from the closed door meeting in Karben.

What was the rush? Mark had helped Oliver with the project to resurrect Riverlea, dismantle the slums and bring hope and opportunity to the people. It all looked good on paper and the numbers were in order. Even Max had agreed to the plan. They'd had it all figured out, but something had clearly changed and Mark was concerned. Now it looked like World United was sending in an army to pacify Riverlea.

Someone knocked on the door, startling Ivy, who was already on edge. It was the right knock so Mark opened the door. The guards never came up to the apartment unless it was really urgent.

"Sābanto's at the river," the guard said.

Mark wished he hadn't had Ivy overnight that day. He'd never have put her at risk if he'd known. Mark grabbed a small electronic tablet from his pocket and handed it to the guard. "It's for Oliver in case something happens to me," Mark said, and the guard nodded. Mark looked around to make sure Ivy wasn't around to hear him before continuing. "I can't go with you," he said. "There's a letter here for Ivy." He took out a yellowish envelope from the case of the tablet and put it right back. "Don't give it to her unless you're sure I'm dead. If my heart stops, this corner will light up." He pointed at a corner of the device. He paused, then added in a more urgent tone, "There's a boat at the river close to the docks. I'll message the operator to be on standby. He'll take you out of the delta and drop you on the south side of Covedale, away from here. Stay far from Riverlea and wait for me. I'll be back for the tablet," Mark said. He spoke optimistically, but he wasn't sure that he really believed the words himself.

Mark turned to Ivy who was sitting on the bed. She looked worried. "The guard will take you to the river," he told her calmly, hiding his own fear and uncertainty. "I'll shut down the equipment and follow."

"I'll wait with you here," Ivy insisted. He noticed that even after being woken up so abruptly, she was still paying attention to her grammar and pronunciation. She was the best student he'd had. He smiled.

"There's nothing to fear, Ivy," he said. He sat beside her and moved a strand of her hair away from her cheek. "Once the displays are down, I'll run to meet you. Sending you ahead means that we'll both be out of here quicker."

She looked at him and nodded. She knew there was no point in arguing. Mark's mind was made up about how they would leave Riverlea. She trusted him. He was the smarter, more careful one. She leaned over and their lips met. Their kiss was brief, but Ivy felt both happiness and sadness in the moment.

She got up and smiled nervously at Mark. "I'll be waiting for you at the river," she said, and followed the guard outside.

The man took Ivy to the river, and they got into Mark's boat which was waiting for them. The operator started the engines without saying a word, and—despite Ivy's protests—they moved away from the shore towards the opening of the delta rather than directly to Covedale, just as Mark had suggested.

"Just a few minutes before we go get Mark from the shore," the operator raised his voice a little so they could hear him over the wind and the engine noise. "He signals, we go back."

Ivy looked at the river, hoping her fear for Mark was unfounded. She could see only endless darkness on her left, and the torch lights illuminating the short, familiar buildings on the right. A shiver ran down her spine.

The signal from Mark hadn't come yet, so they continued along the shore. The boat landed on a pebble beach south of Covedale. The operator helped them to disembark and then went back to wait for Mark. Ivy and the guard were a few kilometers away from Covedale's Main Square, but decided to keep away from possible danger. Ivy had a friend who lived on a farm south of Covedale and she knew she could take refuge there and get the latest news.

When they got there, nothing the radio was broadcasting was of interest to them. The anchorwoman was discussing a new tragedy: workers burned by some chemical spill, and World United was blaming the workers for sleeping on the job. The radio was silent about Riverlea.

"Emergency evacuation!" someone shouted through a megaphone outside.

Violet woke up, not knowing what time it was, but it still looked to be night as no light was passing through the crack in the wall of their shack. She looked at Natalie who was also awake.

"Emergency evacuation!" the same voice yelled, but much closer now. They could hear people shouting. Arguments started outside. "Ya have five minutes," the voice shouted again.

There wasn't enough time. Her money was still hidden away in the ruins in a half-wall between piles of rubble that no one visited and had a loose brick that only she knew about. She wouldn't have time to grab the money now. Seb was eighteen months old. She couldn't take him along, and she couldn't leave him here and be separated. She'd get the money when she got back after the evacuation, or whatever this was all about.

She peeked out of the shack. There were bright lights coming from the far end of the alley. She strained her eyes trying to see what was happening, and saw men dragging people, forcing them from their homes. They wore matching dark uniforms with the white word SĀBANTO on their backs. They were pushing her neighbors and hitting them to make them get up and move. She looked around the place she'd been living for the past few years, but there was nothing of value that she could carry with her.

"Sābanto's here," Violet said to Natalie. "Grab stuff for a couple of days. We be back soon." Violet wasn't sure if that was true, but she was hopeful.

They packed some rags in case Seb needed to be changed, and went outside to join the other people. The three of them walked down the path between the shacks. They kept the boy between them, each of them holding one of his hands.

They were rounded up in a big group on the street and made to sit down on the pavement. There was chaos all around them and Seb was constantly crying. Violet tried to comfort him, but she didn't know if he was hungry or sleepy, or if he simply felt her fear.

A man on the opposite side of the group they were in took out a knife, trying to break free from the troops that surrounded them. Shouting erupted as the armed Sābanto soldiers took the man to the ground and held him down. They heard talk that someone had been wounded.

A woman sitting behind Violet cried loudly, wailing constantly about someone she'd been separated from. She wanted to turn around and tell the woman to shut up, at least for a moment, just long enough for Seb to maybe fall asleep, but she didn't think she had the right. She knew she would have wept just like that woman if they had separated her from Seb.

It didn't take long before they loaded the first people onto the trucks. People resisted boarding the vehicles and being taken away. More fights erupted.

Violet and Natalie held each other close to protect Seb and didn't protest about getting into the truck. They were two women and a toddler, and they knew they wouldn't be able to win a fight against the armed men.

The trucks took them to Covedale using a temporary bridge that they must have laid down specifically for this operation, but they weren't dropped off in town. Natalie only caught a glimpse of the bakery storefront facing the river as the truck rushed by it. She recalled the fresh crispy buns she used to get there just a year ago. The taste of bread felt so distant now.

They were taken to a fenced yard outside of Covedale city limits, with a large new hangar. The three of them walked in together. There were many people arriving, and the soldiers were breaking up the crowd by sending them to different entrances. Violet was carrying Seb in her arms, but she and Natalie became separated inside.

They segregated Natalie from the men. She watched the place swelling as more and more women came in. Soon there was no place to sit or lie down beside the hard floor. After a few hours, one of the Sābanto soldiers came up to her.

"Come," he said, and she got up and followed him without protesting. He took her to a small room with another person sitting at the table. It was a woman Natalie had never seen before. She was definitely not from Covedale.

"Name?" the woman asked.

"Catherine Reed," she replied. She came up with the name on the spot. It was important that no one could find her. There wasn't much left of Natalie's former identity, even her looks were no longer the same. Natalie was dead. She had died in Riverlea.

"Age?"

"Forty." She couldn't believe she had already reached that round number.

"Can you read and write?"

"Yes"

"Profession or last job?"

"Prostitution."

"Family?"

She thought for a moment about Tom. He was gone. It wasn't worth mentioning him anymore.

"None," she replied.

The woman nodded and looked Catherine up and down before speaking. "I'll mark you down as employable. You'll be assessed further later."

Catherine said nothing. She'd find answers to her questions when she reached the compound, she was sure. A Sābanto soldier was already beside her, pulling her by the arm to get up and leave. On the way out, she passed a different woman being brought in for the same interview.

The soldier led her through the narrow passages between the cages. Some were empty, others already had people in them. They moved her to a cage filled with women. She sat in the corner on a thin mattress and closed her eyes.

Stay calm, she heard Max telling her. *Once you get to the fucking compound, you'll be safe. No one is looking for you. Once you're there, find Oliver.* She nodded. *Good luck my Covedale bitch.*

"Fuck you, too, shitface," she muttered to herself.

Now I wait, Catherine thought. *Cat.* Good choice of name, Cat. She smiled to herself.

She opened her eyes and looked around. She saw fear in people's eyes and she wanted to tell them that Sābanto was nothing to be afraid of, but why would they believe her? When another woman looked at her, she gave her a small yet genuine smile, but the woman averted her eyes shyly.

She lay down and tried to sleep. She needed rest.

The next day she was on the truck towards Compound 48, Unit 2.

Violet was carrying Seb because he couldn't walk quickly and she didn't want him to get lost in the crowd of people. They pushed her into a cage with some others, mostly women with kids, and the elderly. No one she knew. She looked at the sign stuck to the door: *Compound 10, Unit 23.* She didn't know what it meant.

She received a good-sized meal, mostly potatoes with some root vegetables, hastily prepared and overcooked, but she didn't complain. Seb had calmed down a bit. The cage they were in was much quieter now, except for the muffled sobs of one of the women. Violet was glad that Seb had eaten some of the meal too. The next day, after sleeping on the hard mattress on the floor, they were loaded onto the truck to be transported somewhere else.

Oliver insisted they leave for home right after he got back from the World United office. Sophia had a whole week's getaway planned with sightseeing, a spa visit, and spending time with Ben and Emma. She wasn't happy they had to leave right away, but she said nothing.

When Oliver got back from the office, he was visibly upset about something. At the chop-jet, Oliver closed himself in the other room on board and talked on the phone for the duration of the eight-hour trip.

"What is it?" Sophia asked Greyson when he passed her, but he just shook his head to let her know not to ask him again. Greyson knew that if there was anything Sophia needed to know, she'd hear it from Oliver, and he was busy.

From the other room, they could hear Oliver's angry voice as he spoke. "Ben, what do you mean the councilors made last-minute amendments to the bill?" he asked. There was a pause before he continued. "What we were planning to accomplish in months we now need to do in a matter of days." There was another moment of silence where only Oliver's steps could be heard as he paced the room. "But why?" he asked Ben on the phone, voicing his displeasure.

When they arrived in Covedale, Oliver gave Sophia a quick kiss. "I'll be home soon," he said and smiled as he dropped her off.

Oliver and Greyson went somewhere else and didn't come home for the night. Sophia knew he was working on that Sābanto project. She'd heard a lot about it, but had never looked into the details. She'd never seen Oliver so upset before.

Sophia paced at home, not finding any comfort in her daily routines or the hobbies she normally enjoyed. Oliver had been away for six days already and she was worried that something had happened to him. She glanced absent-mindedly at the ruins visible from the sitting room as she got up, ready for bed. Normally Riverlea was dark, absent at this time of night because there were no lights illuminating the city. But tonight she could see the ruins in the distance. Sunset was hours ago, so there was only one explanation for the orange hue highlighting the rubble. The city was on fire.

3 2

"WHY DID YOU CALL me?" Oliver shouted over the sound of raging fire as he approached the meeting place White had suggested. It was at the riverbank in the east end of Covedale, sheltered on three sides by woods. Dawn was just breaking, but the fire on the other side of the river illuminated the clearing. It was a few hundred meters away, but somehow felt much closer.

Oliver caught a glimpse of White's face and found it calm. He'd asked him to come alone and so early in the day that Oliver was suspicious of his intentions. He expected the unexpected and had prepared for it accordingly. He carried his loaded gun at the small of his back as a last resort, but he hoped the old man would finally give up his vendetta against him.

"Explain this to me!" White shouted, pointing at the other bank of the river.

"It's something that didn't go as planned!" Oliver replied, standing beside White. Even from afar, they could feel the heat of the flames on their faces.

"Don't you know Riverlea is the biggest source of income for Covedale?"

"Looks like you'll have to find something else!" Oliver took out a cigarette and lit it. There was a slight breeze blowing towards the water, fueling the flames on the other side.

"Easier said than done," White replied, then after a moment he added, "Why do you have to destroy everything you touch?"

Oliver took a puff of his cigarette, then looked at White with annoyance. "Can you—for once—stop talking riddles?"

White continued to stare straight ahead as he replied, "Killing and destroying comes so easily to you!"

Oliver nodded, not in agreement, but to acknowledge White's state of mind, which hadn't changed since their last talk.

"I didn't burn it!" shouted Oliver, his voice strong, trying to make sure White heard him over the roar of the fire.

249

"Just like you didn't kill your friend Eric and his wife!"

"You suggested it, remember?" Oliver was getting angry.

"Did I?" White replied. His voice was calm but loud. "I never said to kill him! That was your own interpretation!"

They stood for a moment in silence, listening to the destruction happening around them.

"Did I tell you to kill two of my men, too?" White asked. "They were good guys! Had families. They just had orders from Friends. That was their only crime!" Oliver said nothing, so White continued. His voice was getting raspy as he tried to shout over the noise. The dryness in the air didn't help. "Strange that when I put these killings together, they trace back to Covedale! I can trace them all back to you!" White thought for a moment. "Tom. Doug, the businessman I lost the contract with in Clamerton. John Leggett. The road to Covedale is littered with bodies!"

Oliver kept quiet. Agreeing or disagreeing was pointless here.

"It's been more than a year since Leo went missing. Was that your doing as well?"

Oliver didn't reply.

"And this is what I don't understand," White continued. "Friends are protecting you! I can't stop you or what you're doing. I can't expose you for who you are and demand justice for the dead. I can't confiscate your money like I would do with anyone else who displeased me. I tried!" White paused to rest his voice before continuing. "I can't even protect my own family."

He paused again, thinking. He then turned to face Oliver and continued, "And now with no Riverlea, Covedale will be ruined!"

There was a moment of silence before Oliver replied. "You smeared Covedale with blood for decades. Every time you stopped the food shipments, people there died!" He pointed at Riverlea. "But of course you couldn't see it. It didn't exist for you because it was there and not here. How can you live with yourself, Steven? You're accusing me, but look at you! Look inside yourself and be honest. You're not the man you pretend to be."

With a quick movement, White pulled a gun from his jacket and pointed it at Oliver, who put his hands up, his unfinished cigarette still in his left hand. The gun charged quickly, but the roar of the fire drowned out the hum.

"Put the gun down, Steven!" Oliver shouted at White and dropped the still-lit cigarette onto the pebbles below. He tried to calm the old man down. "Let's relax and go over this!"

"Friends made me do all that, and I had no say. But I'll stop you!"

"I'm a victim here, just like you are," he replied.

Oliver knew they were too close to each other. If White pulled the trigger, he'd be dead. He scanned his surroundings, but there was nowhere to hide. The woods were his best bet, but he didn't think he could make it.

Oliver had to keep White occupied, so he continued. "What about Sophia? She'll hate you forever!"

The old man replied after a long moment.

"She won't know!" White adjusted his hands on the gun, trying to keep it steady, pointing at Oliver's head.

"You won't be able to hide it! Sooner or later, people will start looking for you." Oliver was focused on White's finger on the trigger. "Think about it!" Oliver felt sweat on his forehead. He was unarmed and exposed, but there was no good way for him to grab his own gun from behind his back. "Your grandkid is on the way!" Oliver tried again to bring the old man back to reality, to what was important, hoping he'd reconsider.

White didn't reply.

To Oliver, it felt like hours passed, and White was still waiting. Hesitating. *Do it or let me go,* he thought. His eyes were getting tired, but a blink of an eye might mean his death.

In a split second, White's finger moved. Oliver's eyes registered it with the speed of light. The blast passed right above his head. White had missed, but Oliver knew it was a close call. It might've even caught his hair. He'd felt the heat of the stream on his face. He was glad White had aimed for his head and that his hands had been shaking. Oliver might not have been so lucky otherwise.

Oliver threw himself to the ground and rolled away from the shot that followed. By the time White's gun was ready to fire again, Oliver had his own gun in his hand and the weapon was a quarter charged—enough for a precision shot and kill. If he aimed at the eye, White would be dead.

He pulled the trigger.

White shouted in agony as Oliver's shot hit the gun he was holding. He'd hit it precisely in a spot that made it too hot to hold, but wouldn't cause it to explode. The old man dropped the weapon. His hand was red, but it would be fine in a few days with some care, Oliver figured. He picked up White's gun and threw it far from where they were standing.

"I won't kill you, Steven!" Oliver shouted angrily. He also threw his own gun in the same direction. "The Gutters. Riverlea. They wanted you dead. They told me to kill you, but I convinced them that killing you won't make a difference because Friends would just put someone else in your place. I found a way out. I made a deal. I traded Riverlea for your life."

"But you need to die!" White shouted. "Let Friends kill me when it's done, but I'm here to end this for Covedale and for my daughter!"

Oliver came closer to White. He was hoping for a more relaxed conversation while they stood side by side, but White took it as an opportunity for another assault. In an act of foolishness, he clenched his fist and took a wide swing at Oliver.

Oliver blocked the blow, effortlessly stopping White's arm in mid-air. He took a step back.

"You have no chance of winning, Steven!" Oliver shouted over the noise, but he was calm. He thought White was being ridiculous by trying to start a fist fight.

White pulled a switchblade out of his pocket and flicked it open. He had the grin of a madman, his eyes sparkling with rage.

"What the fuck are you doing?" Oliver shouted at White, but he knew he couldn't reason with the old man.

White was coming in for another attack and Oliver had to disarm him. With his left hand, he blocked the hand with the knife inches from his body. The knife fell as Oliver's right hand struck the side of White's neck.

The strength of the blow sent White reeling out of control and made him gasp for air. The knife hit the pebbled beach moments before White's body met the ground with a hollow thump.

White wasn't moving. Oliver knelt beside him, trying to wake him up, but the man wasn't responding. There was no blood, but the rock his head had landed on might have knocked him unconscious. He slapped him a few times to get him to come back, but it was pointless. He checked for vital signs and found none.

Oliver looked around. There was no one else in sight. Even if there had been somebody around, the raging fire would have made it impossible to overhear. For a moment he half expected Leo to show up out of nowhere and point a gun at him, but he wasn't there. The burning city had everyone preoccupied. He sat down on the ground and looked at the fire. He recalled the words White had said to him just a moment ago. *Why do you have to destroy everything you touch?*

"Fuck, White." He looked at the man lying beside him. "Why couldn't you accept peace?"

For the first time in a long while, he felt fear. "Sooner or later, people will start looking for you!" he said. These words used to be White's, but hearing them coming from his own mouth gave him goose bumps. He was breathing heavily. That loaded phrase kept coming back to haunt him. Everything he'd achieved was now in jeopardy. He had always been the calm, confident one, but those words were seeds of doubt in his mind. *People will start looking for you!*

Sooner or later, Sophia would learn of her father's death. How would he look her in the eye when she grieved for the old man? He lay down on his back on the rocks and covered his face. It was self-defense, wasn't it? He tried to justify his actions. Should he tell her that, or keep it all a secret? If it was a secret, how long could he keep it? How many more things would he need to keep from her? How many more lies would he need to keep track of? *She can never know,* Oliver told himself.

Suddenly he felt the ground moving beneath him. On the other side of the river, the steel from one of the tall buildings had just given way from the heat and a big chunk had toppled to the ground, sending a shock across the water and up the shore.

White knew too much about the killings and he could have told Sophia everything. Alive, White was a constant risk, a liability, a person Oliver would have to keep tabs on at all times. The fewer people who knew about his contract with Friends, the easier it'd be to keep it a secret. Maybe it was better this way. White was already tired enough of reporting to Friends; how would he have felt having to report to his son-in-law as well?

Oliver sat up. His face now much brighter.

White was free. There was no one steering him anymore, no one pulling his strings. Oliver was free too. He was free of White.

He looked at Riverlea. There was beauty in the fire. The flame kept destroying everything, but it was also the creator of something new. The chaos was just an illusion. The fire had a purpose, the means to change everything, to reshape the world.

When Oliver got back home he felt tired and defeated. He was sure that there was worry on his face, but Sophia didn't bring it up. She probably didn't want to upset him. She was happy he was home, and she was ordering the servants around in order to make his return the best experience in hospitality he'd ever had. Oliver was famished, so they had a big dinner with all of his favorites.

"Did you miss me?" Sophia asked, and Oliver kissed her in reply.

They sent the servants away after dinner so they could spend some time alone on the sofa in the sitting room upstairs. She was on his lap, wrapped in his arms as they kissed.

He touched her belly, checking how much it had grown. "I'm sorry I was away," he said. "And that we had to change our plans."

"How about your penance will be to pamper me forever and always?" Sophia laughed and they kissed again.

"I'd love that," he said, smiling.

Oliver scooped Sophia up in his arms and laid her down on the sofa in one smooth move. He sat at the end of it and put her feet on his lap, then took off her slippers and began massaging her feet, saying, "You know I'm crazy for you." He kissed her foot, and she laughed.

I've done so much wrong just to have her, he thought, looking at her delicate feet as he rubbed them. If not for her, he would have run away, hidden somewhere Friends couldn't find him, maybe even left the continent. But he couldn't imagine telling Sophia that they had nothing. That everything that surrounded them—the house, Covedale, and even World United—was just a big lie, a front. Would she ever look at him again? If he told her how many people he had killed in his lifetime, would she still love him? She could never know how her father had died.

Sophia stirred and took her feet away. She scooched over on the sofa to sit beside him and stroked his hair. He smiled at her and kissed her.

She noticed his glass was empty. He never drank this much. He often had a drink, but he always sipped it slowly, toying with the glass as he did it, never getting drunk on it. Today wasn't an ordinary day.

"Let me get you some more," Sophia said. She smiled and got up enthusiastically. She walked to the table and poured some more whiskey from the carafe, but when she turned around, she froze and her eyes narrowed.

"Is Riverlea really burning?" she asked, confused.

Oliver got up, took the glass out of her hand and put it away. He held her tightly and kissed her. "Don't worry, it's all under control. If it wasn't, I wouldn't be home yet," he said to Sophia without even looking out the window.

She smiled nervously. He picked her up and carried her off to bed. He yanked the curtains closed, shutting out the world for the night.

33

Violet and Seb traveled a whole day on the back of the packed truck. She had watched the Covedale hills disappear in the distance as they traveled along the shore, catching glimpses of the ocean sporadically between the trees. Then the land had flattened and she'd seen meadows and golden fields.

She felt the vehicle stop again. The soldiers were probably just letting people out to stretch. It was just another stop. A few minutes of walking around and they would be told to sit again for a couple of hours.

People were getting upset about being crammed into the back of the truck for so many hours. They didn't know where they were going or what they would find at the end of their journey. There were some who tried to escape, but they were captured and put back on the truck with their hands bound. Others shouted, accusing Sābanto of taking away their freedom and removing them from Riverlea against their will.

The men who escorted them, all dressed in black uniforms, were getting tired as well. They had become more aggravated, shouting at the group more often and pushing them around. They wanted to press on with the transport, but this many people needed frequent stops. Violet worried that it was just a matter of time before someone was seriously hurt.

She was sitting on a wooden bench, deep in the cargo bed. Her head leaned onto the metal partition behind the driver while she waited for her turn to get out to stretch her legs. Just like everyone around her, she wished the journey was over. She was tired and hungry. If someone were to give her even a dirt floor to lie down on, she knew she'd immediately drift off.

The back of the truck was emptying, so she got up and lifted Seb into her arms. He was heavy, but he was sleeping and she didn't want to wake him. When she got to the edge of the vehicle, a young Sābanto soldier—probably not much older than herself—looked up and smiled at her. He wasn't one of the ones that had been escorting them. He was someone new and wearing a green-colored uniform, not a black one like the men from the truck.

"I'm Robert. Let me grab him," he said, and gestured at Seb who had just woken up.

Violet was hesitant, but she knew she wouldn't make it down to the ground with Seb in her arms. Robert seemed nice, and he looked at her with dark, friendly eyes. His smile seemed genuine, so she lowered Seb into his arms.

The soldier looked at the boy he was now holding. "What's ya name, big guy?" he asked.

"Seb," the boy replied shyly, smiling at Robert, who offered a hand to help Violet climb down from the truck. Seb rarely talked much, he was so shy, and it surprised Violet how quickly he'd spoken.

She stepped down onto the ground. There was no concrete or cold, packed soil under her bare feet. There was grass. Living in Riverlea had made her forget how soft grass was. Last time she'd seen this much grass around her had been at the meadow behind the house she used to live in. In the summer, she used to take the goats out so they could munch on fresh greens. She recalled the sunlit emerald carpet where she'd picked flowers. She'd made a wreath from them that day.

She smiled to herself, but Robert must have thought the smile was directed at him and he smiled back. He was still holding Seb, who had already told him his age and volunteered other information, including his mother's name.

"Welcome to Sābanto, Violet," Robert said, handing Seb back to her.

She looked around and saw white buildings to her left and right. Standing side by side, they looked like they stretched for miles. Someone was waving at her to hurry into the building in front of her. She was the only one left from her truck still standing outside.

"Thank ya," she said to Robert, but he was no longer there to hear her. Another truck pulled up by the next building and he was already helping them to disembark.

She took Seb by the hand and walked towards the person who was waving at her and entered the building. It was big inside, with a high ceiling and a set of fans rotating in the air, creating a slight, pleasant breeze.

They asked her to sit at one of the large tables with the rest of the people from her truck, and they were each given a bowl of thick soup as they waited.

Some refused to eat, distrustful and angry about having been brought here, while others started fights trying to steal food from their neighbors.

One by one they were called by the staff, but there were many people. The process seemed to take hours and Violet was having a hard time keeping her eyes open.

When it was Violet's turn, she scooped a sleeping Seb up into her arms and carried him to the desk. An older woman sat there wearing a short-sleeved navy top and matching pants. Violet recognized the name Leggett on the trim of her clothes.

The woman seemed emotionless and was asking questions without looking up. Violet gave her the information she requested—name, age, birth town—to the best of her knowledge and memory.

"Boy's father's name?" the woman finally asked.

Violet hesitated for a moment. "I don't know," she replied. It was less complicated that way.

The woman looked up at Violet and sighed, but she quickly turned back to her work.

After taking pictures of Violet and Seb, the woman handed Violet a key. "House 35, room B," she said absently, and another person in the same navy attire escorted Violet out of the building. They crossed a large courtyard filled with more grass and entered a much smaller building with a big number thirty-five on it. Her attendant left her at the door.

Room B was tiny—just a bed, a crib and a small table—but bigger than the shack they had in Riverlea. She laid Seb, who was still sleeping, down on a soft blanket in the crib. In the corner there was an auburn-colored stuffed toy. Violet picked it up and touched its big ears and tail. "Ya must be a monkey," she said quietly. She smiled, feeling tears swelling in her eyes. She lay the toy down beside Seb. There was a rush of memories of Oliver suddenly occupying her mind, but she brushed them aside.

She walked away from the crib and sat on her bed. She felt the bedsheets with her hand. The linen was fresh and crisp to the touch. She'd never had a real bed just for herself. Even at the farm, she'd shared a bed with her brother.

It reminded her how exhausted she was. The need to sleep was strong, but she suddenly became conscious of the dirty rags she was wearing, and of her hair, crusted with the dust from the road. Earlier, she'd been shown the water pipe that was just down the hall, but she had no strength to wash.

She curled up on the floor with her hands under her head instead of a pillow rather than making the new bed dirty. The room was quiet. She looked again at Seb who was sleeping peacefully.

"I can't say I know where we are, Seb, but we're together," Violet said quietly. She didn't know what the next day would bring. She was anxious but hopeful. *As long as they were together . . .* she thought as her eyes closed.

EPILOGUE

IT HAD BEEN SIX days since Ivy had last seen Mark. Riverlea was still burning. The wind was blowing Ivy's way again as she put a mug of coffee in front of her. She was quite far from the river, staying with her friend at the farm who'd given her refuge. Even here, she could feel the effects of the fire. The thick smog, choking at times, was slowly traveling in her direction, bringing the acrid smell with it.

The sun was up already, but all she could see through the window was an orange glow filling the horizon where the sun should've been.

Ivy was glad to be left alone with her own thoughts. Socializing with the farm occupants was the last thing on her mind. She continued to recall the moment in Mark's when they'd parted. He'd promised that he'd follow her so they could escape together. She couldn't understand why he hadn't.

The radio had said nothing about Riverlea for a long time, but now the news was repeating the same story.

"Due to a tuberculosis outbreak, the town of Riverlea has been evacuated," the anchorwoman said, giving the latest update. "And all people are now receiving treatment. Unfortunately, a group of dissidents calling themselves 'Gutters'—well-known in the area for their exploitation of those forced to live in poverty and squalor in Riverlea—refused to cooperate with the evacuation, threatening the medical response units and putting the lives of local residents in danger. It's believed that this group started the fire that's now raging out of control on the island. Officials involved in the response say there's no way to safely contain the blaze and it will simply have to burn out on its own. It's been confirmed that the rebel leader, Maximilian Walter Owen, as well as his accomplices, are dead. The scientist Dr. Charles Davis who was being held captive in Riverlea is presumed dead, but no body has been recovered."

"You don't evacuate people from their homes because of tuberculosis," Ivy said quietly to herself. "Where did they take them all?" she wondered aloud, but there was no one there to answer.

She took out the envelope with the letter from Mark. The soldier said that the light on the tablet had turned on two days ago, but only now had she decided she was ready to open it. As she read it silently, she felt tears falling down her cheeks.

My Ivy,

If you're reading this, you know I'm gone.

First, I want to apologize for being such a selfish bastard. You have the right to hate me for what I've done to you. Since my son left, I've been a loner, doing things my way, until I let my guard down for you. I don't regret the nights we spent together, but I knew they would only hurt you and I should not have let that happen. I dragged things out for too long, hoping you'd give up and leave me, and I was too cowardly to end it. When the time came, I knew there wouldn't be a future for us. I hope you're safe in Covedale.

I know it will be hard for you, knowing that something happened to me in Riverlea. I want you to know that whatever I had to do, it was with you in mind and for the well-being of the people on both sides of the river.

I have no one besides you, Ivy, so I left you something. Do with it as you wish. It's in White's bank under your name. You will also find there a contract between yourself, Ivy Roberts, as buyer and Oliver Conway as seller of the Leggett factory. He wanted you to know that you deserve the company more than he ever did. Sābanto will take up most of his time now and we could not think of a better person to take over the factory.

Ivy, there was no other way.

With Love,
Mark

SĀBANTO

Sābanto is an English loanword in the Japanese language, written phonetically. Japanese doesn't have a natural V or a hard R. The macron over the A means it's an elongated sound, imitating an R. The word means 'servant'.

ACKNOWLEDGMENTS

I WOULD LIKE TO thank my husband Ian for not only enduring my obsession with writing, but also for his constant encouragement and help in getting the book through the editing and publishing process.

I am especially grateful for my tireless readers, my mom, Barbara Cogan, Peter S. Cramp, Ross Breithaupt and Dawn Kewell for their help with making the book better. Your suggestions were invaluable in having this book see the light of day.

Thank you to Philip Mason and Benjamin Powell for their assistance with Japanese. Dōmo Arigatō.

English is my second language, and I couldn't have published this book without the help of Lara Dwyer, who spent countless hours fixing the manuscript.

Thank you to all my readers and fans of Sābanto who followed me through this publishing journey, and to those who picked up the book and gave it a try. I could never have written this book without your support.

Last, but not least, RIP Joe.

ABOUT THE AUTHOR

Ewa Anderson was born and raised in Warsaw, Poland. When she was eighteen, and with very limited English, she immigrated to Canada. She took the challenges of living on a new continent and learning a new language as an opportunity for growth. Living in Canada as an immigrant increased her awareness of the importance of belonging, acceptance and diversity in society, which she tries to relate in her work.

You can follow Ewa at www.ewaanderson.com